SECRETS AND SINS

Jaishree Misra has written five novels, published by Penguin and HarperCollins, all of which have been Indian best-sellers. She has an MA in English Literature from Kerala University and two post-graduate diplomas from the University of London, one in Special Education and the other in Broadcast Journalism. Until recently, Jaishree worked at the Board of Film Classification in London but she now divides her time between England and India.

For more, see: www.jaishreemisra.com

By the same author

Secrets and Lies

JAISHREE MISRA

Secrets and Sins

AVON

This novel is entirely a work of fiction.
The names, characters and incidents portrayed in it are
the work of the author's imagination. Any resemblance to
actual persons, living or dead, events or localities is
entirely coincidental.

AVON

A division of HarperCollins*Publishers*
77–85 Fulham Palace Road,
London W6 8JB

www.harpercollins.co.uk

A Paperback Original 2010
2

A catalogue record for this book is
available from the British Library

ISBN-13: 978-1-84756-185-5

Set in Minion by Palimpsest Book Production Limited,
Grangemouth, Stirlingshire

Printed and bound in Great Britain by
Clays Ltd, St Ives plc

Mixed Sources
Product group from well-managed
forests and other controlled sources
www.fsc.org Cert no. SW-COC-001806
© 1996 Forest Stewardship Council
FSC

FSC is a non-profit international organisation established
to promote the responsible management of the world's forests.
Products carrying the FSC label are independently certified
to assure consumers that they come from forests that are managed
to meet the social, economic and ecological needs
of present and future generations.

Find out more about HarperCollins and the environment at
www.harpercollins.co.uk/green

Acknowledgements

I have a deep debt of gratitude to Sharmila Tagore who generously described her experiences of being on the Cannes jury to help me research this book. Any errors that may have occurred in interpretation will be mine.

As before, gargantuan thanks to everyone at my agent's and publishers for such touching faith and treating me like a potential Danielle Steele. Lovely women all: Judith, Kesh, Sammia, Kate, Karthika, Lipika, Ratna, Amrita. And not forgetting the men: that enthusiastic army of sales guys who determinedly flog my books, despite their disapproval of the titles.

And where would I be without my ever-present, never-sagging feather-bed of friends and family, always ready to cushion me when I fall, providing warmth and succour and rest.

I dedicate this to Shalini Misra who is no relation and yet showers my Rohini with the kind of love only the closest relatives give.

Prologue

She gazed up at the cinema screen. He was larger than life, the close-up zooming in on his face causing his sleepy brown eyes to look directly into hers as he smiled into the camera. His hair was still black and shiny, exactly as she remembered it from back then. How many years ago was it? Every so often, she counted . . . ten . . . eleven . . . always surprised that the yearning hadn't gone away . . .

Something indefinable caught at her heart as she saw his face soften. She cast a look around at the rows of faces staring intently at the screen, all of them absorbed in the drama of the tender love scene unfolding before their eyes. He continued to be Bollywood's most popular actor, equally loved in action as well as romantic roles – but undoubtedly it was his romantic persona that carried abiding appeal for his throngs of doting female fans.

As he leant down to kiss the heroine on the nape of her neck, the same thought came to her as it always did when she watched one of his love scenes on screen. She sighed and sank down in her seat and wondered, with the same old feeling in the pit of her stomach, what all these hundreds of people watching the film would do if they knew . . . if they only knew that she, Riva Walia, was the very first girl to whom the iconic and adored Aman Khan had ever made love.

1

Chapter One

LEEDS, 1994

The Union Bar was more crowded than Aman had ever seen it since joining the university. Unsurprising, he supposed, seeing that the Man U versus Barça match was due to kick off in fifteen minutes. The din was unbearable but everyone else seemed oblivious to it; both the groups of students gathered around the cheek-by-jowl tables and the bar staff who were by now probably all stone deaf. Aman looked around for the only person he was hoping to see, and soon spotted Riva. She was with a gang at the far end of the room, seated around a scuffed circular table near the back door that was sticky with spilt drinks and littered with crumpled crisp wrappers and cigarette butts.

Shouldering his way through the throng, Aman saw the usual crowd surrounding Riva, including a few people whom he knew by face rather than name. Aman had watched Riva acquire at least a hundred new friends in this first year at uni; she was always surrounded by people. Riva's best friend, the chirpy redhead Susan, was the first to spot him. She said something to Ben that made him look up and give Aman what was definitely an unwelcoming glare. And then Riva spotted him. Her face broke into one of those lovely smiles that did strange things to Aman's insides. She raised her arm and waved enthusiastically at him. He nodded as she pointed to the empty stool next to her, and continued to make his way through the crowd in her direction. Could he really hope that she had kept that seat waiting for him? Ben was still glowering as Aman neared the table but Susan's medical student boyfriend, Joe, was friendlier and moved his bag aside to make room for Aman.

'Hi, can I get anyone a drink?' Aman asked. He licked his lips – his mouth had gone suddenly dry. Everyone had full glasses and so Aman sat down. He would get his orange juice later. It wasn't what he was here for anyway.

'Didn't know you were a football fan,' he said, turning to Riva with a smile.

'Oh, I'm not,' she replied cheerily, taking a long swig from her glass. He watched the golden lager passing through her lips, thinking of how badly he wanted to kiss them. Putting her glass down, she said, 'And I didn't know *you* were a footie fan.'

'I'm not either,' he replied, slipping into the same merry tone of voice she had used.

'Shall we escape this shit then?' she asked. 'Or did you have other plans?'

Incredulous at the unexpected change of fortune and momentarily robbed of speech, Aman nodded dumbly. Then, gathering his wits, he said, 'I was going to make myself something to eat back at the hall, actually. You know, take advantage of everyone being here to get free use of the kitchen.'

'*Make* something? You can cook?'

The truthful answer would have been 'Hmmm, a tiny

4

bit – toast and scrambled eggs mainly.' But Aman, his heart surging with bravado, said, 'Of course I can cook. I'm quite good actually. Why, don't you believe me?'

He couldn't help but imagine the peals of laughter his mother would have broken into had she been around to hear his blatant lie. Luckily Mum was as far away as she could possibly be, probably fast asleep in her bed in Bombay and blissfully unaware of her son's evil machinations.

'I only ask because Sonalika, my mate back at school, used to say she knew no Indian men who cooked,' Riva smiled. 'My dad certainly can't, but I don't know too many other Indian men apart from him, so I shouldn't judge.'

'Chicken makhani's my speciality actually,' Aman said, warming to his theme.

'Cor!' Riva looked gratifyingly impressed. 'Teach me!' she demanded.

'Teach you? Now?'

'Now!'

'But the match . . .'

'Stuff the match! We're neither of us here for the footie anyway. C'mon, let's escape this hellhole.' Riva knocked back the last of her lager and picked up her coat and bag from under her chair. Aman, needing no further invitation, got up and looked apologetically around at the others.

'Hey, guys, Aman and I are off in search of some nosh,' Riva said casually as she pulled on her jacket. 'Be back by the end of the game.'

Aman did not miss the renewed glare from Ben, who looked ready to get up and punch him, but none of the others seemed too bothered as it was nearing kick-off and the attention of the whole bar was starting to focus on the screen. Riva was already halfway out of the back door and lighting up a cigarette by the time Aman caught up with her.

'Don't think Ben was too pleased,' Aman said.

'Ben? Why, what makes you say that?' Riva blew a plume of smoke out into the cold air.

'He is your boyfriend, isn't he?'

'Naaah.' Riva shrugged and asked, 'Have you got the stuff you need, Aman?'

'Stuff?'

'You know, the chicken, onions . . . what else will we need? Rice? Oh, chicken makhani sounds great. I'd love to learn how to cook it.'

'Er, no, I haven't got the stuff . . . I was thinking of buying it from the campus shop on my way back.'

'Okay, we'll do it together then. And I'll buy a bottle of wine – that'll be my contribution to the meal. God, I'm starving! So much nicer to sit down to a proper meal and conversation, rather than spend the evening watching a sport I hate. Overpaid prima donnas who call themselves sportsmen, tribal warfare, loutish crowds . . . I loathe the whole shebang, honestly!'

Aman felt weak at the knees as he walked along beside Riva. He could not tell if it was due to the prospect of a whole evening alone with such a beautiful, clever, sassy girl, or the fact that he had no idea at all how to make chicken makhani. It was his favourite dish at the *dhaba* around the corner from his house in Bombay and, occasionally his mother got the *bai* to cook a version of it at home as well, but the thought of making it himself had never crossed Aman's mind before.

At the shop, he did his best to look masterful, throwing two onions and a bulb of garlic into his shopping basket, next to a cling-filmed pack of chopped chicken. The shape of the pieces (long and narrow) didn't look quite right to him but it would have to do. Remembering in the nick of time that he would need a substance to fry everything in, Aman added a block of butter to his shopping. It stood to reason that chicken makhani would bear some relation to 'makhan', which was Hindi for butter. Good idea to use plenty of it, he reckoned.

Riva was waiting at the till with a bottle of red wine and insisted on paying for it, even though Aman tried to persuade her to let him take care of the entire bill. It was only when they walked into his hall fifteen minutes later, stamping their feet to get rid of the snow and mud from the soles of their boots, that Aman realised he had nothing but salt and pepper by way of seasoning. While Riva went to the toilet, Aman frantically opened a few cupboards, hoping to find a stray bottle of spices. He finally stumbled upon a can of mixed herbs and sniffed its contents. It smelt vaguely of pizza. Quite clearly, no Indian masala had been anywhere near this bottle – but it would have to do. Aman rolled up his sleeves and began to yank the peel off the onions before chopping them into large rough chunks. Riva returned and rooted around inside a drawer to unearth a corkscrew and a pair of wine glasses. As she busied herself opening the bottle she had bought, Aman wondered if he ought to confess that, apart from not having a clue how to cook this meal, he did not drink either. He wasn't sure if Riva had already noticed his variety of fruit juices on the few occasions they had been in bars and pubs together, and he was worried that she would think he was a stick-in-the-mud, rather than just an obedient son to Muslim parents.

'Do you mind if I have OJ?' Aman asked as Riva started to pour the wine into two glasses.

'I'll let you off for now, seeing as you need to concentrate. That's a rather delicate operation you're carrying out there,' Riva replied, watching nervously as Aman ham-fistedly attempted to light the gas cooker.

Eventually (with some help from Riva), Aman got a weak blue flame going and began piling the pieces of chicken, onions and garlic together into the pan and stuck it on the hob. Riva was halfway through the bottle of wine by this time. Aman stirred the mixture together to form a pale white sludge. He continued to stir it in a determined fashion, willing it to change colour and look more appealing, but the best it could do was deepen to a pale brown as the onions started to burn in their pool of butter. Riva did not appear to notice, however, but sat on a kitchen stool throughout his exertions, chatting about her school and family back in Ealing. Aman wasn't sure where exactly Ealing was but, from Riva's few mentions of London, he gathered it was a suburb of the capital. She had questions for Aman about his Bombay upbringing too, carefully referring to the city as Mumbai, even though Aman himself almost always referred to it as Bombay. He kept his answers brief, standing near the stove, terrified that his dish would go up in flames if he did not keep stirring it. It looked terribly pale compared to the chicken makhani that he so enjoyed back at Sardar's *dhaba*, which was usually bright orange and served up with giant wedges of pillowy soft naans.

'I don't have all the spices I need, so it's a bit colourless I'm afraid,' he said apologetically to Riva.

She got up and peered into the frying pan. 'Yes, something's missing. Could it be . . . hang on, you need tomatoes to make a curry, don't you? I'm sure I've heard my mum say that . . .'

Aman froze. Of course a curry needed bloody tomatoes!

8

He closed his eyes and slapped his forehead, making Riva throw her head back and laugh.

'Never mind,' she said, 'as long as the chicken's cooked through, it'll still be edible. I might have mine on toast. Be a shame to waste all that butter.'

Aman looked at her hopefully. 'Now? Shall I make you some toast now? I have bread in the fridge . . .'

'Later. I'm not hungry yet,' Riva said. 'Shall we take this somewhere else?' she asked, picking up the wine bottle. 'Or we'll both be stinking of food. You must have a glass too, seeing that it's my pressie to you.'

'Good idea, let's get outta here,' Aman said, switching off the flame with relief. He washed his hands as Riva poured him a glass. Hopefully, by the time Riva had finished the bottle, she'd be too drunk to remember to eat. Aman took a tentative sip as he followed her down the corridor, the taste making him want to pucker his lips and spit it out forthwith. Aman had never been able to tell why people drank the stuff but it was sure making Riva laugh a lot tonight, her cheeks turning a pretty soft pink as the colour rose in her face. She stepped back for Aman to open his room door and he hoped desperately he'd left it in a reasonable state earlier. Luckily it was neat enough, except for a small pile of discarded clothes that Aman hastily kicked under his bed while Riva wandered around his room looking at the pictures on the wall and table.

For another half hour, they talked, Riva sitting on the bed and Aman at the table. Or rather Riva talked, while Aman gazed at her animated face and shining dark eyes, nursing his glass of wine and pretending every so often to be sipping at it. He thought it incredible that Riva trusted him enough to sit here on his bed, in his room, while

9

everyone else was down at the Union Bar. Especially when all he could think of was grabbing her and kissing that lovely mouth. But Aman did no such thing, of course, having been brought up to be a gentleman. He hadn't had much practice with being alone with girls before, except for his large band of cousins, who didn't really count. But something told him it wouldn't be wise to use this opportunity to shower Riva with passionate kisses. And yet, when the bottle of wine was finished and Riva got up to leave, Aman felt bereft and stupid, his best chance presented to him on a platter before being snatched from under his nose.

He got up from his chair and asked weakly, 'Do you not want to eat? My chicken . . .'

'Ah, yes, your chicken . . . of course . . . you took such trouble and here I am . . .' Riva was slurring slightly. She suddenly swayed alarmingly on her feet. Aman caught her just as she crumpled, stopping her from falling to the floor. For a few stunned seconds, he just stood there, holding an unconscious Riva in his arms, wondering what to do. Then he lifted her up and carried her to his bed, trying to push aside the duvet with one foot. The cheap wine had knocked her out cold and she barely stirred as he pulled off her fleecy boots and covered her with his duvet. Her face wore a slightly anxious expression.

Aman stood next to the bed, unsure of what to do next. He certainly couldn't leave Riva here on his bed, not least because he had nowhere else to go. And now that it was past eleven o'clock, he didn't think he would find Riva's friends down at the bar either. Besides he too was desperate to catch some sleep, the rigours of his hour-long culinary effort having completely exhausted him. He took a pair of sheets out of his cupboard and tried to fashion a bed for himself on the floor, using the small cushion and rug he had inherited from the previous occupant of this room. It was terribly uncomfortable in comparison with his bed, but he was nevertheless pleased to see Riva sleeping soundly, the earlier worried crease in her forehead having cleared as she fell into a deep slumber.

When Riva opened her eyes the next morning, it was with a strong sense of being somewhere she was not meant to be. It was either getting on for late evening or close to dawn because there was a sliver of light showing around the edges of a drawn curtain. Where the fuck *am* I, Riva wondered, raising her throbbing head, alarmed to see a figure huddled on the floor next to her. The events of the previous night gradually returned as she recognised Aman's sleeping form and remembered his dismal attempts at impressing her with his chicken makhani. He'd made a total hash of it and she had fortunately managed to wriggle out of eating any. But her empty stomach was probably the reason why she had keeled over so unceremoniously after just three glasses of wine . . . or was it four? All Riva could remember now was the room spinning around her as Aman had grabbed her. He must have led her to bed and tucked her in . . . bloody hell, and taken off her boots! She felt about her nether regions in sudden panic, relieved to find she was still wearing her jeans. Overcome with mortification, Riva convinced herself there had been no rumpy-pumpy after she had passed out; surely she would remember if she had had sex with Aman?

God, that would have been just terrible, she thought, laying her head back on the pillow in sudden relief. Perhaps Aman was of the slow 'n' steady school of seduction, rather than a fast mover. Riva had recently confessed to Susan how appealing she found Aman's eager adoration of her, and

11

Susan had wagered that Aman's good looks were a hugely contributory factor to Riva's inability to tell him to bog off. Susan didn't know, however, how much Riva enjoyed Aman's company. The fascinating insights his background gave her into her own Indian heritage were a large part of his appeal. Above all, it was his gentleness that drew Riva in, a rare quality in the boys she generally met. And now here she was, wrapped snugly in Aman's duvet while the poor bloke lay shivering in a sheet on the floor . . .

Later, Riva would try to understand what prompted her to do what she did next. After all, she had never been particularly promiscuous. But there, in the early hours of that February morning, Riva raised her head and called softly out to Aman before stretching her hand down towards him to touch his arm. He looked startled as he opened his eyes and his confused gaze met hers in the half darkness.

'You must be freezing,' Riva said, whispering for some unfathomable reason. 'Come up here,' she invited, moving the duvet aside. Aman sat up and she saw that he was still wearing his jeans and a T-shirt. 'Take off those bloody jeans,' she said, smiling, as he got up. When he had done so and climbed in to lie next to her on the bed, she rubbed her hands up and down his cold arms to warm them. By now Aman looked wide awake, his dark eyes shining in the diffused moonlight filtering through the curtains. While Riva rubbed his shoulders and then his chest through the thin cotton of his T-shirt, he cupped her face in the palms of his hands. They kissed gently at first, then more passionately. They began to undress each other, Riva sitting up in bed and raising her arms so that Aman could slip off her top before lying down next to him again. As he kissed her again, pressing her down on the bed with the force of his ardour, she lay down and arched her back to tug off her jeans. Finally, when they were both naked, their bodies shining in the half light, they made love, tentative and fumbling at first. When Riva felt Aman come, she held him close as his body trembled against hers and they stayed like that for a long time.

When they finally drew apart, Aman lay back, his head next to hers on the pillow. Riva could hear him panting slightly. A few minutes later, he spoke, looking at the ceiling rather than at her, his voice shy.

'You might have guessed, that was my first time.'

'I didn't actually,' Riva replied, but she was being kind. Even though she wasn't hugely experienced herself, it hadn't been hard to tell from Aman's nervousness that he had never had sex before. It also suddenly occurred to Riva that they had not used a condom and she cursed her stupidity for assuming Aman would have had one handy.

Aman's next words followed a logical thread. 'Was it the first time for you too?' he asked quietly, now turning his head to look at her.

His expression was strangely hopeful and Riva wondered momentarily if she should tell him the truth or not. But, honesty being one of her unfailing traits, Riva replied, 'No, not really.' Aman continued to look at her questioningly and so she elaborated. 'There was a boy in high school I was quite mad about. And I sort of thought he loved me too. Well, he said he did and I believed him but, the following week, he went on to say the same to my best friend who slept with him too. So that was that!'

They were too tired to talk much more and soon Riva drifted off into slumber again. In the morning, Aman got up while Riva was still asleep and made two mugs of coffee. She deliberately kept the conversation light and friendly as they sipped their drinks, recognising the faint embarrassment that now lay between them. Riva hoped it would soon dissipate, for she was keen to stay friends with Aman. He seemed like such a nice lad, and so different from the boys she had met so far. She was held rapt whenever he talked of India, her own memories of the place she had come from now being far-off and fuzzy. There was, however, little chance of her relationship with Aman going any further than friend-ship – despite his astonishing good looks, they were a bit like creatures from different planets. Besides, it somehow felt wrong to be going out with someone who was even less worldly wise than her! Finally finishing her coffee, Riva got out of bed and pulled on her clothes before going down the corridor to use the bathroom.

Ten minutes later, she popped back into Aman's room to collect her bag and coat. He was sitting on the edge of his rumpled bed, holding his empty coffee mug. Riva felt a rush of sympathy for the little-boy-lost expression on his face. She bent and kissed him on the cheek. 'We must do that curry another time,' she said. Then she grinned, straightening up and waving a forefinger at Aman, 'No, really a *curry*, not using euphemisms now!'

'Shall I walk you back to your hall?' Aman asked.

'Don't be daft, it's broad daylight now so I think I'm perfectly safe. Typically sweet offer, though, Mr Khan. You've obviously been dragged up proper. Not like the boorish lads one usually gets around here . . .'

Nevertheless, Aman did accompany Riva down the corridor of his hall of residence and she kissed him lightly on the lips before stepping out into the morning sunshine.

He stood at the door, unable to take his eyes off her as the black of her duffle coat disappeared around the corner, feeling his body surging with an odd mixture of hope and disappointment.

Chapter Two

LONDON, 2009

The foursome emerged from the Comedy Store, blinking in the bright lights of Leicester Square. Riva shivered as a cold gust whipped around them and swiftly pressed herself up against the warmth of Ben's coat, slipping one ungloved hand into his pocket.

'That was good, wasn't it? Terrific to see Paul Merton return to form,' she said, looking over her shoulder as she talked to their friends.

Joe, walking a few paces behind, replied, 'Good is an understatement. Those guys are so clever. Certainly one of the best uses you can put twenty quid to in London.'

He pulled on an ancient woollen bobble cap, earning an affectionate slap on his behind from his wife.

'For God's sake, Dr Joseph Holmes, where *do* you manage to unearth that ugly bit of headgear every winter!' Susan said in exasperation. 'I thought I'd sent it off to Oxfam last spring.'

'You nearly did. Very sneaky, if you ask me. But no flies on me: I managed to retrieve it in the nick of time,' Joe retorted, putting both hands to his hat and pretending extreme relief.

Susan rolled her eyes skywards. 'I'll soon have to scrape it off your head!' she muttered, linking her fingers with his and dragging him along to keep pace with Riva and Ben. 'Fancy a coffee, anyone?'

'More like a stiff brandy on a night like this, methinks,' Ben said.

'Too right,' Joe grinned. 'There's De Hems just around the corner from here. Hopefully the crowd's thinned out a bit by now.'

'Or Bar Italia just up Greek Street?' Susan chipped in.

'Intent on nudging us in the direction of some cake, ain't ya, Mrs Holmes?' Riva said.

'Oh, you know me so well, Riva,' Susan responded, laughing.

'Well, I have got thirty years' worth of research on your cake-eating habits,' Riva joked.

'Is that really how long you two have known each other?' Ben asked. 'I thought it was more like twenty.'

'For heaven's sake, Ben, *we've* known each other nearly fifteen years now and Sooz and I go back so much further. South Ealing Primary, that centre of academic excellence – remember, Sooz?' Riva asked, putting her arm around Susan's waist.

'Do I remember? Took you a whole week to stop crying for your mum – and then only because I took you under my wing!' Susan said, squeezing her friend's arm.

Ben, who had been counting in his head, interrupted them. 'Fucking hell, Riva, you're right, it'll be fifteen years for us next autumn. 1994!' He turned to Joe. 'In fact, you guys met the same year too. We should have a joint celebration.'

'What a lovely idea,' Susan cried. 'Not quite a wedding anniversary because you two pipped us to the marital post by three years. But we could have a sort of joint the-day-I-laid-eyes-on-you sort of celebration, couldn't we? Couldn't we, Joe?' Susan repeated, nudging Joe with her elbow, who was now busy examining the interior of De Hems through its misted glass panes.

'Hmmm, yes, of course, darling,' he replied distractedly before turning to Ben. 'What do you think, old chap, too crowded?'

'Naah, it's fine,' Ben dismissed, though the throng inside the pub was overflowing onto the windswept street.

'Oh, please, I want to go somewhere where we can sit down. I've been on my feet all day in the classroom!' Susan protested.

'Let's go to All Bar One on the other side of the square, that's usually quieter,' Riva suggested.

'Good idea,' Susan said. The women turned and started to walk back to Leicester Square. Their husbands reluctantly brought up the rear, moaning and grumbling loudly. Susan and Riva ignored them as they walked on, arms linked. Riva fished in the pocket of her coat for some change as they passed an old busker playing 'Moon River' on a saxophone, for which she received a huge toothless smile.

As they passed the Leicester Square Odeon, Susan gazed up at the posters that were being pasted on for the Friday show changes. She clutched Riva's arm. 'Get a look at that,' she said, jogging Riva's arm.

Riva looked up and saw a massive poster for a new Hindi film. The words 'Iske Baad – Afterwards' were printed above an image of Aman Khan's handsome face gazing broodingly into the middle distance.

Susan giggled. 'Goodness, he's still a bit of a dish, ain't he?'

Riva cast a glance over her shoulder, but the men were

still engrossed in their conversation and had not noticed the poster. She looked up again and felt her heart do its familiar flip. She had seen this film at the London Film Festival but hadn't Googled Aman's name for a while, so did not know anything about its wider release. She couldn't help wondering if Aman might be in London for the press junket. Perhaps he was just around the corner, signing autographs or cutting red ribbons or doing whatever it was that film stars did of an evening . . .

Riva did not particularly want Ben to see Aman's poster for a variety of reasons. Luckily Susan seemed to take her cue, and called out in mock exasperation to the two men, 'Come on, you two, this ain't exactly a stroll in the park, y'know! Do let's get moving, chop chop!'

Chapter Three

Two days later, Riva sat in the darkened BAFTA theatre and sneaked another look at the time on her mobile phone, holding it under her pashmina so that its light would not disturb the person sitting next to her. Eight o'clock. Her heart sank. She would need to leave soon as Ben was expecting to meet her by nine at the restaurant.

The film had started half an hour ago, soon after the chairperson of BAFTA had announced that their chief guest was running late, 'held up by the inclement weather'. Despite her disappointment, Riva had not been able to help smiling at that, remembering what a wimp Aman had been about the English weather when he had first arrived as an overseas student from Mumbai. But surely he didn't have to worry about the snow in London now, given the fleet of cars and chauffeurs he probably had at his disposal whenever he visited?

The programme on BAFTA's website had stated that the evening would begin with the Aman Khan interview, followed by the screening of *Afterwards* – the film that, according to reports on various Bollywood sites, had cata-pulted him to international recognition, with talk of an Oscar nomination for Best Foreign Film. Riva's plan had been to watch Aman's interview before slipping out of the hall to make her restaurant rendezvous with Ben. The little porkie she had told about a drink with her agent and publicist couldn't really stretch her evening beyond nine. Now it looked like she would have to leave without seeing Aman after all. But it was probably worth waiting just a little while more . . . after all, the BAFTA man had said Aman was on his way. She frowned again at the screen, trying to concentrate . . .

Although Riva had enjoyed *Afterwards* at the London Film Festival, and was quite accustomed to watching some of Aman's films twice, even three times over, she was finding it hard to focus on the screen today. She cast a glance around the darkened hall, wondering if others in the audience were similarly distracted by the imminent arrival of its lead actor. But all she could see were rows of half-lit faces intent on the screen.

Riva sat back in her chair, trying to settle. Pictures were flickering on the screen – they had come to the part where Aman's character tells a friend he is leaving for Kerala – but, instead of hearing his dialogue, Riva reflected with amusement on the apology that had been made by the hapless BAFTA bod charged with announcing that the film would be stopped as soon as Mr Khan arrived. He had timorously suggested that it would be best not to delay events any longer as heavy snow had been forecast for later tonight. But the crowd had remained cheery and upbeat, someone even whistling very loudly at the announcement, one of those piercing finger-in-mouth toots that had made people turn around in startled amusement. After that, very unusually for a BAFTA screening, the crowd had sung and clapped in time to the song that played under the opening credits of the film, one already popularised by the Asian TV and radio channels. This was a predominantly Indian crowd that had turned up in full force to see one of their biggest stars. Certainly BAFTA would have never seen a fan event like this before: all these Asian women wearing spangly *salwar kameeze*s under drab winter coats, not to mention the air of general enthusiasm and bonhomie. In the crowd was the usual token sprinkling of white faces, most likely movie buffs trying to educate themselves about what they thought of as world cinema.

Aman Khan's handsome face was filling the screen now in an extreme close-up and Riva, leaning her head back on the seat, remembered the young Aman with sudden sharp clarity. The years had been kind to him. Although she had observed his onscreen persona filling out in his twenties, an obvious new health regime in his early thirties had made him leaner and brought out interesting shadows on his face. Oh yes, still the old Aman, and – as Susan had observed – still quite, quite gorgeous.

Riva sighed softly, sinking down in her seat and trying once more to concentrate on the movie.

But the next few minutes brought a flurry of activity at the door – Aman Khan must have arrived because a wave of excitement was passing through the front rows of the audience. Riva felt the surging collective exhilaration and suddenly . . . there he was! The real Aman, being escorted onto the stage by Siddharth Jose, the young British director who was due to interview him. The crowd erupted into a tumult of clapping, some people even leaping to their feet to applaud their favourite star. As the film was halted, the BAFTA chairperson walked over to the lit podium while Aman bowed and waved at the crowd. But the applause kept coming, wave upon wave, and the BAFTA man smiled indulgently, turning to nod again at Aman, who now looked faintly embarrassed.

Finally, when the seemingly interminable ovation had abated slightly, the man tapped the mic lightly and asked for silence. When the crowd had settled, the star and director took their places on two armchairs that had been hastily brought out from the wings for them. Aman looked very fit indeed, slim and broad-shouldered in a black silk Nehru jacket. He leant over to pour water from the bottle placed on the table before him and Riva watched as he put it to his lips.

Aman looked into the crowd as the house lights brightened and Riva's heart heaved as she felt his eyes looking into hers. She reddened as his gaze moved on, telling herself to stop being so fanciful. For heaven's sake, she was sitting about ten rows away from the stage and Aman's long-distance vision had never been very good anyway. On the other hand, it was entirely possible that he knew that she lived in London now – after all, her own name had made it to the papers when she'd won the Orange Prize; Indian journalists had showed particular interest in her at the time. Aman's attention was, however, now on the interviewer who was asking his first question.

'Why London, Aman?' Siddharth was asking. 'It's a city you make it a point to visit every year, I'm told. For someone who lives and works in this grimy old city, I can't help wondering why anyone would leave balmy Bombay for London, certainly not when it's in the grip of winter like this!'

Aman laughed and settled back in his chair. 'I love it here, *especially* in the grip of winter,' he said in his familiar deep voice. To Riva it sounded as though the crowd around her was sighing with happiness as Aman continued to speak. 'Don't forget how sultry it gets in Bombay – and how unrelenting the heat can be. There's something very . . .' he searched briefly for the right word '. . . very *appealing* about the changes of season when you live in a place that doesn't have them. And London's so full of energy, it's such a great city. I love being here in any season really, and so does my son apparently. Although I think when he says "London", it's the inside of Hamleys he's thinking of! But a winter trip has always been compulsory anyway, so that my wife can wear her Gucci coat and Prada boots, which otherwise never get the chance to be worn in Bombay.'

He paused as the crowd laughed affectionately. Salma Khan's shopping penchant had been much written about in the gossip magazines and Aman had hit just the right note of affectionate exasperation in his voice. His English had improved considerably too, Riva noticed, trying to remember whether she'd ever heard him use words like 'unrelenting' before. Of course, they had been mere freshers when they had last met and, although Riva knew that Aman had never gone on to complete his graduate studies, such a big star as he would almost certainly have had the advantages of media training.

The audience around her was laughing again and Riva realised with dismay that she had missed something amusing. Aman was looking relaxed and responding to a question he had just been asked about his early life in England.

'It was only for a year, although it gets mentioned quite a lot – as if I spent all my college years in Oxford or Cambridge or some grand place like that! Actually it was Leeds University and I only spent first year there – in the English Department.' Siddharth Jose cocked an enquiring brow at Aman who explained. 'You see, my uncle was working in Leeds and, because my parents were worried that I was just hanging around in Bombay, not doing anything after school, he sponsored me to come here for my studies. Didn't last! I just wasn't good enough and so, at the end of that first year, I dropped out of the course and went home.'

'Ah, but that was what took you to the Film Institute, was it not?' Siddharth Jose cut in. 'So, if you had been "good enough", as you say, for Leeds' English Department, Bollywood – and all of us – might have missed out on one of our finest actors!'

'Indeed, who knows – Bollywood's loss may have been Leeds University's gain!' Aman joked, making the audience laugh again.

And mine . . . maybe, Riva thought, recalling that long ago time up in Leeds. How torn she had been between Aman's attentions and Ben's for a few days before she had made her decision. Irrationally now, she tried to will the interviewer to quiz Aman further about the decisions he had made as a young man. Such as, '*Why*, Mr Khan, had you not thought to fight just a little harder for Miss Riva Walia's affections before upping and leaving Leeds University?' Annoyingly, however, interviewer and interviewee had already moved on to something else.

Aman was talking about his early career. 'Well, I took what I got in those days,' he was saying to Siddharth Jose. 'Beggars and beginners can't be choosers, as they say. When I was offered my first role, I did not even stop to ask what type of film it was or even if I was to be a hero or a villain. I just jumped at it and asked all my questions later, once I was signed up and safely on the set.'

His candour and lack of pretension was disarming. Riva could see that he certainly had this audience eating out of the palm of his hand. But now Siddharth Jose was leading him into less personal areas and they talked about his film career for the next half hour.

When the interview ended, Riva used the short break before the film restarted to slip out of her seat. She tugged on her coat and gloves as she hurried through the foyer. It was now a quarter to nine and, even if she took a cab to the restaurant, she would be late. Ben did so hate to be kept waiting, she thought with a sense of slight panic as she ran down the stairs towards the main entrance. She drew in her breath at the sudden cold outside, annoyed with herself for forgetting to carry her umbrella and woollen cap. As had been predicted, snowflakes were now drifting against the tall streetlights of Piccadilly while a brisk wind, bitter with cold, stung the tips of her ears and nose. A small gaggle of people was huddled against the railings outside BAFTA and Riva heard one of them loudly cry out Aman's name. Unthinkingly, she joined the crowd of fans, momentarily forgetting her lateness and the no-doubt steadily growing impatience of her husband awaiting her in the restaurant.

Standing on tiptoe, Riva saw that Aman had emerged from BAFTA's main entrance – perhaps he had been just a few steps behind her! He was now getting into a long black limousine along with a couple of other people. As it pulled away from the kerb, the group of fans started waving and blowing kisses at the car. Riva joined them, running a little way down the pavement to where the crowd was thinner. Inside the car, Aman's head turned to look back as he was driven away. The car disappeared into the distance, leaving Riva with the distinct impression that Aman had spotted her.

Chapter Four

It was twenty past nine by the time Riva finally spotted the garish neon sign of Maroush glinting through the curtain of sleet that veiled everything in a thin grey. The normally colourful and welcoming shops of Arab Town had their doors closed against the wretched weather and the windscreen wipers on passing cars were going nineteen-to-the-dozen. Despite the rain, pedestrians were thronging Edgware Road as usual. Who *were* all these people out shopping and celebrating on a ghastly night like this, Riva wondered, elbowing her way past wet shopping bags and umbrellas. Despite her shortness of breath, she sped up again, imagining Ben's irritation when she eventually stumbled into the restaurant. He had been in a bad mood for the last couple of days and only the other night he had complained, 'You're never ever on time, Riva. Well, not for me anyway. Deadlines for publishers, yes. Appointments with that agent of yours, of course. Lunches and meetings with friends, oh, it goes without saying. You're on impeccable behaviour for all of them. But the simple matter of being on time for *me* seems completely out of the question.' He hadn't seemed angry when he had said it – merely sort of weary – and Riva had not argued, knowing that the remark had emerged from his present depressed view of the world. She sighed. It wasn't easy for an ambitious man like Ben to find himself in the unlikely position of househusband.

She ducked under the awning with relief, her head and clothes momentarily lit pink by the flashing neon sign of the restaurant. She knew she must look a right old state, her hair wet and in clumps, her Ugg boots soaked through. She had hopped on a bus at Piccadilly and ended up trotting the half-mile distance from Marble Arch rather than hailing a cab, quite simply because there had not been one with its light on. But it would annoy Ben if she said that she had walked – he was quick to assume these days that her habitual frugalities were due to his being out of work. Every so often he took pains to remind her of the fat payout he had received from the bank when he had been made redundant. In Riva's view this was quite unnecessary – she hadn't been financially dependent on Ben for many years as her own account now received regular injections of royalty payments. But it was curious how even a man as liberated as Ben preferred to be seen as the breadwinner rather than an equal partner in the kind of joint endeavour they had always agreed their marriage would be.

Riva stamped her boots outside the entrance and tried to retie her mussed-up hair with a wooden clip. Of course she wasn't going to confess to Ben that Aman and his film were the reason for her lateness. She had always hidden those little jaunts to the cinema from Ben, assuming that he would be jealous of the unlikely success of their old classmate, particularly as he was also her old flame. It was one of Riva's more awkward memories when Ben had once spotted a cinema ticket to Feltham Cineworld in her purse, *after* she had told him she had been to see a Hollywood film starring George Clooney. He had had the good grace to laugh off her white lie, and even jested a little at the memory of Aman's crush on Riva back at uni. But Riva had, of course, been mortified to have been caught redhanded with the ticket to *Ishq* in her purse, a feeling akin to the time her father had spotted seven Crunchie bar wrappers in her bin, bought using the change she had pinched from the bowl in the hallway.

Riva thought up her excuses now, rehearsing them as she stepped through the doors of the restaurant and spotted Ben sitting by one of the tables at the window, looking out at the rain. She slipped off her coat and handed it to the waiter before making her way across the crowded room towards him. Her heart melted at sight of his slumped shoulders: everything about him spelt out his depression.

'Oh, Christ, sorry to be so late, love,' she said, lightly kissing Ben's cheek and sinking into the seat facing him. 'How long have you been here?'

'What excuse do we have today, huh?' Ben asked, raising his left arm and waving his watch at her, his voice uncharacteristically peevish.

'Oh, don't ask! No cabs to be had for love nor money on a night like this. And the meeting at Gideon's just dragged on and on. Antonia, the PR girl from the publisher's was there too, and wanted to discuss the digital media campaign for the new book. You'll never believe this but they're talking about a seven-city tour across Europe, which, of course, would be lovely, except . . .' Riva realised that Ben was no longer listening, his attention focused quite deliberately on the wine list.

Riva lapsed into silence, glad to have been stopped in her tracks while lying so shamelessly to her husband. It really did make her feel quite hateful. Not that all of her utterances were *lies* exactly, as Riva had indeed had several conversations with both Gideon and Antonia in the course of the day, but it was certainly not true that she had been in a meeting with them this evening. It suddenly crossed Riva's mind that Ben may have read something online about Aman Khan being in London to promote his new film. She flushed at the thought – it would not take much for him to put two and two together and guess that she had gone to see him at BAFTA. Nervously, she reached out for Ben's glass of water and watched him over the rim as she sipped. His face looked more drawn than usual today, his grey-blue eyes bloodshot, and Riva wondered if he had spent all day staring at his computer screen. She sighed and sat back in her chair, feeling an inexplicable surge of sadness overcome her. Riva had always striven not to rub Ben's nose in the success of her publishing career, conscious of the fact that Ben had been the one with real writing ambitions back in college. Of course, he had greeted Riva's unexpected book deal with excitement and good grace at first, perhaps anticipating with typical confidence that his own chance would surely follow before long. He had even joked of how they might one day become the 'golden couple in publishing', both of them enjoying flourishing literary careers. But, as the years passed with submission after submission of his being turned down, Ben had not been able to help becoming just a tiny bit bitter. Riva had done her best to assist in whatever way she could, but she cringed when she recalled the weary look that would come over her publishers' faces whenever a husband with writing ambitions was mentioned. The most brutal blow had come when Gideon, Riva's own literary agent, had returned Ben's manuscript with a terse and uncomplimentary letter of rejection. Ben had found it astonishing that the man had not even done him the courtesy of a phone call and angrily reminded Riva that it was her sizeable royalties that were keeping Gideon ensconced in his fancy Covent Garden offices. In Riva's opinion this wasn't true at all – Gideon had many other successful writers on his list – but Ben had not wanted to hear that, and accused her of taking sides with her agent. They had ended up rowing that day and Riva had subsequently stopped advocating on Ben's behalf. Recently he had complained again about the stand she had taken, claiming to be writing much better material now that he no longer had his job at the bank distracting him from concentrating on the book, but Riva had held firm, quite sure that he should try his chances like all other aspiring writers did, rather than expecting favours merely because he was married to a published author.

'What do you want to drink?' Ben passed Riva the menu, interrupting her train of thought. 'There's a rather nice Bordeaux listed . . .'

'You choose, Ben. Although I think I'll have a mint tea first, to warm my poor icy fingers,' Riva replied. Once, a chance remark like that would have had Ben promptly reaching out for her hands to massage warmth into them. But Riva rubbed her own palms together now, feeling saddened again by the distance that had crept into their marriage somewhere along the way. Where did these cold gusts fly in from, she wondered, blowing aside all life in a marriage and leaving only the carcass of something that was once so warm and loving?

Riva folded her pashmina and pushed it into her bag before running her fingers through her hair and sitting up in her chair. She was determined to enjoy her evening out with her husband and hoped – both for her sake and Ben's – that she had managed to cover up her silly secret outing to BAFTA. It suddenly seemed so terribly sad to have snuck off to gawp at a film star she had once vaguely known – one who, in all likelihood, would probably look right through her if he saw her today! But it was even sadder, Riva thought, that she should have to hide such a thing from the man she was married to. It was daft and mean and Riva resolved she would never do such a thing ever again.

Ben, sitting across the table from Riva, scanned the extensive menu without seeing it. He had spent the past hour assiduously reading its contents in minute detail while waiting for Riva to turn up and knew exactly what he was going to order. What was preoccupying his mind was not Riva's lateness. Nor was it anything to do with her carefully elaborate explanations of her whereabouts this evening. He and Riva never questioned each other about whom they had met in the course of the day; theirs simply wasn't that kind of a watchful, possessive relationship. Tonight, however, Ben simply could not erase from his mind the conversation he had overheard between Riva and her dislikeable little sister, Kaaya, the previous night. It had left an acrid taste in his mouth and Ben wondered now if he ought to tell Riva about how hurt he was feeling. It would, of course, ruin their meal out and Ben knew that would only make him feel more wretched. It was true what they said about eavesdroppers never hearing good things about themselves – although he had not been eavesdropping, but had merely stumbled upon an accidentally overheard conversation. It must have been close to ten o'clock by the time he had come in from the pub. He had entered through the kitchen door and the sisters, sitting in the living room, had not heard him come in. He was just about to stroll into the hallway to say hello when he heard Kaaya's loud voice ring out in her horrible brassy manner.

'Admit it, you're just too, too soft on Ben, Riva, constantly tiptoeing emotionally around him and thinking up various imaginative excuses for what is plainly typically selfish male behaviour.'

As Ben froze at the kitchen door, he had been relieved to hear Riva respond tetchily. 'Look, it's not as if he's never worked, Kaaya. Don't you go forgetting, honey, that Ben not only supported me for the time it took to complete my creative writing course at East Anglia, he bailed *you* out too with that loan for your PR diploma. Besides, he was a rock to us all when Papa died.'

But Kaaya – in Ben's opinion, a self-seeking opportunist who mysteriously had every single man in her immediate circle seemingly wrapped around her little finger – was typically ungrateful. He could imagine her waving a dismissive manicured hand in the air as she spoke.

'I paid back Ben's loan years ago, in case you've forgotten! Yeah, sure, he even helped Papa once financially. But Ben was a different man then. Not the grumpy old git he is now. People change and you're mad to keep clinging to some lost notion of what he once was. Chuck him out, sis,' she advised coolly, as though Ben were no more than a carton of something going slightly whiffy in the fridge. It had taken superhuman self-control to keep from striding into the living room to let the pair know he had overheard their conversation. But Ben had stopped himself. Not to save Kaaya the embarrassment but, quite simply, to hear Riva's response. Surely, surely she would spring to his defence.

Instead, he had heard Riva laugh. Perhaps it had been with astonishment or wryness, rather than amusement – it was hard to tell without seeing the expression on her face. But Ben had been so incensed by the sound of Riva's laughter at Kaaya's suggestion of 'chucking him out' that he had turned on his heel and walked out of the house, leaving the kitchen door swinging open on its hinges for the two women to puzzle over later. He had subsequently stayed at the pub until closing time, getting more and more drunk and wallowing in sadness and self-pity, trying desperately to convince himself that Riva would surely have defended him after his departure.

The worst part of it all was that, at some level, Ben knew Kaaya was right – what was Riva doing with a man like him anyway? It wasn't like it had been when they'd all been young and full of promise back in their university days. After all, any one of them – Riva, Susan, Joe, Aman – could have turned out successful back then. It was all a matter of luck and chance. Despite one's best efforts, life had a totally arbitrary way of dishing out favours, Ben knew that now. The pity of it was that back at uni, it was he, Ben, who had seemed most likely to be going places, the only one in the gang to be hand-picked by a bank when the milk rounds had started in their final year. It would be no exaggeration to claim that he had once been the most popular student on campus, not just a top student but also an ace debater and captain of the cricket team. Would anyone even remember now that he had been the first among them all to have landed a job, one that everyone was so certain would lead to a glittering career as a banker?

Twelve years down the line, however, events had taken a direction that no one would have predicted back then:

Riva was a successful, award-winning novelist; Joe a consultant psychiatrist at one of London's biggest teaching hospitals; Susan, the special needs co-ordinator at a primary school praised for its innovative teaching methods; and, most gallingly, Aman Khan of all people was now a fucking film star, earning megabucks in Bollywood, gracing magazine covers and being worshipped by droves of women in the farthest corners of the world. To Ben, Aman Khan's resounding success had been the biggest surprise of them all. Kaaya's came a close second – vacuous, self-absorbed Kaaya who had done amazingly well for herself as a Hollywood film publicist. Who in their right mind would have ever imagined that brain-dead *Kaaya* would one day turn into a better have-it-all feminist than her much brighter and nicer sister? Whenever Ben reflected on life's vagaries (something he had a lot more time for since the bank had laid him off two years ago), he could see it all quite clearly: Riva Walia, one-time president of Leeds University's student union and founder of *Bitten Apple*, the campus feminist rag, had merely got unlucky and was now trapped in a lacklustre marriage that was like a drug habit, impossible to break. And there, in her swanky Holland Park apartment across town, was Kaaya Walia – once considered the pretty airhead sibling – having her cake and eating it (and by God, was she eating it) with an office overlooking Soho Square, a designer apartment in Holland Park, two flash sports cars in the double garage, a wealthy investment banker husband and, as if all that wasn't enough, an endless string of admiring men on the side. Ben had seen them, hanging adoringly around Kaaya at the fancy parties she threw – a besotted young colleague here, a well-heeled client there, men went mad for her. As they would have done for Riva too, had she been a different sort of woman. Riva was equally, if not more, attractive than her sister, but was not given to the sultry come-ons that Kaaya was so adept at. Riva was hard-working, sweet-tempered and persevering but, when all was said and done, it was Kaaya who was materially more successful. How unfair was that?

It made Ben feel wretched to think how easily his golden prospects had gone dark and sour, and how he had dragged Riva down with him. It was incredible to think that he, Ben Owen, should be out of a job. Incredible but true. Perhaps Kaaya had been right last night: he was holding Riva back and she was too kind to admit it herself. He ought to do the right thing by her and leave. Vanish into the ether. Perhaps allow her to pick up with Aman Khan where they had last left off. Which had been at the end of that first year at university when he, Ben, had thought he was king of the world, simply because he had got the girl, while poor luckless Aman Khan had left uni with neither a girl or even a degree. And now, there was Aman Khan gracing posters overlooking Leicester Square, gloating at the tiny luckless mortals that passed beneath!

Chapter Five

Kaaya delved into her handbag for her BlackBerry, wondering how illicit love had been managed in the era before mobile telephony. Perhaps spouses just caught each other out more frequently in those bad old days, when lovers had no choice but to use home phones after work hours. Kaaya, of course, called on Joe's home phone only if it was Susan she needed to speak to. Which wasn't often, as Susan was really her sister Riva's friend more than hers. Nevertheless, there had been the occasional call – to invite Susan and Joe to dinner or, more recently, to help organise Riva's surprise birthday party. Kaaya would be the first to admit that there had been a curious thrill in speaking to Susan, knowing that Joe was probably listening in at the other end of their conversation, longing to grab the phone and shower kisses into it.

She glanced at the time on her phone. This was the best time to catch him, just as he would be finishing his daily workout. He was in fact probably just settling down before one of the computer terminals at his snazzy wi-fi enabled gym, from where he used his new secret email account to write her long and sentimental emails. Kaaya preferred telephone conversations to emails, writing being much more Riva's thing than hers. Besides, tapping on a keyboard was murder on her delicately French-manicured nails.

She inspected their perfect pearly sheen now as she stretched out on her chaise longue, listening to the distant buzz of Joe's phone. On her face was the smile that Riva used to describe as 'Kaaya's cat-smile' when they were children. But Kaaya's smile faded as the ringing tone continued and she realised that the answering service was going to kick in. Kaaya was accustomed to having men grab hurriedly at their phones to answer it without delay when her name flashed up on their screens. Still, she reckoned she could give Joe the benefit of the doubt this once. He had, after all, proven to be a most attentive lover this past month. Unsurprisingly, actually, given that she was his first (and, quite likely, would be his only) extramarital dalliance in the ten years he had been married to Susan. He had, in fact, all the gauche charm of the first-time adulterer, as eager as a puppy with his affections. Kaaya was familiar with the sort, and she found she enjoyed their attentions rather more than those of the more blasé seasoned cheats. The only problem with a lover as ardent as Joe was that there was every danger he would get too serious and start talking divorce and remarriage. And that was *definitely* territory Kaaya was not interested in. She already had a husband, for heaven's sake, and a rather high calibre one too! No, Joe was merely a timely emotional prop to help her through this rather bleak time.

Kaaya's thoughts stopped drifting when Joe's phone stopped ringing. 'This is the Vodaphone messaging service. Please leave a message after the tone.'

Kaaya kept it brief. 'Hi, it's me. Call when you can.' She did not need to specify who she was and that she was alone. Joe already knew that Rohan was in Japan for a week and had vowed to see her every day in his absence. Or rather, every night after work. Except Tuesday, he had said, as it was his old classmate's birthday. Kaaya glanced at the digital calendar on the wall. Of course – Tuesday, that's where he was. The bloody birthday party!

Kaaya clapped her phone down on the coffee table, trying to quell her rising irritation, and used the tip of her forefinger to pick up a fleck of dust that was shining silver on the glass surface. It wasn't like Manuela, her fanatically hard-working housekeeper, to miss even the tiniest smear or speck. Kaaya glanced around the room, forcing herself to take pleasure in its perfect designer chic – the Italian sofa in soft cream suede, the sweeping chrome down-lighters, the bunches of fresh yellow rosebuds arranged on the mantelpiece in small square glass vases. It was the perfect setting for an elegant woman like her. After all, Anton, Kaaya's Parisian jeweller, had once explained how even the highest quality gold was just metal without the embellishment of a perfect stone. But what a waste to be looking as fabulous as she did tonight when there was no one around to appreciate it.

Kaaya got up, sighing as she walked into her bedroom. She peeled off her Chanel jacket and hurled it onto the floor. Manuela would put it on its upholstered hanger and return it to its rightful place in the walk-in wardrobe when she came in tomorrow morning. Divesting herself of the rest of her office clothes, Kaaya riffled through her vast collection of home outfits, wearing only her mauve lace lingerie and a towering pair of purple patent leather Jimmy Choos. Without too much ado, she chose one of her many Joseph silk kaftans and threw it onto the clothes horse. Then she slipped off her bra and panties and surveyed her curvy but gym-toned naked figure with momentary satisfaction before finally pulling the kaftan over her head. Kicking off her five-inch stilettos, Kaaya slipped her feet into a pair of gold chamois slippers and padded her way back across the pile carpet to fetch herself a drink from the cabinet. As she walked, she could feel the soft fabric of her kaftan brush rather pleasurably against her bare nipples. Oh, *what* a bloody waste to be feeling so sexy on a night when her lover was unavailable. If Kaaya had been a little more adventurous, there were numerous others she could have summoned with a click of her fingers – suave old Rodney Theobald from the art gallery, for instance, or Henry from the accounts department at work, the latter no doubt ready and willing for a quick bonk at five minutes' notice! Henry had held a candle for her ever since she had joined Lumous PR a year ago and, last Christmas, he thought he had hit the jackpot when she snogged him in the broom closet and allowed him to slip one hot hand under her bra. But he – single, adoring, available – was far too easy for Kaaya. She generally preferred a chase to be more exciting, even when it was a new client she was wooing at work. Which was why affairs with seemingly happily married men were the bigger challenge. But they certainly came with some irritating constraints. Damn Joe and his friend's birthday party! Kaaya considered calling him anyway, to make him sweat just a tiny bit under the scrutiny of his wife and friends . . . That would serve him right for leaving her in the lurch on a night like this, she thought, picking up her phone again.

She stopped short, deciding to call Riva first. The juicy tidbit of news she had for her sister could not wait any more. The din of a noisy restaurant was apparent in the background as Riva's voice came down the line. She was shouting to be heard over the clamour. 'Hello? Hello? Kaaya, that you?'

'You sound like you're in the middle of a railway station,' Kaaya said, enjoying, as always, being rude about the kind of downmarket places her parsimonious sister tended to hang out in.

'It's a restaurant, actually, Kaaya dearest.'

'Really? I don't exactly detect the hush of discreet waiters and thick white linen in the background . . . or the tinkle of crystal, for that matter,' Kaaya said, her voice dripping with sarcasm.

'What? Can't hear . . . hang on, I think I need to walk towards the door,' Riva said.

'I said, it – sounds – too – noisy – to – be – a – *restaurant*. Oh, never mind.' Kaaya sighed but Riva had heard her this time.

'Well, I'm hardly one for shelling out six months' worth of royalties on a minuscule platter of nouvelle cuisine, just because it's got some jumped-up cheffy name attached to it, am I?' she retorted, refusing to rise to her sister's snobbishness.

'Now, I can think of various responses to that, Riva darling, but I'll spare you while you're dining, lest you choke on your sausage and mash. Who're you with anyway? Not that sad specimen you call a husband, by any chance? In which case, you must be dining at the finest greasy spoon. Or – I know – a greasy chopstick basement in cheapest Chinatown. Yes?'

Riva laughed. 'Cheapest Arab Town, actually. Wassup, anyway?'

'Okay, won't keep you. Just that I have news for you. You'll never guess whom I met this arvo.'

'Who?'

41

'A college mate of yours . . . said he remembered you
. . . Care to wager a guess? Oh, I can't bear this so I'm
just going to tell you. It was Aman Khan, King of
Bollywood, no less!'

There was a pause before Riva spoke again, her voice
calm. 'Aman Khan? Where on earth did you meet *him*?'

'At my office, believe it or not. He came with a director
– some oily bloke called Shah – to talk about getting a
publicist for a forthcoming crossover film of his. Indrani
down in reception recognised him from her regular diet
of Bollywood. She was all aflutter, near fainting point, I
can tell you. And I do have to say he's really quite a looker
in the flesh. You never said he was so dishy or I'd have
taken more trouble keeping up with his films!'

'How did my name come up?' Riva asked.

'Oh, we got chatting and I told him that my big sister
was his classmate at Leeds Uni.'

'I wish you hadn't. He's hardly likely to remember me,
is he?'

'That was the peculiar thing, Riva: he did! He suddenly
got all animated too, telling me about how you cornered
him on his first day on the campus to stick a placard in
his hand. Typical of the shop-stewardy sort of thing you
would do, come to think of it!'

'How curious he remembers *that*!'

'Or was the placard just a chat-up ruse on your part?
Clever, if it was. He still remembers it anyway . . .'

'Of course it wasn't a chat-up line! There was some
kind of protest on in uni when he joined, if I recall.'

'Well, I told him you were still a bit of a trade unionist
and rabble-rouser. Putting pamphlets through people's
doors and doing your soapbox thing down at Speaker's
Corner every Sunday morning.'

'Kaaya, you didn't!'

'Sure did.'

'Oh Kaaya!'

'Course I didn't!' Kaaya cut through Riva's wail. 'What do you take me for? He wasn't there to talk about you anyway so we swiftly moved on to other things.' Her voice became smug. 'Think I may have netted a big fish today, sis.'

'Well done, you,' Riva said quietly, not sure if Kaaya meant that she had netted a new client in Aman – or a new admirer. The latter was not an unlikely scenario, given the earthy sex appeal Kaaya oozed in such abundance. Surely Aman Khan, like most men, would not be impervious to Kaaya's beauty? Riva wondered why the thought should make her suddenly feel so despondent.

But Kaaya was now ending the conversation in her usual abrupt manner. 'Better let you get on with din-dins, then,' she said, before adding a cheeky postscript. 'Love to you but none to that crabby hubby of yours. Oh, and mind you don't choke on a bit of cartilage, eating all that cheap meat.'

Chapter Six

Aman walked up the metal stairs to board his flight for Dubai. He was impressed by the sheer bulk of the massive Airbus A380, remembering a letter he had recently received, signed by Sheikh Al Maktoum himself, which contained all sorts of lavish promises to revolutionise the whole concept of luxury air travel. But even Aman Khan, for whom luxury was now a byword for existence, found himself impressed with the private suite the air hostess was now ushering him into. He looked around with pleasure, feeling comfortably cocooned, as the air hostess hung up his Armani coat in a small closet. Since becoming a star, he had learnt the value of privacy, but air travel had remained the one arena in which no amount of money could buy this precious commodity. He had toyed many times with the idea of a private jet, but had not taken it any further because of his fear of small aircraft. Sitting down in a capacious seat, Aman resolved to get his secretary to write to Sheikh Al Maktoum and thank him for coming up with the idea of private cabins on board flights. He kicked off his Loake loafers and settled himself down. After the rigours of the publicity hoopla for his latest film release in London, the air hostess's standard patter about his seat converting to a flat bed was unobtrusive and reassuring. Adopting his usual method of tackling long-distance air travel, Aman asked for lime juice with soda and angostura bitters.

'No, nothing to eat, thanks,' he insisted, ignoring the anxious expression on the woman's face. The food earlier in the evening at the Mayfair house of the Bindra brothers had been the usual rich Punjabi fare and was still sitting heavy in his stomach. The Bindras were the biggest distributors of South Asian films across Europe and a visit to their home had become compulsory on his London trips; which wouldn't have been too trying, were it not for the fact that Mrs Bindra always assumed he must miss Indian food terribly when he was travelling abroad. And she sure went to town on all those ghee-laden gravies, when all he really wanted was some soup and toast.

After the air hostess had left, closing the door to the suite softly behind her, Aman strapped himself into his chair, feeling his spirits lift as the behemoth he was ensconced in started to trundle down the runway, picking up speed before it pulled upwards into the eastern sky. Very civilized, he thought, fiddling with the technology around him after his drink had been served. Aman picked up the in-flight magazine and leafed through to the entertainment section. He had over a thousand films on demand – and only seven hours to watch them in! He decided to order a second drink before turning the privacy button on, which, as the air hostess had explained, meant that he would be left alone to watch as many films as he liked until ten minutes before landing. 'Except in the very unlikely case of an emergency, of course, Mr Khan,' she had said, smiling. He had smiled back, not voicing aloud the passing thought that, in his current bleak state of mind, the idea of an emergency was not such a worrying proposition.

He looked out of the minuscule window at the empty vastness beyond, dark and purple at its edges . . . Who would ever imagine that an unsatisfactory marriage could bleed so much of the happiness out of life?

Still, he had many other things to be grateful for. Aman picked up the remote control to search for one of those . . . Ah, here it was, the Bollywood selection, including eight films in which he played the lead! He scrolled downwards to the earliest of them – *Krodh* – and clicked on it. He watched his younger self appear in a few fragmented black and white shots under the opening credits. Only the tie he was wearing was imbued with colour, glowing an arty fluorescent red. Very James Bond, he thought, breaking into a sudden grin. He sat back as the film started and watched himself appear on the screen alongside Amitabh Bachchan. As a twenty-something sidekick, in comparison to the great Bachchan, the towering *real* hero of *Krodh*, the young Aman Khan was just a boyish young runt! Perhaps it was true what the rags said . . . Aman *had* grown better looking over the years, although it wasn't due to plastic surgery, as some of the magazines had imputed.

Aman leant his head back on the leather upholstery, remembering his excitement at being offered that first big break. It was a year after Aman had returned from England, having decided to give up on university there. And the break couldn't have come at a better time, when his life appeared to have ground to a complete halt with a failed attempt at a university education and a broken heart. Even now, it wasn't hard to recapture the gut-wrenching disappointments of that summer.

Aman took a deep breath, searching his memory . . . Had he *imagined* Riva's face in the crowd as he had left BAFTA earlier this evening? He'd always thought of her as a Londoner, an idea he'd picked up from a small newspaper piece he had read in India when she had won that prize a couple of years ago. He had never heard of the Orange Prize before but, from the tone of the piece, it appeared to be something fairly major in the world of books. It had come as no surprise to Aman that Riva had gone on to become an acclaimed author. She had always been so intelligent, even as a teenager, and had diligently read every single book on their reading list in that first year, sometimes helping Aman by giving him compact précis of the more difficult ones. She'd been unfailingly sweet to him during all that time, and Aman had been sure she had been as much in love with him as he had been with her. But in the end Riva had succumbed to Ben's persistent attentions and Aman had stupidly allowed her to drift away. Looking back now, Aman knew he ought to be kinder to himself. It hadn't been stupidity that had led to his losing Riva but a lack of confidence; today, of course, he would have dealt with things quite differently. Then Riva had seemed so superior to him, so clever and so smart. It was no surprise she'd chosen the English guy over him really . . .

Aman looked unseeingly at the pictures flickering on the screen before him. He'd never forgotten that distant past, even though he had firmly walked away from it and not stopped to look back. But this afternoon, he had thought about Riva a lot, his memories sparked by that chance meeting with her sister at the PR firm. The sister had confirmed that Riva did indeed live in London. And – this was the bit that still stuck slightly in his craw – that she had finally gone on to marry Ben. At least, the sister had mentioned the name Ben; it had to be the same guy. It sounded exactly like the kind of golden life Aman would have expected Riva to be enjoying by now. So what would she have been doing lurking among a crowd of his fans at the BAFTA entrance today?

Aman shrugged. As before, he must have imagined seeing Riva in the crowd. It was silly but quite often he imagined he had spotted Riva when travelling in England, seeing her standing on railway platforms or across crowded shop floors. Aman pulled out the small clutch of business cards that was still in his pocket. 'Kaaya Walia' was the name printed in a large curly font, flamboyant gold on ivory. Aman had never met Riva's sister before, and during their meeting this afternoon she had mentioned still being in school when Riva had joined university. She was a good-looking woman, though not a lot like Riva, being harder and far more sophisticated than the teenage Riva of Aman's memories. But then, Riva might by now have changed a great deal herself.

Aman picked up his drink again, reflecting on how Riva's success – unlike his own – was completely unsurprising. Even as a first-year student, she'd shown signs of making it big some day, being so bright and focused and determined. And yet she was one of the most gentle girls he had ever met. People like her deserved their success. Unlike him, who had merely got lucky. His own mother sometimes joked that fame had dropped into his lap when he had been half-asleep and lounging on the sofa one lucky day.

Aman took a long swallow of his lime soda, wondering, not without embarrassment, if Riva ever watched any of his films. Perhaps she and Ben laughed at the thought that the shy and rather silly young suitor she had humoured (and Ben had had to fight off) back at college was now a film star. Famous enough to be featured on the cover of *Time* magazine recently. He looked out of the window and, in its black emptiness, saw his own face looking back. The *Time* article had described him as 'handsome' and 'aloof' but what Aman saw when he looked at his own reflection was the rather diffident and uncertain man he had always been. Stardom hadn't changed him that much. It certainly hadn't made him any happier.

Aman smiled now, wondering whether he could blame his 'aloofness' on his early heartbreak over Riva. If he were honest, he had never completely gotten over her. The easiest explanation was that Riva had been the first girl he had fallen for and maybe it was true what they said about the first cut being the deepest. Or perhaps it was something to do with the fact that *she* had dumped *him* – in contrast to all his subsequent relationships where he had been the one to end things. Aman became pensive again. The most likely explanation for the warmth with which he remembered Riva was that his marriage to Salma had turned out to be such a calamity. It was wrong but, every time Salma behaved in a difficult fashion, Aman was unable to stop himself imagining what it would have been like to have married someone as kind-hearted and lovely as Riva instead.

Their becoming classmates had been something of a happy accident. That English degree had been a disastrous choice of subject for Aman but it was all that had been on offer for a green school-leaver from India with un-impressive grades. The course apparently demanded A's and B's but his Uncle Naz had been breezily confident about getting him admission, assuring his anxious parents back in Bombay that British universities were now desperate to get full fee-paying international students to join up. 'Better than having the boy hang around a city like Bombay, getting bored and getting into trouble,' Naz *Chachu* had cheerily assured his parents on the crackly long-distance line from Leeds. Aman's parents had agreed without too much hesitation. Bombay colleges had all closed their admissions, even their second lists. And, after all, Naz himself had once been the family black sheep, whom life in England had straightened out in a way no one would have imagined when he had first left India with a few hundred rupees in his pocket. Just ten years down the line, Naz *Chachu* not only owned a string of petrol stations, he was branching out into motorway cafés and – three years ago – had shown further good sense in marrying a girl from a moneyed family. In a move that signified his total and complete redemption, he was offering to take the next generation's black sheep into his home in Leeds to sort him out.

But Aman had arrived in Leeds in the midst of a grey autumn, and he could recall that the only thing that had prevented him from jumping onto the first flight back home was the sight of a pretty young Indian girl in a red miniskirt who had accosted him on his very first day at the university outside the Chancellor's office to insist that he join the Union's protest. 'But what are you protesting against?' he had queried half-heartedly, not keen at all to spend his very first day at college being thrown out of it. Not after the trouble and expense poor Naz *Chachu* had gone through.

'The hike in the tuition fees that overseas students are required to pay! It's downright shameful,' the girl had replied, her face frowning and pink with annoyance. And Aman had been too shy to confess that, despite being an overseas student himself, it was an issue he knew absolutely nothing about. Besides, the girl was far too attractive to be disagreed with, and so he had meekly allowed himself to be press-ganged into joining the small band of predomin- antly brown-faced students, all of whom were carrying placards and shouting a great deal. She had disappeared into the crowd with a pert flash of her skirt after that but, fortunately, soon popped up again, handing Aman a dustbin lid and a wooden ladle with instructions to 'Make as much noise as you possibly can, okay? Yell, if you must. That's the only language they understand.'

Even though he did not know whom she was referring to as 'they', Aman had obediently made as much of a din as he could, shouting and clanging for all he was worth, all the while keeping an eye on the red miniskirt as it flashed around the quadrangle. Its pretty owner appeared to be quite definitely in charge of events as they unfolded. Aman recalled how, finally, about an hour later, a great cheer had broken out among the protestors as the Bursar emerged from his office. He wore a harassed expression on his face as he beckoned to the miniskirted girl. When she disappeared into his office along with a couple of others, the remaining protestors seemed to lose both interest and momentum and Aman heard the word 'pub' mentioned as, one by one, people started to put their placards down and drift away. Only Aman continued to stand there, shivering in his too-thin jacket as the sun set over the roofs of the college buildings and the evening drew in.

When she emerged from the Bursar's office an hour later, the girl looked startled to see him still standing under the tree, holding the dustbin lid and ladle she had given him.

'Goodness, you're not still protesting, are you?'

'Well, I'm not shouting any more but I had to return these to you,' Aman said, handing her the dustbin lid and ladle as though they were prize possessions. She took them from Aman, looking around at the empty quadrangle with a huge frown.

'Don't tell me they left you here by yourself to decamp to the pub? What utter bastards!' she declared, looking in concern at Aman's thin, shivering frame. He nodded dumbly and was astonished when she proceeded to take his arm. The discomfort of the cold autumn evening was instantly forgotten as she beamed up at him and squeezed his arm. 'Well, our victory makes it all worthwhile, eh? We won! The Bursar's going to take the matter up with the uni's governing council so it's only a partial victory at this stage. But well worth a celebration.' She took her hand from his arm and added, a little more shyly, 'Hey, thanks for joining in. Can I buy you a drink for your pains? Least I can do. I'm Riva, by the way.'

Aman leant back on the headrest of his aircraft seat, remembering that long-ago time. No doubt anyone who knew him then would declare that he had changed unimaginably – and not necessarily for the better! Fame had converted his boyish shyness to 'aloofness' and his open, trusting nature to cynicism. Even the susceptibility he once had to the sort of kindness Riva had shown him was now transformed into the deepest suspicion of people's motives. But, back then, he had been so easily touched by Riva's friendship and the manner in which she had firmly taken him under her wing. That day outside the Bursar's office, she had marched him into the smoky warmth of the Hare & Tortoise and introduced him to everyone as though he was her best friend. The others had been faintly curious but eventually accepting of him, despite his being a bit of a fish out of water: a teetotaller, fresh out of India and completely clueless about some of the jokes they tossed about so nonchalantly. Looking back, Aman realised that they had all been nice enough – all except for Ben. Aman had soon worked out that the fellow was already madly in love with Riva and consequently jealous of the attention she was showering him with. Ben wasn't to know that she was only feeling sorry for the lost soul Aman had been back then! In fact, it was probably pity that had led to her first sleeping with him four months later too. But, mere weeks after that, she had gone off him again, and slipped back into her own circle of friends; people who were like her and with whom she would naturally feel more at home.

Aman chewed on a slice of lemon, trying to recall the names of all the others . . . Susan was Riva's best friend, a gregarious redhead who had been to the same school as Riva and had joined Leeds Uni too, but in the History department. Her name had stuck in Aman's head for some reason but, try as he might, Aman could not now remember the name of the medical student Susan had been going out with . . . a tall, gangly, serious type who talked a lot about joining Médecins Sans Frontières when he had completed his MBBS . . . Jack? John? No, it had gone . . .

With all those young faces now floating around in his head, Aman tried to settle into his aircraft bed. But, after half an hour of trying to fall asleep, he was still awake, wondering if, like Riva, Susan had gone on to marry her college sweetheart. They had seemed a well-suited pair, the chatty redhead and her medical student boyfriend who had such a grave and serious air about him. Aman had heard them talk about joining VSO together . . . Perhaps they had, and were now working side by side in some corner of the world, helping the poor and dispossessed. Some couples were like pieces of a jigsaw slotting in perfectly together, Aman thought as he finally fell into a troubled sleep.

Chapter Seven

The sudden clear knowledge of Joe's infidelity came like a physical blow to Susan's stomach. The unease had been growing for days but she had so far had nothing definite to put her finger on. One could not possibly make an accusation, or private judgement even, on the basis of such vague observations as a spouse's far-off look, for heaven's sake! Not if she did not want to be seen as completely paranoid.

There had been other things, though. Until last month, Joe's BlackBerry had been an instrument carelessly strewn about the house, often beeping insistently while Joe raced about the house searching frantically for it, or nearly getting chucked into the recycler along with the Sunday papers. Now, however, Susan had observed the damn thing become a permanent accessory to her husband, looped around his neck on a cord, and glanced at frequently and surreptitiously. If Joe had been seventy, Susan would have understood the neck-cord thing but he was thirty-five, for God's sake, and far from requiring memory aides! Before the suspicion had crept in, sitting like an unmoving lump between them, Susan had quite casually asked Joe about his sudden attachment to his mobile phone. He had looked confused for a moment – clearly not realising he'd made it so obvious – before speaking quickly, thinking on his feet. He was considering dispensing with wearing a watch, he said, and had Susan noticed that youngsters never wore watches any more? Their whole array of technological needs was now being met by their phones, apparently. Susan had at first accepted Joe's explanation without question, even agreeing that most of her older students had in fact dispensed with wearing wristwatches.

What was more difficult to ignore was Joe's more recent tendency to veer from overblown expressions of love to irrational snappiness, as though Susan had simultaneously become both her husband's most loved person, and his most hated. There had even been that ghastly scene last month when they had been driving up the M4 to visit her parents in Stoke Poges. Joe had been silent for much of the journey, responding to Susan's attempts at conversation with monosyllables or grunts. He had also been driving unusually fast and, when Susan had reminded him that they were in no particular rush to get there, he had slammed on the brakes and swung onto the hard shoulder in a quite terrifying manoeuvre, only narrowly missing a coach travelling on the inside lane. The angry blare of the coach's horn was still ringing in their ears as Joe turned on Susan in a fury to yell, 'Do *you* want to drive then?' Startled by the unexpected aggression, Susan had silently swapped places with her husband and taken the wheel, unwilling to let Joe drive when he was in such an agitated state. Joe had calmed down just as rapidly, soon reaching out to cup his hand over Susan's on the gearstick and mutter an apology. But, needless to say, the lunch at her parents' home had been awkward.

Despite Susan's rather affable and trusting demeanour, she was no fool, and had contemplated the possibility of

Joe having an affair with a pragmatism that had impressed even her. Then she had hastily put the thought away, feeling disloyal for even considered it. Besides, the very idea was too exhausting in its potential for grief.

But now, tonight, proof was here staring her in the face.

Curious how the tiniest of actions could escalate into an event so big, so devastating. Who would have thought that five minutes could change your life? All she had done that evening was to excuse herself to use the ladies' at the restaurant. Wending her way through the other tables, she had seen Joe leave the gents' just ahead of her; but he did not return to their table as she expected, instead walking out of the restaurant into its herb garden, all his attention on the keys of the BlackBerry he was jabbing. Still thinking nothing of it, she had followed him, planning to give him a mischievous private snog before they returned to their table of celebrating friends. It had been a noisy evening, with everyone congregating at the River Café after work, and Susan had barely managed to grab a few words with Joe before they had been caught up in the general merriment of gift-giving and catch-up chatter. A hug was now in order, especially seeing how unusually tired Joe had looked as he had walked into the restaurant, his tie askew, that distant expression on his face again.

She could just about hear Joe's deep voice as she came up behind him, expecting him to turn at the crunching sound of her heels on the gravel path and smile at her. But his attention had seemed consumed by his call, his head bent, his voice low and caressing. Perhaps it was that which made Susan stop – the intimate tone of voice that she had always previously assumed was reserved for her. She came to a halt just before she reached out to touch him, her heart lurching sickeningly when she heard him say, 'I have only a couple of minutes, darling, but I had to call you . . . Where are you?'

Oddly, there was a part of her that, instinctively recognising an intensely private moment, had wanted to slink away. Later, talking to Riva, Susan would even exclaim ruefully at that memory – laughing at her typically doltish instinct to be considerate to her husband, even at her own expense. But then that irrational moment had passed, and she reached out to touch Joe's elbow. He had swung around and visibly flinched at the unexpected sight of her; almost as though she were not his wife at all but a crazed mugger carrying a knife. Their eyes had locked for a few confused seconds in the moonlight. Susan could see Joe struggling to remember what he had just said that might have been overheard. Comically, the silence between them was filled by the unmistakably female voice that continued to emerge from the mouthpiece of Joe's phone, crackling from somewhere far away, unaware that it was not being responded to any more. Then Joe had cut the line dead, muttering a lame excuse to Susan about a patient needing emergency advice, before stuffing his phone back into the top pocket of his shirt. Susan had nodded, looking blankly at the small bulge that the phone formed against Joe's chest, almost as though expecting it to involuntarily start speaking and offer a more credible explanation than the one she had been given.

Susan had accepted her husband's blatant lie, quite simply because it was far less devastating than the truth. Then she had swiftly and silently walked back into the restaurant, Joe following her. They had weaved their way past all the other diners, making painfully slow progress back to their own table at the far end of the restaurant, and soon were swallowed up once more in the noisy warmth of their celebrating group of friends.

It was the fortieth birthday party of David, Joe's oldest friend, now a paediatrician at Great Ormond Street Hospital and one of Susan's best chums too. David's plump face was by now quite pink from all the Shiraz he had been consuming. As Susan now slipped back into her chair, he enveloped her in a bear hug, slurring fondly, 'Dear, darling Ginger . . .' (David was the only person Susan ever allowed to call her Ginger) '. . . where have you been? I was quite lost without you, y'know . . . don't be running off like that again . . .'

Susan, still trying to calm her racing heart, smiled at David, but, over his head, she could see Joe excusing himself from the table again, walking swiftly back in the direction of the toilet. Of course, he was going to call and apologise to the person he'd so rudely cut off – Susan knew that without a doubt. And, despite the smile for David that was still frozen on her face, she could feel her heart break into a million bits inside her chest.

Chapter Eight

Joe woke on the morning after David's party, unsure for a moment of where he was, blinking in confusion at the sun streaming in through the thin linen curtains. Then he groaned as he felt his stomach churn and a dull ache hit him between the eyebrows. He'd drunk way too much last night. But that had seemed the only option after that ghastly mishap with Susan and the phone call. He wasn't sure how much she'd overheard of his conversation, especially as she'd seemed fine later, laughing and joking with David as usual.

He recalled feeling his knees physically buckle underneath him when Susan had materialised behind him in the garden of the River Café, while Kaaya's voice had been caressing his ear. How strange was this thing called guilt – on the one hand, it had the power to make him feel as if a knife was slashing away at his insides and yet . . . yet, there were times when he was so completely inured to it, he could look straight into his wife's face and lie, coolly and blatantly, without the slightest pang. Why, there had even been the day – at the birthday party Susan had recently thrown for Riva – when he had lost control and kissed Kaaya full on her lips, his hands running all over her lithe body as he pressed her against the fridge, all the while hearing Susan's laughter in the next room. If it hadn't been for the fact that he was himself a psychiatrist, he would have thought this behaviour a form of madness.

But that was what women like Kaaya did to men like him. She was just so beautiful and so captivating, he was like a ball of putty in her hands. Joe knew he wasn't a weak man, never had been. Not with alcohol, not with women. It was something he prided himself on. But it was literally as though he had had no choice at all once Kaaya had set her sights on him. Of course, they had met many times over the years – he had even attended her wedding to Rohan, for Christ's sake – and although he had long thought of her as the most gorgeous thing he had ever laid eyes on, he had never even considered flirting with her. Not least because he would never have dreamt of hurting Susan with that kind of behaviour. Now Joe realised, of course, that the only reason he had not fallen for Kaaya before was because he had thought her completely inaccessible; he had never once imagined that she would spare him more than a moment's thought. Until that night, when they were all gathered quite casually at Riva's house and Kaaya had caught him looking absently at her cleavage. Instead of doing that thing that women like Susan did – rather sheepishly adjusting their necklines and swiftly looking away – Kaaya had deliberately bent over to pick up an almond out of a bowl, further revealing the alluring swell of her breasts. Then she had looked up at him through her lashes and smiled knowingly as she delicately placed the almond on her tongue and chewed on it, leaning back and running one finger along the rim of her wine goblet.

That had been the start of it and Joe still felt giddy at the memory of the days that followed – the snatched flirtatious conversations at parties and restaurants edging them closer to very dangerous territory, that first kiss on Riva's wet driveway last Christmas, stolen while the others were busy collecting their brollies and drunkenly kissing everyone else in the hallway, and finally, one frozen day in January, a long, lingering lunch at China Tang, which he had managed by pleading a trumped-up illness at work to be able to leave at midday. It was only after that lunch, convinced by Kaaya's passionate air and seeming sincerity, that Joe had finally plucked up the courage to take their relationship to the next logical step, one he was quite sure he would not have taken for a mere physical fling. It was something he had only rather wildly dreamt about before, listening with some amusement to other people gossiping about such things in half-horrified, half-admiring tones. Adultery. Infidelity. Big words, as though it required more than a couple of syllables to express such major transgressions. At what stage exactly did one describe a relationship as adulterous? When a man first held his wife's body and imagined she was someone else? When he first lied to a woman he barely knew about the state of his marriage, allowing a near stranger to believe that his wife of ten years could not make him happy? Even if it had to be a physical act, at what precise point in the continuum between kissing and having full-blown sex did an affair slip into the realm of infidelity? The simple truth was that, by the time Joe had decided to have sex with Kaaya, he had seemed to have no choice in the matter at all. He was, in fact, so ready to burst with love and longing for this beautiful, beautiful creature, so convinced that it was nothing short of a gift to be offered her love, that turning away from it would have seemed the bigger travesty. He had loved Susan well enough, but now it was as though he simply loved Kaaya more.

It had been a perfect day too, nothing about its clean white snow and crisp sunshine indicating that something immoral could be afoot. They had driven out that morning through the peaceful Oxfordshire countryside bathed in winter sunshine, heading for Bray. After a light lunch at a country pub – both of them being too nervous to eat very much – they had checked into a local B&B, and made fervent love all through the afternoon. It was only when the sun had started to set beyond the fields, and the plane tree outside their window was filled with the noise of returning birds, that Joe had even remembered they both had homes and spouses to get back to.

He had told Susan he was attending a day conference at Oxford and she seemed to think nothing of it when he returned late that evening, exhausted and unwilling to talk. Odd that he had never before noticed how tatty Susan's pink bathrobe was, or how annoyingly she slurped on her mug of bedtime cocoa while watching TV. But he had managed to blank it all out, turning away from Susan in bed and pretending to be asleep until he could hear her breathing lapse into soft snores. But sleep did not come easy to him that night, his nerves jangling from being on edge – not from guilt, surprisingly, but because of the plan that had been made to spend a whole night at Kaaya's apartment the following week. Luckily, Rohan's job involved a great deal of travel and Susan was not unaccustomed to Joe needing to do the occasional night shift. It would not be difficult to manage.

All Joe knew that night, as he drifted into sleep remembering Kaaya's warm, luscious body in the hotel bed, was that he could not wait – not just to make love to Kaaya all night but to experience the magic of waking up in the morning and seeing that she was not just a dream he had conjured up in the night.

Susan prepared a cafetiere full of coffee before calling up the stairs for Joe to wake up; it was a habit formed over the years since they had moved in together – eleven this year, ten since they were married and fifteen since they had first met. Susan noted the figures with sudden shock, never having been one for showy anniversary celebrations. For fifteen years, she had loved one man so wholly that the possibility of losing him now seemed so tragic it was almost laughable!

With one ear cocked for the creaks and sounds of Joe moving about upstairs, Susan made her sandwich, wrapped it in a bit of foil and tucked it into her handbag alongside an apple. Normally by the time this was done Joe would have appeared in the kitchen – tousle-haired and sleepy-eyed in his pyjamas – just in time to collect a kiss from her before she left for school. It was his job to clear away after her, of course, collecting the milk and newspaper from the doorstep and waving her off as she reversed her car down the drive.

Today, however, there was no sign of Joe, even after the sandwich had been made, and things had gone very still upstairs. Susan wondered if she ought to go up to the bedroom to make a pretence of saying goodbye. She took a quick look at her watch and hesitated. It wasn't the lack of time – she still had ten minutes to spare – but the wrenching memory of the overheard phone call last night that was stopping her. There had been no point confronting him with it last night, not when they were surrounded by their friends and everyone had been so drunk. After that, either because of the alcohol or sheer exhaustion induced by shock, Susan had slept the sleep of the dead, waking up far too late to do her customary half hour of yoga. And there wasn't the time to start hurling accusations at Joe right now, not when she had so little time before she needed to leave for work. It would have to wait till the evening. Or perhaps she needed to 'gather more evidence' first. There was every chance Joe would just deny it outright, telling her she had imagined it. Would premature questioning not merely present him with the opportunity to cover his tracks more efficiently, giving him time to come up with a plan to deceive her better? Perhaps he would even put his head together with the person he had so casually addressed as 'darling' to come up with a finer plan to fool her and string her along a bit more . . .

Who *was* this other woman? And why on earth would she have gone after a married man? *If* she knew Joe was married, that is . . . Susan felt her stomach twist and quelled a sudden desire to retch. What was she to do? There had never been a template for responding to a husband's infidelity in all the books she'd read. As far as she knew, infidelity wasn't something anyone in her inner circle had ever had to cope with anyway. Not her mum, her two sisters, or her best friend, Riva. And it was much too late to go rushing out to buy those trashy magazines she saw at the dentist's that emblazoned problems across their covers such as: 'My husband is gay' or 'He slept with my mother' . . .

Keeping her voice calm, Susan shouted upstairs again and this time heard Joe's muffled voice as he emerged from the bathroom.

'I'm off now,' she called, before picking up her bag and shutting the door behind her. She was managing to impress herself with all this calm, poised behaviour. Of course, everyone at school had probably always seen her as impossible to ruffle, whatever the crisis at hand. Even that time when little Patrick Hoolihan had badly cut his arm and blood had gushed out of the wound in a jet that flew across the art room, it was Susan who had kept her head, stemming the flow with a tourniquet and silencing the child's screams with a swiftly made-up story involving an ambulance that was too polite to flash its lights and scream its way through the traffic.

It was only once Susan was in the car, driving down her leafy Wimbledon road, that the magnitude of what she was so coolly coping with hit her. A social worker had once told her that cars did that to people – something about their rocking, womb-like environment making children suddenly disclose abuse and other horrors kept hidden from the world. More effective, the social worker had said, than a hundred carefully controlled psychotherapy sessions. So that was it, then. All it took was sliding into the front seat of her little blue Mini and, suddenly, Susan could feel everything magically well up inside her: a huge wave of anger and sorrow and pain that she could not hold at bay any more and that now threatened to drown her as she drove along the A23. She would have to pull in somewhere, she thought in panic as the tears started to slide uncontrolled down her face, blurring her vision. But the traffic was heavy and moving along in brisk single file on this busy Friday morning.

She tried to stem her tears. It would be shameful to walk into the school with her face all red and blotchy; what would the poor children think! But, for now, it was such sweet relief to simply let go. Susan drove on, feeling the tears roll down her cheeks and drip off her chin onto the woollen fabric of her skirt.

Somehow she made it from the car park to the school toilets without bumping into anyone. Once she had washed her face, Susan felt calmer and took out her phone. She had to talk to someone, to help restore that terrible lost sense of reality that was overwhelming her, as though she had somehow managed to wander into one of her worst nightmares.

Riva. Her best friend was the only person who could possibly help sort this tangle out.

Chapter Nine

The phone started to ring just as Riva jabbed with relief on the full-stop key. Chapter Nine done, hallelujah. More importantly, her main character had reached the cross-roads she had spent five chapters propelling him towards and had finally decided which way to go. The rest of the book would be a freewheeling exercise downhill, Riva knew. With one successful book under her belt, she was starting to get familiar with the routine.

Her mind still miles away in a fictional town in the Peak District, Riva said 'Hello?' absently into her phone, her eyes still scanning the screen of her laptop. Instead of an answer, she got a strange muffled snuffling at the other end of the line. Just as she was contemplating hanging up, she heard the sound of Susan's voice suddenly emerge, not bubbling with laughter as usual, but drowning in a flood of tears.

'Sooz?' Riva called out in alarm. 'Is that you?'

The snuffling gave way to a horrible low wail. 'It's me, Riva. The most terrible thing's happened,' Susan said, her voice suffused with tears. 'Joe . . . he's . . . oh Riva!'

'What is it, Susan? What's happened to Joe, for God's sake?'

How many conflicting possibilities was it possible to

have racing simultaneously through the mind in the space of a few seconds? Riva's brain collected them all: accident, heart attack, cerebral thrombosis, serious domestic spat . . . until it stopped short at the one possibility that Susan was now blurting out through distraught tears.

'Affair . . . Riva, he's having an *affair*!'

'What?'

'I said, Joe's having an affair.'

'*Joe!* An *affair?*' Riva asked, unable to match up those two words, even have them occupy the same sentence. Nevertheless, she repeated the words slowly and blankly, trying to digest them. 'Joe's having an affair.'

Perhaps her reaction wasn't so obtuse. Of all the people in Riva's very wide circle of friends and acquaintances, the one person who seemed furthest removed from the possibility of an extramarital dalliance was Joe. Good-natured, serious, contented old Joe, who had loved no one but Susan since day one at uni, who had steered a steady course through their years of separation when he was at med school, and who had married his college sweetheart the moment he had started earning a pittance as a junior doctor because he had said he could wait no longer.

'Susan, are you *sure*?' Riva asked, knowing it was a stupid question but waiting, biting her lip, hoping that Susan was only joking. Not that Susan was given to puerile pranks, so it really was a very stupid hope. While her friend noisily blew her nose, Riva enquired more gently, 'Where are you, Sooz? I just realised it's a weekday – are you at school? Are you able to talk from where you are?'

Susan had recovered herself a bit by now. 'Yes . . . I'm at school but I can talk for a bit. I desperately needed to speak to you, Riva.'

'Okay, so tell me what happened.' Riva tried to sound calm while quelling her own growing panic.

'Oh, Riva, I'm as sure as I can be about it. The suspicion's been growing for days now but I hadn't mentioned it before because I wasn't sure. But yesterday . . . yesterday I overheard Joe on the phone to someone, Riva. I wasn't imagining it.'

'What did you hear?'

'Not a lot. But he had sneaked away from the crowd and he addressed her as "darling" . . .' Susan broke off again in sobs.

'Was *that* it?' Riva asked, relief flooding through her.

'What do you mean, was that it? Isn't that enough? Pretty much confirmed it for me, I can tell you,' Susan replied, reverting momentarily to her more spirited self.

'Hang on,' Riva replied. 'People often get away from crowds to take calls, Susan. It doesn't necessarily mean they're *sneaking* off . . .'

'Yeah, right. In a freezing garden and without a coat. That's why I followed him, actually, to tell him off for being outdoors without a coat . . .' Susan's voice was edging into tears again.

For want of anything else to say, Riva tried another tack. 'Besides, addressing someone as "darling" means nothing in most circles, right?'

'Joe doesn't address anyone as darling, Riv, not even me!' Susan was now sounding quite indignant.

'His mum?' Rev asked, clutching at straws.

'Christ, no! How many men do you know who call their mums "darling", Riva? For God's sake!'

'I don't know . . . maybe I was thinking of Indian men and their mums . . .' Riva trailed off. Then she added, 'Where were you when you overheard him, Sooz?'

'At the River Café. David's birthday party. And it wasn't just the fact that I'd overheard Joe, Riva. It was his reaction to seeing me appear suddenly behind him. He was guilty as hell. It was written all over his face.'

'What did he do? Did he say anything?'

'That was the other thing, Riv,' Susan said, weeping again at the memory. 'He lied . . . he . . . he . . . he looked me in the face and *lied* so idiotically. Said something about a patient who needed medical advice, for God's sake. As if he would have *ever* given his private phone number out to a patient and as if they'd *ever* call him close to midnight. That was the really grubby bit, Riva, that he actually thought I'd be thick enough to buy such a fucking unlikely story.'

'Oh, Susan,' Riva whispered, recoiling at Susan's un-characteristic use of strong language. The import of what Susan was saying was only just starting to permeate her consciousness. 'Did you tell him, Sooz? Tell him you didn't believe his fib, that is?'

There was a small pause before Susan replied, 'No I didn't, Riva. And, before you ask me why not, it was because . . . because I just couldn't bear to hear the truth. I . . . I preferred to have Joe stand there and lie through his teeth to me, rather than have him be honest and tell me he's having an affair with someone.'

Riva felt her chest squeeze painfully as she heard her friend's voice dissolve in tears again. In her confusion, she offered another stupid alternative. 'Maybe he isn't . . . sleeping with her, Sooz. I mean, maybe it's not that sort of an affair but some kind of friendship thing . . .' Riva trailed off, realising that an emotional attachment was perhaps worse than a physical affair.

'For God's sake, Riv!' Susan cried. 'Even if he isn't fucking her now, he obviously *wants* to, doesn't he? I mean, why the fuck would a man sneak away from his wife and call another woman and address her as "darling"? Why the fuck, if it isn't to shag her . . .'

Riva nodded, her head reeling from Susan's uncustomary flurry of f-words. Even 'shag' seemed too strong for someone so well brought up. The strongest language Susan normally used went no further than 'damn' and 'bloody'. Riva gathered her thoughts together again, trying to stay calm for Susan's sake. 'Have you any idea who he might have been talking to, Sooz?'

'You know, I haven't even got as far as that, Riva. Because what I still can't cope with is that *Joe's* been lying to me. It's almost as if it doesn't matter who she is. You know?' Before Riva could respond, Susan added angrily, 'But when I do find out who she is, I swear I'll kill her.'

Kaaya eased herself into the leather seat of her Lotus Elise and, after turning on the ignition, pressed the electronic buzzer for the garage doors to open. Usually the deep throb of the engine filled her with a sense of well-being but this morning Kaaya was in a bad, bad mood. Bloody Joe! First he had abandoned her last night, leaving her to spend a boring evening watching reruns on TV, and then he'd woken her in the morning babbling on about how worried he was that Susan may have overheard their conversation last night. Before even asking her what sort of an evening *she'd* had all by herself.

Apparently, Susan had walked up behind him when he had been kootchie-kooing her from outside the River Café. Susan hadn't *made* any accusations yet but Joe was *quite* sure she'd smelt a rat. It was written all over her *face*, she

73

was *real* quiet this morning, she left for work barely saying *goodbye* . . . blah di blah di blah . . .

'Pathetic,' Kaaya muttered under her breath as the garage doors swung open and she reversed her car out onto the quiet cobbled mews. What the fuck had Joe expected would happen when he embarked on an extramarital affair – that he could blithely carry on and never be found out? The way he had bleated this morning, it was as if he'd never even considered the possibility. Married men were such morons sometimes, imagining they could live different parts of their lives in convenient little bubbles that, if they ever collided, would simply cheerfully bounce off each other and float away!

When the traffic lights on Holland Park Avenue turned green, Kaaya pressed her foot on the accelerator, hearing the wheels of her car squeal against the road. She had half a mind to call off this whole stupid thing with Joe. Affairs were meant to be fun and uplifting, not a bloody mill-stone around the neck, pulling you down. It was piteous, the way Joe had gone on this morning, blithering on about how he really, really didn't want Susan to know. How he couldn't bear to hurt her. It wasn't that Kaaya wanted him to leave Susan for her – that was the last thing on her mind, for heaven's sake! Nor, for that matter, did she particularly want to hurt the bloody woman. She had nothing against her and Susan was, after all, her sister's best friend. But Kaaya certainly wanted Susan kept well away from the fun she was having and Joe's insistence this morning on shoving his wife's pain down her throat was such a drag.

Stopping at the next set of traffic lights, Kaaya sensed someone's gaze on her. She glanced out of her car window and felt the familiar old frisson as she saw a man – oh, and a pleasant-looking man in a silver Ferrari – eye her appreciatively. As their eyes met, he smiled and nodded his short-cropped grey head. It could have been at her sports car or it could have been at her lustrous brown hair, tousled by the breeze. It certainly fitted her mood to decide it must be the latter and Kaaya slowly smiled back at him, her enigmatic I-could-be-interested-in-you-depending smile. Then the lights turned green and she shot ahead of him, leaving the faint smell of burning rubber in her wake.

Kaaya was feeling calmer by the time she wafted into her office half an hour later, the man in the silver Ferrari having provided further entertainment by racing her down Great Western Road before finally disappearing in the direction of Regent's Park.

Henry from accounts was doing his customary hang-around reception, waiting for her. His crush on her had got so bad since the last Christmas party, he no longer even bothered hiding it from everyone. Sarah, the girl behind the reception desk, gave Kaaya a quick smile of relief as she walked in. The poor girl was probably quite exhausted from Henry's stubbornly clinging presence – half an hour extra today owing to Kaaya's lateness.

'Hello, Sarah, sorry I'm late. Any messages for me? Oh, hello, Henry,' Kaaya said, stopping by the reception desk and casting glowing smiles all round. Greeting Henry with more warmth than usual would only refuel his cloying adoration but, after Joe's behaviour this morning, Kaaya would be willing to charm Idi Amin himself.

'Oh, Kaaya, Pamela was looking for you a few minutes ago. And these people called,' Sarah replied, shoving a small pile of notes towards Kaaya.

'All well, Henry?' Kaaya asked, collecting her messages

and turning the full blast of her 100-kilowatt smile on the hapless Henry. Henry gulped and nodded, a virulent pink creeping up from under his collar at the vibrant presence of Kaaya in a swishing purple miniskirt and fishnet tights within touching distance of him.

'H-hello, Kaaya,' he whispered, unable to look her in the eye. Kaaya decided to spare him further agony and spoke over his shoulder to Sarah. 'Tell Pam I've just got in, Sarah, sweetie, and I'll pop upstairs soon as I can.'

She riffled through her notes as she walked into her office. Aha, two from Joe. Evidently he'd gathered she wasn't too pleased with his panic attack this morning and was trying to make amends. She'd keep him waiting a bit before calling him back. Kaaya really didn't like clingy love-sick dimwits, so perhaps she would keep Joe at bay for a while. She did, after all, have a job to attend to.

Chapter Ten

It wasn't working. Riva closed her laptop and leant back in her chair, suddenly exhausted. It had been a messy writing day, starting off with a couple of extremely productive hours first thing in the morning. But, after that phone call from Susan, her work had been patchy, thoughts swinging wildly from what suddenly seemed like trivial fictional diversions to the terrible earth-shattering stuff of reality. In her time as a fiction writer, Riva had discovered that, usually, it was real life that was the crucible for the most powerful dramas. Poor Susan. Riva hadn't heard her friend sound so distraught in years. In fact, she probably hadn't heard Susan sound so distraught *ever* – Susan being the kind of placid soul who had steadfastly done nothing wrong all her life. Suddenly the carefully made-up problems of Riva's protagonist seemed so very inconsequential in comparison to what Susan was facing at the moment. Riva clicked shut the Word document that was the growing manuscript of her third book. There was no point. Whatever she wrote on a day like this was bound to be complete rubbish and guaranteed to be trashed when she returned to it later.

Riva looked at the kitchen clock as she slipped her

laptop back into its case. Three pm. Enough time to grab a shower before heading out to Susan's school. They had agreed to meet at the Portuguese café down the road from the school so that Susan would not be interrupted by her colleagues or students. She seemed to want Riva's help in preparing a strategy before Joe got home that night but, although Riva had given it extended thought, she had not come up with any ideas beyond boxing Joe's ears if indeed he had been cheating on Susan. She still couldn't believe it though. Not Joe, ideal-boyfriend-then-ideal-husband Joe Holmes, the kind of guy all their single female friends were looking for.

Riva shoved her computer case onto the bottom shelf of the bookcase with some force. Then she sprinted up the stairs, gathered her towel from the airing cupboard and disappeared into the shower.

Towelling herself dry a few minutes later, Riva wondered where her own husband had gone. Ben had left the house first thing in the morning to go to the British Library and certainly had not said he wouldn't be home for lunch. The ham sandwich Riva had made for him when she stopped for a bite at midday now lay in the microwave with its edges curling. She sighed. No doubt Ben would be expecting a hot meal when he got back, seeing as she'd been in the house all day, and would not be amused at the sight of a dried-up sandwich awaiting him instead. Riva sighed again, more deeply. The business of both of them being full-time writers did rather complicate the domestic arrangements sometimes. Never mind that Ben found more excuses to leave the house than she did, the nonfiction he wrote apparently requiring more trips to the library than fiction writing, which Ben always seemed to imply required less hard graft. Never mind the fact that she was the only one of the two of them with an actual publishing contract!

Riva sighed and gave herself a reproachful look in the bathroom mirror. She knew she shouldn't be uncharitable to poor Ben, even if it was only in her thoughts. It was downright mean to regard his writing plans as dubious merely because he hadn't been published yet. She, more than anyone else, ought to understand how much determination it took to spend hours working on a manuscript, completely uncertain of whether it would ever get published or even read.

Shivering in her underwear, Riva sprinted to the pair of tall mahogany wardrobes in the bedroom. She cast a glance out at the steely sky. It had remained a stubborn grey all day, reluctantly leaking meagre sunshine through leaden clouds like an afterthought. And now it was barely three o'clock and the day was already resolutely darkening into night! She hurriedly pulled on a thick jumper over a T-shirt and dragged on her Levi's, feeling altogether miserable. She had always hated these short February days, when night and day were barely discernible from each other. Something to do with her Indian birth, she reckoned, or the two sunny years she had spent in the Punjab before her parents had emigrated to England. Despite all these years, she had never grown used to the unrelenting greyness of the English winter and never would.

Of course, today everything was made infinitely worse by the misery of her best friend, but something had been palpably infecting her feelings for Ben of late, even though today, of all days, she should have been appreciative of her faithful husband. Perhaps it was something to do with her beloved father's recent death, which had rather curiously brought into focus Ben's own shortcomings as a husband.

'Well, Ben,' Riva muttered, sitting on the edge of her bed to yank on a pair of fleecy boots, 'I *could* have roused myself to rustle up a *pulao* or a soup, *just* to keep you feeling like a man who's just come in from a hard day's work. But, you know what? My best friend, Susan, has just found that the man she's lavished every ounce of love she's had to give since she was eighteen may be having an affair. As though he were just another *dick* and not the fine, intelligent, upstanding man we always thought he was. Maybe, just maybe, she needs me a tiny bit more than you do tonight, Ben.'

That was the other thing about a writer's life: these ridiculous monologues that had recently become a habit, everyone assuming that a writer's life was easy simply because you could hang around in your pyjamas while doing your day's work. Would anyone stop to consider, Riva wondered, that she hadn't spoken to another soul all day? Except for Susan this morning, which was a most unusual event. Even the routine trip to the newsagents had been dumped in favour of finishing Chapter Ten because there was every danger of being sucked into reading something in the papers that would gobble up a precious couple of hours. Deadlines, deadlines, did publishers know how sapping of creativity these bloody deadlines could be? Ben certainly didn't.

Riva looked at herself in the mirror to dab a bit of powder over her face and run a kohl pencil over her eyes. That would do. She really ought to wipe this unseemly frown off her face before she got to Wimbledon. For Susan's sake. God knows she needed some cheering up, although Riva didn't feel terribly well qualified to be that person tonight.

She picked out a small leather satchel and slipped her

travel card into it, making her way downstairs. It was only as Riva was pulling on her coat in the hallway that she saw the letter sticking out of the postbox. The envelope was creamy and expensive looking, and had a French postage stamp bearing a Cannes postmark. Riva ripped it open and nearly dropped it in her excitement. She reread it to be sure it wasn't a mistake. This was incredible! She, Riva Walia, was invited to be a jury member at the sixty-third Cannes Film Festival this summer!

In disbelief, she ran her eye once again over the details, savouring every word . . . At the Palais des Festivals et des Congrès . . . Nine jury members . . . Chaired by Isabelle Huppert . . .

Then she sucked in her breath sharply as she read the names of the other eight judges and came to the fourth on the list . . . Mr Aman Khan from India.

Riva leant heavily on the sideboard, suddenly dizzy. Perhaps she had wished for this somewhere in her deepest subconscious, in some kind of stupid yearning fan-like dream. Without an author carefully plotting events on a timeline and playing God with a bunch of helpless characters, choreographing their every move, how else could such an astonishing thing possibly happen?

Riva slid the letter under a pile of newspapers and left the house, resolving to contain her excitement until after she had met poor Susan.

Chapter Eleven

Aman was met at Dubai airport by a small posse of dangerous-looking men who whisked him into a fleet of cars. Although he enjoyed relative anonymity in this city, like London, it was too full of Indians for him to hope to pass completely unnoticed.

He looked out of his darkened windows at the other opulent cars passing by, imagining how excited he would have been as a boy to see a Bugatti, a McLaren and a Maybach all in the space of ten minutes. Now everything seemed so lacklustre.

It was not long before Aman saw the tall mast-shape of the Burj Al Arab rise from the waters of the Arabian Gulf as the chauffeur steered his Rolls-Royce expertly through Dubai's lunchtime traffic. The car swept along a freeway that was flanked by palm-fringed emerald lawns on one side, the ocean glittering blue-gold on the other. Soon his car was rolling up the hotel's vast drive, the ocean on either side giving Aman the illusion that they were wafting all the way up the gangplank to a massive ship.

The Indian doorman gave Aman a delighted smile as he disembarked. After a polite exchange of words with the man, who seemed quite overcome by a film star paying him so much attention, Aman sprinted up a set of sweeping marble stairs to the entrance. No matter how many times he walked through the doors of the Burj, Aman couldn't help being dazzled all over again by the quantities of gold leaf that seemed to cover everything; the walls, the floor, the ceiling were brighter than ever as the afternoon sun poured in. This was his fourth or fifth visit but Aman reckoned he would never entirely cope with the garish opulence of the Burj. It was Salma who insisted on staying at this hotel when she was in Dubai, mostly for the privacy they guaranteed all their guests, but also, Aman knew, because she simply would not settle for anything less. If there was a seven-star hotel in a city, it would be unthinkable that Salma Khan should stay anywhere else!

'Has my wife arrived yet?' Aman asked the butler, who was walking a few respectful paces behind him down a gilded maroon corridor towards the lift.

'Mrs Khan arrives in an hour's time,' the man replied in soothing tones. As if he understood already that soothing was what Aman really needed with the imminent arrival of Mrs Khan. Aman smiled wryly. Salma would appear, as she always did, in a whirl of secretaries and beauticians and hair stylists, barking orders into a phone that was permanently glued to her left ear. The habit had grown worse with her recent acquisition of a cricket team that was playing in the Indian Premier League, the long-distance negotiating and strategising seeming to give her a special buzz. It was as if she thrived on the power of being in charge of things, no matter how far away she was. She certainly had a strange way of robbing not just Aman, but the very air around her, of peace and tranquillity.

Aman sighed as he was escorted up to the Royal Suite on the twenty-fifth floor. He'd suggested going for one of the smaller suites this time, given that this was not a personal visit but one organised and paid for by the Khalili brothers. But Salma would never agree to anything but the very best, of course, and the ever-courteous Khalili family had been quick to respond.

'Least they can do, Aman,' Salma had urged. 'After all, you are charging only half what you normally get to attend their function.' She was right but, typically, she was overlooking the fact that the discounted rate was because the Khalilis were known for their philanthropic work and the function was a fundraiser for Autism Awareness, a cause the oil tycoons were committed to because of the autistic twin sons born to the elder of the two brothers.

Aman entered the mustard and gold expanse of the Royal Suite, wondering how the hell he would cope with leopard-print carpets for three whole days. The two bedrooms upstairs were a necessary requirement, as he'd asked Salma to bring Ashfaq along on this trip and she would no doubt turn up with his regular entourage of nanny, governess and playmate. But a living room this size, a dining room *and* a private cinema was definitely overkill for such a short stay, much of which would be spent in the Khalilis' ocean-view mansion anyway.

Aman flung his shades down on a console table and kicked off his shoes, enjoying the cool of the Carrara marble underfoot. Running up the stairs, he entered one of the two bathrooms and washed his face vigorously under water as cold as he could stand. After towelling his face dry, he picked up a bottle and splashed something that smelt faintly like citrus fruit on his face – Eau de Hermès, the lettering on the bottle discreetly pronounced. Salma would be pleased.

Aman wandered out into a bedroom whose centrepiece was a huge circular and canopied four-poster bed. He remembered this bed from an earlier visit four or five years ago – a time when he and Salma had been getting on better, for he could recall how they'd laughed while experimenting with its various spinning and vibrating functions. It was hard to imagine such a time now, given the frostiness that had crept into their marriage in the past few years. Looking back, the surprising bit hadn't been that he'd married Salma in the first place. She had been a beauty, after all, daughter of the legendary Noor, India's top actress in the sixties. Aman had spotted Salma at one of his first film parties – a lavish affair celebrating twenty-five years of Rajshri Studios – and had found himself unable to take his eyes off the fair-skinned, svelte beauty that Salma had been then. She was, in fact, the spitting image of her mother, as Noor had been in her prime, and Aman was overwhelmed by a feeling of déjà vu, imagining he was watching an old Noor film (and he had seen them all in his misspent schooldays) as he watched Salma, clad in a sparkling white *gharara*, sitting demurely by her father, the powerful and influential Abdullah Miandad, then Bollywood's top director.

Aman had managed to inveigle an introduction to Salma at the party and they had spent some time chatting about inconsequential things. But Aman had picked up a sense of an ambitious girl trapped in a traditional setup and had felt a rush of sympathy that only added to the sensation of being quite smitten. Old Miandad had been pleased as punch when, a month later, Aman made a tentative enquiry regarding the possibility of seeking his daughter's hand in marriage. The positive response had surprised Aman at first, but he realised later that Salma's canny father had probably already had some inkling of Aman's star potential with *Krodh* having by then catapulted him to hero status. Aman's parents had been nonplussed by the Bollywood princess they had suddenly been landed with as a daughter-in-law, but Aman's new-found money and status was by then bringing them a life of substance too, so it hadn't been a totally unequal union. In the early heady flush of that youthful marriage, Aman had for a short while genuinely believed he was happy and in love.

That was *then*, Aman mused, staring out at the waters of the Persian Gulf sparkling into the distance. He had certainly never bargained for Salma turning into a lazy, complaining wife who considered it his duty to keep her in comfort. Even his tentative suggestion that she try taking up the acting career she had seemed to so desire was met by a disbelieving look.

The blazing blue of sky and sea was broken only by the occasional boat or aircraft and, as Aman watched a helicopter approach the hotel, he guessed that it was making for the helipad on its roof. He grinned, remembering a tennis match he had witnessed on the helipad a few years ago – a Roger Federer–Andre Agassi tournament that the smooth British MC had described as 'strawberries and cream meeting the mile-high club'. Aman watched the helicopter progress slowly in the direction of the Burj and it slowly dawned on him that Salma had taken the option of using a helicopter transfer from the airport, despite his firm instructions not to do so. He felt bile and fury rise in his stomach as he thought of how heedlessly she had taken to ignoring his every request. She would, doubtless, accuse him of being tight-fisted but it wasn't that at all. It was not just Aman's fear of small aircraft but also his ever-present terror that something bad would happen to Ashfaq when he wasn't near enough to help; an anxiety born from being forced to spend so much time away from his son. Salma would have been fully aware that a helicopter journey with Ashfaq would make him deeply unhappy – and yet she had chosen to do exactly that. Aman watched the small distant dot of the helicopter and felt his jaw clench in helplessness and fear.

It was a full fifteen minutes before the chopper landed and he could breathe easy again. He watched wearily as Salma's arrival in the Royal Suite was preceded by three hotel flunkeys carrying an entire set of Louis Vuitton suitcases. Behind them came Hameeda, Salma's chief maid who, when required, also doubled up as general foghorn and fixer. She was certainly doing her best impression of the former, blaring out instructions to the hotel staff in her brassy voice, ceasing only when she spotted Aman standing against the windows. She swept her arms and head downwards in a low grovelling *adaab*. The respect was all surface stuff, Aman knew. Hameeda's loyalties had been with Salma ever since she accompanied her from her childhood home and it had always been patently clear that she would happily kill anyone – even Aman Khan – if they ever crossed her beloved mistress.

And there she was now, Mistress Salma herself, sweeping into the room in her customary cloud of rose attar, her phone clamped to her ear, as was her habit, while she talked nineteen-to-the-dozen, both into the phone and at everyone around her.

'Mummy,' she mouthed at Aman as he walked across to give her a welcoming kiss. She could have been talking to Allah Himself for all Aman cared as, bringing up the rear of the party, was Miranda, Ashfaq's *ayah*, carrying in her arms a precious bundle clad in D&G Junior. He was beaming from ear to ear at the sight of his father.

'Ashfaq!' Aman said, taking his son into his arms, feeling joy and relief coursing through his body as the small sweaty bundle clung to him. Was he imagining it, or were their periods of separation getting harder and harder to bear? He kissed the boy's slightly damp head before lifting him into the air to see him better and hear the squeals of pleasure this action always produced.

'Dadda!' the child screamed, clinging to his father's arms as he was wafted up and down a few more times. Aman gave him one more hug before setting him down and watching him toddle away.

Salma came off the phone now and gave him a peck on one cheek. He touched her forehead with the back of his hand. 'You're hot,' he remarked.

'Oh *hanh*, we took the helicopter transfer from the airport. Ashfaq was *sooo* excited.'

Salma was clever enough to know that mentioning his son's name would defuse Aman's annoyance. Besides, they were safely here now so there was little point in making a huge fuss about the helicopter ride. Aman nodded, deciding to overlook the incident. Unusually, they were to be together for three full days here in Dubai – it was best not to ruin it at the start. But, just as quickly as she had appeared, Salma was off again, wafting up the stairs this time, her chiffon *sari pallav* trailing after her as she yelled various instructions to the bellboys and Hameeda to begin unpacking the suitcases. Aman joined Ashfaq at the floor-length windows of the living room and dropped to his knees in order to share his son's view. Ashfaq had both chubby fists pressed to the thick glass.

'Car!' he said solemnly, pointing at a distant yacht.

'Boat,' Aman corrected.

'Car,' Ashfaq insisted, illustrating his point with a guttural 'Drrrrrrrr', small hands holding an imaginary steering wheel.

'Oh, okay, car-on-water,' Aman laughed, sitting back to enjoy the sight of his baby son take off for a spin in a pretend car around the carpet. Returning a few seconds later, Ashfaq clambered onto his father, changing tack to say informatively, 'Coppen.'

'Coppen?'

He nodded. 'Elicoppen!'

Aman looked enquiringly at Miranda who was hovering nearby.

'Helicopter,' she explained. 'New word, learnt today.'

'Ah, helicopter! Yes, you came here in one, didn't you, Ashfaq? Did you enjoy it?'

Ashfaq nodded. 'Elicoppen drrrrrrrr,' he yelled, scrambling off his father's lap to do another small circuit on the carpet.

Salma reappeared, phone clapped to her ear again. In her other hand was a bundle of letters that she waggled in Aman's direction before throwing them onto the coffee table. She returned to the bedroom, still talking nonstop into her iPhone.

Aman reached out for his mail but stayed where he was on the floor, sitting cross-legged and leaning on the glass while leafing through the bundle. Pillai, his efficient PA back in Bombay, would have already sorted out the wheat from the chaff so this was all probably important stuff. It was the one right at the top of the pile that caught his attention. An invitation to judge the Palme d'Or entries at Cannes this year. It was quite an honour but he would have to check his shooting schedules first of course. He had a vague memory of having verbally promised dates in May for Ritesh Shah's Indo-French venture. It had to be summertime, in order to catch the Parisian setting at its best, the director had said. Perhaps the festival could be fitted in around those dates as he would be in France anyway.

And then he spotted her name . . . Riva Walia, award-winning novelist from the United Kingdom, the letter said. How curious that this should happen just a day after he thought he had spotted her in London – almost as if that had been an omen! It had certainly led to his thinking about her a great deal on his flight out from London . . . their long walks on Woodhouse Moor . . . her concerned words of advice when he was unable to cope with the course. Lovely, gentle Riva, whom Aman had thought he would never see again. It had seemed the most decent thing to remove himself from her life when she had chosen Ben over him. And so he had not just left uni but England too, in order to get as far as possible from his disappointments. What would it be like to meet her again after all these years? Of course he was quite ready to face her now. So many years down the line and so much water under the bridge . . . they were both grown-up now, and married and successful. Aman felt sure he would be able to look Riva straight in the eye and not give away a thing.

He looked up from the letter, seeing the blueness outside, sea melding into sky somewhere far off, and barely noticed that his son was clambering onto his back to play at being a helicopter again.

Chapter Twelve

Riva held her friend's hand across the table, looking wanly at the top of Susan's bowed head. For the first time, Riva noticed that a bit of grey had crept into Susan's plentiful auburn mop, gathering around the central parting, oddly curlier in texture than the rest of her hair and standing upright, as though begging for hair dye.

Their mugs of coffee had long since grown cold on the table and a handful of crumpled tissues lay strewn across its marbled pink Formica top. It was at times like this that Riva gave thanks for London's big-city anonymous indifference. Susan had cried nonstop for about ten minutes once they had got to the café and the only reaction from people around them had been an occasional concerned sidelong glance and a second round of coffees that had magically appeared, which the kindly woman behind the counter had refused to take money for.

'Why would Joe do such a thing to me?' Susan asked for the tenth time.

Riva shook her head. 'I wish I knew, darling Susan. All I do know is that it simply couldn't be anything that *you've* caused or brought on. I've seen you two for long enough to know that much for sure.'

'Maybe your perspective's a bit skewed too, Riva. I

mean my best friend's hardly likely to be objective in all this . . .'

'True. But I honestly don't think you can have contributed to Joe doing such a thing, Sooz. Only he can offer a proper explanation.'

'Something tells me he won't . . .'

'And that would only be because perhaps even he doesn't know the answer. It's probably a totally illogical, stupid, unthinking thing on his part, like affairs so often are.'

'You sound like you're forgiving him, Riva!'

'Oh, Susan, it's not forgiveness exactly. But I think I need to try and understand it, before judging him. I mean, he's been a friend too for many years.'

'But you just said it couldn't be anything I'd done! Surely that must mean the blame lies with him.' Susan sounded close to tears again.

Riva took her hand and spoke gently, 'Of course, the blame lies entirely with Joe and, at the moment, I do hate him for what he's done to you. But something's obviously happened to rob Joe of his normal equilibrium. This is just not typical of him, is it? I mean, you meet some married guys and know straightaway that Jack-the-lad lurks just under the surface. But Joe? He's always been so solid. So dependable. The one we all turned to for counsel even when we were eighteen, for God's sake!'

'Is it an early midlife crisis, do you think? Can you *have* a midlife crisis at thirty-five?'

'Oh, come on, isn't Joe too intelligent to fall victim to such an obvious thing as a bloody midlife crisis?'

'Think about it, though, Riva. We started going out so young: I was eighteen and Joe twenty. Maybe it's suddenly dawned on him that he never really had a chance to sow his wild oats and wants to catch up now, before it's too late.'

'Of course it's possible. But I just don't think Joe processes things in such a . . . a base manner, you know? His mind's too refined for that kind of panicked reaction.'

Susan shook her head forlornly. 'Maybe *she* tempted him. This woman he's fallen for. Maybe she's really special, Riva, y'know, really beautiful . . .' After a pause Susan added, her eyes widening as a new terrifying possibility occurred to her, 'Maybe she's half our age, Riva! A sixteen-year-old, sex-crazed nymphet!' She jabbed at a sugar cube in the bowl, pulverising it as she muttered, 'I keep seeing a woman in a sexy Lycra nurse's outfit for some reason . . . and – wait for this – I've taken to going through Joe's pockets and checking the call history on his mobile phone whenever I can . . . It makes *me* feel cheap and tawdry, that's the irony.'

'And?'

'And nothing. Not a sausage. It's quite amazing how organised he's managing to be, deleting all incriminating evidence as he goes along.' Susan threw her head back as though in agony. 'God, I really, really need to find out who she is!'

'Why though? If you did find out, would you want to confront her?'

Susan thought for a minute before responding. 'Actually, you're right. Why *would* I want to confront her? After all, my contract of trust is with Joe, not her, whoever she may be.'

Riva nodded. 'Poor you,' she said softly. 'It must be so hard to remain sensible at a time like this. But you're managing it bloody well from what I can see. Better than I'd have done.'

'Oh, don't bank on it,' Susan replied, mustering up a faint smile. 'Don't be too surprised if I suddenly crack up when I get home tonight and stick a knife between Joe's ribs!'

The women laughed briefly but Susan must have seen the flicker of fear passing across her friend's face, for she added quickly, 'Oh for God's sake, I *won't*, Riva! All said and done, I think I still love the silly bugger. Don't ask me why – and whether the feeling will last – but, at the moment and despite everything, the last thing I want is to lose Joe.'

Riva gathered herself together and sat up, trying to sound more purposeful. 'So what do you think you'll do?'

'Tonight?'

Riva nodded. 'You did say you wanted to come up with a plan before going home and confronting him,' she reminded her friend.

'Confronting him,' Susan repeated in a flat and dull tone. She heaved a sigh. 'Oh, how exhausting the thought.' Then she laughed. 'Normally, I'd be driving home at this time, planning what we'd have for dinner. Or which film we'd watch after dinner. You know, *innocuous* stuff. We never do stop to thank our lucky stars when we only have normality to worry about, do we? I'd give my right arm at this moment if someone could magic up a boring domestic evening for me. Instead, here I am, wondering how best to broach the subject of infidelity with my beloved husband!' Her voice broke briefly.

Riva sat back, thinking. After a pause, she said, 'You don't have to confront Joe with it right away, you know.'

Susan looked at her quizzically, so Riva explained, speaking slowly as her thoughts unfolded. 'I mean, all you have at the moment is a half-heard conversation. One-sided and incomplete. When you were probably a little drunk yourself . . .' Riva raised her hand as Susan

96

tried to interrupt, carrying on speaking in as calm a voice as possible while Susan subsided back in her chair. 'Nothing, Sooz, nothing like the kind of proof you need before you make an accusation. Especially one as huge as this. *Infidelity*, for heaven's sake. Maybe . . . maybe you need to be more sure of exactly what Joe's up to before you do . . .'

'More sure! I couldn't be surer he's having an affair, Riva!' Susan cried, unable to remain silent any more. 'Don't forget those uncustomary mood swings and temper tantrums last month. I read in a magazine that those are often signs of infidelity. Anyway, I've been with Joe fifteen years and know him like the back of my hand. Well, okay, I *thought* I knew him until this!' she added bitterly.

'Granted. But what would be the harm in holding back, Susan? Just for a bit. Until you know for sure. With as little as you have, Joe could just deny it completely and then where would you be?'

'On the other hand, he may crumble, when he realises I've guessed . . .'

'And then what? What if he does crumble and tell all but doesn't promise to end it? I hate to suggest it but there is that possibility, you know, that he'll want to leave you to be with her. You'd have to be prepared for that. Are you?'

'No!' Susan said so loudly and tearfully that the people at the next table briefly glanced their way. She dropped her voice and spoke more softly. 'No, of course I'm not, Riva. But can't I just think about that later?'

Susan looked so despondent, Riva's heart wrung itself out in her chest. 'Darling Susan, the more I think about it, the more I feel you ought to wait a bit. There's two reasons really: one being that you might be able to gather a bit more evidence you can use to confront Joe properly – you know, not allowing him any wiggle room if he's going to play coward and lie to you. And the other is to prepare yourself better for whatever this may lead you to. And I do mean whatever. Because we don't know yet what your choices may be.'

Susan nodded, looking downcast. 'Won't be easy to stay silent and play-act as though I still haven't guessed . . .'

'Of course it won't be easy,' Riva said sympathetically. 'None of this is.'

'Hiding such huge knowledge . . .' Susan muttered, 'it's almost like walking around with a gun in my handbag.' Then she smiled, giving Riva a brief glimpse of her more normal self again. 'Hmmm . . . a gun . . . now there's a thought.' But Riva could see that her friend's eyes were twinkling through her tears.

Riva's heart twisted with pain on Susan's behalf. She could willingly kill Joe at this point. Or, even better, the woman he was canoodling with. What *was* it that prompted some women to take up so carelessly with married men? Did they have no concept at all of a sisterhood, within which women protected each other rather than set out to make their own struggles worse? Who the bloody hell was this woman who was wreaking such havoc in Susan's life?

Kaaya lit the last of the tall vetiver and frangipani candles and looked around, inhaling deeply. There was nothing more flattering than buttery soft candlelight falling on a woman's face and here was a whole row of candles, flickering with tiny crackles and filling her living room with fragrant light.

Joe had said seven and Kaaya still had fifteen minutes to touch up her make-up. She had more or less forgiven

Joe by midday, when he made his fifth call to apologise for his thoughtless behaviour of the morning. However, it had amused her to keep him guessing for the rest of the afternoon, pretending to be in various meetings and leaving instructions with Sarah to say that she was lunching with the boss. That would drive him crazy, no doubt. A contrite lover was a particular amusement but, in Kaaya's experience, one that was both contrite and insecure could be manipulated to a remarkable degree.

When the bell rang with a soft bonging sound, Kaaya walked unhurriedly over to the door. She swung it open and leant on the door jamb, arms crossed and a small smile on her lips, allowing Joe to take in the sight of her naked body beneath her kaftan, so sheer and insubstantial that she might as well have not been wearing it. He looked a little tired and drawn but Kaaya could see colour return to his face at the sight of her. Not that she wasn't used to having this instant effect on men but it was increasingly reassuring to see that her touch was as infallible as ever as she approached that looming milestone, her thirtieth birthday, next month.

'Darling,' she purred as he walked into her arms, bending his head to kiss her deeply, gradually losing breath as his tongue continued to hungrily explore her mouth. She wondered if he and Susan had stopped kissing each other on the lips as many married couples did, given the way he was now probing her tonsils. Kaaya was in a position to assess that Joe was a reasonably good kisser, but he was also a very tall man and, despite her own not insubstantial height of five foot eight, she suddenly felt a little overwhelmed by his weight bearing down on her. Gently extricating herself, she closed the front door, suddenly fearful that one of her neighbours might choose to take the stairs rather than the lift and catch sight of her necking with a man who wasn't her husband.

'Drink?' Kaaya asked as she walked to the cabinet, knowing that Joe's eyes would be hungrily taking in the sight of her shapely bum rolling under the translucent white silk of her Joseph kaftan. He followed her to the cabinet and, unable to keep his hands off her, slid his fingers through the open slit of her garment while her back was still turned. She stiffened with pleasure as his palms cupped her breasts and he turned her around by the shoulders to face him again. He searched for her lips once more and she could feel him hardening under his trousers. Laughing, she playfully thrust him away.

'I don't know about you but I'm parched,' she said. 'I was waiting for you to get here before pouring myself a drink actually.' That was the right cue for a man like Joe and, ever attentive, he instantly let go of her to fetch their drinks.

'What would you like, my love?' he asked, kneeling before the drinks cabinet.

'There's a Sancerre in the wine chiller,' Kaaya said, pulling out a pair of glasses from above his head. 'Or would you like whisky?'

'I'll share the wine with you, if that's okay,' Joe replied, reaching into the chiller for the wine. He took the corkscrew Kaaya was holding and opened the bottle before handing it up to her. Joe stayed on his knees while Kaaya poured the pale liquid into two glasses and wrapped his arms around her hips. He sank his face into her crotch and kissed it as she lifted the two glasses and looked down at him. Her voice was only half-joking as she said, 'And I thought I'd seen the last of you, the way you were going on this morning about Susan.'

Joe looked up at Kaaya, the adoring expression on his face going momentarily blank at the sound of his wife's name. He didn't want to talk about Susan any more. Not after Kaaya's reaction this morning and certainly not when he had just been forgiven with this invitation back into her home.

'Seen the last of me?' he asked, his expression agonised. 'God, how can you even think that, Kaaya, when I can't get you out of my head for as much as five minutes!' Joe got to his feet. He kissed Kaaya tenderly on the mouth once again before taking a glass off her.

He kept one arm around Kaaya's slender waist as they walked towards the sofa and sank into the creamy leather. Joe pulled Kaaya's legs over his own and waited, holding both glasses, while she adjusted the cushions behind her so she could recline comfortably, draping her legs over his knees.

'Nice day?' she asked, reclaiming her glass and taking a long sip of the Sancerre. He nodded, his mind clearly no longer on the previous night's mishap with Susan.

'Well, it was the usual busy day at work,' he mumbled, before turning his attention to the subject they were both more interested in. 'You?'

'Hmmm,' Kaaya replied lazily. 'Paul – you know, the managing partner at the firm – took me out for lunch to a lovely little Italian place in Covent Garden.' Kaaya was only trying to rouse a tiny bit of jealousy in Joe and wasn't prepared for the tortured look he gave her.

'Why was he taking you out for lunch? Trying to get your pants off, I bet,' Joe said, unable to mask his anger.

'Now, now,' Kaaya laughed. 'We aren't getting a bit jealous, are we?'

'Of course I'm jealous. Jealous of every single man

who gets to be near you when I can't. What do you expect?'

'How will you cope when Rohan returns then? You'll want to murder him!'

Joe was silent for a moment, remembering that Rohan was due back from Japan the following day. He spoke up, his voice thick with emotion. 'I'll miss terribly not being able to come here after work,' Joe said, running the fingers of one hand over Kaaya's ankles and calves. She wiggled her toes and he took the hint, putting his drink down on the side table to take her feet in his hands and rub her soles. He'd already discovered how much Kaaya enjoyed massages, anywhere and everywhere on her luscious body. And what seemed like a chore when Susan wriggled up against him, pointing to her shoulders, was a complete pleasure when Kaaya demanded a massage. Especially considering the fabulous sex that usually followed.

'Ohhh, lovely doctor's hands,' Kaaya said, sipping wine again and arching her neck in pleasure as he worked his thumbs upwards to her ankles and calves.

'Nice doctor's mouth too,' Joe murmured, lifting one shapely foot and slipping Kaaya's toes between his lips. She lay back, watching him through half-closed tawny eyes, closing them only when he rolled her kaftan over her smooth thighs and put his face to her newly Brazilianed pubis.

One busy hour later, they were lying panting and sweating on the sofa. Joe lifted his head from Kaaya's bosom and ran his hands through his damp dark curls before sinking back onto a cushion.

'Kaaya, Kaaya, beautiful Kaaya,' he groaned softly, unsure of whether to be agonised or ecstatic at her beauty. He watched her adoringly as she got up from the sofa and disappeared into her bedroom, returning a few minutes later, her confident naked form making its way across to the chiller. She bent to stick a glass under the ice-cube dispenser, turning her pert bottom squarely in his direction. Looking at her striding back to him, Joe couldn't help thinking of how self-conscious poor Susan had grown over her own body lately, slipping into her nightshirt or bathrobe the minute they had finished having sex. He suddenly stopped short, realising with sudden insight how disrespectful it was to be remembering Susan while looking at Kaaya; though for a few confused seconds, his mind couldn't process whether the disrespect was to Susan or to Kaaya.

Kaaya was holding out the glass of chilled water to him and he sat up to take it.

'That was good,' she said casually, sitting next to him while he downed the water in one thirsty gulp.

Presuming she meant the sex, Joe smiled at her before replying in a tone that still sounded faintly incredulous at his fantastic luck, 'Who would've thought, eh? Even a mere six months ago, who would've thought . . .'

'Thought what? D'you mean about you and me?'

'Yes, you and me, lovely Kaaya. And all this,' Joe replied, waving an arm around at the smoky fragrance and melting candles, their clothes scattered all over the floor as testimony of their wanton passion.

'Why six months ago?' she laughed. 'Who would've thought when we first met that we were headed for this one day, huh? Do you remember it, Joe?'

'When we first met?' he asked. She had turned to face him and he couldn't quite look her in the eye as he nodded. The truth was that Kaaya had been a pretty but completely dim-witted sixteen-year-old when Joe had first set eyes on her. She had been sitting at her parents' dining table in Ealing when he and Susan had driven Riva down to London from university once, and he had barely noticed Riva's sulky-faced kid sister while they had all had lunch, newly in love as he had been then with Susan. Oddly, it was his first meeting with Susan that was etched deep into his mind – the girl with freckles and tousled red hair who was being treated for mild concussion when he was doing a stint at Leeds General Hospital in his third year. She had apparently bumped her car into a tree and, later, noticing the bright blue Mini zipping madly around campus, he discovered why. She was rash and mad and had the sunniest smile and it was not long after that he had found himself a regular, if terrified, passenger in the Mini and completely head-over-heels in love with its flame-haired owner.

'Remember?' she persisted and it took Joe a few seconds, as he was jolted out of his thoughts, to realise that it was Kaaya and not Susan who had asked the question.

'Of course I remember, my sweet,' he replied, tracing one cold finger over the side of Kaaya's fulsome breast before arriving at her nipple.

'No, you don't,' she laughed, kicking his shin with her bare foot. 'You don't remember a thing, admit it!'

'Course I do!' he protested. 'Ealing. 1995, wasn't it? Or '96 perhaps?'

'See, I told you,' she said, pushing his hand away in mock anger. 'I should punish you, really, for having looked right through me that day. The only people you were interested in at the time were Susan and Riva.'

'Well, they were closer to me in age and, at the time – what was I then, twenty, twenty-one – you would have seemed very young.'

'No, it's not that,' Kaaya said, her mood turning suddenly flat as an imperceptible darkness shadowed her beautiful face. 'You see, when people meet Riva and me together, it's always Riva they notice first.'

Suddenly she didn't look that different from the scowling teenager of that first meeting. Joe put his glass down and took Kaaya's hands in his. 'That's not true at all, Kaaya! Riva's lovely, of course. Why, half the campus was in love with her by her second year. But you . . . you're simply beautiful, Kaaya. You know that.'

'Well, it's nice of you to say so, Joe,' Kaaya said, getting up to slip her kaftan back on. 'But it's something I've known since I was a little girl. Perhaps it's because Riva's so clever but, when we're together, people almost automatically start talking to her and not me.' Kaaya stopped for a moment, pouring herself another glass of wine and pondering darkly, before opening up again. Joe's sympathetic bedside manner was drawing her into a confessional mode that she knew she would later regret but suddenly she couldn't stop. 'It's not just Riva's cleverness, actually, she's just so . . . so *good* . . . it shines through somehow. She's kind and generous and warm and has never – incredible as it sounds – never done anything wrong. Anything! Can you believe that? Is it any wonder that everyone, even my mother, loves her more than they love me?'

Chapter Thirteen

'Come with me, Ma,' Riva pleaded, 'You can't ignore it any more. And the GP *has* given you an emergency appointment after all.'

But her mother shook her head, her small plump frame squashed firmly in the armchair as though glued to it. Riva quelled her rising frustration. After all, it had been less than seven months since her father had succumbed to that shocking heart attack and it was perhaps too early to expect her mother to have gotten over the trauma. What Riva hadn't anticipated, however, was this heart-breaking regression to childhood, her mother seeming to think that her two daughters would replace her husband, making sure she ate properly and went to the doctor, at least until her husband got back. That was the really frightening part: Ma's apparent hope that Papa's absence was a temporary thing. Despite being gently corrected a few times, she insisted on referring to him in the present tense, as though he had merely popped out for a pint of milk and would come wandering back in, newspaper tucked under one arm and whistling 'Kuch kuch hota hai' as he always had.

Riva decided to try another tack. 'Look, I may let you off the hook, Ma, but Kaaya never will. You know that.

And she'll be here in less than ten minutes seeing that she was already on Hanger Lane when she called.'

To her relief she saw her mother's grip on the arms of the sofa loosen slightly at the sound of Kaaya's name. Even in her current depressed state, she obviously did not want to get on her mouthy younger daughter's wrong side. Then she collapsed back against the cushions again, her face crumpling as she pressed a ball of tissue to her mouth.

'Oh, Ma,' Riva cried, squatting next to the armchair and putting her head on her mother's lap as she held her knees. 'Don't cry. I know it's unbearable trying to manage without Papa. I miss him terribly too.' She looked up, her voice getting clogged with tears. 'But think how upset he'd be to see us like this . . .' Riva reached out for a box of tissues from the side table – there was always one at hand in her mother's house these days. She handed a fresh tissue to her mother and took the sodden balled-up one from her before blowing her own nose.

The sound of keys in the front door was followed by the sight of Kaaya's tall figure walking in. Riva had never been more relieved to see her sister.

'Oh, thank goodness you're here,' she said, adding, 'Oh, hi, Rohan,' as Kaaya was followed into the room by her husband. 'When did you get in?'

'Less than an hour ago,' Rohan replied, kissing first his mother-in-law and then Riva. 'We're on our way home from Heathrow actually.'

'So, what's happening here then?' Kaaya asked, taking off her coat and chucking it onto the sofa. She bent and gave her mother a kiss. 'Have you two been crying again?' she asked, looking at Riva's reddened nose.

Riva gave her a warning look not to set their mother off again. 'Ma's tummy pains are worse and she won't come with me to the surgery, even though I've managed to get an emergency appointment.' Riva tried not to sound too querulous.

'I told you, I am all right,' Mrs Walia protested. 'Why don't you listen to me?'

'But just yesterday you said it was hurting again when I called,' Kaaya said.

'That was yesterday. Today I am fine,' her mother said firmly. 'And you know I never like going anywhere without your father.'

Riva felt the usual panicky flutter in her stomach at the reference to her father in the present tense.

'Does anyone fancy a cuppa? I'm going to do that Brit thing when things are going awry and stick the kettle on,' she said, trying to lighten the mood.

'Oh, yes please to a cup of good British tea, Riv,' Rohan said, trying to fold his lanky frame to sit on the arm of his mother-in-law's chair.

Kaaya followed her sister into the kitchen, unwinding her cashmere scarf and throwing it on the banister.

'Tea *pour vous*?' Riva asked.

Kaaya nodded, perching herself on a bar stool while her sister filled the kettle.

'You look rough,' Kaaya observed, eyeing her sister's unkempt hair tied carelessly into a loose knot on the nape of her neck.

'Christ, it's been a pretty grisly weekend so far,' Riva sighed, getting four mugs and the tea canister out of the cupboard. 'Ben's in a foul mood for one . . .'

'Well, you only have yourself to blame for that, sis,' Kaaya said unhelpfully, pulling the spice tin across the breakfast bar and helping herself to an elaichi. 'We went over all this the last time we met,' she said, trying to extricate a cardamom seed from its pod without chipping her immaculate nail polish. 'Ben's clearly not the same guy he was when he was a high-flying banker. Unemployment does funny things to men, you know, and you should leave him before it gets any worse. It's certainly not as if you *need* him.'

Riva sighed again (she had noticed lately how often she had taken to releasing these huge, heartfelt sighs) as she threw tea bags into four mugs.

'As if nothing else counts, Kaaya, for God's sake!' she said wearily.

'What else?' Kaaya looked genuinely puzzled as she chewed on her cardamom.

'Oh, I don't know. Loyalty? Gratitude? Memories? . . . Hope?' Riva, waiting for the kettle to boil, saw her sister toss her head dismissively.

'I notice you didn't mention love,' Kaaya pointed out tartly.

Riva ignored her. 'Besides Mamma adores Ben . . .' she said with finality.

'Oh, that's just Ma's Indian thing – son-in-law is king and all that!' Kaaya laughed. 'And since when have *you* gone all Indian, doing the right thing by the family rather than yourself, huh?'

'Oh, Kaaya, just think how it'll break Mum's heart if I split with Ben. Last thing she needs in the midst of everything else, I should think. Get me the milk please,' Riva said, pouring boiling water into the mugs.

Kaaya fetched the milk from the fridge and, handing it over to Riva, picked up a strand of her sister's hair that had worked its way loose and was now hanging onto Riva's face. 'For crying out loud, look at those split ends!'

Replacing the milk bottle on the counter, Riva retied her hair. She smiled at Kaaya's sisterly concern and said mildly, 'I know, I know . . . been postponing a haircut to time it alongside the book launch. I'm planning a big treat for Susan and me at Cobella's next week actually. And I'll make the appointment tomorrow, I promise! It's not as if anyone but the postman sees me when I'm in the throes of finishing a book anyway!'

'Treat for Susan? It's not her birthday, is it?' Kaaya queried, her voice studiously casual as she returned to the breakfast bar.

'No, her birthday isn't till August. It's just that she's not doing too great herself . . . that was the other thing keeping me up last night. It's as if the whole world's turning upside down.'

'Oh?'

Riva stirred the tea, her back still turned. 'Well, Joe's been behaving pretty weirdly too, can you believe it? Worse than Ben, as it happens!'

'Joe? Why, what's he done?'

Riva, busy searching the cupboards for her mother's sugar-free tablets, did not notice Kaaya's expression as she replied with a distracted air, 'Not sure, actually. He's behaving a bit strangely.'

Kaaya persisted. 'Strangely?'

But Riva was silent as she got the tea tray ready, placing the mugs on it and getting a handful of custard creams out on a plate. She picked up the tray to indicate the conversation was over and Kaaya knew that Riva's loyalty to her friend would prevent her from saying anything further. She felt a small flutter of apprehension at how much Susan might have guessed about Joe's affair, mixed with relief that Riva had not the faintest idea that she was Joe's lover!

They returned to the living room and found Rohan

making their mother smile, recounting an incident from his travels in Japan that involved chopsticks and slippery mushrooms. Riva smiled gratefully at her brother-in-law as she handed him his tea, although what she wanted was to give him a huge hug for bringing a smile back to her mother's face. She put the tray down and rumpled Rohan's hair affectionately on her way to the sofa, then sank into it with relief.

'Where is Ben?' her mother asked. 'Ben should also have been here. So rarely do I see all four of you together . . .'

'Oh, sorry, Mamma, but Ben had to go get some stuff posted.'

'What, on a Saturday afternoon?' Kaaya remarked, never missing an opportunity for a dig at Ben.

'Yeeesss, Kaaya,' Riva replied patiently. 'The one up at King's Cross is open all day on a Saturday, and this was an urgent task.'

'Another manuscript?' Kaaya asked. Her face was innocent but it didn't take much to guess that the query was sarcastic.

Riva ignored her, turning back to her mother. 'I have news for you all, actually. Big news. Wait for this – I've been asked to be a judge at the next Cannes film festival. Apparently Isabelle Huppert read the French translation of my book and personally recommended me!'

'*Cannes!*' Kaaya squealed, suddenly rid of her bored tone. 'Ooo, can I come? I'm sure I can swing some PR work while we're there. I could share your hotel room, perhaps. They're like gold dust when the festival's on and I'm sure you'll be put up somewhere swish.'

'Hey, Cannes jury's quite a coup, Riva,' Rohan said. 'And having a fan like Isabelle Huppert can't hurt. Good on you!'

Only Mrs Walia looked unhappy. 'You should not go alone, or even with Kaaya. You should go with Ben.'

'Oh, Ben can look after himself!' Kaaya expostulated. 'Take me!'

'The invitation's only for me, I'm afraid,' Riva said firmly. 'And Kaaya's right for once, Ma, Ben can certainly look after himself for ten days.'

'Oh, is *that* what Ben's all upset about then? That you're off to tread the red carpet at glamorous Cannes?' Kaaya asked, not seeing the second warning look her sister was flashing at her.

As expected, their mother took the bait instantly. 'Ben is upset? You never said Ben is upset, Riva.'

Riva sighed wearily. 'Do you seriously think I would tell you whenever Ben's upset, Mum? No, it's nothing to do with Cannes. He's just going through a small bad patch.'

'I'll bet it *is* about Cannes,' Kaaya said, receiving a third warning look, from her husband this time, but ignoring it all the same. 'Strange things happen to men when their wives start getting more successful or popular than them. Look at Charles and Diana.'

'I am very worried about Ben,' Mrs Walia said gloomily. 'In that matter, Kaaya is right, Riva. It is not good for a man to be sitting at home all day.'

'But he's working from home, Ma, not just "sitting", as you say!' Riva said indignantly.

'Yeah, right,' said Kaaya, rolling her eyes.

'Enough!' Rohan cut in softly, finally making his wife subside.

Mrs Walia was sitting up now, looking more businesslike than she had all morning. 'I think, Riva, that you should write to these Cannes people and tell them you are not in a position to be a judge when your husband is at home,' she said in her firmest voice. 'After he gets a job, it is okay. Go wherever you want. But as long as he is at home, you should be there with him, *beti*. A wife's place is next to her husband.'

Normally, a line like that was the cue for their mother's face to start crumpling into tears again but Riva was too incensed for the time being to consider that possibility. '*After* he gets a job?' she cried. 'That could be a long, long time, Ma. There's a small recession on, you know.'

'I know, I know all about the recession and credit crunch and all. I also see the TV news. But everyone is saying it is now lifting, with the green shoots coming. Ben will soon get a job, you wait and see.'

'Who's everyone?' Rohan asked, mildly amused.

'Oh all the TV *wallahs*,' Mrs Walia replied vaguely. 'Let Ben get a job, Riva. Then you can go to Can-van and all.'

'He's not even looking for a job, is he?' Kaaya giggled.

'How do you know?' her mother demanded. 'Maybe he is looking secretly. No point in announcing to everyone until you have something to say. Your father is also just like that. Maybe that is where Ben is right now, *hain na*, job hunting?'

Suddenly Riva was smiling too. Her mother's faith in everything – the end of the recession, Ben's job prospects, her two daughters' blissful marriages – was touching. And she had to admit there was an odd sort of comfort to be had in assuming that the traditional order of things her mother relied on so implicitly would return, along with those elusive green shoots. The recession would lift, men would be out there, successful in their job-hunting, head-hunting, jungle-like masculine activities, while their wives would stay loyally, waiting for them at home. Why, in her mother's version of utopia, Papa too was no doubt simply out on a temporary trip, being head-hunted by some very important corporation. Riva felt both amused and saddened by how far from reality her mother's idea of perfection lay.

Chapter Fourteen

As that weekend progressed, Susan started to wonder if perhaps she *had* imagined that strange phone call in the River Café garden on Tuesday night. For one, Joe had been in all weekend – surely, if there had been a secret lover, he'd be trying to sneak off at the weekends to a motel, or wherever it was that secret lovers went. And he'd been his usual self, pottering about his beloved car on Saturday morning, later turning his hand to a fabulous dish of pasta with black olives and leftover Parma ham slivers, which they'd had for dinner with a bottle of chilled sweet Riesling. In the evening, they had watched a movie on their home cinema, a rom-com of the sort that Joe normally hated but had teasingly said he would watch for her sake. They had made love too after going to bed on Saturday night, Susan observing Joe's every move to figure out if there was anything new about the way in which he made love to her. But she had not discerned anything vastly different; Joe always closed his eyes when in the throes of passion, there was nothing new about that. Besides, Susan had been so pleased at the sudden return to normality, she had accepted it gratefully, like an unexpected gift. By Sunday morning, when all the waiting and watching was starting to wear Susan out, she decided she really had no reason to feel suspicious as she watched Joe pack for his usual trip to the gym.

'I'm thinking of throwing a party for Riva,' she said, taking washed clothes off the airer and folding them into neat little piles.

'Oh? Any particular reason?' he asked.

'You know, just to toast her on the Cannes jury thing. It's quite a major achievement when you think about it.'

'Sure is,' Joe agreed. 'Good old Riva, we always knew she'd go into the big league at some point, didn't we?'

'Yeah, I just wish Ben would find it in himself to appreciate her better.'

'But he does, doesn't he?' Joe asked absently, unzipping his toilet case.

'Not any more, I think. Hard to recall now how madly in love he was with her back at uni, eh? Pursued her about for ages, virtually from day one. Pipping young Aman Khan at the post too. Remember? God, how young we all were back then . . .' Susan got no response from Joe, who was busy searching for a pair of socks in his drawer. She changed tack. 'How many people do you think we should call?'

'Call?' Joe asked vaguely, shoving a pair of white towelling socks into his kit.

'You know, to our party.'

'Oh, Riva's celebration. I don't know. The usual gang – seven or eight?' He looked up at her. 'Or did you want to make it bigger?'

'Yeah, let's go the whole hog. We haven't had a party in such a long time. Be lovely to catch up with a few others from the old uni crowd too. I could drop Tony and Fidelma an email. And Grace, Ravi, Vicki . . . Chris and Neil, maybe? You could ask David – he likes Riva. Loves her books. I'm sure he'd want to know about her new one.' Susan started to count on her fingers. 'So that's about eight, plus Riva and Ben, Kaaya and Rohan, of course, and us . . . about fifteen of us?'

Joe had picked up his kit, a thoughtful expression on his face. 'When were you thinking of doing this?'

'Next month sometime, I guess. If we're calling folks like Vicki and Ravi, we'd have to give them plenty of notice.'

'So, April then? Middle of April?'

'I guess. Haven't thought that far yet. Why? You weren't thinking of going anywhere in April, were you?'

Joe shook his head, slinging his bag over his shoulder. 'Nope, just asking. A party for Riva's a great idea and I can always adjust my work schedule closer to the time anyway.' He kissed the top of Susan's head before saying, 'I feel a mammoth session coming on at the gym. I may be a couple of hours.'

Susan watched from the bedroom widow as Joe reversed his car down the drive. Her every instinct still screamed that there was something wrong but she simply could not put her finger on it. Somehow, Joe's niceness felt like acting, although she was willing to acknowledge that the fault might lie with her own suspicions of him. It would be cruel and unwise to accuse Joe of something as terrible as infidelity when all she had at the moment was a half-heard whispered phone call that night at the River Café. But there was still no viable explanation for it – why would he go off into a dark corner of the garden like that? Why *whisper*? For whom would Joe use the word 'darling' and why would he need to ask, in a tone of such concern, what she was doing at that time of night? Susan got up from the bed and started to stack the clothes in the cupboards and chests of drawers, still feeling that inexplicable flutter deep in her stomach that had been plaguing her for days.

Joe drove to the bottom of the road before pulling in. It had been pretty damned unbearable not being able to call Kaaya all of yesterday but she had said she would be collecting Rohan from the airport and then going across to her mum's. They had, however, agreed to a short phone call on Sunday and, although Joe knew that she would prefer to call him, he felt a curious sense that he might drown if he did not hear her voice for another whole morning. Never before had he experienced being so out of control of his life. He tapped Kaaya's number into his phone. It had never been saved on his contacts list, unlike Riva's, because Susan would surely find it strange that he had suddenly acquired Kaaya's number on his phone. He had also learnt to diligently erase her number from his list of calls and texts every time phone contact was made, just in case Susan checked. Surely she would think something was amiss from that conversation she'd overheard on the night of David's birthday? Although it was now starting to look, much to Joe's relief, as though she had perhaps not heard very much. Susan would have certainly quizzed him if she had: being blunt and open was much more her style. It was also clear that Kaaya was the last person she'd suspect of having an affair with him, although it had given him a small shock to hear her mention Kaaya's name so casually a few minutes ago while they were talking about Riva's party. If there had been some telltale sign on his face, Susan had luckily not been looking at him at the time.

Joe listened now to the ringing tone on Kaaya's phone with some trepidation, ready to hang up swiftly if someone else answered it. Luckily it was Kaaya herself and Joe felt his chest momentarily cave in at the sound of her husky voice, remembering the last time he heard it, when she had bid him goodbye at her door late on Friday night, nibbling his ear as she did so.

'Darling,' he said softly, 'Can you speak?'

'Oh, hi, Vinita!' she said cheerily.

'Hi . . .' Joe replied, unsure of what to say next.

'Where have you *been*?' she asked as though they had not met in years.

'Er . . . at home . . .' he offered gingerly.

'You hardly call these days,' she accused.

'I guess Rohan's around,' Joe said. 'You can't speak, can you?'

'Yes!'

'You can?'

'No, no, of course not.'

'Well, I'd better hang up then . . . call me when you can?'

'No, I meant we should really arrange something, just us girls.'

'Yes, we really should. Just us girls,' Joe laughed, suddenly getting into the spirit. 'When?'

'Well, lemme see now . . . I should be free on Wednesday evening. Should we arrange something? Drinkies in town?'

'Now, if you're talking to *me*, Joseph Holmes, rather than Vinita, I'm afraid I can't do Wednesday. Hospital night, you see.'

'Oh, that's a shame!'

'But tomorrow? After work? Please, I've got to see you soon, Kaaya!'

'Ha, ha, that's very funny,' Kaaya replied.

'You mean you can't?'

'I'm sure we can come up with something. Look, I don't

have my work schedule on me right now as I'm in the car, driving up to Leicester to visit my in-laws, you see. But I'll call you tomorrow, shall I?'

'Oh, Christ, this is driving me crazy!' Joe threw his head back on the car seat, running his hand through his hair in frustration.

'Oh, Rohan's fine, thanks. And your Jaspal?'

'Kaaya . . .'

'Good . . . good. Look, email me and we'll make a plan.'

'Email? Okay, yes, I can do that! Right away – from the gym – I'm going there now actually. Look, call me if you can, Kaaya. The phone will be in my pocket all day. I'll be waiting. Whenever you can . . .'

'Okay, doll, lovely hearing from you, byeeeeee.'

And with that she was gone. Joe sat for a few minutes, looking at his phone as though it had personally let him down. Joe put his phone back in his pocket and started up the car again, feeling completely dejected. He sat for a few minutes as the engine idled, feeling worse than a lovesick teenager. The curious thing was that he had never been a lovesick teenager even as a teenager, having spent most of that period of his life agonising about getting into medical school! Then he had met Susan and he had considered himself the luckiest man to have found, so easily and uncomplicatedly, the girl whom he knew straightaway he wanted to spend the rest of his life with. Why indeed was he now setting about with such mad determination to ruin his own happiness?

Chapter Fifteen

Ben read the letter that had come for Riva from Cannes once again, that dark hole deep inside him which seemed to grow a little every day, greedily sucking up all his positivity like a malevolent sponge. He was losing Riva, of course he was losing her. It was only a matter of time before she would be gone for good. And there was nothing at all he could do about it.

Ben looked at Riva's duffle coat, hanging obediently on the row of wooden hooks in the hallway, as though reassuring him that she was still there. Of course there were things he could *try* to do to keep from losing her: an unexpected gift box from Jo Malone might do it, seeing that she never bought expensive things for herself . . . or a romantic meal at that new tapas place in Kensington he'd read about recently . . . a holiday somewhere warm. If only he could muster up the energy. After all, on certain days, it took only a subtle reminder of their teenage relationship to make Riva's face soften and break into a smile. She too must remember how much in love they were back at uni. How could she not? But the name, printed right here on the letter from Cannes, was also from those days, Ben couldn't help reminding himself. Aman Khan. Who couldn't have come jolting back into their lives at a worse

121

time. Ben had never felt smaller about himself than he did this year – twenty months since being made redundant from the bank and with a writing career headed nowhere. How could Riva not fail to notice the difference between his failure and Aman Khan's success? From what Ben could see, the man had everything,: money, good looks, adulation, fame . . . it was impossible not to be struck by what the unimpressive lad he'd known at Leeds had gone on to make of himself. And now he would be hobnobbing with Riva in the South of France for ten whole days!

Ben wandered listlessly into the kitchen to pour himself another mug of coffee from the cafetiere (his third of the morning). It was lukewarm and so he placed the mug in the microwave oven for a minute as he munched absently on a chocolate digestive. He reached out for another and realised with sudden horror that the cookie jar, which had been refilled only yesterday, was already nearly empty. Ben hastily withdrew his hand and screwed the lid back on, feeling his small growing paunch with some horror. The view from the kitchen window did not provide much succour either as the back garden looked even more unkempt than usual on such a wild and wet day. The storm that had lashed London overnight had left all the plants looking bedraggled, the strong winds having managed to topple a couple of the garden chairs right over. They now lay on their sides on the patio tiles, helplessly waiting to be rescued and righted, but Ben was in no mood to step out into the cold just now. He took the mug of coffee back to his computer, suddenly guilty that he had skipped out of going to his mother-in-law's again today. Yesterday it had been the knowledge that Kaaya would be there too that had prevented him going. He hadn't laid eyes on his sister-in-law since the day he had overheard her bitching about him with Riva. It was best to postpone that as far as possible, lest he be tempted to smack that smug, pretty face. But he certainly could have gone today, since Riva had mentioned that Kaaya was spending the day in Leicester. Riva would have appreciated some help at Tesco, seeing that she was doing her mother's shopping alongside their own. But how could he explain the blackness of mood that had overwhelmed him as soon as he had woken up in the morning? It had been so bad that he had been unable to drag himself out of bed until he'd heard Riva's car drive off. The minute she'd left, Ben had regretted not accompanying her. But in those few short seconds that lay between selflessness and selfishness, he had seen in a flash what it would be like trawling around Tesco's crowded aisles while politely fobbing off earnest enquiries from his mother-in-law about his nonexistent job prospects. Sweet as she was, Mrs Walia had recently shown a terrifying capacity for nagging, leading him to wonder if Riva would become like that in her seventies.

Ben looked blankly at the colourful Windows icon dancing and bobbing cheerily on the screen as the computer continued to hibernate. He had not written a word so far this morning and already it was past midday. The first hour had gone with the online newspapers. There was always so much more to read on a Sunday. Then he had played a bit of poker and done the crossword and, before he knew it, the grandfather clock in the hallway was chiming twelve.

Fifteen minutes later, Ben was still sipping his coffee, immersed in a clip on YouTube from the latest Springsteen concert, when there was the sound of keys in the door. Hearing Riva throw a couple of bags of groceries onto the floor of the hallway, he clicked the YouTube window shut and got out of his chair to help her.

'Oh, hello,' Riva said, returning from the car, this time with a twelve-pack carton of Diet Coke and a carrier bag full of fruit slung on one arm. Ben took them off her at the door, feeling the winter chill stab at him through the thin fabric of his T-shirt.

'Is there lots more?' he asked. 'I'd have come out but I'm barefoot.'

'No, that's fine, just another couple,' she said, going back towards the car parked in the drive.

Ben slid the Coke carton into one of the lower cupboards before taking the fruit across to the sink. As was their habit, he filled the smaller sink with tepid water and immersed bunches of red and green grapes in it. Behind him, he could hear Riva stamping her boots on the doormat and curse under her breath as she slammed the front door shut.

'Just filthy out there,' she said as she came into the kitchen in her socks, still wearing her red woollen cap. Her nose and ears were pink from the cold. Ben contemplated cupping her face between his hands and kissing her nose to warm it but Riva looked irritable as she fished out the till receipt from her handbag. 'Just as I thought, damn woman hasn't given me the discount!' she cried.

'What discount?'

'*Damnation!* I should've thought of checking it before leaving the bloody store!' She yanked off her cap, causing long curls to tumble about her face.

'What was it for?'

'Papayas!' Riva replied, throwing both hat and receipt on the breakfast table. 'There was a sign up on the shelf saying that they were at half price but the labels were falling off. And I bought *four*, two for mum!'

'Never mind, couldn't have saved you more than a couple of quid,' Ben, trying to assuage her anger, but receiving an annoyed glare instead. He changed the subject. 'How's your mum?'

'Oh, don't ask!' Riva snapped, ripping off her gloves to noisily stack the butter and cheeses in their fridge compartments. 'You should've come, she asked after you at least twenty times,' she said, not looking at Ben.

'I hope you told her I was in the middle of a really important part of the book?'

'Yeah, right. Like she's a total idiot and won't figure at some point that something's wrong.' Riva was now unloading a bag of potatoes into a wicker basket with some force.

'But nothing's wrong,' Ben protested. When Riva remained silent, her attention fiercely focused on the vegetables she was arranging in their tray, he persisted, 'What do you mean by "something's wrong", Riva? Nothing's wrong as far as I know. Unless there's something *you* want to tell me . . .' He could hear the sarcasm creeping into his voice and stopped.

Riva clattered the tray into the bottom of the fridge and straightened herself to finally look at him. The colour in her face was still high but her voice was now calmer. 'Ben, for God's sake, would it take too much to try seeing things from someone else's point of view for a change?'

'Whose point of view? Yours? Your mum's? I don't understand. Can we talk specifics please?' Ben enquired coldly. He knew he was being deliberately obtuse and unreasonable but could not help himself.

'Oh, for God's sake, don't pretend you don't know what I'm talking about,' Riva cried.

'I don't! If you have a complaint about me, I suggest

125

you come straight out with it.'

They stood at either end of the kitchen glaring at each other. Then Riva returned to her groceries, turning to cut open a bag of muesli and pour its contents into a Tupperware box. Ben watched her for a couple more seconds, silently challenging her to speak her mind. But her lips were tightly pursed and, when she tapped the knob on the DAB radio and a voice from Radio 4 filled the kitchen, Ben turned and walked out. He went upstairs and changed into jeans and a fleece jacket. He needed to get out of the house and as far away as possible from a wife who had clearly stopped loving him months ago.

Riva was kneeling on the floor to reach the back of the cupboard when the front door slammed decisively. From previous experience, she knew that Ben would now absent himself for most of the day. Riva never knew where he went on these long sulks as he kept his phone turned off and often returned only long after she had gone to bed. Even after they had made up, one or the other of them tentatively attempting conversation the following day, she never queried him about the periods in which he went AWOL, understanding that he needed to feel he was in control of some aspect of his life.

As sadness washed through her, Riva sank onto the limestone tiles and started to weep. Tears ran down her face, dripping off the end of her chin and onto the front of her mohair sweater. On the radio, the Chancellor was justifying his use of public money to pay for tax advice – saying the kind of things that would normally have Riva either snort with laughter or spit with rage. But that was when Ben was around to chat with and bounce ideas off. That was what had first attracted her to him back at uni, she remembered with sudden stabbing pain: a shared political sensibility and sense of humour. No one else in her circle at college – not Robbie Crampton, not the very handsome Alex Wright, certainly not Aman Khan – had quite measured up to Ben's smartness and charm and quickfire wit. Where, oh where, had it all gone wrong for them?

Finally getting up, Riva twiddled the knob on the radio, searching for something that would make her feel better. Planet Rock's inane slogan filled the kitchen: 'If music be the food of love, get ready for a good rogering.' She and Ben always shared a laugh at that and now, rather than being with her in this nice warm kitchen, he was tramping around the cold, leaf-strewn streets. It was as if he was deliberately pushing her away. What was *wrong* with him? Riva wandered across the kitchen to click the kettle on. She heaved a huge self-pitying sigh as she reflected on the terrible morning she had had so far. First a crack of dawn start to make sure she got to Ealing before Ma started on the biscuits. Ma had casually revealed that she had run out of porridge oats just as Riva had been leaving yesterday. Concerned questioning had been received with a shrug and 'Oh, I will have something, don't you worry.' Which Riva knew full well meant that the jar of custard creams would be gone by midday. Her mother's blood sugar, previously a strictly monitored and much discussed business, had soared alarmingly after Papa's death. The doctor had said that stress sometimes had that effect and Riva also suspected that her mother was comfort eating, having recently found a half-eaten box of chocolate profiteroles thrust deep inside the freezer. Ma had tried to wave her enquiries away, claiming with a distant, vague expression on her face that the profiteroles were 'just some leftovers from a tea party'. Riva recognised the blatant lie, given that her mother had not thrown a tea party since Riva and Kaaya had last celebrated childhood birthday parties at home. Besides, Papa's death had caused Ma to withdraw in anxious confusion from even her kindliest friends and neighbours. Even old Mr Simpson from next door had complained cantankerously to Riva the other day that her mother had refused to answer the door to him, although he could clearly see the curtains upstairs twitching. 'All he was trying to do was deliver a parcel he had signed for when you were out shopping, Ma,' Riva had cried in frustration but, as Kaaya had observed, their newly widowed mother had taken to behaving as though all single men were potential rapists. Riva had tried to rationalise her mother's behaviour to herself, knowing how hard it must be for her to live alone, having never been in that position before. Nevertheless, she had point-blank refused to move in, even temporarily, with one of her daughters, unable to bear leaving the house she had lived in with her beloved husband. Further quizzing on the profiteroles had also merely made Ma clam up with a terse, 'You worry too much, Riva. Just like your father you are in such stupid, silly matters.'

Riva blew her nose, feeling more and more sorry for herself. Was she imagining it or was her world increasingly being peopled by adult delinquents. 'Children, badly behaved children, the whole lot of them!' she muttered, her teaspoon hitting the sides of the cup with vehemence. 'Ma, Ben, Joe, let's see now, who's the worst offender . . .' She scowled at her distorted reflection in the steel kettle. 'Maybe it's *you*, Riva Walia. Yes, you. Slowly but surely going potty. Loopy woman, jabbering to herself all day!'

She took her tea into the living room and straightened

the floor cushions with her foot before sinking into her favourite, now slightly faded, Jaipuri bolster. She leant her aching back on it with a groan. Ma was a fine one to accuse *her* of worrying, going on and on this morning about Ben and his nonexistent job. Of course, Riva knew that the discipline of a job would be good for Ben but, short of bundling him down the job centre, what was she to do? Nagging him would only make him feel worse and she could not very well force him out of the house to do any old job, especially when he seemed so convinced by his writing talent.

'But he can write *along* with a job,' Ma had said in a puzzled voice as she trotted around Tesco's aisles next to Riva, maintaining one proprietorial hand on the trolley. It was as Riva had swerved to avoid crashing into a free-wheeling toddler that her mother had grabbed her arm. 'You should tell Ben, Riva, that writing is something you can do anywhere, at any time. You're an author. He will listen to you. In the meantime, I think he should find a job. A nice, good job. Even if the pay is not as good as before. That does not matter. But a man . . . a man *must* have a job.'

'For heaven's sake, leave it, Ma, he'll find something soon enough. It isn't as if he's floating in a sea of jobs, y'know,' Riva had snapped, making her mother finally subside. Except, unaccustomed to having her normally mild-mannered elder daughter talk so rudely to her, this exchange had caused Mrs Walia to dissolve into a sudden bout of tears. Despite a fumbled hug and abject apologies right there in the middle of the supermarket, her mother had carried on weeping all the way to the tills, causing the woman at the checkout to look at Riva as though she were an axe murderer.

Riva stretched her legs out towards the radiator, feeling welcome warmth travel through her thick woollen socks and into her cold feet. Her fingers, wrapped around the mug, were also finally feeling less frozen. She thought of Ben forsaking the peace and comfort of their house and tramping London's wet streets merely to avoid her.

'He can go slip on a leaf and bump his head on a tree trunk and lie there in the rain half-dead for all I care,' Riva muttered, draining her tea. She put the empty mug down and stretched out on the carpet as close to the radiator as she could get. Before she knew it, she was drifting into fitful slumber punctuated by dreams full of shopping trolleys and runaway toddlers and tearful, angry faces glaring at her. Among the angry faces was the woman in the supermarket and, strangely, both Ben and Aman.

Chapter Sixteen

Kaaya gazed listlessly out at her mother-in-law's garden. From where she was seated on the red leather sofa near the French windows, Kaaya could see hanging baskets devoid of flowers, balding bird-feeders, a mossy bird bath, a wrought-iron pergola, a wooden swing-seat, a set of plastic garden furniture and a whole scattered family of garden gnomes. She shuddered and turned her attention to the room in front of her.

The scene indoors was even more crowded. Rohan's parents were well off and their house far larger than their current requirements demanded. But Rohan's mother had made it her business, from the moment the house had been bought twenty years ago, to gradually fill it with every conceivable material possession that she could lay her hands on. Despite the three reception rooms and four bedrooms, she had so far done a competent job of stuffing her house to such an extent that it was hard to walk through any room without bumping into something en route. Rohan's father, who owned three restaurants in Leicester, was seemingly content to allow his wife her indulgences in the form of furniture and rugs and artefacts and paintings, as long as she kept her hands off his beloved restaurants, all designed in minimalist Scandinavian style with beech tables and chrome and leather chairs.

Rohan's mother had explained it to Kaaya on her very first visit to their house. 'We have a very good understanding. Rohan's daddy dare not tell me what to do in my home and I dare not tell him what to do in his business. It is good for husband and wife to have separate-separate interests.'

Kaaya could hear her mother-in-law banging about her kitchen now and sighed at the thought of getting up to join her. Rohan and his father had just left for the Melton Road restaurant to investigate a leaking pipe and Kaaya had felt forced into volunteering to stay back and help with the lunch. Finally dragging herself off the sofa, Kaaya thought of using the opportunity to call Joe, but he would probably be in the gym right now, and if she left a message there was every chance he would call back just as the family were sitting down to lunch or at some other such inopportune moment. Having another conversation of the sort she'd had this morning, with Rohan sitting right next to her in the car, was risky. Luckily, Rohan's attention had been on the cricket commentary and so he had barely noticed the phone call. But, whatever Rohan's antecedents, he was far from brainless, his parents having not only produced two intelligent sons but also given them the benefit of private educations. While Rohan had gone to Cambridge followed swiftly by Goldman Sachs, his younger brother – less of a star and still at university – was being groomed to take over the family's restaurant business. That was exactly the way Kaaya would have wanted things to pan out too – for who in their right mind would want to give up the glamour of London for three trying-to-be-trendy Indian restaurants in Leicester and life with the in-laws? Avoiding such a fate was worth the small sacrifice of the occasional weekend up here to see the folks.

'Can I do anything, Aunty?' Kaaya asked without enthusiasm as she strolled into the kitchen.

'Oh Kaaya-*beti*, please take out the plates from the dining room cabinet. I will bring the spoons and forks.'

Kaaya wandered without haste into the dining room and eyed the vast array of plates that had been stuffed higgledy-piggledy into a large glass cabinet. She was sure that if she slipped so much as one plate out, the entire edifice would come crashing down about her ears. Gingerly she turned the ornate tasselled brass key and opened the door. Stacks and stacks of plates glinted at her in the afternoon light.

'Which plates did you want?' she called out to her mother-in-law.

'The Weera Wang lacy gold ones, *beti*,' came the distant reply. As no one else was around, Kaaya could freely grin at her mother-in-law's ongoing inability to put a 'V' and 'W' together.

'Okay, *Weera* Wang, where are you?' Kaaya said, pulling up a chair to stand on it for a better view.

'Oho, *beti*, be careful!' her mother-in-law said, bustling in with a dish of rice. Kaaya carefully climbed off the chair, imagining it was her safety that Rohan's mother was concerned about. But her mother-in-law dusted the chair's upholstery with the tea towel before reaching up for her plates. 'Here, lay these nicely,' she said to Kaaya before scurrying back into the kitchen. 'Your father-in-law and Rohan will be home soon, they just rang to say they are on their way,' she called over her shoulder.

Kaaya, looking around for the place mats, blinked back a sudden uncustomary tear. She hated Rohan's mum for subjecting her to this routine humiliation, even if it only rolled around once a month. Kaaya was sure her mother-in-law trotted out these commands only to make her look inept in front of Rohan. All that saccharine *beti-beti* stuff was an ineffectual front for a woman who really hadn't cared to have her son married to a beautiful working woman with a highly glamorous job.

Kaaya searched fruitlessly on the top of the hostess trolley before opening and closing a few drawers on the sideboard, still searching for the place mats. Damned domesticity, it was an art Kaaya knew she'd never master, even if she lived to a hundred and seventy. And why should she? It wasn't for a life of domestic drudgery that her beloved papa had brought her and Riva up. He was the kindest, sweetest soul Kaaya had ever known – 'the first original feminist', Riva had always teased – and it was his gentle bespectacled face Kaaya was thinking of now as she slammed shut the last of the drawers, unsuccessful in her search for the place mats, and collapsed onto a dining-room chair in an abrupt flood of tears.

'*Beti!* What has happened?' Rohan's mother cried in astonishment when she came back into the dining room a few minutes later and saw that her daughter-in-law's face, normally so composed and beautiful, was suddenly all blotchy and flustered.

'I can't find any place mats!' Kaaya wailed.

'*Ooffo*, they are here, you silly girl,' her mother-in-law said, opening a corner cupboard to reveal stacks of place mats in wood, plastic, linen, lace and bamboo. She smartly laid out four wooden mats, clattering the plates down on them before rushing back to the kitchen, the expression on her face seeming to say she had no time for weepy girls in her efficient household.

Kaaya jumped as her phone buzzed deep in the pocket of her jeans. She hoped it wasn't Joe again as she stood up to get it out. The number was unfamiliar but she answered it.

'Hello, Kaaya,' said a familiar voice. 'It's Susan here.'

Kaaya felt a quick lurch of fear and guilt. Why the *fuck* would Susan want to call her and where the fuck was Joe? Keeping her voice steady, she replied, 'Oh, hi, Susan.'

'I hope I'm not calling at an awkward time?'

'No, no, course not,' Kaaya replied, still trying to calm herself.

'Well, I thought a Sunday would be better than trying to call on a working day, y'know, seeing how madly busy we all are in any given week. But tell me I'm not interrupting lunch or something? Riva tells me Rohan's back from his travels to Japan.'

'No, we're at his parents' but we're not lunching yet,' Kaaya replied. Get to the bloody *point*, she thought, agonising at what might be coming next; though she knew Susan was hardly likely to indulge in small talk as a prelude to accusations of adultery.

'Rather jammy, the frequency with which Rohan goes to Japan. You should go along sometime. Have you been?'

'Yes. No. No, I mean, I plan to go soon. Just need to organise myself at work, you know, and Rohan's trips are usually pretty last-minute.'

'At least you don't have to wait for the damned school holidays to go away somewhere nice like I do. Everything's three times the price and all holiday destinations are chock-a-block with kids. I can't seem to get away from them!'

Kaaya forced a small laugh. She had already heard Joe moan about this once, using almost exactly the same words.

After a small pause, Susan spoke again. 'Well, I shouldn't keep you chatting while you're at your in-laws'. I was just calling to ask if you're free on the twenty-ninth, or the Saturday after maybe? I'm trying to get a few people together to throw a party for Riva. You know, something to celebrate her going to Cannes in June. It's such an achievement, isn't it?'

'Sure is!' Kaaya said, relief flooding through her. 'Yes, fab idea, Susan. I'd love to come. And the 29th would suit us fine as Rohan probably won't be travelling for a bit now. I'd love to help, actually, if there's anything I can do?' She stopped short, aware that she was now babbling with relief.

'Don't think so really, Kaaya, though it's good of you to ask. I'll let you know closer to the time if necessary. I may merely order some stuff from Carluccio's and Joe will take care of the drink, of course. In fact, his mate who runs the Oddbins branch at Primrose Hill will probably come – I don't know whether you've ever met Joe's old schoolfriend, Ross? Well, he's a lovely guest to have because he just turns up an hour or so in advance, with all the whites beautifully chilled in his refrigerated van, and, Bob's your uncle, we're ready to party!'

'Is it meant to be a surprise for Riva?' Kaaya asked.

'No, I didn't think we should risk that,' Susan replied. 'Just in case she took off somewhere to finish her next book and we lost our guest of honour! No, no secrets, she knows, so it's safe to talk.'

'Oh, okay, fine,' Kaaya said.

'Good-oh, I'll try to see how many people I can get for next Saturday then. If I need to push it back by another week, I'll let you know of course. Well, okay. Enjoy your Sunday up in Leicester. I hope it's nicer there than it is here – it's pissing it down something awful here in London!'

After Susan had rung off, Kaaya sat at the dining table holding her phone for a few minutes. For the first time since her affair with Joe had started, she felt a small flicker of guilt deep in her stomach. Perhaps it was down to Susan's cheery manner. Or perhaps she was still recovering from her earlier bout of missing Papa so dreadfully it was as though she had only just realised he was gone for good. These past few weeks, that knowledge had developed a terrible way of rushing in on her at the most unexpected moments. Numb with shock in the weeks following her father's death, it wasn't until two full months later that the pain and rage had overwhelmed Kaaya to such an extent she had felt a sensation akin to drowning. Rohan had been on one of his interminable business trips on that occasion and Kaaya had tried holding back from calling either her sister or her mother, knowing that both were barely dealing with their own loss. In the end, however, she had taken a taxi across to her sister's house, bawling most uncharacteristically as she had walked into Riva's arms, clutching a bottle of wine. She had to admit that Riva had been wonderful that day, silently absorbing Kaaya's pain like a sponge, even as tears were coursing down her own face. Joe and Susan had swung by later to check on Riva and that was the evening Kaaya had first become aware of Joe's attraction for her, catching him looking at her so intently, it was as if he was seeing her for the first time. It was while Susan and Ben were fussing around in the kitchen that Joe's gaze and hers had locked and, in one single swoop, that small action had swept away the darkness of the day. It had been so easy, so very easy to be blinded by the light of Joe's attentions after that, and it was with a sense of gratitude and relief that she allowed it to melt away and distract her from some of the sadness of her father's death.

Kaaya had thought about Joe endlessly that night while trying to get to sleep all alone in her bed. She reflected on his quiet, serious manner, feeling suddenly incredibly attracted by it. Joe was a fair bit older than many of her own and Rohan's friends and came across as a kind and gentle soul, not unlike her father in fact. What had followed in the next few weeks had almost seemed like a gift she was being offered to help her get over her father's death. Joe was adoring and gentle and, more importantly, right there and available when Rohan was usually away on business. It had also felt, quite suddenly, as though the only thing that she and Rohan really had in common was a shared love of the high life. Was it any wonder that she had grown to need Joe in a way that even she couldn't have predicted? Now, despite Susan's trusting cheeriness (and the rather terrifying thought that Riva would kill her if she found out about the affair) the thought of losing Joe seemed quite unbearable. And what of the fact that Joe was by now madly in love with her too? From what Kaaya could see, it was much, much too late to try turning back the hands of the clock. It wasn't exactly love she felt for Joe, but Kaaya knew she was as close to that emotion as she would probably ever get.

Chapter Seventeen

Aman picked up his sleeping son as the doors of the aircraft swung open to allow the first-class passengers off. Ashfaq whimpered slightly but rubbed his face with little fists before flopping back onto his father's shoulder. Aman kissed the soft curls on the child's temple, feeling moved by the trust of such heavy slumber. He waved the approaching nanny away. Ashfaq had been quite fractious on the flight, demanding his father's attention the whole time.

'I'll carry him, don't worry,' Aman said to Miranda. 'Don't want him crying again when he wakes up.'

The *ayah* nodded and retreated. Aman watched her gather Salma's belongings together instead. Salma looked groggy as she stood up, her eyes puffy from sleep and her *sari pallav* askew.

'Are you okay?' Aman asked her as she tottered slightly and grabbed his arm.

'Really uncomfortable flight,' she said, 'so bumpy, I thought it would never end.'

'Well, something was certainly bothering Ashfaq,' Aman said, resting his cheek against his son's head.

'Next time we should stay at least a week,' Salma grumbled. 'Three days away is really so unsettling.'

'Well, there was nothing to do in Dubai after the charity dinner . . .'

'*I* could have done some shopping. But would those Khalili women let me out of their sight! Come and see our special education unit, oh, meet all our lovely teachers, now let us visit the Grand Mosque – oh, dull, dull, dull, all these charity types!'

'Perhaps you should have stayed back then,' Aman responded tersely. 'Done all your shopping after getting rid of the do-gooders.'

'But *you* said you wanted to get back to Bombay for the *Duniya* shoot.' Salma's voice had become a whine now. 'And you wanted to take Ashfaq back with you. I can't really send him back and not be there, can I? We really should have stayed another two or three days. It wouldn't have been a big deal.'

'Try telling the producers that,' Aman snapped. 'Sorry, guys, please hold up the shoot, my wife wants to go shopping, you see.' He dropped his voice to speak more softly. 'I asked you to come back with me, Salma, because I don't get to spend enough time with Ashfaq, that's why.' Aman patted Ashfaq's back as the child shifted uneasily in his sleep. 'The least you can do is be in Bombay with him when I'm shooting here. It's not too much to ask, is it?'

To her credit, Salma refrained from taking the argument further, disembarking from the aircraft in sullen silence behind her husband and son. The usual tremors of excitement went around the airport as the Khans walked into the terminal building, passengers and airport staff nudging each other and staring.

Salma ignored the curious stares, sweeping along in her husband's wake with her nose in the air.

'I just hate being seen in public with you,' she muttered to Aman under her breath.

'Sorry, but it can't always be avoided,' Aman replied cheerfully, not sounding sorry at all.

'Well, you may be the star but people are always more inquisitive about me than you,' Salma said crossly. 'Though somehow I always attract the negative stories too.'

'Well, let's be thankful word doesn't seem to have got out that we're on this flight. No paparazzi hanging about the gate, see?'

'Thank God,' Salma mumbled, 'or they would surely have got a few pictures of me with this puffy face and crumpled sari and all.'

'You don't look that bad,' Aman said, trying to sound sincere.

But Salma was unconvinced. 'For some reason, even if they get *good* pictures, they always print those in which you look really handsome while I am caught standing next to you in the most unflattering poses: opening my mouth to eat, or with the wind blowing my hair about like some mad *bhoothni*. It's deliberate, I tell you. All those female journalists just hate me!' Salma stopped to catch her breath.

'Come on, it can't always be deliberate,' Aman tried to reassure Salma but she was on a roll now.

'Of course it is! I'm not a fool, Aman. It's just jealousy, plain and simple. They can't stand that I had such a privileged upbringing. Don't forget, as the daughter of Noor and Abdullah Miandad, I was famous before marrying you. Why, people even said when I was a teenager that I would be a wonderful actress. It was my marriage to you that ruined all that. And then your rise to stardom after our marriage has brought even more envy my way. So much good kismet in one person's life, it just turns everyone's stomachs.' Salma sniffed and tossed her hair, adding angrily, 'May curses rain down on all their heads!'

Aman ignored the familiar spiel. It was true that Abdullah Miandad would never have allowed his only daughter to go into films and perhaps it had been a grave disappointment to Salma to realise she would never be allowed her own career. But Aman had run out of sympathy long ago, not least because he had always made it plain that he would help Salma if she wanted a break in films, and she had always shown a curious disinterest in his offer.

It was the usual custom for the airline to send their luggage on after them and so the small group swiftly left the airport to board the two shiny black Land Cruisers that were awaiting them. The maids got into one with all the hand luggage, while the Khans boarded the other.

Aman, pleased to see the smiling face of his old driver, leant forward to clap him on the shoulder in a friendly greeting.

'Fareed Mian,' he said, '*kaisey ho?*'

'Fine, sir, fine, sir!' the man responded with a beaming smile.

'Good, good, and how is *amchi* Mumbai?' Aman responded.

'Very good, sir, very good.'

Aman grinned, remembering that, despite Fareed's best efforts to learn English these past ten years, his stock tended to run out at this point. He switched over to Hindi to ask what the latest events in the city were and, more specifically, enquire about the latest film news. Fareed was always up-to-speed with new releases and able to inform Aman quite reliably of what the word on the street was regarding likely hits and misses.

As they left the airport behind them, Aman looked out at his city, readying itself for the night. Hawkers were covering up their fruit and vegetables with lengths of damp sacking, while beggars, having given up their business along with the city's last commuters and shoppers, had already dissolved away into the gateways and porches of deserted offices, forming dark bundles barely visible among the shadows. As they stopped at traffic lights, Aman saw an urchin – no more than eight or nine – pull a discarded leaf plate from a bin before licking it clean. He felt in his pocket for some money, realising he only had *dirhams* on him. A Bombay urchin would no doubt know exactly where to go to get any currency changed and so Aman hurriedly lowered his window to give the astonished boy a few notes before his car pulled away from the lights to head for Juhu.

Half an hour later, the guards were opening the gates of the Khan residence to allow the two cars to pull into the drive. Aman got out of the car, still holding his sleeping son. He turned to Miranda. 'Shall I take him up to his room?'

'I will take him, sir.'

'It's all right, Miranda, I'll put him straight into his bed. He may just sleep through the rest of the night.'

'Okay, sir,' the nanny replied, hurrying up the stairs to turn down the sheets on Ashfaq's cot before Aman reached the room. Softly, he bent over to slip Ashfaq into his bed, patting his shoulder as the child mumbled and half-opened his eyes enquiringly. After Ashfaq had settled back into slumber, his forehead clearing as he sensed the familiarity of his bed, Aman raised himself up. He left the bedroom and closed the door behind him, leaning gently on it for a moment before walking down the corridor to his own suite of rooms.

Salma was bathing in the *en suite* bathroom, so Aman pulled out a fresh *kurta-pyjama* from his wardrobe in order to nip to the shower room that was attached to the study. He turned on the lights and cast a glance at the pile of magazines and publications awaiting him on his desk. He barely got the time to even glance at all the press coverage he received any more, but he knew that Pillai, his PA, would keep him informed of anything out of the ordinary. Luckily there had been no scurrilous stuff of late. Perhaps the press pack was losing interest in him as potential fodder for their gossip columns, ever since that story about him and glamour model Reeta Malkani had been proven completely unfounded. Not that it *had* been untrue, of course, but having a well-oiled publicity machine whirring along twenty-four/seven was one of the blessings of money and fame.

Aman stripped off his clothes and, leaving them on the floor of his study, walked under the power shower. He turned it on and felt needles of cold water bounce off his neck and shoulders, finally forcing his muscles to relax. Keeping his palms flattened on the tiled wall, he wondered at his fatigue. He had just enjoyed three restful days in Dubai, free of shoots and schedules, and should be feeling rested. But Aman had worked out a long time ago that a mere two hours in Salma's company now had the most exhausting effect on him – three days stuck in a hotel suite together had been an ordeal. Even Ashfaq's cheering presence and the overbearing hospitality of the luxury hotel had not leavened the tension that now lay between them. Who had changed most – was it her, or was it him?

Aman watched the water swirl around his feet before it drained away with a few dissatisfied gurgles. Of course, love had a strange way of dying sometimes, even between people who started off madly in love. He had not married Salma for love exactly – he had barely known her, after all – but Aman had intended with all his heart to love Salma when he had married her. That much was true. He had already lost Riva when he had left England, and the few relationships that had followed at film school had all come to nothing. So it certainly was not as if he was still pining for anyone else when he had met Salma, and their courtship had consequently been completely sincere. She had been sweet enough then – just turned twenty and, despite her father's wealth, innocent in the ways of the world. Their first year of marriage, perhaps even two, had been a process of eager mutual discovery. That tentative exploration and growing together had definitely been a kind of love. Aman could not tell if it was his own rapid rise to success that had changed things some time after that but, by God, how things had changed. Aman barely recognised the brittle, selfish, complaining creature that Salma had become. Perhaps he had changed too. Surely that's what she would say if anyone asked her.

He turned off the shower but stayed where he was, allowing the last water droplets to fall onto the back of his neck as he kept his unseeing gaze on the floor. Suddenly he felt terribly depressed again, feeling pushed to tears by the knowledge that he would probably never be able to rekindle love with the woman he was married to. And how strange that – at the exact time that terrible knowledge was coagulating around his heart – Riva Walia was about to re-enter his life. The first girl he had loved . . . when such things were *real*, rather than attached to his fame or fortune. Surely Riva would have heard of his own success in the intervening years? And how would that make her react to him?

Aman's new-found cynicism couldn't help making him wonder if perhaps Riva regretted slightly having dumped him so unceremoniously back then. But he checked his thoughts as he pulled a towel off the rack. Reconnecting with Riva would be one way to discover if he had genuine feelings left within him. There were days when he felt like an automaton, churning out schedules and churning in money. Friendship, love, these were all the things that Aman knew he had gradually lost as he had gained fame. Perhaps with Riva he could have hoped to find them again . . . if she hadn't been happily married to Ben . . . and if he hadn't so much to lose.

Aman towelled himself vigorously, trying to stop his uncontrolled thoughts, deliberately reminding himself of his sorry little pursuit of Riva back in England. His competitors had been well-spoken British boys like Ben, who came from the same sort of world as Riva. Either them or that whole gang of Indian and Pakistani students who, like Riva, had been born and bred in England, comfortable second-generation kids who slipped in and out of their two worlds, taking what they wanted from both. Aman had struggled to fit in with them as well, the brand of English they spoke being swift and witty, often too fast for him to grasp, especially over the hubbub of the Union Bar where he sat with his orange juice, trying to look as if he belonged. Some of the things they talked about were a complete mystery to him too: football, for instance.

Aman smiled as he remembered that it had been on one of those big match nights that Riva had first returned with him to his room. Of course, he had used a lame pretext – bloody chicken makhani, surely she must have seen through his ruse! But they had opened a bottle of wine and Riva had got quite drunk. She'd fallen asleep on his single bed and, when she woke, had invited him under the blanket with her. It had been nothing short of heaven, climbing into that bed next to her warm body in the early hours of that dawn. Aman remembered holding her face, being quite content to merely drink in Riva's loveliness, which was even headier at such close quarters. But then they had kissed and undressed each other and made love. Perhaps the memory of that night had etched itself in Aman's mind because it had been his first time, although Riva told him later that it had not been hers.

Aman had assumed that the night had moved them miles away from just being friends, but had been puzzled when Riva had kissed him on the cheek and left his room with a cheery joke. Regardless, Aman had thought he could not have been any happier in the days that followed. He and Riva had spent a lot of time together, going for long walks after their classes, once also hiring a pair of bikes to go cycling in the Yorkshire Dales. On that occasion, they had ridden into a wood and made love under a canopy of leaves. But, try as he might, Aman had almost never been able to get her all to himself. Being so gregarious, Riva was always surrounded by friends and admirers and, despite his best efforts, Aman had felt himself slipping away and out of Riva's charmed circle somewhere along the way. Gradually (there had never been any one precise moment), Aman started to realise that Riva and Ben were getting closer. When, feeling threatened, Aman had asked Riva if she loved him, she had looked at him as though it was the most confusing conundrum she had been faced with.

'Oh, Aman, I wish there were an easy answer to that,' she had replied and it had made him wonder if perhaps the boy who'd broken Riva's heart when she was at school had broken it so hard she had ended up behaving a little bit like him. But Aman consoled himself with the knowledge that Riva was still inordinately fond of him, even after it became official that she was going out with Ben. She seemed to think they could still be friends, but Aman knew he would not have been able to handle that. Nonetheless, it comforted him for a long time after to see that, on the day he announced he was giving up his course to return to India, Riva had looked genuinely stricken. He had said something about not being able to cope with the course and she had accepted that. Then she had given him a long hug before he had shaken Ben's hand and walked away.

Aman threw his wet towel over a chair and pulled on his *kurta-pyjama*. He contemplated staying in the study for a while, or slipping down to the basement theatre, so that Salma would be asleep by the time he went to bed. For a while now she had been talking about separate bedrooms but Aman had so far resisted, seeing this as the final irrevocable step in a broken marriage. Now he wondered if it was worth clinging to the mirage of a happy marriage any longer. Wearily, he walked back to his bedroom, running his hand through his damp hair.

Chapter Eighteen

Riva smiled with relief when she spotted Susan's head among the crowd emerging from South Kensington tube station. She had been starting to wonder if her friend had chickened out of the planned makeover. Typically, Susan had resisted the offer at first, eventually succumbing only when Riva said it was she who needed moral support.

'I can't go to Cannes looking like this,' Riva had wailed, holding up her split ends. That had finally swayed dear old Sooz and so here she was, happily convinced she was doing her friend a favour, rather than the other way around. Her tousled mop of hair, much in need of taming (and a colour job), was wilder than ever today, and teamed with an anxious expression on her face that cleared only when she saw Riva outside the tube station.

'Sorry, darling,' Susan huffed. 'Bloody long hold-up at Earl's Court and no signal, obviously. You haven't been waiting long, I hope?'

'Few minutes, not a problem. I couldn't help wondering if you'd bottled it though.'

'Oh, I wouldn't do that. Never look a gift horse in the mouth and all that,' Susan replied, taking Riva's arm as they started to walk down the road. She took up the conversation again after they had crossed the busy road.

'Still not sure you should be doing this, though, two heads to be transformed at an expensive salon, that'll be one large dent in your wallet, honey.'

Riva laughed. 'Never you mind about that. My publishers have given me a decent advance this time, don't forget. And what better way to spend it than on much-needed makeovers for us both?'

'True, but at least you're spending yours on a worthwhile cause – for God's sake, being on the Cannes jury isn't to be sneezed at! The world's media will be watching you . . .'

'Well, your makeover's worthwhile too. For me at any rate, because I have to keep looking at you, you see. So do stop jawing.' Riva squeezed Susan's arm affectionately as they arrived at the salon. She instantly regretted her joke as Susan's face turned pensive.

'Not forgetting the crucial role makeovers play in keeping errant husbands from straying,' Susan said with a wry laugh as they stepped into the salon. 'The timing may not be quite right on this one, though, Riv. Y'know, stable door, horse bolted and all that?'

'Don't, Susan,' Riva said, taking off her coat, 'don't let whatever Joe's doing rob you of your self-confidence. Hard as it may be, you have to believe that it's got nothing to do with you, okay? Nothing.' She held her friend's gaze for a minute before turning to the girl who was waiting politely to take their coats off them.

An hour later, left finally in a quiet corner of the salon with foil bits in their hair, Riva was relieved to see that Susan was looking more cheerful again. She smiled as she turned to ask Riva a question that was bound to have come up at some point.

'Talking of Cannes,' Susan said, putting away the tattered

copy of *Hello* she had been reading while her colour was being applied, 'are you looking forward to seeing Aman Khan again? You know, I barely spoke to him that year he was at uni with us.' Susan laughed, remembering. 'Poor lad seemed so painfully shy, he'd go beet-red the minute I got too matey with him. Although he seemed quite happy to be matey with *you*, pushy even! Inviting you back to his room, well, I never!' Susan shook her head in mock disapproval, grinning.

Riva ignored the friendly barb, continuing to deliberately leaf through her magazine but Susan persisted. 'You haven't answered my question, Riv. *Are* you looking forward to seeing Aman again?'

Riva lowered her magazine and considered Susan's question carefully. Not that it needed careful consideration, for she had thought of little else since the invitation had arrived, but she was too embarrassed to admit as much, even to her best friend. She tried to fob Susan off with a muttered response. 'He'll have changed a lot, I reckon . . .' she said doubtfully.

'Of course, he'll have changed. A top Bollywood star, for heaven's sake. But surely he wouldn't have forgotten *you*!'

'Oh, I don't know . . . he may have.'

'C'mon, Riva! He fancied you something rotten, didn't he? One never forgets one's first love.'

'First love! Think that might be overstating it a bit, Sooz.'

'Well, he did admit it was his first time, that night in his room, didn't he?'

'Oh, Christ, I was hoping you'd forgotten that! You do have an elephant's memory, don't you?' Riva laughed. 'Not one of my more edifying memories, I can tell you!'

'Oh, it was sweet, you said he was lovely.'

'He *was* lovely – so gentle and anxious and eager to please, and so different from the boys I'd met up to that point. I must say I felt like such a heel later when I took up with Ben.'

'On the night of the Blur concert, was it not?'

Riva grinned, 'Goodness, your synapses are working well!' She paused, remembering the start of her romance with Ben. 'Yes, I'd been vacillating terribly but it was the night at the Town and Country Club that finally decided it for me. Ben had been so generous, queuing up overnight in the rain to get tickets and poor Aman didn't even have a clue who Blur was! It was such a little thing but it did rather suddenly bring home to me how far apart we were in so many ways and what a big mistake I'd be making if I went with him. I think I mistook my fascination over him being Indian for love but, honestly, there were times when I felt we were speaking different languages even when we were both conversing in English!'

Susan nodded. 'You can't discount the importance of shared cultural reference points, I think. When all's said and done, you were much more like Ben, despite your Indian origins.'

'But Aman didn't seem to get it and looked all wide-eyed and hurt every time he saw Ben and me together; it was awful!'

'Hey, you don't think that was the reason Aman left uni, do you? Heartbreak at losing you?'

'Course not! For heaven's sake, Susan Holmes, you're reading far too much into what happened. Aman Khan probably forgot it all a long time ago. World at his feet and so on. Goodness, he must have millions of women chasing him now!'

'Did you ever tell Ben about your little dalliance with Aman?' Susan asked.

'I didn't need to! Aman's feelings were always written all over his face. But . . . if you're asking whether I ever fessed up to Ben about sleeping with Aman, oddly enough I never did. Which is strange, considering I used to believe that there was no room at all for secrets in good, healthy relationships.'

'Why didn't you tell him? Surely he wouldn't hold against you what happened before you two got together . . .' Susan queried, puzzled.

'Not sure . . . but I guess I sort of knew, even way back then, that Ben was the possessive sort. Some kind of sixth sense told me to keep a lid on it. And, before I knew it, Aman was gone anyway.'

Susan nodded. 'Just as well you didn't tell Ben, I reckon. It would have made it harder for him to accept your being with Aman in Cannes next month if he'd known about your fling. Fling? Affair? What *would* you describe it as? Somehow it sounded like a sweeter encounter than those words usually mean . . .'

Riva tried making light of what still felt like a slightly awkward memory. 'Hmm . . . not sure it was that sweet to be robbing an innocent of his virginity.'

'Oh, come now, that innocent was begging for his virginity to be robbed!'

'Susan Holmes, you appal me!' Riva laughed, happy to see Susan back to her old animated self.

'Well, it's hard to think of such a hunky young chappie as Aman Khan as being "innocent", you know. Even back then he had a certain smouldering charm. I can certainly see what made him such a star in Bollywood.'

'Oh yes, Aman was certainly a looker. But, hand on

heart, it wasn't that which attracted me to him, Sooz. There was something . . . something sort of little-boy-lost about him. And I'm *such* a sucker for vulnerability! In fact, it's that incorrigible weakness for the underdog that probably makes me so patient now with Ben's occasional tantrums.'

'I meant to ask you about Ben, actually. There've been no more moods since that last one, I hope? When was it you called and said he'd stormed off into the pouring rain?'

'Well, that was the last time, actually. A month ago. He seems to be making a real effort now, but I can't help thinking we're always in a state of temporary truce. I'm sure he's doing his best, and I've heard him make a few calls to employment agencies, but I keep thinking that the next row is simmering just below the surface. Besides, I think he has very mixed feelings about my going off to Cannes without him. And soon after I come back, there's the European book tour. I did ask at one point if he wanted to come along but he was in a strop about something and said no. I think he's just a bit grumpy that I'm taking off like this, you know. At exactly the time that his own career has sort of ground to a halt.'

'He can't possibly be grumpy about you going to Cannes, for heaven's sake! I mean, it's such a fabulous opportunity . . .'

'Well, I don't know if it's fair to describe it as "grumpy". He's just a bit depressed, I suppose.'

'But it's hardly your fault he's out of work, is it? Shouldn't he be grateful that at least one of you is doing something lucrative? *Men*, what is it with them?' Susan said, shaking her head, obviously now thinking again of her own errant husband.

Riva looked at her carefully in the mirror. 'Male ego's a strange thing, isn't it? Kaaya could be right when she refers to men as emotional infants. Usually with reference to Ben!'

'Pity that she and Ben have never managed to get on. Her Rohan seems nice, though. Or is he an emotional infant too, in her view?'

'Oh, Rohan's an absolutely terrific husband, if you ask me. But I'll grant that you only ever get to know someone by living with them. And, according to Kaaya, he's a complete mummy's boy.'

'Hmmm . . . she was with her in-laws when I called to invite her to your party and didn't sound half bored, I can tell you!'

When Susan was led away to have her hair washed, Riva looked at herself in the mirror. The foils on her head made her look like a prize idiot. *Was* it all to impress Aman? Pretty damned ridiculous, if that was the case, not least because Aman was probably surrounded by the most gorgeous women at all times. And what the hell did all this beautification say about her own brand of wishy-washy feminism, ready to fall away the minute she thought that a good-looking man was likely to pay her a little attention? Nevertheless, Riva looked at her face again, trying to assess the changes Aman was likely to see. She was thinner now, having still had a bit of puppy fat on her in the first couple of years at uni. Her hair was longer, and would soon have a few highlights running through to her waist. But what of these laughter lines, and the occasional smudges under her eyes when she hadn't slept well? It was Aman who would have changed for the better: all sculpted body and sophisticated man-of-the-world now, no doubt. Riva had seen enough of his movies to know that his body was now rippling muscle, a far cry from the boyish frame she had held in her arms that night in his room back in Leeds. Contrary to what she had said to Susan, Riva did remember Aman a lot more than she dared confess to anyone. One particular memory had lingered – from an autumn afternoon when they had gone cycling in the woods and Aman had told her of his family back in Mumbai. Riva had drunk in his descriptions of rambunctious family gatherings when people sat around an old harmonium singing Hindi songs and children tumbled around in play. It was the sort of Indian child-hood Riva had longed for when she had been smaller, having grown up in Ealing without an extended family of grandparents and cousins.

She had made passionate love to Aman that day, and felt deeply content when she had lain in his arms, her head on his upper arm. It was a curious sensation and only much later – after she had taken up with Ben – was Riva able to intellectualise her reaction and work out that it was the idea of her lost Indian identity she had felt attracted to, rather than Aman himself.

Or so she had firmly told herself whenever she later regretted Aman's departure . . . Riva now looked ruefully at her reflection in the mirror of the salon, seeing a much older and wiser woman than the one who had so unthink-ingly let as true a love as Aman's go.

Chapter Nineteen

Susan pulled the baking tray out of the oven and prodded at the asparagus spears wrapped in streaky bacon. They looked just right, the asparagus still plump, the bacon curls crisp and golden at their edges, held in place by toothpicks. Straightening up and clattering the tray down onto the marble surface of the pastry board, Susan smiled for the first time in the day. The broccoli and Stilton quiche she'd made earlier had turned out pretty perfect too, as had the tiny caramelised onion tarts, a recipe she hadn't followed in years. Apparently, she hadn't lost her touch, despite the black mood she had woken up with. Previously Susan had almost never suffered the mood swings she'd heard other women talk about, having the kind of temperament that was generally described as 'sunny' or 'cheery' or, annoyingly, 'jolly hockey sticks'. Even if she was angered by something, Susan's tendency was to let rip openly, never the type to hold onto grudges. But her moods these days were linked to Joe's and he was certainly still behaving very strangely; his old, pleasant self one minute and a cold stranger the next. Susan sometimes caught him looking at her with a small crease in the middle of his forehead, as though he was wondering who the hell she was. His irrational outbursts of temper hadn't stopped either. Just yesterday he had flown off the handle at her for forgetting to recycle the cans before the council's collection service. And – rather than asking him why he hadn't done it himself if it mattered so much to him – she had apologised (actually apologised!) before promising not to forget the following week. What the hell was *wrong* with her? More gallingly, she was still going through Joe's pockets whenever anything went into the laundry and checking call lists on his mobile. Nothing had emerged, so Joe had probably grown remarkably adept at deleting incriminating evidence. In the meantime, however, the business of sleuthing on her beloved husband was surely turning her slowly potty.

Susan pulled out a stack of quarter plates from the kitchen cupboard. She had kept her promise to Riva all right, not yet openly accusing Joe of any wrongdoing and never once questioning him on the overheard phone call at the River Café. It had seemed to make sense to follow Riva's advice and allow the situation to unfold and become clearer. Anything said before that would only damage their relationship permanently, as Riva had warned. But the waiting and watching was getting to her, as Susan had admitted to her friend on the phone earlier today.

She put the tea towel down and surveyed the kitchen. Order was beginning to prevail. The quiche and cheese sticks were covered in foil and warming gently in the oven, the fridge was stacked with cling-filmed bowls of crudités and dips, while smaller lacquer bowls filled with nuts and Japanese rice crackers were neatly lined up on the kitchen counter. Susan assessed her mood, convincing herself that she was feeling stronger. This was the best part of a party after all, when the bulk of the work was done, and she could look forward to spending an evening in the company of good friends. Perhaps that was one of the things she had let slip a bit over the years, both she and Joe getting too busy with their respective careers to stop and have fun often enough. The evening was sure to be good for both of them as a *couple*. She resolved instantly to do it more often.

As Susan started inserting little paper serviettes between each plate, she heard the sound of Joe's car pulling into the drive. She cast a quick glance at herself in the dining-room mirror before trying to smooth down her hair. That was the other thing getting her down – the constant struggle to look pretty and smell nice. She had been as pleased as Punch after emerging with Riva from Cobella's with a new hairstyle, her confidence and self-esteem mysteri-ously restored by a shiny new barnet. It had, however, got the two women talking about being totally failed feminists in their ridiculous bids to save their respective marriages – Susan by succumbing to the temptations of Clairol's Burnished Bronze Number 09 and Riva by running herself into the ground to make Ben feel better about himself. It didn't help either that neither of the two men appeared to have even noticed their wifes' efforts, Joe needing to be prodded into a half-baked compliment when Susan had finally demanded a response.

Despite all her angry thoughts, Susan summoned up a big smile for Joe as he now came in through the kitchen door.

'Hello, darling,' she called cheerily.

'Mmmm, great smells, what's cooking?' Joe asked, kicking off his trainers and unloading his gym kit on the floor. Susan noticed that, instead of coming up to kiss her, as used to be his wont, he went around the other side of the kitchen island to sift through the small pile of post awaiting him on the sideboard.

'Stuff for Riva's party tonight,' she responded, using a wooden spatula to gently slide the now cool tarts off the baking tray. 'God, I haven't made these in ages. Do you remember, we used to make them every time we entertained back at Werther's Close? I could just rustle them up in a matter of minutes back then.'

'Mmmm . . .' Joe muttered, not really listening as he tore open envelopes, separating their contents out into piles that would either be filed or shredded.

'Oh goodness,' Susan continued, undaunted. 'Werther's Close . . . remember how minuscule the kitchen was – and yet we had people over all the time, all those spontaneous parties . . .' Susan looked out at her vast garden, feeling sentimental for the innocent joy of those days. She gulped back the stupid lump that had suddenly formed in her throat (it appeared there quite unexpectedly these days) and turned to offer Joe the last of the tarts that was still on the tray.

He shook his head. 'Best not, actually. Having just spent two hours trying to get rid of this damn thing.' He patted his belly with a rueful expression on his face.

'Oh, silly, the way you talk, it's as if you have a great big beer gut hanging there! There's nothing to you there and you're as handsome as ever; go on, have one,' Susan beseeched, cringing inwardly at how far she was willing to go in order to pander to Joe's ego.

Joe shook his head, ignoring the compliment, although he looked a little shamefaced, Susan thought.

'What time's everyone coming?' he asked.

'Well, I've said seven to everyone except Riva and Ben who'll come at half seven. Be good to have all the rest assembled before the guest of honour's here. David's the only exception – he can't be here before eight because he's on call.'

Joe glanced at the time on his phone. 'Gosh, it's nearly six already. Are you ready . . . did you want a hand with anything?'

'Blimey, Ross will be here soon with the wine and I need a shower. Here, let me show you how to do this.' Susan moved up to make room for Joe next to her, telling him how she wanted the asparagus spears to be arranged on their platter, in an orderly ring around a small pot of yoghurt dip. They did the job together, standing side by side for a few minutes, Susan suddenly silenced by the huge big stupid lump that had formed in her throat again.

Kaaya stood before her mirror, as usual pleased with what she saw. The black Versace shift dress was a beauty, clinging exactly where required and, when worn with a pair of sheer tights to keep her legs warm, just right for a late spring evening like this. The new pewter Manolos completed the picture quite marvellously. Kaaya screwed on a pair of antique pearl earrings, brushed her hair down into a sleek chignon and pulled a pale grey pashmina out of her wardrobe. Sophisticated, toned down, that was exactly the impression she wanted to create tonight. The last time she had been with Joe, she had been wantonly naked, lying on a hotel bed and watching him pull on his clothes in preparation to leave before it got too late. Her sober attire tonight would present a nice contrast to that last rather disreputable tryst, no doubt driving him quite wild.

Rohan wandered into the room, whistling, towel around his waist. Kaaya waited for the obligatory compliment as she continued to preen, looking over her shoulder at the view from behind. Her bottom did indeed look shapely in this little number. But compliments were not forthcoming,

Rohan merely opening his cupboard and asking a little peevishly, 'What should I wear, Kay? It's casual, isn't it?'

Kaaya sighed. If this was what happened after a mere three years of marriage, what hope was there for the future, she thought. Never mind, Joe would surely shower her with compliments – if they managed to get away from the others for a bit, that is.

'It's too early yet for a linen jacket,' she replied, picking out a small silver clutch purse to slip a minuscule bottle of perfume and her mobile phone into. 'Your Armani blazer maybe?'

'Isn't that a bit over the top? What are you wearing?' Rohan turned finally to look at his wife. 'Gosh, you're all dressed up! Didn't think it was that dressy tonight?'

'I'm not all dressed up!' Kaaya protested. 'Just needed to wear this once more before sending it to the dry-cleaners.'

Rohan's attention returned to his wardrobe, and he began riffling through his jackets again. 'Okay, the Armani then. Teamed up with a pair of jeans, it won't look too OTT, I guess.'

'Which car are we taking tonight?' Kaaya asked.

'Don't mind. No, actually, let's take the Beemer. I'll drive. Don't think I want to drink much tonight.'

'You sure?' Kaaya asked.

Rohan nodded. 'Yeah, think I should give it a break for a while. Been drinking far too much of late.'

Kaaya wandered through the lounge, checking that the light timers were on, before collecting the BMW keys from the black Japanese glass bowl on the console table. When Rohan emerged from their bedroom a few minutes later, they left the flat to walk down to the garage together.

The drive from Holland Park to Wimbledon was an easy

twenty minutes on a Saturday evening and Kaaya relaxed as Rohan expertly took the wheel. That was one thing she'd give him over Joe, who was a terrible driver, always in a state of high distraction. It had occurred to Kaaya that it was perhaps merely her presence that made Joe drive badly but it wasn't a particularly flattering thought when he was seconds away from driving into the path of an oncoming bus. Normally, Kaaya would have had little reason to be driven anywhere by Joe – in fact, it was rather risky to do so – but as Rohan's travels had come to a temporary stop, she and Joe had recently taken to meeting for snatched rendezvous in a small hotel in Paddington. Kaaya had initially baulked at the sleaze-factor but, in a strange way, checking into a faceless hotel for the specific purpose of having sex had added a definite frisson to their secret meetings. On their last assignation, Kaaya had even taken a dinky little vibrator along with her, a gadget she had recently bought from the Harmony store around the corner from her office in Soho. Joe had vaguely heard of sex toys like fluffy handcuffs and vibrators but had clearly never seen one before.

'Lipstick?' he had queried as she slipped the vibrator out of her handbag once they were both naked. Silently, she had held his stomach down with the palm of her hand before turning the appliance on and running it gently over his thighs and his scrotum, watching the expression on his face turn from surprise to pleasure to an almost pained ecstasy. The sex that had followed had been excited and frenzied and Kaaya had been delighted to see a side to Joe emerge that was far wilder than she'd ever anticipated. When he finally flopped back, hot and sweating on the pillows, he had croaked, 'Bloody Nora,' in a weak voice before looking at Kaaya with renewed passion and admiration springing in his eyes. Clearly, all the years of respectful lovemaking with Susan had never brought him as much pleasure as that one evening with her, making Kaaya wonder why wives were so poor at being ingenious in bed. Didn't they realise how easily bored men were? They were like children, in need of new amusements every day! But Kaaya had to admit that was easier said than done. Despite having vowed to keep her own sex life with Rohan as spicy as possible, a certain staid sameness had indubitably crept in over the months. And it was certainly not beyond the bounds of possibility that Rohan had also taken to playing the field while on his business trips. If that was the case, then Kaaya was glad she had got there first!

She looked out at the passing streetlights as they drove on, idly contemplating what it would be like to meet Joe alongside Rohan and Susan tonight, surrounded by all their friends. While there would be a certain thrill involved in pulling the wool over everyone's eyes, it was her sister Kaaya couldn't help worrying about. Riva was a keen observer of everything, and there was no knowing what her authorly insight would cause her to see, even though Joe had promised to keep his head.

By the time they pulled up outside the Holmes's Wimbledon residence, it looked as though the party was already in full swing. The curtains had not been drawn and Kaaya could see about ten people in the living room, all with glasses of drink in their hands. Platters of food were being passed around and vases filled with flowers crowded the windowsills.

'No sign of Ben's car yet,' Rohan observed as they got out of their vehicle.

Kaaya pulled her dress down over her hips after she had disembarked.

'Susan's given them a later time than everyone else, I expect,' she muttered distractedly, hoping the dress wouldn't ride too far up her legs every time she sat down.

'Of course – chief guest!' Rohan replied, bleeping the locks. 'It's sweet of Susan to do this for Riva. Perhaps we should have thought of it – you know, a party at home to celebrate your sister's success.'

Kaaya shrugged as they walked up the drive. She was far more accustomed to having Riva think up these sorts of things on *her* behalf; habits like that were probably formed way back in childhood. Besides, Kaaya thought sourly, she never needed to bother to do all that sisterly stuff when Riva had best buddy Susan to think of such things.

A loud burst of laughter emerged onto the street as Susan opened the door to them. She was already hot and red-faced from playing hostess, but Kaaya took in Susan's new hairstyle as they kissed, a huge improvement on the tangled bird's nest she had sported previously. Then, as Rohan kissed Susan and handed over the bottle of wine they had brought as a gift, Joe emerged from the kitchen, holding a bowl of pistachio nuts. As her back was turned to everyone else, Kaaya raised her eyebrows and gave him a significant smile, amused that he could only respond with the utmost politeness and decorum.

'Hello, Kaaya,' he said, perhaps slightly overdoing the courtesy as he gave her a chaste hug, barely touching her.

'Joe, lovely to see you,' she breathed, naughtily tickling his ear lightly with her tongue as she air-kissed him. She watched as he greeted Rohan and took the bottle of wine off Susan. When he disappeared into the kitchen again, Kaaya and Rohan accompanied Susan into the living room. Most of the people Kaaya could see were unfamiliar faces but she spotted a couple of Riva's old friends from university. She had met them at various parties before but always had difficulty remembering their names, especially the people she called 'Riva's loony left-wing brigade'. After the round of introductions had been completed, Kaaya seated herself on the sofa, conscious of Joe's presence in the room as he circulated, holding a few empty wine glasses by their stems, a bottle of Sancerre in his other hand. It was bizarre seeing him behave in such a meek and domesticated manner – a far cry from the man who had groaned and writhed so ardently under her hands four days ago. Kaaya mischievously considered being slightly naughty in some way tonight. Just for a bit of fun, although she knew it would make sense to hold her horses until everyone was a little more drunk, of course. For the time being, she turned to chat with a bland-looking woman wearing a voluminous flowery skirt who was seated at the other end of the sofa, scoffing vast quantities of breadsticks dipped in olive tapenade. She said her name was Ada and explained that she was an old friend of Riva's from *Bitten Apple*'s editorial team, although she now wrote for the *Big Issue*. Riva did pick up the weirdest of acquaintances, Kaaya thought, trying not to look instantly struck by boredom.

Ten minutes later, Riva and Ben came through the door to a small round of applause and some good-natured cheering. Riva, blushing slightly, waved her hands, trying to dismiss the attention but Kaaya thought she looked happier than she had in a long time. She noticed too that Riva also sported a new hairstyle, her long black hair subtly highlighted with strands of gold and blow-dried to look halfway decent. Kaaya hadn't realised that Riva had lost a bit of weight recently too. She looked almost too thin, clad in a black polo-neck sweater and a pair of skinny jeans. Her sister had even gone to the trouble of wearing a smart pair of stilettos; perhaps it was all a part of her preparation for Cannes. Which was quite out of character, given that she'd even refused to buy a nice frock for her Orange Prize night, turning up at the South Bank venue in an old chiffon sari belonging to their mum, with a black bikini top masquerading as a blouse!

After Riva had gone around the room greeting everyone else with hugs and kisses and cries of delight, she gave her sister a quick embrace. They hadn't met since spending an evening together at their mother's house the previous weekend, an occasion that had been fraught with unspoken tensions between Kaaya and Ben. Kaaya ignored her brother-in-law now as he followed Riva around the room, giving Rohan a particularly warm handshake and thump on the shoulder while giving Kaaya a perfunctory greeting. She told herself she didn't really care. Ben and she had never shared the affectionate warmth Riva and Rohan did, but she had not been able to help noticing that, of late, Ben's behaviour towards her had deteriorated considerably. Kaaya wasn't sure why but guessed it was something to do with Ben's general shitty mood about his redundancy. Strange that he still seemed able to talk pleasantly to other people – her mother, for instance, who had always (rather mysteriously, in Kaaya's view) liked Ben and had, this past weekend, spoilt him silly, cooking him his favourite *channa daal* and insisting Riva took a Tupperware box of the stuff home for his lunch the following day.

Kaaya saw Ben now engage in animated conversation with Rohan, no doubt sucking up to him in order to find out about goings-on in the City so he could nose down a job. Annoyed at the cold-shouldering she was getting from Ben, Kaaya threw him a dirty look and decided to wander towards the kitchen in search of Joe instead.

She found him at the sink, rinsing out a whisky glass. 'Need any help?' she asked, making him jump.

Joe smiled when he turned and saw Kaaya. 'Nick's just asked for a single malt and we hadn't got any whisky glasses ready. You know how you expect people to drink only wine at these shindigs. Can never be prepared enough, I guess . . .'

It sounded as though Joe was wittering and Kaaya wondered if her presence in his house was making him nervous. She also saw how easily he had slipped into that casual married-person use of the word 'we', a pronoun he was normally careful to avoid using in her presence. She was about to open her mouth to playfully point this out to him but Susan came bustling into the kitchen at that moment, carrying an empty platter.

'Joe, darling, would you refill this for me please? Oh hello, Kay – do you need something? Has Joe given you a drink?'

'No, no, I just wandered in to see if I could help in any way. And, yes, I'm all nicely topped up, thanks,' Kaaya replied, waving her glass in the air. She was really not very keen to get her fingers messy with onion tarts and hoped Susan would not ask her to help. Luckily Susan, observing Joe's wet hands, was now getting the miniature tarts out of the oven herself, picking them off their tray and dropping them one by one onto the serving plate. Clattering the tray back into the oven, she offered Kaaya one first, before bustling right back out of the kitchen again.

After she left, Kaaya surreptitiously swung open the lid of the Brabantia bin to throw the tart away and wipe her hands on a kitchen towel. But Joe spotted her and threw his eyes upwards.

'She's been making them all morning – she does rather work herself up into a lather over these things,' he said apologetically.

'And you? Do you work yourself into a lather too?' Kaaya enquired silkily, raising her eyebrows over the rim of her large wine goblet.

Joe laughed sheepishly. 'Not sure what you're referring to,' he said, wiping the whisky glass with a tea towel, unable to meet her eye.

'No? Get worked up, I mean . . . into a lather . . . doesn't sound too unfamiliar to me . . .' Kaaya breathed sexily before taking a sip of wine and adding in a more prosaic voice, 'Albeit, not over onion tarts.'

Joe gave Kaaya a long look, still wiping the glass mechanically but dropping his voice to say softly, 'You look just gorgeous tonight, you know . . . it's driving me crazy . . .'

'Is there somewhere we can go?' she asked suddenly.

Joe stopped wiping the glass. 'What do you mean?'

'Oh, I don't know – the garden, your car? I've got to kiss you or I'll go mad, right here, in the middle of your kitchen,' she warned, enjoying being mischievous.

Joe looked alarmed, looking over her shoulder towards the door and keeping his voice low. 'But you were telling me to go easy tonight . . . we can't possibly . . .'

'Why not?' Kaaya demanded.

She could see Joe wrestling with himself for a minute before he gestured at the door to the garden. In a flash, Kaaya had opened the door and dragged him out by the hand. The night was cold and the garden dark, except for dim light trickling through the slats of the wooden kitchen blinds. Kaaya reached up for a kiss and Joe grabbed her bottom with both hands, yanking her roughly towards him. His mouth pressed down on hers with a passion that robbed her of breath and she felt his hands searching for her breasts as she moulded her body against his. Reaching down, she assisted his hand to reach under her dress and felt him plunge his fingers down her stomach and into her pants. Suddenly she was moist; but a burst of laughter from inside the house made him freeze. As though coming to his senses, Joe withdrew his hand. He gave Kaaya a long look before kissing her gently on the lips and whispering, 'You beautiful, beautiful creature, you're driving me quite wild. But we mustn't, Kaaya, not here. It's way too risky.'

'I'm not scared,' she said stubbornly, sticking out her chin.

'Of course, you are,' he laughed softly, smoothing down her hair. 'You don't want Rohan to know, do you, or your sister? C'mon, let's go back in. Before someone spots that we're missing.'

Kaaya exaggerated a disappointed moue with her lips. 'Chicken!' she accused in a scornful murmur.

But Joe kissed her sulky mouth again, trying to get her to smile. 'Not chicken at all. You'll catch your death out here so it's doctor's orders. I need you to be in the pink of health . . .'

'Oh yes? Whatever for?' Kaaya enquired innocently.

Joe held her by her arms and gave her a serious look. 'I love you, Kaaya. You know that, don't you? We'll meet tomorrow, yes? At the Holiday Inn, same time, same room.'

Kaaya finally nodded.

'Love me?' he asked. She nodded again and, looking relieved, Joe released her to propel her back into the warmth of the kitchen.

Kaaya stepped back in through the door and drew in

her breath sharply. Riva was at the kitchen counter, picking up the empty whisky glass that Joe had left on the counter. She looked up, startled to see Kaaya coming in from the garden, followed closely by Joe.

'Oh, Nick was wondering where the bottle of single malt was,' Riva blurted. Looking confused, she added, 'I told Susan I'd get it because she's been running herself off her feet . . .' Riva trailed off, probably realising she was babbling.

'We just stepped out for a bit of fresh air,' Kaaya explained.

'Kaaya wanted to see Susan's herb garden,' Joe added.

'*Herb* garden? But you're hardly interested in gardens, Kay, let alone herbs,' Riva said, puzzled.

'I . . . I insisted,' Joe said. 'It's beautiful out,' he added weakly.

While Kaaya was mentally instructing Joe to stop over-explaining, she saw a look creep over her sister's face. Almost imperceptible at first, it grew slowly into one of recognition. Kaaya was not sure what exactly Riva had identified but she had learnt way back in her childhood that there was little that escaped her oh-so-clever big sister.

Joe, still trying to cover up, was now blithering on about single malts and decanters as he fussed about looking into kitchen cabinets, but both sisters were now oblivious to him, looking at each other as though seeing one another for the first time.

Riva had seen everything she needed to in that one instant. Kaaya. *Kaaya* was the woman Joe was having an affair with!

The rest of the party passed in a blur for Riva. Through her churning thoughts, she registered that Joe and Kaaya did not disappear anywhere together again. In fact, they hardly spoke or acknowledged each other. But Riva knew she had not imagined the tension in the kitchen earlier, and that look on Kaaya's face was one she was well familiar with from their childhood. It was one that Kaaya used whenever she had done something wrong but thought (usually erroneously) that she had got away with it.

Despite a sense of sudden and unbearable anguish, Riva maintained her composure at the party, answering everyone's questions about her new book and the impending Cannes trip. She continued the party patter, circulating among her friends – some of whom she had not met in weeks – trying to catch up on all their news.

Later, when some of the guests, including Kaaya and Rohan, started to leave, Riva helped Susan clear the glasses and put them in the dishwasher. When only David and Ross were left, the women left Joe and Ben to chat with them in the living room while they sat at the kitchen table with a bowl of salad between them. Riva allowed Susan to add a couple of falafels and a generous dollop of hummus onto her plate, although – when she tried to eat – the food got stuck in her craw. Helping it along with quantities of Chianti, Riva was quite drunk by the end of the evening. But, try as she might, and even in her extremely inebriated state, she could not bring herself to look Joe in the eye for the rest of the night. Not even when it was time to leave and Joe offered to walk down the road with her and Ben to their car.

'Don't worry, we'll let ourselves out, mate,' Ben said at the door, pulling on his coat and helping Riva with hers.

'No, really, I'll see you to your car,' Joe replied in his usual genial manner.

'I guess you do need to make sure your neighbours

don't complain later about drunken and disorderly behaviour from the Holmes's guests,' Ben joked.

'You're not over the limit, are you?' Joe enquired, worried. 'You can always sleep over, you know . . .'

'Nah, I only had a couple of glasses,' Ben replied. 'Thought I should let Riva get plastered, seeing as it was her party.'

'Nice!' Riva said, rousing herself. 'Hardly plastered, I'll have you know. Mildly pickled, perhaps, but not plastered.' She knew she was slurring slightly even as she said it.

Joe laughed. 'I don't think I've ever seen you plastered, Riva, not even back at uni.'

They reached the car and Riva pulled the keys out of her purse to hand over to Ben, waiting a few agonising seconds next to Joe as Ben walked around the car. Open the damn thing, it's got central locking, she thought, hoping desperately that Joe wouldn't attempt to speak to her. Certainly not to offer any more explanations regarding what he was up to with her sister. She was sure she would hit him if he did.

After what seemed an eternity, Ben bleeped the doors and Riva got in, Joe holding the door open for her. Ben opened the windows as he adjusted the mirrors and the driver's seat and Joe bent over to say goodnight to them. Riva stared straight ahead, unwilling even to kiss Joe in her usual fashion, but he leant in and gave her a peck.

'I hope you enjoyed your party,' he said.

Riva finally forced herself to look at Joe. It was a pointed look, aimed at forcing a guilty look out of him with a deliberate mention of Susan's name. 'It was lovely of Susan and you to do this for me,' she said stiffly as Ben started up the ignition.

'Gosh, it was certainly worth breaking open the bubbly for,' Joe replied cheerily. 'Don't think I know anyone who's done anything as tremendous as getting on a Cannes jury. You go show them, girl!' Joe gave Riva a fond smile, his hands resting on the window frame. But the second he moved his hands away, Riva jabbed on the button to send the electric window back up again. It was almost as though she needed to put a physical barrier between herself and Joe before she did something unfortunate.

'Are you okay?' Ben asked as he negotiated past all the parked cars on the street.

Riva heaved a sigh to slump down in her seat. 'Yes, why do you ask?'

'I dunno, you seem preoccupied.'

'Did I? At the party, you mean?'

'Well, you did seem a bit out of sorts by the end. I wondered if you were tiring from all the attention.'

'Sweet of you to notice, Ben. Yes, I think I was a bit overwhelmed. Plus I'm not used to bloody stiletto heels!'

They drove on in silence, Riva still mulling over the horrifying possibility of Kaaya and Joe having an affair. It was hard to know which of them to feel more enraged with but, for the time being, it was Kaaya she focused on. Not that Joe could be let off the hook but Riva knew that Kaaya always set out to get what she couldn't have. When they were children, it was Riva's toys she had always wanted, and Riva's bike, even when she had hundreds of toys of her own and was still only at the tricycle stage. Riva could still remember with frightening clarity how Kaaya had wept and screamed on the day Riva's first shiny new cycle had been delivered. No amount of explaining by both their parents about it being dangerous and her legs being too short had any effect and Kaaya had finally

174

been lifted onto Riva's brand-new cycle, still hiccupping and red-faced. Riva had watched with her heart in her mouth as Kaaya had wobbled down the drive, the stabilisers trembling madly. Of course, Kaaya had fallen down as soon as she had reached the pavement, grazed her knees and dented the cycle. Her renewed howls of pain made everyone forget that she had just ruined her sister's eighth birthday gift, the dent on its front mudguard a permanent memory of that incident. That was Kaaya. And Riva knew Joe would be just another casualty of her sister's horribly acquisitive nature.

Chapter Twenty

Aman sat by himself in the privacy of his air-conditioned home theatre. Billy Mehta, the director of *Zulmi*, his forthcoming summer release, had sent him some of the rushes and Aman was scribbling notes in a small book. With the right marketing, it could be the year's biggest grosser, Aman reckoned. And it had all the ingredients to appeal to the overseas markets too, being a slick, taut thriller shot partially in Scotland. He chewed the end of his pen, thinking about the overseas markets. Were Bollywood films indeed starting to appeal to mainstream audiences in the US and UK, as Billy had insisted earlier today during their phone conversation? Or was it merely the increasing prosperity of the Indian diaspora that was turning these films into hits abroad? Aman smiled. He'd ask Riva when he met her later this month in Cannes, he thought. It was the kind of question she'd be sure to give him an honest opinion on.

He laid aside his notebook and sank back in his leather seat, both amused and perturbed by the number of times he had thought about Riva Walia since the Cannes invitation had come. She seemed to pop into his thoughts at the slightest excuse these days. It wasn't even as if he intended raking up their old attraction – if indeed there had been anything like that from her side at all back then, rather than just a passing fancy. Besides, she was no doubt very happily married to Ben. She might even have children; her sister had mentioned that Riva was married, but had not said anything about kids.

Aman got up from his chair and picked up his notebook. He turned off the projector using one of the many remote controls lying on the console. Waiting for the blue screen to turn white again, he mulled over why he hadn't stayed in touch with anyone from Leeds University. For that matter, he hadn't stayed in touch with the people he had met at film school either. Absently watching the screen retract into the ceiling, Aman wondered whether it was a form of snobbery when successful people claimed difficulty in making and maintaining friendships. As he got older, however, he was certainly starting to feel the lack of true friends.

Aman's phone rang as he climbed the stairs to the ground floor. It was his mother. '*Beta*, I have been trying and trying to call you.'

'Oh sorry, Ma, I was in the theatre in the basement. No signal there, as you know. Is everything okay?'

'It's your Papa again, *beta*. I don't want to worry you but he was getting all breathless again and . . .'

'Have you called Dr Tandon?'

'No, I thought I should not worry him every time . . .'

'Call him, Ma, tell him it's urgent. I'm on my way . . .'

Aman dialled Fareed, his driver, to bring the car around the front of the house. He didn't know where Salma was, he hadn't seen her all day, but she knew where to call him if he was required for anything. Barely waiting for Fareed to pull the Mercedes into the portico, Aman jumped in and asked him to drive as fast as possible for Andheri.

His father's health had become a source of worry this past year and his mother was not always the most efficient carer, swinging between overindulgence and overcaution, treating her husband as though he were one of her nursery charges. It was at times like this that Aman sometimes found himself wishing for a job that involved less travel. His father was a gentle soul and Aman would never be able to forgive himself if he were not around when he needed him. Luckily, the roads were free of traffic jams today and Fareed got Aman to Andheri in a record twenty minutes, even managing to stop off at a magazine kiosk en route so that Aman could pick up a few items for his father.

As they pulled into Desai Road, Aman spotted his parents' high-rise flat, rising alongside many others into the horizon. It was a sight that always pleased him, as the Jaivilas penthouse had been his very first property purchase in Bombay, bought after his second blockbuster hit. Four years ago, he had felt almost boyishly thrilled to hand it over to his parents when the construction work on his Juhu bungalow had been completed. He had subsequently tried, unsuccessfully, to get his parents to move into his house, which was so palatial it could easily absorb another two families without anyone noticing. But they had always refused, citing a variety of ingenious reasons. Aman suspected the real reason was Salma. She had never liked them much and was scornful of their social status, though they were perfectly respectable. Aman's father had been an engineer with Air India all his working life and his mother a nursery school teacher. Compared to Salma's father's wealth, however, anything would seem paltry and insignificant, Aman supposed.

Aman's mother opened the door to him, a worried

expression on her face. 'I think he is better already,' she said.

'Well, I spoke to Dr Tandon too. He's on his way,' Aman remarked, walking into his parents' bedroom. His father was seated cross-legged on his bed, wearing a blanket over his shoulders and an annoyed expression on his face. 'Hey, Pops,' Aman greeted him cheerily, throwing the clutch of newspapers and magazines onto the bed.

'Treating me like an invalid,' Mr Khan muttered, throwing a dark look at his wife.

'He is trying to go out and meet his friends,' she said helplessly, looking to her son for support.

'You keep me in prison here, you think I will get better?'

'Prison! Look at him talk!' she cried.

'I am not meeting my friends for going wild or anything, woman! Just for a bit of *gup-shup* and taking the sea breezes. Is that unhealthy, tell me?'

'Hey, hey, no fighting now,' Aman intervened, smiling as he sat on the edge of their bed. His parents' squabbles were never serious. If ever a couple were deeply devoted to each other, it was his mum and dad. But his father's recent retirement had led to their spending far too much time in each other's company and Aman was sure the 'heart ailments' were caused by his father not having enough to do. Mr Khan was already looking through the pile of magazines Aman had brought and pulled out *Sportsweek*, the expression on his face cheering considerably as he saw that the special feature was about the latest IPL tournament.

'Where are my specs?' he asked his wife, who threw her eyes upwards before going in search of them. Thank goodness for wall-to-wall cricket coverage, Aman thought as his father squinted, holding the magazine at arm's length in an attempt to read its contents page without his glasses.

His mother returned with the spectacles and gave them to her husband, but not before waving them at him and chiding, 'Look at you, your son is here and you are reading *Sportsweek*!' She turned to Aman. '*Beta*, you want some tea?'

Aman smiled at her. 'With lots of elaichi, Mum, only you know how to do *masala chai*.'

His mother went off again, beaming, and Aman turned to his father who had obediently put his magazines away. 'She's right. I don't get to see enough of you as it is. How are you, *beta*? No travels for a while, I hope?'

'Not much this month. I'm shooting with Yashraj at Lonavla for three weeks. But at the end of the month, I have to go to Cannes, as you know.'

'Ah, but that will be pleasure more than work, I hope. Is Salma also going?'

Aman shook his head. 'I don't think partners of jury members generally go as they keep the jury very busy, from what I hear. Nandita Das, who went a few years ago, emailed to warn me that we'll be watching three or four films a day. I'm rather looking forward to it but I don't think that would be Salma's scene at all!'

His father nodded. 'Why didn't you bring Ashfaq with you today?'

'Well, I left home in a bit of a hurry when Mum called. But I'll come back later this evening with him.'

'Good, your mother will be happy. We have not seen him for a while.'

'Why? When did you last see him?'

Mr Khan thought back. 'He came about two weeks ago, I think. His *ayah* and Fareed brought him when we called up to ask if we could come to see him there . . .'

Aman's mother came back into the room with two mugs

181

of tea. 'Nine days back,' she corrected her husband, holding the tray out to him. 'We would really love to see a little more of Ashfaq, *beta*,' she said as she turned to give Aman his tea.

'Well, there's no reason why you shouldn't see him every day when he's in Bombay. Juhu's not that far, for God's sake.'

'Once he starts school, of course, it will be difficult,' Mr Khan said mildly.

'All the more reason why we should try to see more of him now,' Mrs Khan countered firmly. 'Of course, we could come to Juhu but it's hard to know when he and Salma are at home or at her parents' house.'

'And when did you last see Salma?' Aman asked. He couldn't help noticing the small exchange of looks that passed between his parents, signifying much more than the bland reply he got.

'Maybe we saw her last month?' his mother replied, looking doubtfully at her husband. Aman's father was silent and then he picked up his magazine again, refusing to get drawn into criticising his daughter-in-law. A couple of seconds later, the doorbell rang and Dr Tandon was ushered in.

Aman used the opportunity to walk onto the balcony and call Salma. He took a few deep breaths as her phone rang, trying to quell the seething feeling in his chest. He got straight to the point when he heard Salma's voice.

'Salma, I'm at my parents' house and I want you to bring Ashfaq here immediately.'

'Why?' she asked.

'Because I say so,' he snapped.

'*Arrey!* What is the matter with you?'

'Will you only ever do what *you* want, Salma? Never anything for anyone else?'

'What are you talking about?'

'The fact that my parents have not seen either you or Ashfaq for weeks, that's what.'

Salma's voice became hard. 'They have been complaining about me to you?'

'No, of course they haven't been complaining about you!'

'Then who told you this? A passing bird?'

Aman clenched his fists. 'This is not the time or place for sarcasm, Salma.'

'Then what am I to do? Laugh? How dare you call me when I am in the middle of a meeting to shout at me.'

'What meeting? And I'm not shouting.'

'Yes, you are. Shouting. When I'm here in a meeting with the coach and captain of my team. This is business, Aman, not acting. Okay?'

Before Aman could say any more, Salma had hung up, leaving him standing on the balcony of his parents' penthouse, feeling ready to throw himself off it. What had he done, Aman wondered furiously, to deserve a wife like Salma who did not care enough to do him even the smallest of favours? Had it all been his fault? Had he perhaps, in the early years of his marriage, been too caught up with establishing his career to have befriended Salma, and made her love him? Had he inadvertently driven her love away?

Aman tried to calm himself by looking out over the busy metropolis that he loved and that now avowedly loved him. Everyone who lived behind each of those millions of windows, every occupant of the hundreds of cars he could see crawling on the roads below would either be a fan or have seen at least one of his films. That kind of adoration came to so few people in their lives. And, yet, to Aman, that love suddenly seemed so insubstantial, so very trifling and inconsequential. What was the point in being so loved when the person closest to him had no love for him at all?

Chapter Twenty-One

Kaaya had lain low for a whole week after Susan's party. Clearly her canny sister would have guessed what she and Joe had been up to in the back garden. Kaaya had, however, conferred with Joe and reassured him that, however angry Riva got, she always came around in the end.

'She's a loyal family-is-everything type, Joe. She'll sulk for a bit and then grill me, at which point I'll come up with some explanation that'll convince her, don't worry,' Kaaya had said breezily, even though she still quailed inwardly at the thought of what Riva would say when she finally confronted her.

The situation was unusual, though. When eight days had passed and Riva had still not called, Kaaya knew her sister was seriously upset. She decided to visit her mother first to see if she could pick up any useful clues.

On Saturday afternoon, Kaaya pulled her Lotus Elise into the drive of her mother's house in Ealing and cut the engine. Kaaya had made sure before coming that her sister had no plans to visit their mother today; Riva was on Sloane Street, shopping for her Cannes trip, apparently. That was another thing that alarmed Kaaya, who had no confidence at all in her sister's ability to pick out decent designer wear. For heaven's sake, this was the most important celebrity event

Riva would ever attend in her life and she was quite capable of turning up in Gap khakis when all the other women would be draped in Versace and Prada! Kaaya wondered if she ought to feel cut up that Riva had not asked for her advice or help with her shopping . . . but then again, she had a very good idea why she hadn't.

'Hello, Ma,' Kaaya said, bending down to kiss her diminutive mother at the door.

'Thinner! Every time I see you, you are thinner, Kaaya,' Mrs Walia grumbled. 'Are you not eating properly?' She put her hands on her daughter's slim hips, as though feeling hopefully for a roll of fat.

'Ma, if anyone is eating properly, it's me – *properly*, as in large portions of salad and greens. Not sure one can say the same of you, though! Have you been taking your insulin shots?'

'Oho, always you two are after me. Worse than your father.'

'Have you?' Kaaya persisted, following her mother into the kitchen. She took in her mother's shape with alarm, noting that she had put on even more weight around her stomach from the last time she had seen her.

'Yes, yes,' Mrs Walia replied irritably, filling the kettle. She added in a peeved voice, 'Last time Riva was here, she even *counted* my insulin packs and wrote it all down in a diary – what cheek, I tell you!'

'Well, I don't blame her, Ma. Sometimes I feel tempted to do the same. You've become so careless about your diet.'

'Tea?'

Kaaya shook her head. Her mother invariably forgot that Kaaya only ever drank mint tea and, even if she did manage to find a pack, it would no doubt be well past its sell-by date.

'So, lucky Riva, out shopping all day today then?' Kaaya asked, seating herself at the breakfast bar.

'You should have gone to help her since she's buying things for this Cannes trip. Even though actually, I am not happy at all that she is going.'

'It's the chance of a lifetime, Ma!'

'But then she should take Ben along. Husbands and wives do too many things separately-separately these days. It is not right, not *healthy*.'

'But this is like work, Ma. Riva couldn't possibly take him along. She's a jury member and will probably be kept madly busy viewing all those films. And what would Ben do then?' But Mrs Walia shook her head, muttering something indistinct in a low voice. As she stirred two sweeteners into her tea, Kaaya spoke again. 'So when's she off? She did tell me but I can't remember now . . .'

'She goes next weekend. Ten whole days for Ben to be alone. I really don't like it.'

'Oh, he'll cope, Ma,' Kaaya said irritably, following her mother into the living room.

'At least you and Rohan should look after him, take him out for some nice dinners or outings. I have asked him to come here for his meals but he says it is too far. I think he feels a little shy when Riva is not around. Poor boy.'

Kaaya held back the various caustic remarks that sprang to her lips. As far as she could tell, her mother had never figured out just how little Ben and she liked each other. Papa had been the sensitive one, always picking up on the unspoken. Kaaya looked at her father's picture on the wall and felt the customary constriction in her throat. The colour in the photograph had faded a bit but he was looking straight into the camera, wearing a gentle half-smile on his face. It was the best likeness the family had of him and both his daughters had taken copies before their mother had had the picture framed and placed above her TV set. Riva had set her copy in a Perspex box on her writing bureau but Kaaya kept hers tucked away inside her cardigan cupboard. She still sneaked a look at it every day, but invariably put it hastily back, fancying that Papa could now see everything, even look right into her thoughts.

'So tell me all the news, Ma,' she said, slipping off her Bally driving pumps and tucking her feet under her.

'My news?'

'Your news, Riva's news . . .'

'Well, I don't think I have any news to give you, *beti*. Just the usual things that one has to do here at home.'

'And Riva?'

'How do I know? That girl does not tell me anything. She must be telling you more of her news than me!'

'Nope. She doesn't tell me anything either. I guess it's because she's got Susan for that.'

'Ah, Susan is like her big sister,' Mrs Walia replied fondly, taking a sip of her tea. 'She never forgets that you are the *little* sister, though. She was saying that she threw her a party to celebrate her going to Cannes. Such a sweet girl.'

Mrs Walia's habit of using pronouns liberally often left even her daughters mildly confused, but Kaaya guessed the compliment was intended for Susan. 'Yes, I was invited to that.'

'Oh, were you? She never said. Was it a nice party? Lots of people?'

'Hmm-mm.' Kaaya nodded. 'Didn't Riva tell you about it – the party, I mean?'

'That's what I mean – she never says anything about

anything. Never even told me that you were there at her party, can you imagine! Never does she get the time to sit like this, like you do, just to talk and . . . and *enjoy*, you know. Always busy doing the shopping and the cleaning for me, even though I tell her she doesn't have to. Then running out to buy medicines and counting them and making notes in her diary. Last time she came, she even insisted on weeding all the flower beds, saying that Papa would have done it at this time of the year.'

Mrs Walia did not see the passing look of guilt on her younger daughter's face who had clearly not thought of such things. As the sudden realisation that her husband was not around to do all the usual springtime chores suddenly overwhelmed Mrs Walia, she started to weep, using the end of her sari to wipe her eyes. Kaaya sighed and got out of her armchair to comfort her mother. It didn't look like she was going to be able to get much more about Riva from their mother now.

Kaaya patted her mother's back absently, feeling ever stronger stirrings of nervousness at the length of this silence from Riva. She could not, in fact, recall any occasion on which Riva had remained incommunicado for longer than three days. Of course, Kaaya knew her sister was angry and perhaps she had good reason to be, seeing how fond of Susan she was. But mild flirtations went on all the time, and that's all Riva should assume it was. Why, in some social circles a lot more than mild flirtations went on between friends. Kaaya had recently heard about wife-swapping parties on Indian tea estates, for God's sake! Only Riva was morally stuck in some sort of nineteenth-century Victorian world. She simply had to ease up a bit, in Kaaya's opinion.

But as her mother continued to weep, Kaaya grew more

and more miserable at the thought that she had upset her only sibling to such a great extent, and so soon after their beloved father's death. It was as if their tiny family was fragmenting into many unglueable bits.

Chapter Twenty-Two

Ben pulled out the Samsonite from the garden shed and wheeled it down the path. Before taking it into the kitchen, he gave it a vigorous rub down with an old flannel, trying to remember when the suitcase had last been used. He and Riva hadn't travelled anywhere for a while now and he realised suddenly that they hadn't had a holiday together since he had left the bank.

Stepping back into the kitchen, he placed it on the floor. 'There you are, I've given it a bit of a clean but you may want to take a J-cloth to it too.'

Riva turned from the bowl into which she was shredding lettuce. 'Oh, ta, love. Goodness, it does look like it's seen better days, doesn't it? When was it last used?'

'I was trying to remember too,' Ben replied. After a minuscule pause and as Riva turned back to her shredding, he added, 'We should plan a holiday somewhere. It's been a while.'

'Good idea. Maybe tack something on to my book tour later in the summer?' Riva replied.

Ben had forgotten. 'When is that?'

'Be sometime after the launch here so I guess that'll take up most of June, perhaps a bit of July.'

'Have they said yet where they're sending you?'

'Six countries, I believe. Be the obvious ones with big publishing territories – France, Italy, Spain, Germany, Holland, Greece . . . wherever I've sold translation rights, I'd have thought. It's a bit of a new game for me too so I'm not sure how long the tour will be for, and whether it's just the main cities . . .'

'Exciting times,' Ben said, trying to sound more enthusiastic than he felt.

Riva laughed. 'Well, don't forget that this book tour is coming three years after the first page was written! That's how long this one's taken anyway.'

'I suppose they have to cash in on the Orange win of the last one before people forget.'

Riva was spinning the lettuce leaves in her salad spinner when the phone rang.

'I'll get it,' Ben said, regretting it the minute he picked up the phone and heard Kaaya's voice.

'Hello. Riva there?' she asked coolly.

'It's your sister,' Ben said to Riva, placing the cordless handset on the kitchen table, without a word to Kaaya. Riva wiped her hands and picked up the handset as Ben wandered into the living room in search of the newspapers. Only half-listening, he heard Riva speak a few monosyllables into the phone before she hung up.

'All well?' he asked as she came into the living room.

'I guess. She went to see Ma yesterday and apparently she's on a bit of a downer again, poor Ma.'

'Anything in particular?'

'Don't think so, sounds like the usual sort of thing. It'll be a long time . . . in fact, I wonder whether she'll ever get over Papa's death.' Riva's voice was tired and dispirited.

'The human spirit is more resilient than you think,' Ben said, trying to offer comfort.

Riva threw herself into an armchair. 'Kaaya says she'll take me to Heathrow tomorrow.'

'Oh, why? Any special reason?'

Riva shrugged. 'Dunno. We haven't seen each other for a bit.'

'It's not like her to be so selfless,' Ben said. 'Well, she doesn't have to. I'll take you.'

Riva was silent for a couple of minutes before she replied. 'Actually, Ben, I think I will take Kaaya up on her offer.' Ben looked at her quizzically and she explained, 'There's just a couple of things I need to discuss with her, y'know, Ma's medication and stuff. It might be our only opportunity to speak.'

'You can tell her all that on the phone, can't you?' Ben asked, suddenly feeling his earlier good cheer depart dramatically.

But Riva was too distracted to notice. 'No, I think I do need to talk to Kaaya face-to-face, Ben. It's okay, I'll have her pick me up.'

'Suit yourself,' Ben said, getting up from his chair. Suddenly he needed to get out of the house, to clear his head of these dark thoughts that had reappeared so un-expectedly.

'Where are you going?' Riva asked as he picked up his keys from the mantelpiece.

'Out.'

'Don't you want lunch? The salad's nearly done, I just need to dress it with some vinaigrette . . .'

'Nope,' Ben replied, opening the front door and letting it slam shut behind him. Striding briskly down the garden path, he realised that he had promised to accompany Riva to her mother's this afternoon. No doubt she would be on the phone to him soon to enquire about that. He felt in his pocket, realising that he had left his mobile phone behind in the house. But he was certainly not going back for it. Riva could go wherever she fucking wanted on her own, or with her sister, for all he cared. His own presence was clearly a total irrelevance in her life.

Walking down the road, Ben felt that familiar gnawing feeling begin to eat away at his stomach as his anger slowly receded. Of course Riva was at liberty to ask her sister to take her to the airport, and he ought not to take it as a measure of the regard she had or did not have for him. He was being unreasonable, he knew – but surely she should understand what he was going through these days too?

Though puzzled by Ben's abrupt departure, it was Riva's earlier phone conversation with Kaaya that continued to aggravate her. Riva's original intention had been to refrain from seeing her sister until she had got back from Cannes, needing time to cool off. But Riva had spent the past week worrying that, by the time she got back from Cannes, the situation between Kaaya and Joe would have deepened to a stage beyond reason or control. Riva knew she had no choice but to accost her sister with her suspicion. She would need to do that before telling Susan, certainly. That's if she *did* tell Susan. Christ, how that would hurt! And what would she say? 'Oh, Sooz, you know the woman you think your husband's having an affair with? Well, it's my kid sister, how about that?' Damn Kaaya, damn her pretty little face, Riva thought, leaping to her feet, unable to sit still when she felt so enraged.

Riva saw the suitcase in the kitchen and, picking up a damp J-cloth, knelt next to it to rub at its hard grey plastic with all her might. Using far more vigour than was required, she felt herself slowly run out of breath. As she stopped to wipe her face with the back of her hand, it suddenly occurred to her that perhaps Kaaya had offered her a ride to the airport in order to explain things. Perhaps even to seek her help in ending the affair before either Susan or Rohan found out. Oh God, what would poor Rohan do if he did find out? Despite his adoration of Kaaya, he surely wasn't the kind of man who could ignore a wife's extramarital fling. And he would surely find it unforgivable if he thought Riva had known all about it and hadn't told him.

Riva mulled over the different possibilities, sitting back on her haunches in the middle of her kitchen. The terrible thing was that she couldn't talk to anyone about this. Not Susan, obviously. Not her mum who would just curl up in horror and die. Not Ben, who already hated Kaaya . . .

She started rubbing at the suitcase again. And what was eating *him* now? Another marathon sulk from Ben was the last thing Riva needed just before her departure to Cannes. They hadn't rowed for a couple of months now and he had seemed to be making a huge effort to be sweet and helpful, accompanying her to her mum's and even helping her with some of her shopping for Cannes. And now, suddenly, he'd stormed off again! Of course, Riva knew it was something to do with her having said she'd go to the airport with Kaaya. But what was she to do? There was no point suggesting he come along too for it would defeat the purpose completely if she couldn't talk to Kaaya in private.

She pulled out her mobile phone and texted Kaaya. *Will take you up on offer of lift to airport tomorrow. Come at 8 am.* Then she tried to soften her feelings towards Ben, aware that her mother would feel much happier to see both of them together on the eve of her departure to Cannes. Shoving aside her pride, Riva clicked on Ben's number. But as she heard the ringing tone kick in, a curious echo of the ring became audible, and Riva saw Ben's phone sitting on the sideboard, ringing away for all it was worth. Damn him, damn the world, Riva thought, feeling overwhelmed by other people's problems as she slammed her phone down.

Chapter Twenty-Three

Kaaya watched her sister emerge from the house, lugging a suitcase behind her. There was no sign of Ben, fortunately. Perhaps he was still asleep. Typical, Kaaya thought, climbing out of the car to help open the boot.

'Morning,' Kaaya said, but Riva only grunted in response as she hoisted up the suitcase. The two women got into the car and Kaaya started up the engine. Stopping for a stream of oncoming traffic at the T-junction, she sneaked a quick look at her sister's face. Even in profile, Riva looked grim. One would hardly think she was off on a once-in-a-lifetime trip to the South of France, Kaaya thought with a sigh.

'Looking forward to Cannes, then?' she asked cheerily.

Riva finally relented with a mumbled, 'You bet.'

'Lucky you, hobnobbing with the likes of Isabelle Huppert and Robin Wright Penn! And, best of all, Aman Khan! Perhaps you could persuade him to take you somewhere swanky for dinner. Get chatting about the old times at uni or something . . . and remind him about me! He hasn't come back on that deal yet.' Kaaya flicked the indicator to change lanes, recalling that Aman had never been part of the set that had occasionally come down from Leeds in Riva's uni days. Riva had, in fact, only casually

197

mentioned that he had been a classmate when they'd been watching a Bollywood film at their mother's house one Sunday years after she had left university.

Riva roused herself slightly to say, 'It's hardly likely Aman Khan will want to consort with the likes of me.'

'You never know. He did seem to remember you quite fondly. Why, he may even have read your book and be a fan! And want to buy film rights. After all, he was studying English at uni, wasn't he? It does rather depend on how starry he's become, I suppose. He may be all nose-in-the-air, did-I-ever-have-a-*normal*-life-before-becoming-a-star? Y'know what I mean.'

'Hmm,' Riva responded, looking out of the window.

Kaaya took a deep breath. It would seem her sister was intent on not forgiving her that little misdemeanour with Joe. She tried another tack. 'Ma said you bought some new clothes for Cannes. Get anything good? You could have called me for help, y'know . . .'

At this, Riva suddenly snapped, turning in her seat to face Kaaya more directly. 'Don't you think you have a bit of explaining to do, Kaaya?'

'Explaining?'

'You know what I'm talking about. Joe. That night at their party.' It was a statement, not a question, Riva's voice sharply sarcastic.

Conscious that Riva was studying her face closely, Kaaya tried to remain expressionless while thinking of how to respond. There was no point trying to cover up, Kaaya knew that well enough. Riva was far too incisive and was perhaps the only person who really knew her inside out. But aggression was worth a try first. 'For God's sake, it was a minor flirtation, Riva. Get a grip!' she said, trying to sound angry.

'*Flirtation*! Get a *grip*? You have some fucking cheek, Kaaya!'

'Oh, c'mon, Riva,' Kaaya wheedled. 'I know you're conservative but there's no need to be quite so fuddy-duddy! Flirtations between friends aren't that uncommon, y'know. For heaven's sake, you'd have thought I'd committed a murder, the way you're going on.'

Riva was silent for a moment and Kaaya thought she might actually have managed to convince her sister of her overall innocence. When Riva spoke again, her tone was quieter than before. 'How far has the affair gone?'

'*Affair*? Who said anything about an affair?' Kaaya said, hoping she wasn't overdoing the injured innocence.

'For fuck's sake, Kaaya! Susan overheard a conversation between you two. You may as well stop pretending now.'

It was now Kaaya's turn to say nothing as she tried to gather her thoughts. Riva could merely be calling her bluff – on the other hand, there was every chance Susan *had* overheard one of their calls. Joe was hardly adept at dealing with this kind of thing. So how much did Susan and Riva already know?

Riva wasn't letting go. 'How far have you gone with Joe, Kaaya?' she asked, very slowly and very deliberately.

'What do you mean "how far" . . . I don't get it,' Kaaya was now openly flustered by Riva's direct and uncharacteristically aggressive approach.

'For fuck's sake, Kaaya, have you had sex with him?' Riva was shouting now.

Kaaya suddenly felt very cross at being interrogated in this manner. She was not a child any more and did not owe anyone – least of all her bossy big sister – any explanations. She pursed her lips and muttered, 'I don't need to take this from you, Riva,' although she knew she sounded far from convinced herself.

Riva threw her head back onto the leather headrest and said in an incredulous voice, 'I don't believe it. I just don't believe it. You and Joe have been sleeping together . . .' When Kaaya remained silent, now stepping on the gas and thundering as fast as her Lotus would go down the dual carriageway, Riva spoke again, her voice sounding almost tearful. 'For how long, Kaaya? How long has this been going on, damn it!'

'It doesn't *mean* anything, Riva,' Kaaya replied, realising how like a little girl she suddenly sounded. Without even noticing, she had slipped into the same cajoling tone of voice she used to adopt when she wanted to wear one of Riva's favourite tops or had inadvertently given away a precious first-edition book of Riva's to someone who would not return it.

After what seemed like a terribly long time, Riva replied quietly, 'You mean it doesn't mean anything to *you*, Kaaya. But then it never does mean anything to you, does it? Not even if it means a whole lot to other people. What makes you think you can take what belongs to others without a second thought for what it may do to them, Kaaya . . .'

Kaaya stuck her chin out, her voice petulant. 'If you're talking about Susan, shouldn't it have been Joe thinking of her, rather than me?'

Riva shook her head. Still speaking in the kind of quiet, saddened voice that Kaaya hated (she'd have much preferred a screaming row), Riva muttered, 'Yeah, like Rohan doesn't matter at all.' She took a deep breath and said, 'Look, drop me off here. I'll get a cab. I didn't really want your lift. I just wanted a chance to ask you about Joe and I've got as much as I want. Stop the car.'

'Don't be silly, Riva, Heathrow's not far now.'

'STOP THE FUCKING CAR!' Riva yelled so loudly, Kaaya swerved a little but she continued driving.

'It's a bloody motorway, I can't stop!' she shouted back, flustered. 'Besides, you'll never find a cab here. And then you'll miss your flight.'

Luckily Riva wasn't doing anything as dramatic as reaching for the door handle and leaping out. She must have remembered that her suitcase with all the designer clothing was in the boot. Kaaya sneaked another look at her sister, whose expression was now unreadable. She had to say something to repair the damage.

'Look, I'm sorry, Riva,' Kaaya said, speaking swiftly. 'I didn't mean to hurt anyone, really. I'll do something to sort it out. By the time you get back . . . I promise!'

But Riva was silent and remained that way until they got to Heathrow. Taking the exit for Terminal 1, Kaaya pulled into the set-down area and turned to her sister, hoping to make one last explanation or apology. But Riva was already halfway out of the door by the time she had cut the ignition. Kaaya released the boot lock from inside the car as Riva started to wrestle with the handle. Disembarking hurriedly from the driver's seat, Kaaya walked across to help Riva but she had already pulled her suitcase out and was starting to walk briskly towards the entrance door of the airport without looking back. Kaaya stood for a few minutes next to her car, watching as her sister was swallowed up by the swing doors. She felt, for the first time since her affair with Joe had started, a genuine clutch of fear. This wasn't anything like the exciting little frisson she sometimes experienced while talking to Joe on the phone, knowing that either Susan or Rohan were within earshot. This was *real* fear. Dark and sickening and clawing away at the inside of her stomach like a living being. Kaaya had already lost one family member this year – she simply could not afford to lose another.

Back at the house in Kingston, Ben finally dragged himself out from under the duvet. He had been wide awake when Riva had risen and, lying on the futon in the study, had listened to the sounds of her getting ready upstairs to leave for Heathrow, feeling angry with himself and yet completely unable to do anything about it.

Ben had not seen Riva at all since he had walked out on Sunday morning, having spent the night in the study. He had returned to the house at some point in the evening, having gone for a long walk via a couple of pubs. But, by the time he had returned, the house was empty. 'Gone to Mum's' a scribbled note on the kitchen table read. He had used the chance to grab a duvet, a pack of water biscuits and a handful of Babybels, planning to hole himself up in the study, thereby avoiding Riva when she got back to the house. In the event, she had not returned until half past ten and Ben, exhausted from the quantities of fresh air he had ingested on his marathon walk (not to mention the six pints of lager in three different pubs), had been barely aware of her return.

In the morning, the creaking of the floorboards from above had woken Ben and he had lain there, listening to the familiar sounds of Riva getting ready; the sliding open of her lingerie drawer, the creaking of the shower door, the sound of water splashing on the tiles. She appeared to be going about her routine more quietly than usual in an effort not to wake him, perhaps out of consideration – or a desire to avoid him. Either way, he could not bring himself to open the study door and make amends before she left. It felt as though she was leaving, not just for Cannes, but for an entirely new life. One that was glittering and high profile and involved international film stars. Where was the room for the likes of him in such a brightly shining picture?

Ben gazed blankly up at the ceiling, considering how doubly galling it was that Riva should be going to meet Aman Khan in Cannes, the man whom – fifteen years ago – Ben had stolen her from.

Of course she had been in love with Aman back then; it had been written all over her face, despite what she had said. Ben had watched miserably as the pair hung around the campus with their heads together whenever they were out of class. And it didn't help that they were on the same course, while Ben was reading Economics and Commerce. But Ben, who had himself fallen hook, line and sinker for Riva in the first week of uni, wasn't going to give up without a fight. The Blur concert was his golden opportunity to make up some brownie points and he had patiently queued up all night under a minuscule plastic tent in order to get into the gig. Ben's delight at getting a pair of tickets was unbounded, though he had then had to spend an hour at the entrance of the Town and Country Club wondering if Riva would even turn up. It had been a wet night; Ben could still remember the cold ache of his fingers curled tightly around the tickets, which were slowly turning damp and sodden in the pocket of his jacket. And then she had come! Like a small miracle, Ben had felt Riva steal up behind him to wind her arms around his waist. He had turned to face her, they kissed, and something about the way Riva clung to him made Ben aware that she had reached some kind of turning point. He had never stopped to question what it was that had caused her to choose him over Aman. It had been good enough to know that she was finally his . . .

For a long time after Ben had heard the deep throb of Kaaya's Lotus disappear down the road, he had lain on the futon, looking at the shadows cast by their elderflower tree against the sunlit cotton curtain. He and Riva had planted that tree together ten years ago, when they had bought the house, and had at first tended it carefully, measuring its every growing inch with pride and glee. Then, at some point that Ben couldn't remember, it had shot upwards and taken over one whole corner of the garden.

Now, a full two hours later, Ben climbed out of bed and, zombie-like, went through all his routines; putting the futon back together, making a pot of coffee and reading the sports pages of the previous day's *Telegraph* along with a bowl of muesli. He had set a mental test for Riva, keeping his mobile phone charged up and at his elbow all day. But she had not called from the airport, either on the mobile or landline. Of course, she might have been waiting for *him* to call, especially seeing that it had been mean of him to leave her to visit her mum on her own the day before. But the way Ben reasoned it to himself, Riva was the one with the upper hand – the lucrative career and all the trappings that went with that. Surely she, who prided herself on being sensitive and empathic, would understand that he was crying out for her help. But Riva hadn't called. And, by evening, tired of staying in the house, hoping she would call on the landline, he had finally stepped out.

Dusk was falling as Ben took his usual route to the park through Seymour Street, a road flanked by large plane trees and neat rows of Victorian townhouses. Some houses already had their lights turned on, their owners perhaps back early from work. As Ben walked past them, he could not help looking into the windows of the basement flats, most of which had neither curtains nor blinds, as though happy to advertise their normalcy to the world. In one, a group of three people was gathered around a dining table on which a wine bottle was cooling in a bucket of ice. In another, a woman's denim-clad legs were visible as she stirred something at the hob while a child played with a set of blocks on the floor. In the third, a couple sat together, watching television. Ben wasn't usually given to staring, but today he felt drawn to these squares of light and life. He felt a sense of terrible despair that his own home was one in which love was slowly dying away.

Chapter Twenty-Four

Joe wondered why Kaaya was being so weird. Most of his calls to her in the day had been ignored and, when she had finally replied, her tone had been brusque.

'Are you still at work?' Joe asked when she finally answered the phone.

'No, on my way home now.'

'Driving? Are you able to talk?'

'Yes, I have Bluetooth on.'

'Are you all right, Kay?'

'Hmm-mm.'

'Nice day?'

'Hmm-mm.'

'Kaaya, what's wrong?'

'What do you mean?'

'Something's wrong . . . you're being so . . . curt. And you've avoided me all day.'

'I haven't!'

'Yes, you have. Seven missed calls?'

'Well, I've been at work, y'know.'

'Of course, I know, my darling. I just wanted to see you . . . hold you. Please tell me when.'

Kaaya was silent for a few minutes and Joe could hear the deep roar of her Lotus negotiating the evening traffic in his ear. When she finally spoke, his heart started to plummet inside his chest.

'Look, Joe . . . I've been thinking,' Kaaya said slowly, deliberately. 'I think we should give this a break for a while.'

'What do you mean "this"? Do you mean *us*?' Joe asked in an incredulous voice. Kaaya did not respond and so Joe spoke up again, agonised. '*Why*, why do you want to give it a break, Kaaya?'

Finally, after what seemed like forever, Kaaya spoke. Her voice was uncharacteristically sober. 'I think they all know about us.'

'They? Who's they?'

'Well, Riva does. She confronted me this morning, before she left for Cannes. And she said Susan knows too.'

'*What?*'

'That's what Riva said. And she doesn't usually lie.'

'But it wouldn't be like Susan not to ask me if she knew. I'm sure as anything she doesn't know,' he asserted emphatically.

'Maybe she's watching and waiting?'

'Naaah,' Joe said, although he felt suddenly queasy. 'What did you say to Riva when she confronted you?'

'Nothing. But I didn't have to say anything, Joe, she's no fool.'

'No, no, of course not. Bloody hell. No wonder you went all silent on me. I can hardly blame you.' Oddly, relief was Joe's first reaction, relief at the knowledge that Kaaya was angry not with him but with having been found out. Then he suddenly thought of Susan again, feeling sick at the thought that Riva might have called and told her everything before leaving for Cannes. Denial seemed the easiest way forward and so, in the voice of a small boy, he asked, 'We can still meet tomorrow, can't we? Tuesdays are our day, after all . . .'

'Don't be daft, Joe! Don't you get it – they *know*! Riva knows, Susan knows. Don't think Rohan does yet but it won't be long before he's in on it too. Bloody hell, I thought Riva was going to kill me this morning.'

'Oh, Christ,' Joe said, running his free hand through his hair. 'I'm so sorry, my darling. I feel terrible about you having to face Riva's wrath. Must have been awful. Christ, we've got to think of something. I'll think of something,' he said, babbling, trying to talk the icy tone out of Kaaya's voice. 'I think we should deny it. Yes, that would be one way forward – deny it.'

'It's too fucking late for that, Joe! Don't you see – they know, it's out there. Stable doors . . . horse bolted . . . geddit?'

'What if Susan asks me tonight?'

Joe sounded genuinely worried and Kaaya thought for a minute before replying. 'She might not know for sure. Unless Riva called her from Heathrow, of course . . .'

Joe let out another strangled cry. 'Christ almighty, it's all going horribly wrong, isn't it, Kaaya? When it's such a beautiful thing we have. Look, Riva's not back for a week so nothing's going to happen at your end at least for a bit. I suggest you just carry on as normal for now. As for me, I'll face Susan when it comes up. Even ask for a divorce, if it comes to that. You could do the same with Rohan, couldn't you? I'll marry you, my darling Kaaya, you know that, don't you? God, I'd marry you like a shot if I could.'

But Kaaya made no response to that, muttering something about bad traffic before hanging up. Joe sat back on his office chair, listening to the gentle hum of the air-conditioner in his room at the hospital. This bland little room, with its papers on the desk and medical posters on the wall, suddenly felt like a safe little cocoon he was most reluctant to leave. Nevertheless, he got up and started to push papers into his briefcase, his mind still buzzing. For some peculiar reason, a line from a Ted Hughes poem he had learnt in high school was jumping around in his head; he couldn't remember it exactly but it was something about love flying into his life like a hawk into a dovecote. That's what his love for Kaaya had been like, flying in and turning mad his small, twee, dull dovecote life . . .

Joe straightened a pile of folders on his desk, still thinking furiously. If Susan did know about the affair, as Kaaya had suggested, it was most peculiar that she had not confronted him yet. Why would Susan not ask? She had far too much self-respect to quietly accept a philandering husband. Was she – as Kaaya had suggested – waiting in order to gather evidence to use against him? Or could it be that Susan could not bear the idea of losing him, and preferred to close her eyes to any possibility of that happening?

Joe left his office and closed the door gently behind him, the sickening feeling continuing to mushroom within him. Despite his earlier impassioned offer to Kaaya, he had not really given much more than a passing thought to divorcing Susan and marrying Kaaya. Besides, Kaaya had never given even the tiniest indication of wanting to marry him. Joe prided himself on having emotional intelligence (wasn't that the term that was used these days?) and it had not been hard to see that, throughout their affair, Kaaya had always maintained a kind of cool non-committal distance. Whatever it was, it wasn't marriage she had wanted from him. Had he been a different sort of man, it would have made it bloody convenient to carry on having great sex with no commitment on either side.

210

But Joe wasn't like that. He had never given up hoping that he would eventually succeed in melting Kaaya completely. Now the knowledge that Kaaya would merely drop him when he became an inconvenience was making him feel like a punctured balloon.

'Night, Dr Holmes!' Angela called from behind the reception counter.

'Good night, Angela,' Joe replied, trying to smile at the pleasant middle-aged woman who had cheerily seen him off virtually every night for the past seven years he had worked at the hospital. He wondered what Angela would think if she knew he was a philanderer . . .

'Mind how you go, it's pouring outside, Dr Holmes,' she warned. 'Did you want one of our spare brollies?'

Joe looked through the glass doors, surprised to find that it was indeed raining quite heavily. He shook his head. 'No thanks, Angela, the car's not far. I'll manage.'

And, with that, he walked out into the downpour, feeling cold needles of rain pierce the top of his crown and slip down through his collar into his neck. Horrible, but he felt it was just a measure of the punishment he deserved right now.

Chapter Twenty-Five

Despite a very comfortable flight in a BA first-class cabin, it had taken Riva a while to calm down, her thoughts spiralling between her confrontation with her sister, confirming Kaaya's affair with Joe, and Ben's petulant behaviour the previous day. Once again, her mother had been upset at what was now a familiar sight: Riva minus Ben, standing on her doorstep. But she had nagged and worried all through dinner, reminding Riva over and again of her earlier advice not to accept the Cannes invitation.

'You are a wife first and a writer only after that, Riva,' she had said. 'Do not let your marriage suffer because of your writing, please! Such a precious thing, a good marriage, so easy to lose. Just look at me.'

Although Riva had initially argued, that final remark had caused her to eventually collapse into silence. It made her feel awful to even think it, but she was now, less than a year since her father's death, completely exhausted by her mother's grief.

It wasn't until halfway through the flight that Riva finally felt the first stirrings of excitement at actually being on her way to the glamorous South of France. She had held her feelings of anticipation at bay all these days for so many reasons, but now, finally, it was starting to take hold; a small warm glow in the pit of her stomach, which she explained to herself as being part exhilaration and part nervousness. As the plane started to descend, Riva looked out of the window and caught her first glimpse of the famed Côte d'Azur. She had seen the Mediterranean on previous trips to Cyprus and Sicily, but here its colour was more turquoise than anywhere else, calm and flat and dotted prettily with a scattering of yachts. The town of Nice itself, as the plane banked over it, looked surprisingly mountainous, pale purple peaks rising up lazily to meet a peaceful azure sky.

Riva stepped out of the airport terminal at Nice and blinked at the warm blueness of it all. A man with a placard bearing her name in bold letters was awaiting her in the small crowd that was gathered outside the airport and Riva followed him to a sleek black car parked nearby. She slid into the capacious back seat, feeling like a queen as the vehicle started to glide silently down the road. In the distance, Riva could see paparazzi with their cameras, no doubt awaiting the arrival of some big star.

As she sank back in her seat, Riva hoped the car would take a coastal road, seeing that both Nice and Cannes were on the sea. But the Med was only briefly visible before disappearing as the car whisked her towards a wide and busy autoroute.

Less than half an hour later, Riva was on the outskirts of Cannes and, in another ten, she had reached the sweeping palm-fringed boulevard recognisable from pictures as being the famous Croisette. There was a festive atmosphere in this part of town, most buildings and shops draped with enormous posters for all the latest films. People were milling about everywhere, holding cameras and maps and looking eagerly into all the cars with official badges, no doubt hoping to catch sight of the stars. Riva, given a choice of hotels, had plumped for the Carlton, a historic luxury five-star hotel overlooking the sea. The car pulled in at a colonnaded entrance and Riva was shown up a small flight of stairs into a spacious lobby. She walked up to the reception counter, delving into her handbag for her passport and a printout of the email with her booking reference for the hotel. She handed it over and received a warm smile from the well-groomed woman with a chignon standing behind the marble counter. So much for the rudeness of French hotel staff on her previous visits to Paris, Riva thought with a hint of amusement. If one had to travel here, it obviously had to be as a VIP, no less!

'Ah, Ms Walia, welcome to the Carlton,' the woman said in impeccable English with a charming French accent. 'We were expecting you. I hope you had a good journey?' She paused as Riva nodded before glancing at her computer screen. 'Now let's see . . . your room number is 511 on the fifth floor, overlooking the sea, of course.' The woman looked up and smiled at Riva's pleased expression. 'Would you like to go up to your room first and I can send your luggage and the paperwork up afterwards? The lifts are through that archway over there, on your left. Monsieur Gilles Jacob has left a message for you and also Monsieur Grasso from Camera D'Or, who will come to meet you at your convenience. You will find information about the screenings and your schedule in your room. Also many party invitations, which I hope you will enjoy . . .'

'Oh, thank you, that sounds wonderful,' Riva said, looking around to locate the archway for the lifts. Then, on an impulse, she turned back to the woman. 'Oh, could you tell me please if Mr Aman Khan is staying here? He's one of the other jury members and an old friend, you see . . .'

Riva waited while the woman studied her screen again. 'Ah yes, Mr Khan is also staying with us. I saw him maybe just ten minutes ago. But I think he has gone out, according to the information on my screen. So sorry, Ms Walia, but I can take a message?'

Riva felt a pang of disappointment to know she had missed Aman by minutes. But, despite herself, she was excited to know he was staying at the same hotel; they would surely meet before long. She turned to make her way to the lifts but, crossing the lobby, she nearly walked into someone approaching the desk. Riva looked up and stopped dead as she found herself facing the very man she had just been enquiring about: Aman Khan!

He looked calm and completely unsurprised to see her – no doubt he too would have seen her name on the list of jurors. Joy of joys, his expression told her that he remembered her very well!

'Riva Walia,' he said bowing with exaggerated courtesy, one hand crossed over his chest. Riva tried to read his expression but it was inscrutable.

'Aman!' she yelped. She curbed her silly desire to hurl herself into his arms, finding herself overwhelmed by uncharacteristic shyness instead. He looked a lot taller than when she had known him at university, and altogether bigger as he had filled out considerably since then. Even the view Riva had of him on the BAFTA stage back in winter had not done him justice. Now, up close, she could see what a magnetic presence he had become. 'Aman,' Riva repeated, swallowing hard in order to find her voice again. 'Believe it or not, I was just asking for you . . . back there at the desk, I mean . . . ' Riva stopped talking for fear of sounding gushy.

Aman, perhaps noticing her discomfiture, smiled with

one brow cocked quizzically. 'I was expecting to see you before long too. But what a surprise it was to see your name on the list of jurors, Riva.'

Riva noted that Aman had not specified what a *pleasure* it was to have seen her name on the list, and then chided herself for even noticing.

'Have you only just arrived?' Aman continued, looking at Riva's rather scuffed suitcase that had been placed on a small brass trolley nearby.

Riva nodded and took a rash decision to try to ease the formality of this meeting with Aman.

'Oh, come here,' she said, finally giving in to her every screaming instinct and reaching out to give Aman a warm embrace. 'Not starry enough to give an old friend a hug, I hope?'

Her mouth was perilously close to his ear as she felt his arms wind around her. Close enough to give it a little nibble, she thought mischievously, which of course she refrained from doing. Luckily Riva was wearing her brand new six-inch Gucci wedges and the extra height they provided allowed her face breathing room over Aman's shoulder; otherwise her face would have been squashed unceremoniously into Aman's chest. She was enveloped for a few seconds against his muscular torso, and her nostrils filled with some kind of musky aftershave. Breathless from that heady scent and needing to steady herself again, Riva pulled away. She saw that Aman was now smiling more freely, looking down at her through those famous long eyelashes with an amused expression on his face. She laughed self-consciously. 'And here I was wondering if you'd even remember me,' she said, a little out of breath.

'How could you think I wouldn't remember you?' Aman asked, smiling.

'Well, you're a top Bollywood star,' Riva said shyly.

'So? You're a world-famous author,' he countered.

'Hardly world-famous!' Riva laughed, pleased that he knew that much about her.

'I bet more people read your books than watch my movies!'

'You reckon? I don't think so somehow!' Riva responded.

Aman seemed less detached suddenly and his voice now took on a joshing air. 'Actually, if it's a numbers game, I think I may beat you – thanks to India's billion Bollywood fans!' he said, grinning.

Riva's initial attack of nerves was waning and she felt herself slipping back into her naturally easy manner. She ought to try to forget Aman was now one of the world's most famous film stars, lest she start behaving all fan-like. They had, after all, been classmates and friends once, and surely Aman wouldn't have forgotten that his first sexual encounter was with her? That was another memory Riva hastily shoved away deep at the back of her mind, lest she disable her vocal cords all over again. She ploughed on.

'Look, shall we find somewhere quiet for a drink? We have lots to catch up on. I'd love to know how you got to where you are now. The long journey from Leeds to the very top of Bollywood! You never wrote or made contact with anyone after you left uni, Aman.'

'Well, I never was the writing type, unlike you.'

'You didn't have to be. Just an occasional line and I'd have written pages to you, you know. I still write old-fashioned paper letters to people, would you believe it. Even my emails are far too long, people say!'

Aman laughed, now looking much more like his old boyish self as he relaxed. 'It is very good to see you again, Riva. You haven't changed one bit. Did you want that drink now or would you like to go up to your room and freshen up first?'

'Oh, God, why? Do I look like I need freshening up?' Riva asked, mildly flustered and smoothing her hair.

'You look great,' Aman said. His face was serious again, making the compliment sound as though it came from the very bottom of his heart. Riva scolded herself for feeling so flattered, reminding herself that he was, after all, an actor.

'Charmer!' she said lightly in response, noticing that Aman flashed a quick glance up and down her person. What did he see, she wondered, and how would she compare with the gorgeous actresses he was used to hanging out with, or even his very beautiful wife for that matter, whose fondness for fabulous designer wear was legendary?

If she were completely honest with herself, it was with that in mind that Riva had taken more trouble over her appearance today than usual. She was dressed in a pair of navy Chanel jeans and a lacy white top, her long hair blow-dried to tumble around her shoulders to her waist. Even her feet were shod in a pair of white Gucci sandals with cork heels much higher than she was accustomed to. She wasn't normally given to dressing so expensively, but she had surprised herself when she had gone out to shop for this trip last weekend, using her credit card with almost aggressive abandon in those smart Sloane Street boutiques that she had never stepped into before.

'Perhaps I *should* go and check my room out and freshen up a bit actually. You're staying at this hotel too, Aman?'

Aman nodded. 'There wasn't much choice – it was either this or the Majestic and this seemed to be nearer things.'

'What's your room number? Shall I call you when I'm done?'

'It's 517, just down the corridor from yours. I asked when I came in,' Aman explained. He flashed a sudden cheeky smile at Riva. 'Not quite like the men-only halls back in uni, huh?'

Riva felt another flutter, pleased that Aman had taken the trouble to enquire which room she was in. And was that an oblique allusion to the night they had spent together back in his uni digs? She chided herself for being so fanciful. Aman Khan had quite likely slept with far too many women since then to even remember which was which!

'Where will I find you when I come back downstairs?' she asked tentatively.

Aman replied, 'I'll be right there, on that sofa next to the window.' He pointed at a sunny corner masked by a huge floral arrangement.

Riva turned to pick up her room card and smiled again at the woman behind the counter before making her way to the lift. Conscious that Aman might be watching her, Riva hoped she wouldn't trip or do something silly. She tried to calm herself as she got into the lift. It was strange, this breathless feeling she had not experienced for years. She looked at her face in the mirrors lining the lift and willed herself to be more sober. Sure, Aman was an extremely good-looking man and he seemed to have been flirting with her. And – if she were totally honest – she'd been flirting with him too. Riva stopped the puerile train of thought she was embarking on like some star-struck teenager. She had no doubt been quite starved of fun recently, but that was no reason to lose her head. No reason at all.

*   *   *

Aman walked back to the sofa and sat down, his knees suddenly weak. So, it had happened again, the minute he had laid eyes on Riva. She was thinner than when he had last seen her perhaps, her hair longer. She also looked more sleekly groomed. But otherwise Riva wasn't that different to the girl he had fallen for so badly all those years ago back in Leeds. And, while Aman had fully intended to be a little cool and distant, he had found his carefully created air of reserve melt within minutes of facing the full blast of Riva's customary warmth.

Now, as Aman waited for Riva to return from her room, he wondered what the hell he was going to do about his confused feelings. He certainly wasn't looking for a one-night stand or a brief dalliance – those were never too difficult to achieve, his fame providing him with as many women as he should desire, and whenever he should want them. Having run through the whole gamut of gold-digging women since he had become a star, and been stuck for the last five years with a cold and unfeeling wife, Aman was looking for something altogether deeper and more real. If for no other reason than to re-engage with his own nicer side, which on certain days he feared had gone forever. If there was any chance of his being able to find that kind of love again, it could only be with a woman like Riva.

Aman threw his head back on the sofa, trying to quell his frustration. Riva was married, he reminded himself, and to her teenage sweetheart. But he had ten days ahead in colourful, romantic Cannes with her; and he imagined the pair of them watching movies together in darkened halls and sitting in on the jury's deliberations. Then there would be the red-carpet premieres, banquets in fabulous restaurants, parties on board private yachts, the famed jury session at the Château Marmont, dinner with the Mayor of Cannes . . . Perhaps he and Riva would have a chance to play at being the couple he had once dreamt of, an imaginary relationship far removed from the sorry cold life he had with Salma. Could it be that he was being offered a chance to reclaim what he had lost fifteen years ago? Aman shook his head to clear it of such futile thoughts. A serious relationship was out of the question, not least because of the risk of losing Ashfaq, for that was surely how Salma would punish him when she found out . . .

Riva emerged from the lifts, as she had promised, ten minutes later. She had not changed her clothes but had tied her hair back with a large white scarf so that it now bounced in a ponytail down her back.

'Ready,' she said, sticking an oversized pair of sunglasses on her nose. Aman hoped he was not making his admiration obvious as he stood up for her.

'Did you *see* the stack of invitation cards in our rooms?' Riva asked as they stepped out of the Carlton onto the sun-washed street together.

'Ah yes, the famous one is Donatella Versace's do,' Aman said. 'She apparently takes over three terraced suites at a hotel and stuffs it with *haute couture* and things – hoping to tempt rich moneybags like you to shop a bit during the festival.'

'Moneybags, ha, chance would be a fine thing, Mr Khan!' Riva shot back. 'Haven't you heard of the poet-in-a-garret?'

'Come on, bestselling authors must live the high life sometimes.'

'Well, I certainly have no objection to a bit of high

life, I must admit,' Riva replied cheerily. 'So where's this party then?'

'The Martinez, which is not too far from here. Shall we go together? I was told they serve endless quantities of Louis Roederer at those sumptuous Versace shindigs. You could always pretend we're buying stuff while downing as much champagne as possible before being chucked out.'

'Like they can't spot people who turn up with exactly that in mind!' Riva laughed.

'No, I know the routine perfectly,' Aman reassured. 'All you have to do is look snooty and disinterested and pick up a piece occasionally before throwing it down in disgust. That'll have them running after you.'

Riva was tempted to ask if Aman had learnt that kind of behaviour from his wife but she did not think their affectionate banter had given her that much freedom yet.

'Do you think we should be trying to meet the other jurors too?' Riva asked as they stopped for traffic. She laughed as, quite suddenly and magically, a whole fleet of horse-drawn carriages appeared from among the cars. The carriages were fluttering with colourful ribbons as the horses cantered past, trailing a banner promoting a new perfume.

'Naaah,' Aman responded, enjoying the feel of Riva's hand as she slipped it into the crook of his arm to cross the road. 'The other jurors will be scattered all across Cannes anyway, seeing that people choose their own hotels.' He looked at Riva and grinned. 'We could put heads together before meeting the other jurors, couldn't we? And give the prizes to all our favourites. But we'll meet the rest before long, no doubt. Probably at the President's dinner.'

'I found it strange, didn't you,' Riva said, 'that the jury won't necessarily be watching all the films together. I'd always imagined they'd hold special screenings for the jury, but apparently we just slip into screenings when we can, and keep our own notes for the discussion later.'

'You and I could go for our screenings together, though,' Aman replied. 'It all seems incredibly relaxed and easy-going.'

'Well, the gala opening is Pixar's *Up*, did you see? I saw the posters everywhere as I was driven in. That should be fun! In 3-D too.'

'Which means we'll all look silly together, wearing those glasses!'

'I haven't seen a kids' film in years, you know,' Riva said, which gave Aman the opening he had wanted.

'Have you got children of your own yet?' he asked.

Riva shook her head. 'No, there never seemed to be the right time,' she said, and Aman wondered if he imagined a small shadow pass over her face. 'You have one though, haven't you?' she asked, looking up at him.

'Ashfaq,' Aman said. 'He's nearly two, and the sweetest thing that's ever happened to me.'

'Are you a proper, involved sort of dad then?' Riva asked.

'Well, I don't see enough of him. But, when I'm in Bombay or whenever he and Salma travel with me – he's stuck to me like glue. More fan-like than my most devoted fans!'

'Do they travel with you much, Salma and Ashfaq? I half wondered if they might be here too.'

Aman shook his head. 'Salma prefers Bombay to anywhere else. Her parents and friends are all there. Can't be much fun travelling with me, I guess. My schedules can be quite gruelling sometimes.'

'And you travel a lot?'

'More and more these days, it feels like. Partially because tax breaks in some countries have made it more attractive for Bollywood films to be shot abroad than in India.'

'You sound like you don't enjoy the travel much.'

'I used to love it, actually, but now I find I miss Ashfaq terribly. And my parents. They're getting on a bit and I worry about them when I'm far away. I have no siblings, if you remember, so they depend on me a lot.'

Riva nodded. 'God, I understand that. My own dad died last year.'

'Oh, I'm sorry to hear that, Riva. That must have been devastating.'

'And my mum's not the strongest person,' Riva continued. 'It's as if I've had to become the man in her life, which she sometimes resents, I think. So it's all very complicated.'

'And Ben?' Aman asked. When Riva looked at him questioningly, he explained, 'Your sister told me you married him. She did tell you I met her recently?'

Riva nodded but refrained from replying.

'Well, how is Ben? What does he do?' Aman persisted. He couldn't help noticing that Riva's expression had darkened slightly but he could not tell if it was at the mention of Ben or her sister.

They had arrived at a promenade marked 'Palmafasetany' and Riva unlinked her arm from Aman's as they came to a halt. A group of breakdancers were practising a clever routine on a makeshift stage and Riva watched them for a few seconds before replying, 'Ben went on to become a banker after uni. He's fine . . .'

Aman shot a look at Riva's profile. The smile had definitely gone. 'You don't sound very sure,' he said, trying to keep his tone light.

But Riva was silent and shook her head slightly, while a warm breeze ruffled the tops of the palm trees around them. Then she took off her shades and looked at Aman, speaking in her more familiar direct manner. 'Ben lost his job at the bank a while ago, Aman, and that's affected him rather badly.'

Aman tried not to show his surprise – he'd always been so quick to assume that Riva and Ben would be living some kind of charmed life in England.

'I heard that the recession's been terrible for banks in the US and UK,' he said carefully. 'But Ben was always such a smart guy. I would never have thought someone like him would be affected.'

'Ben's smart all right but perhaps he didn't play his cards right on this occasion. He took up the offer of voluntary redundancy because he wanted to be a writer himself, you see. But his alternative career's not going anywhere either.' Riva suddenly laughed. 'Oh God, Aman, look at me dumping on you within ten minutes of meeting up again!'

'Hey, don't worry about that!' Aman responded gently. 'That's the best thing about meeting an old friend – it's easy to pick up where you last left off.'

'Ah, but if we were picking up where we last left off, I'd be getting drunk and passing out in your room, would I not?' Riva shot back before putting her shades back on again. She started to read the inscription on a statue of Georges Pompidou, which Aman thought was just as well, so she did not see his expression. If she had, she would have seen how pleased he was that she recalled that night back in Leeds – it remained such a strong memory for him. Aman looked unseeingly at the inscription too, trying to figure out from Riva's jocular tone if she remembered her time with him with as much sentimentality as he did. Or perhaps it was just one of those things she joked about with her girlfriends – telling them of her clumsy tryst with a fellow who went on to become a film star . . .

Chapter Twenty-Six

Riva looked at her reflection in the mirror of her hotel room, trying to recall when she had last lavished so much attention on her appearance. She often regarded sitting around in pyjamas all day as one of the best things about being a full-time writer. But now, so unexpectedly cata-pulted before the full glare of the world's media, Riva found she was enjoying the business of dressing up rather more than she had ever thought she would. She had been informed by the festival organisers that the jury members would be required to dress glamorously for the opening and closing ceremonies, and also whenever attending any of the premieres, even though most of the partying was by choice. Having at first been unsure about attending too many bashes on her own, Riva now suddenly felt more confident, knowing that she had a willing (and very handsome) escort in Aman.

Today's ensemble for the gala opening had been care-fully chosen back in England. Being the only Indian woman on the jury, Riva was keen to reflect her own heritage but without detracting from the more classic look that was her usual style. She slipped on the slinky vintage dress she had found in a small shop in Chelsea, pleased now that she had bought it despite its staggering price tag. In deep burnt orange silk, the top of the dress cupped her breasts quite demurely at the front, revealing just a hint of cleavage, while its generously scooped-out back revealed her smooth golden shoulders and back all the way down to her curve of her waist. It had all the flowing sexiness of a sari without actually being one. Back in London, Riva had rooted through her collection of Indian jewellery and found a necklace that had belonged to her grandmother to make a perfect match for the dress. She now took it out of its velvet pouch and looped the thick chain of dull gold around her neck, imaginatively draping the old, pitted coral pendant down her back. Riva turned to look at the view of her rear, pleased with what she saw. The hairstyle she had given herself, pinning her tresses up to allow only a few longer curls to fall onto her neck, showed both the coral pendant and her back off to best advantage. After running a comb gently over the hair framing her face, she picked up the bedside phone to call Aman's room.

'Ready,' she said when she heard his deep voice.

'Great. Be with you in five,' he replied.

Riva stood looking out of the window into the distance, where blue sky met sea. Puffs of light cloud were drifting across the horizon while a few yachts bobbed lazily below. It was a lovely calm scene and Riva thought again of Ben. It wasn't the first time she had thought of him on this first day in Cannes, worried that he was still sulking. He had not called, after all. But then, nor for that matter had she. Despite his behaviour, she felt deeply sorry for the state Ben had got himself into. Of course it was not easy for a man to cope with a successful wife when his own life was in the doldrums. But it was hardly her fault – and Riva was certainly not inclined to call Ben if he was going to be snappish with her when she was having a well-deserved break from everything that had recently happened in London, not least her father's death.

She sighed and picked up her purse, a lovely antique clutch covered in semi-precious stones that Kaaya had given her for her last birthday. She had quite deliberately not thought of her sister since leaving London, those thoughts being still far too painful to deal with right now. But the memory of their argument on the motorway had come rushing back to Riva when she had opened her suitcase earlier in the evening and spotted the purse amid her clothes. It caused her to remember Kaaya with a twist of physical pain in her chest. Her sister had given her many generous gifts over the years; she was really far more loving than she often let on. Now, opening the purse, Riva slipped a lipstick and a couple of tissues into it. Perhaps she had been too quick to judge Kaaya – not even giving her the chance to explain what had happened to cause an affair with Joe.

Returning to the here and now, Riva tried to weigh up her own rather confused feelings about Aman's reassuring presence here in Cannes. He was turning out to be exactly the tonic she needed to help her forget Ben's recent black moods back in London. Riva also found it immensely touching that her old classmate was being so warm and unstarry with her. After all, Aman could have decided to hobnob with the other film stars who had arrived in Cannes from both Hollywood and Mumbai, and ignored her completely. But he had shown little interest in seeking out their company, seeming to prefer walking around and exploring the town with her earlier today. When they had been out on the promenade, Aman had even received a phone call from a Bollywood director who tried pressing

231

him into attending a party on board a luxury yacht. But Aman had cut him off, abruptly hanging up on him before saying to Riva with apparent sincerity, 'I'd really *much* rather hang out with you.'

Riva's thoughts were interrupted by the buzz of the doorbell. She opened the door to Aman, unprepared for the look that crossed his face at sight of her – admiration and something else she couldn't quite place – before he clutched his chest and pretended to stagger back into the corridor.

'My God, Riva Walia, you look stunning. They'll all be asking who the new film star is!'

'Flatterer,' she laughed. 'You don't look too bad yourself, you know, Mr Khan. What is that suit? It looks like it's been poured onto you!'

'Ever the poet, Riva Walia,' Aman replied. 'And I'm enjoying seeing you slip into Cannes-speak already: "Who are you wearing, darling?" "Oh it's nothing, just Valentino."' Aman shrugged with a blasé expression and fluttered his hands in a camp way, making Riva giggle again.

She used her purse to smack him gently on his upper arm as they left her room. 'I'm trying to behave starry. This may be my only chance!'

'Shall we go?' Aman asked, looking ready to sprint down the corridor. 'Ready for the paps? Remember not to blink when all the flashing starts, or your pictures will look terrible. The first few pictures of mine in film magazines all had me looking like a drug addict.'

'I'm not worried about the paps. They won't be after me. It's you they'll all want,' Riva said as she closed her door behind her and they started to walk down the corridor to the lift.

'Don't be too sure. Not when you turn up looking all scrumptious like that! They'll be asking Angelina Jolie to get out of the way so they can snap away at you.'

'Keep going, Aman! Silly as you're being, my ego is liking you very much.'

In the lift, Riva looked at the multiple reflections of her and Aman standing together: a handsome man in a Valentino suit with a sophisticated woman wearing a vintage gown the colour of an Indian sunset. They certainly made a striking picture, a far cry from the jeans-clad students they had been when they last went anywhere together. Riva knew she ought to be missing Ben's presence by her side but her sudden freedom from his recent moodiness was making her feel strangely exhilarated. As she and Aman stepped out into the lobby, people turned to stare, and Aman placed a reassuring hand on Riva's waist, steering her to the door. She felt his hand, warm and gentle in the small of her back, remembering in a flash the first time they had made love as teenagers. Then she instructed herself sternly to put the memory away.

A long black and gold car discreetly drew up outside the front of the hotel as they walked down the stairs. Someone held the door open for Riva as a couple of photographers standing outside clicked them in a slightly desultory fashion.

'The really keen ones will be at the Palais des Festivals, crowding the red carpet,' Aman warned as they got into the back seat.

The drive was short but took a while, the car travelling slowly through the celebrating crowds choking up the roads. Tourists armed with cameras peered into passing cars, trying to spot the stars, but Riva felt safe behind the smoked-glass windows of her vehicle. As they approached the big modern structure that was the Palais des Festivals, Riva felt a flutter of apprehension, seeing crowds spilling out onto the street. The car carrying Riva and Aman joined a queue of other official vehicles and slowed to a crawl. She leant forward to look as far ahead as she could out of the windscreen and saw banks of paparazzi standing on specially constructed steps, their cameras flashing so furiously the effect was as fierce as lightning. Aman patted her hand that lay on the seat between them, and she turned to him, suddenly lost for words.

'Nervous?' he asked and she nodded. He squeezed her hand briefly. 'Don't be,' he said softly. 'You look lovely, they'll all be bowled over. And, even if anyone does ask you anything, you'll probably have much more intelligent things to say than anyone else here.'

Their car was now second in the queue, the one in front having stopped to unload its extremely glamorous-looking occupants. Riva saw a pair of women emerge in beautiful couture gowns and preen like a pair of exotic birds showing off their plumage. The cameras clicked madly, photographers shouting for more poses. Now that it was nearly their turn, Riva was too jittery to even speak. Their car had stopped and someone was holding her door open. Riva stepped out, hoping she wouldn't totter on her gold stilettos with the world's cameras flashing at her. She stood waiting for Aman to walk around the car towards her, too terrified to walk up the carpet on her own and quite forgetting that she might compromise his image of being a good family man. Then, catching herself just in time, she held back, realising that it was Aman the photographers would want to catch. He seemed oblivious to all such possibilities, however, and grabbed her elbow, walking her right up to the photographers' stand.

'It's not me they want to photograph, Aman!' she hissed, trying to extricate herself. But Aman's grip was firm. She tried again, still speaking frantically through clenched teeth. 'Please, Aman, before they ask me to step aside!'

But Aman looked completely relaxed, waving at the cameramen and at one point even holding both arms out in Riva's direction as though presenting a new star. The photographers duly obliged and one even called out to Aman in a cockney accent, 'Ooo's the laavely girl then, Mr Kaan?'

'They know you!' Riva whispered.

'Only that guy. He's an old mate of mine. I think he thinks I'm related to James Caan from the way he pronounces my name but he turns up whenever I'm doing anything in London. And his pictures always end up in the *Asian Age* newspaper so make sure your mum gets a copy tomorrow.'

Riva watched Aman perform for the cameras and sign a few autographs before folding palms in the traditional Namaste gesture for the benefit of the small clutch of Indian TV reporters standing to one side. As he returned to her and they walked up the red carpet together, she hoped Aman's wife wasn't watching him on her TV screen back in Mumbai, wondering about the woman in the orange dress who was so closely shadowing her husband. Going by Salma Khan's reputation, Riva knew she would surely be dead meat if she suspected her of dallying with her husband! For that matter, Riva also hoped Ben wasn't watching his TV back in London – he would not be amused at all to see her and Aman looking so matey on day one of the festival!

There was, however, no chance for further apprehension as Riva and Aman were escorted to a small, more private arena to meet some of their fellow jurors. After a quick round of greetings, it was soon time for the main ceremony inside the Palais and silence fell as they readied themselves for the show. One by one, the MC announced the names of the jurors as they walked through the doors leading to the massive Palais auditorium. Some names were met with more applause than others and Riva smiled at Aman when his name was greeted by what sounded like a real roar of appreciation. When her name was announced, Riva walked through the door that had been pointed out to her, finding herself facing a massive audience in what was probably the biggest theatre she had ever seen. She joined the other jurors who were standing applauding her from one side of the stage. Riva knew that the Cannes panel had a long history of recognising the place of auteurs and storytellers in the business of judging films but it was clearly the film stars the crowd had turned up to see. Nevertheless, she felt a surge of pride to have got to such a position of eminence herself and – acknowledging the sight of Aman clapping generously for her – Riva felt suddenly very sad that her husband was not there to enjoy her moment in the sun.

Chapter Twenty-Seven

Kaaya sipped her mojito, looking blankly at the small LCD television screen Rohan had recently installed in the kitchen which was playing an adaptation of *Tess of the D'Urbervilles*. But, as had been happening increasingly these past few days, her mind started to wander half an hour into the film and she was now miles away, thinking of everything but Thomas Hardy's story. There were, in fact, so many things playing on Kaaya's mind, she didn't even know where to start. It was unlike her to spend too long worrying about anything, but the truth was that Kaaya had never before felt as depressed as she had after her recent argument with Riva. Even her father's death, devastating as it had been, had not made her feel so wretched – although Kaaya considered that perhaps the shock of her father's death was in some undefinable way bound up with her affair with Joe. Kaaya, not given to analysing things too much, could not explain it; all she knew was that Joe had made her feel better at a terrible time. She jumped as her phone started to buzz on the glass kitchen counter near her elbow. She picked it up, hoping it wouldn't be Joe. Instead Rohan's name flashed up on her screen. She tapped the green key on her phone.

'Hello, darling,' her husband's voice said. 'What's up?'

'Nothing, really,' Kaaya replied in a dull voice. 'Just got in from work and mixed myself a drink.'

'Anything nice?'

'Just a mojito.'

'Nice. Hey, do you fancy going out for some sushi tonight?'

'Sounds good. Where?'

'Shall I try to get a table at Sake No Hana?'

Kaaya perked up slightly. She did so love their Wagyu beef. 'Oh yes please!' she replied, starting to feel a bit more cheerful.

'Okay, I'll get a booking.'

After Rohan had hung up, Kaaya felt another rare stirring of guilt. He was such a considerate guy – most women would kill for a husband like him. What had happened with Joe was just such an unthinking, banal thing, it was difficult to rationalise, even to herself. So how could she now make Riva understand? Riva, with her high morals and principles. Strong, practical Riva who could cope with everything, even their beloved father's untimely death. No, Riva would never be able to comprehend all those things that had drawn Kaaya towards someone as kind and gentle as Joe when Papa had gone and Rohan had been far away. Kaaya looked bleakly around her gleaming brushed steel and glass kitchen, wondering if her sister would ever forgive her for what she had done.

On an impulse, she picked up her phone again. This time she dialled Riva's landline.

'Ben?' she asked as her call was answered.

'Yes?'

'Hey, it's Kaaya here.'

After a moment's surprised silence, Ben said, without even a touch of warmth, 'Hello, is all well?'

'Yeah, yeah, fine. We were just wondering how you were?'

'We?'

'Well, us – Rohan and me. And Mum, of course. Seeing that Riva isn't here . . .'

'I'm fine, thanks,' Ben replied. His voice still sounded guarded. Kaaya knew he was wondering why she was calling him. He wouldn't have been surprised if either Rohan or her mum called but he was probably remembering, not inaccurately, that she never ever called him. All communication between them usually always took place via someone else, usually Riva.

'Has she called?' Kaaya enquired.

'Who?'

'Riva, of course.'

'Nope.'

'No? That's strange.'

'Why should it be?'

'Well . . . she would call, wouldn't she? Either there or here. But she hasn't called here either. Maybe she's called Mum . . .' Kaaya trailed off, just slightly alarmed.

'Yes, maybe.'

After an awkward pause, Kaaya spoke again. 'Do you need anything?'

'Need?'

'As in need us to do anything for you? While Riva's away, I mean . . .'

'No. Thanks.'

Ben sounded as though his teeth were gritted and so Kaaya hesitated for a moment before wading in further. 'Ben, listen. Don't mind my saying it but we've got to get over this thing . . .'

'What thing?'

'This thing . . . this uneasiness between you and me. For Riva's sake.'

'I don't need to do anything for Riva's sake,' Ben replied coldly.

'What?'

'You heard.'

Kaaya was confused. 'Are you drunk or something, Ben?' she asked tentatively.

But, instead of replying, Ben hung up.

Ben put the phone down on Kaaya, shaking with rage.

'Are you drunk?' He said Kaaya's words out loud and then repeated them stridently, shouting the words into the silence of the house. '*Are you drunk?* What the *fuck* do you mean by that, *bitch?*' Ben stormed into the living room, still shouting aloud, even though there was no one to hear his rant. 'Anyone who fails to fawn on you must be either mad or drunk. That's what it must be, Kaaya. I don't like you, so I must be *drunk*. There can't possibly be any other explanation.'

Ben threw himself onto the sofa, trying to calm himself and feeling an unusual prickle of angry tears in his eyes. He didn't need anyone's pity, least of all Kaaya's. If Riva couldn't be bothered to call, the last people he wanted to be bothered by were her fucking family. But he knew exactly why Riva hadn't called. He had seen her on Sky News earlier this evening, wearing an orange gown with a plunging neckline and trailing after bloody Aman Khan. Quite the fool she had looked too, all wide-eyed and rabbit-in-headlights, facing the cameras that were going wild, not for her she seemed to have forgotten, but for Aman bloody Khan. Then he had watched Aman take Riva's arm and lead her up the red carpet, the pair of them looking like besotted lovers!

Ben had lunged at the TV at that point, clicking it off before it broke his heart any more. If it was a divorce Riva wanted, he would have it ready and waiting for her when she got back from France. He certainly wasn't going to hang around being a millstone around her pretty neck.

With this thought, Ben leapt off the sofa and took the stairs to the bedroom, pulling a suitcase from the top of the wardrobe. Opening it, he started to hurl clothes into it, enough to last him at least a month. He would be gone by the time Riva came back. Not that he knew just yet where to go but his father's house in Denby would be a start. All he knew for certain was that he was not going to stand by and let Riva destroy him any more than she already had.

Ben lugged his suitcase down the stairs, not caring that it was scraping on the wall and leaving large black streaks on its clean white surface. He was still fuming over the sight of Riva canoodling publicly with Aman Khan. It was truly a kick in the teeth, aimed especially at him. Especially because he knew how they had felt about each other back in college. Ben had seen for himself the way Riva's eyes had softened for Aman, and that special laugh when he spoke, even though the guy usually had very little by way of knowledge or wit to offer. The fact that Aman thought the sun shone out of every pore of Riva's body was common knowledge but it wasn't that that had bothered Ben – after all, there were others who had fancied her too. It was Riva. Ben knew that something obscure about Aman Khan had captured Riva's heart all those years ago, never allowing her to forget him. Well, if they wanted to get back together again, they were bloody welcome to each other.

Chapter Twenty-Eight

Riva removed her make-up before stepping into the shower, her nerves still tingling from the excitement of the evening. The earlier attack of nerves before the opening gala had proven completely unnecessary as the media had seemed to love her at the press conference that had followed, three journalists even asking for one-on-one interviews.

After the film, the jury had been taken to the Majestic for the President's grand banquet. Riva had seen nothing like it before, losing count after the fourth or fifth course had been served and giving herself up to enjoying the massive magnums of Mumms and fine French wines that flowed with every course. She now had only a vague memory of the *pièce-de-résistance* being served: a full roast suckling pig, complete with an apple in its mouth, unable as she was by that stage to eat even a morsel. Luckily, Aman (who had only sipped in token fashion at a glass of champagne) had kept his head throughout the night and steered her towards the right car and hotel when it had ended. He had shown her all the way to her door and kissed her gently before she had let herself in.

She now touched the side of her mouth, feeling the part that his lips had brushed. She could still smell his musky aftershave. It had been a far from lascivious kiss, but it was nevertheless a rather heady moment, partly due to all the wine she had consumed, Riva supposed. After Aman had left to go to his own room, she leant her back against the door for a few moments. Then she had finally regained her senses, slipped her gown and shoes off and stumbled to the bathroom.

Now, post-shower, Riva stood before the fogged-up bathroom mirror, water droplets shining on her face and shoulders, feeling a little more sober. Sober enough to realise that she was a married woman and could not any longer keep from calling her husband waiting back at home. Ben was clearly waiting for her to make the first move, as was often the case, and, typically, Riva felt she should oblige. She was the one out having a grand time, after all, and she couldn't help feeling a rush of sympathy for poor Ben. She picked up her watch to glance at the time. It was very late but she was sure Ben would rather hear from her late at night than not at all.

Riva wrapped herself in a generously sized bathtowel and made her way across the dimly lit room to the telephone. She listened for a few seconds as the phone rang but, before the answering machine could kick in, she disconnected and dialled again. Perhaps Ben needed more time to answer. Riva imagined him being fast asleep on the sofa before a flickering TV. But the phone kept ringing the second time round too and, rather than leaving a message, Riva hung up. She tried Ben's mobile number. Once again, she listened to the ringing tone, wondering if she ought to give up and try again at a more reasonable hour. Then, just as she was about to hang up, she heard the ringing abruptly stop and the line come alive.

'Hello? Hello, Ben?'

The response was muffled.

'I can't hear you, Ben. Where are you? Can I call on the landline?'

Now Ben's voice came through more clearly. 'No, you can't.'

'Why not? This is so muffled, I can barely hear you.'

'Because I'm not at home.'

'Oh, where are you?'

'What should that matter to you?' he snapped.

Taken aback by her husband's cold response, Riva wondered if she had misheard. He couldn't still be angry with her, surely – what the hell had she done that was so wrong anyway? She tried being conciliatory. 'Well, because it's late, that's why, Ben. Aren't I allowed to ask?'

There was a moment's pause before Ben spoke, slowly and deliberately, the anger in his voice apparent even across the miles. 'No. No, Riva, you can't ask. Not when you're gadding about with all sorts of people.'

Riva's reply was indignant. 'All sorts of people? It's the Cannes jury, for heaven's sake, Ben!' she retorted.

'Yes, how impressive. Well, why don't you fuck off with the Cannes jury then and stop bothering me, huh?'

The line went dead. Riva sat for a moment, looking at the handset in disbelief. Then, as the tears started to roll, she slowly replaced the phone on its cradle. The shock of Ben's reaction combined with the aftereffects of all the alcohol she had imbibed made her feel suddenly weak and miserable. Riva slipped off the damp towel and climbed into bed. This wasn't how such a glorious day was meant to end, she thought, sinking her face into her pillow and starting to weep in earnest. She froze when, a few minutes later, the phone at her bedside started to ring. Leaping up, she lunged at it. Ben must have returned to his senses.

245

'Ben?' she said into the mouthpiece, relief flooding her.

There was a second's pause before she heard Aman's voice. 'No, it's not Ben, sorry. It's me, Aman.'

She tried not to sound disappointed. 'Aman, hi. My apologies – it's just that I was sort of expecting Ben to call.'

'Oh, sorry. I'll hang up then.'

'No, no, it's okay. It's late. I don't think he'll call, actually.'

'You sure? I was only phoning to be sure you'd got into bed and hadn't passed out on your way to it.'

Riva forced a laugh. 'Yes, safely tucked in! Even managed a shower, believe it or not.'

'Are you all right, Riva?'

'Yes, why?'

'Your voice sounds strange. Like you have a cold coming on.'

'No, no, I'm fine.'

'Careful you don't overdo it in the first few days and fall ill. Perhaps a good night's sleep will help; I won't keep you up. Good night, Riva, sleep well.'

'Good night, Aman,' Riva said before hanging up. She lay back and pulled the duvet up around her bare shoulders. She had not drawn the curtains and, from where she was lying, she could see the dark peaceful Mediterranean stretching out into eternity. Somewhere beyond that sea was Ben, her husband and the love of her life, lonely and depressed and terribly angry with her. Too exhausted to think any more, Riva soon fell into a deep and dreamless slumber.

Two rooms down the corridor, Aman lay sleepless on his own bed, longing to be with Riva. He could tell she had been crying and he had not missed the desperation in her voice when she picked up the phone with her husband's name on her lips. Aman was no fool and it didn't take much to ascertain that all was not well with Riva's marriage. And yet it was Ben her heart was still crying out for.

His sleep that night was disturbed and he woke up several times, at one point pulling open the long windows that led to the balcony to get some fresh air. He stood there listening to the suck and swell of the sea, pondering why he was not more contented with his very enviable lot in life. Was Riva really the solution to his unhappiness? At the moment, it looked like falling in love with her would only bring more despair and grief, given how deeply she still cared for Ben. Warm sea breezes caressed Aman's face and hair but offered little comfort.

In the morning, he woke early and went to the gym for a brisk workout. He spent his usual forty minutes warming up on the treadmill before doing his routine on the weights. On the way back to his room, Aman passed Riva's room but the door was firmly shut. Briefly wondering if he should knock, he decided to get showered first before giving her a call, having agreed yesterday to meet her for an eleven o'clock screening. But when he walked into his room, he found the red light on his phone flashing: it was Riva telling him at half past nine that she was going downstairs for breakfast followed by a stroll on the beach.

Breakfast arrived in Aman's room just as he emerged from the shower and then, typically, his mobile started to peal – most people who knew his routine were aware that he never answered calls until he had finished with his exercise routine and had had something to eat. He tipped the waiter before answering. It was Ritesh Shah again, the director who had tried unsuccessfully to persuade him to attend a party on board the yacht of an Indian construction magnate yesterday. He talked to the director while spearing a cube of watermelon with one hand.

'*Haanji*, Shahsahib. Good morning, good morning,' he said, putting a forkful of toast dipped in egg yolk in his mouth. He chewed hurriedly, grimacing slightly as Ritesh Shah embarked on another long moan about the dates that Aman had reneged on due to this invitation to attend the festival. Finally Aman managed to shake him off, but not before the man had extracted a further promise from him to attend a party on board the *Mastaani*, his friend's yacht, currently moored in Cannes harbour. Then, with one eye on the time, Aman hurriedly started to get ready, brushing his teeth before donning a pair of tan slacks and a crisp white shirt.

Emerging from the lift, Aman scanned the lobby for Riva but there was no sign of her. He called for a car to make the journey to the Théâtre Lumière by himself. Perhaps it was just as well. Yesterday's heady initial meeting with Riva, followed by their spending virtually the whole day in each other's company, had perhaps been too intense, leading to some crazy notions that now, in the cold light of day, felt near nonsensical. Her midnight tears for her husband had brought him back to his senses, luckily; Aman did not fancy another sleepless night. He decided to keep a more formal distance from Riva for the rest of the day and for the rest of the festival too. In the car, Aman spoke on his phone to his parents and then, briefly, to Salma and Ashfaq, their voices reminding him that he had another, very different life awaiting him once he had left Cannes and returned home to Bombay.

*   *   *

Riva watched Aman striding into the lobby of the Lumière and felt a rush of relief. After a sleepless night worrying about Ben's hateful words, she had eagerly looked forward to seeing Aman's friendly face. But he hadn't either called or shown up by the time she had returned from her walk on the beach and Riva had finally left for the Lumière, reluctant to call Aman's room in case he was still asleep. But now here he was, keeping his word about joining her for the eleven am screening and walking across the crowded vaulted lobby in her direction.

'Morning!' she called out as he neared.

'Hello,' he responded. His voice was friendly enough but Riva couldn't help noticing that there were no kisses for her this morning.

'I've already signed in at the jury office,' she said, pointing her sheaf of papers in the direction of the office behind her.

'Okay, won't be long,' Aman replied, turning and disappearing through the doors. A few minutes later he emerged again and they were escorted into the massive theatre that was already full of expectant viewers. The jury booth was set apart slightly and Riva was pleased to see that they were the only occupants. She leant over to Aman once they had settled into their seats.

'I'm so looking forward to this, being a complete sucker for British period drama,' she said.

Aman pulled a face. 'Not my favourite genre,' he replied shortly.

They fell silent as the film started, Riva keeping assiduous notes on her netbook as the film progressed. Aman, she noticed, was also jotting down notes, using a pen and writing pad. When the film drew to a close and the audience behind her stood up to clap through the closing credits, Riva saved her document and took her fingers off the keyboard with a feeling of satisfaction.

She turned to Aman. 'I enjoyed that! Did you?'

Aman nodded. 'It was all right. Not really my kind of film though.'

'Ready for the next one?' she asked.

'Now?'

Riva laughed. 'Well, I guess there are screenings all the time but we can do our next one after a spot of lunch. In the afternoon?'

'No, you carry on with your viewings, Riva. I have a couple of meetings anyway. I'll see you around later maybe.' And, with that rather abrupt farewell, Aman turned to go.

Riva watched his tall figure leave the cinema through a small side door, feeling suddenly a little rebuffed and confused. Was Aman cross with her for some reason? If so, it would seem she was making a habit of upsetting people, and without trying very hard too. She racked her brains but could not for the life of her think of anything she might have done to annoy Aman in any way. All she could see was that he was fine yesterday and suddenly not fine today. Not that different from stupid old Ben, then. And it was the female sex that was accused of indulging in moods!

'Men, damn them all!' she muttered, getting up and making her own way out of the cinema. She cut through the crowd and made her way to the jury office. A working lunch had been laid out and Riva helped herself to a plate of fruit and a couple of very dainty sandwiches, finding a corner where she could plug her netbook in so it would recharge as she ate. After she had finished lunch, she strolled outside the Lumière for some sunshine and fresh air. Seagulls were soaring and screeching noisily. Standing at the top of the steps, Riva could see boats lined up in the marina. It was a pretty sight, far removed from London's damp grey. On an impulse, she decided to call both her mother and Susan and pulled out her phone from her shoulder bag.

Her mother was pleased to hear from her but, predictably, rapidly got onto the subject of Ben.

'He has not called me at all. I think he is really upset that you have gone without him, *beti*,' she said, as though Riva did not already know. Making an excuse about Ben being off on a walking holiday, Riva changed the subject. She wasn't willing to receive any news of Kaaya just yet either and so she quizzed her mother about her diabetes medication instead. Finally, making an excuse about extortionate global roaming charges, Riva hung up on her mother and called Susan, hoping she was not interrupting a class. At least with Susan, conversation would not be like a chess game!

'Goodness me, it's our celeb from Cannes!' Susan's cheery voice came floating down the line.

Relieved to hear her friend sounding upbeat, Riva laughed. 'Just wanted to know if all's well back home, Sooz?'

'All's well here in Wimbledon certainly.'

'Joe?'

'He's fine. You know, I feel quite sure that whatever was going on back then is now all over.'

'Good, pleased to hear that. How can you tell?'

'All kinds of little things but mostly instinct. Listen, I won't rack up your phone bill talking about it now, Riv. Suffice it to say, all seems very well. Dare I say, back to an even keel and where we were six months ago.'

'Thank God for that,' Riva said with feeling. So it looked like Kaaya was keeping her promise after all.

'We haven't heard from Ben at all, though,' Susan continued. 'And he's not answering his phone. Have you heard from him?'

'Well, I spoke to him yesterday. Or tried to. He's still being a complete shit about my being here.'

'Oh dear. I'll try calling him again this evening. Tell me what it's like there, though. Are you having fun? And Aman? Have you met him yet?'

'Yeah, I've met him. He's okay.'

'*Okay?* What do you mean "okay"? Did he remember you? Does he still fancy you? C'mon, dish the dirt!' Susan asked mischievously.

Riva laughed again. 'Silliness doesn't become you, Mrs Holmes! Since you ask, yes, Aman did remember me and at first seemed rather endearingly down-to-earth. But I can't help thinking that, all said and done, he's probably no better than all the other jumped-up, self-important celebrities that are crowding this place. Having been all matey yesterday, I got a definite brush-off this afternoon. Maybe he had Angelina Jolie waiting for him around the corner.'

'Never mind, better have him jump into bed with her than you. Don't pay him too much attention or he'll think you're interested only because he's now a film star.'

'I guess,' Riva agreed. 'Look, I gotta go. Do keep trying Ben off and on, Sooz. And send me a text if you make contact. There's a part of me thinking, let him stew. But I can't help worrying about the silly bugger too. This isn't his usual self, is it?'

'You're right about that. But who'd have thought losing his job would make for such a sea change? Of course I'll keep trying his mobile. You just enjoy every moment there and stop thinking about things here. *Carpe diem!*' Susan ordered before hanging up.

Slipping her phone back into her bag, Riva walked down the steps of the Lumière. Of course, it was natural that everyone would assume she was having the time of her life. But the truth was that she had not felt so conflicted nor so lonely in a very long time.

Chapter Twenty-Nine

Ben walked slowly down a path he was familiar with from his younger days, carrying a long thin switch. As he had done when he was a boy, Ben now swung it ahead of him, using it to get rid of any stray wasps, and to cut through the taller grasses that were springing up on the path. As he crested the hill, however, Ben started to run out of breath – a small reminder that he was no longer the boy he had been fantasising he still was. This place – his childhood home – had obviously retained its power to cleanse and calm him though. Already he was feeling better, the intensity of his rows with both Riva and Kaaya fading in his mind with every minute he spent here.

Ben caught his breath at the top of the hill and looked down at the small village in which he had grown up. His father's house, washed pink, was just visible behind the church steeple, partially masked from view by the large apple tree that had virtually taken over the back garden. Ben remembered the first summer that the apple tree's branches had grown long enough to tap at his window pane. It had been a windy night, and he (then an anxious five-year-old) had lain frozen in his bed, terrified that someone was trying to break in. He had finally managed to call out to his mother and that was one of the few memories he had retained of her; the feel of a soft flannel dressing gown against his cheek and the faint smell of violets. Apart from that, Ben could barely remember his mother, who had died when he was six. Her picture still hung above the fireplace in his father's house, but he sometimes felt as though she was a stranger smiling sweetly down at him.

Ben sat down on a rock and unwrapped his lunch. He took a bite of his sandwich, wondering why his father had never remarried, despite being one of Denby's most eligible widowers. Nevertheless, Ben had to admit that his father had coped admirably with single life, even taking up baking at one point and turning out some rather decent pies and cakes.

'Resilient, us Owens. And resourceful too,' Ben's father had said proudly to Riva the first time she had visited him and they had sat down to a hearty meal of freshly baked bread and homemade Lancashire hotpot. She had been deeply impressed with his dad, Ben could tell, giving him an enormous hug when it was time to return to Leeds. Since then they had maintained a warm relationship with each other, Riva calling his father every weekend regardless of whether Ben already had or not.

Ben put his flask of orange juice to his lips and drank deeply before screwing the cap back on. Yes, he would be resilient too, if Riva decided to leave him. Ben sometimes surprised himself with the coolness with which he could consider and weigh up such earth-shattering possibilities. Perhaps it was something to do with the early loss of his mother, but he was a far cry from the nervous little boy he had once been. If Riva did decide to run into the arms of her teenage lover, Ben knew he would manage a single life, just as his father had done all those years ago.

Chapter Thirty

A week into the festival, Aman's head felt ready to burst with all the images and storylines he had imbibed. Shading his eyes from the sun's glare, he leant back on the waterproof cushions, flipping through his notebook and trying to make sense of the thoughts he had hastily jotted while he had been watching the films. But some of his notes made no sense at all now. What did this mean, for instance, 'light and shade playing on her face distracting from emotion', and which film had he been referring to anyway? He had never been very good at organising his work, even as a student. Aman, stretched out on one of the plastic chaise longues provided by the Carlton on their private beach, riffled through the pages, feeling a slight sense of panic as he counted. He had seen twelve films so far, which meant that he had a whole lot of catching up to do in the three days he had left in Cannes. Riva was no doubt well on top of everything by now – not greatly different from that first year back at Leeds, then, when Riva would be the first to hand in a beautifully crafted essay while he could barely manage two scribbled pages hastily stapled together the night before!

He looked out at the sea through his Ray-Bans, unable to quell his feeling of sadness at the wasted week so far. With Riva so near and yet so far. He had caught only occasional glimpses of her since that first day they had spent together: once at breakfast in the Carlton's dining room and a couple of times at film screenings. So all his eager anticipation before arriving in Cannes, of spending every moment of these ten days in Riva's company, had eventually amounted to nothing. Perhaps it was just as well. Riva was a married woman and still deeply in love with her husband from what Aman could see. There was no room for him there and so it had been wise to maintain this cool distance.

The crunch of shingle behind him made Aman turn his head and he looked around, startled to see Riva approach him unexpectedly. She was wearing an ivory bikini top with a sarong wrapped around her bottom half. She looked so lovely, Aman wondered how he would maintain his air of reserve.

'Hello,' Riva said in a friendly voice, although her smile was tentative behind a huge pair of sunshades.

Aman gave her a guarded smile but tried to keep his words from sounding too unwelcoming. 'Hmm . . . how come some of us have to work while others can go sunbathing, huh?'

'Oh, sorry, am I disturbing you? Didn't realise you were working . . .' Riva replied, glancing in confusion at Aman's notebook.

'Well, if serious work was what I wanted, this is hardly the least distracting setting, is it?' Aman laughed, sitting up and tipping his head in the direction of a couple of women who were sunbathing topless at the other end of the beach. 'It's okay, you're not disturbing any complex analysis here. Come and sit,' he said companionably, patting the deckchair next to him. As Riva settled herself, he added, 'Maybe I can get you to decipher my notes. You writers are supposed to be good at this sort of thing, aren't you?' He couldn't help

258

feeling pleased that, despite not having seen much of Riva these past few days, it had only taken seconds to revert to their friendly banter. So much for trying to avoid her!

'Are you struggling to come to a decision?' Riva asked, smiling. 'The Palme d'Or is a huge deal, y'know. Can't take our responsibilities lightly!'

'Too right. I don't know how the hell I'm going to decide in another couple of days.' Aman shook his head.

'It's going to be tough,' Riva agreed. 'But what a treat most of the films have been so far, don't you think?'

'Maybe not *all*,' Aman countered.

'Ah, I forget that you probably get to see quite a few films in your line of work anyway. But, for me, merely not being closeted away in a silent study all by myself is such an extravagance.'

'Have you been to any of the premieres yet?' Aman asked.

'No, that's what I was coming to ask actually, Aman,' Riva said, turning hesitantly towards him. 'I know Isabella said that our presence on the red carpet was only compulsory at the opening and closing galas but I think I'd like to attend at least one premiere too.'

'The Brad Pitt film, I bet?'

Riva nodded. 'Tonight. And I'm a bit reluctant to fetch up there on my own. Would you come as my escort?' she asked in a rush.

'I'd love to,' Aman replied quickly, adding, 'if you promise not to drop me the minute you spot Brad Pitt, that is!'

'Oh, I don't know, that's a tough call . . .' Riva teased, making Aman grin at her. She looked even prettier than usual today, more like her college self, with her face scrubbed of make-up and her hair tied back with some kind of band that had a ridiculously large pink flower in it.

'You going in for a swim?' he asked, glancing at her bikini.

Riva cast a quick rueful glance down at herself. 'I'd been warned that beachwear in Cannes is much more about style than substance. Or swimming, for that matter. But it feels silly to be here, so close to the Med, and not venture in for a paddle.'

'I'm game, if you are,' Aman challenged. She gave his Lacoste polo shirt and Bermuda shorts a questioning look. 'Don't worry, I wasn't thinking of going in like this. Or skinny-dipping, which is, I believe, illegal in Cannes,' Aman grinned. 'I've got my trunks on under these shorts. Coming?' he asked, standing up and stripping off his shirt in one swift move.

Riva suddenly looked reluctant. 'I'm not the most confident swimmer, I have to say . . .'

'Come on!' Aman ordered, pulling off his Bermuda shorts and waiting while Riva unwrapped her sarong. One glance revealed that her body was still trim, not that different from her teenage figure, though she was now more curvaceous. Together they picked their way across the shingle beach that separated them from a very blue sea.

'And I'd imagined golden stretches of sand for some reason!' Riva said, wincing as the sharper stones pierced her soles.

Aman looked down and noticed her bare feet. 'Here, take my footwear,' he said, stopping to slip his blue flip-flops off.

'No, no, I couldn't possibly,' Riva protested. 'I don't know, those feet of yours are probably insured for millions of rupees or something,' she added cheekily. 'I'll be to blame if a pebble as much as blemishes them!'

'Okay, I won't take them off then, but maybe this will solve the problem of one pair of sandals between two people,' Aman said, suddenly scooping Riva up. Holding her in his arms, he ran along the last sandy bit of the beach, ignoring Riva's surprised yelps at being swept up so unexpectedly. Soon he was splashing his way through the warm waters of the Mediterranean while she turned her face away from the surf, still screaming. Once Aman was waist-deep, he released Riva, but now she clung to him, laughing and looking apprehensively at the water all around.

'Are you all right?' Aman asked her. 'Sorry, I couldn't resist that. Thought we'd never get here, the way you were mincing about.'

'Mincing! I was barefoot!' Riva objected, still out of breath. Aman noticed she was still clinging to his arms as she felt cautiously with her feet for the bottom of the sea.

'Are you really nervous of the water, Riva?' Aman asked, keeping hold with one arm.

Riva nodded. 'I'm nervous of swimming pools, let alone the great big sea!' she admitted, looking shamefaced.

'But this isn't even a swimming pool, it's just a giant bathtub!' Aman said, waving his free arm at the flat sea around them. But Riva refused to let go of his arm, her teeth chattering slightly.

'I'd rather be a bit closer to the beach, actually, Aman. Could we edge a bit that way please? I really don't like not being able to feel terra firma under my feet,' Riva said, sounding breathless as she tried treading water unsuccessfully.

He laughed and spoke in his most reassuring voice as he adjusted his arm to hold her more firmly around her waist. 'You're with me, Riva, so don't worry, okay? I'm a strong swimmer and I won't let go. Okay?'

Riva nodded, but did not look much more confident. She looked around and, after a moment, said, 'Now this will sound really, really silly to you, Aman, but I also worry a bit about crawly sea creatures and sharks and . . . passing submarines even . . .'

But, by this stage, Aman was not listening any more. Later he figured that the exhilarating mix of sun and sea and the feel of Riva's body in his arms had just got too much for him. But there, in the middle of the beautiful Med that was trailing pink and orange flames from the sun sinking slowly into it, Aman turned Riva around to kiss her full on the mouth. The astonishing thing to Aman, whenever he would later recall this moment, was that Riva struggled not a bit against him. Instead, all her previous fright seemingly forgotten, he felt Riva draw willingly into his embrace, her legs and her body sliding up against his as she looped her arms around his neck and, amazingly, kissed him back.

Riva barely knew what she was doing as they emerged from the sea and returned to her room. There was no thought for the risk of being spotted by the media or anyone else as she and Aman walked hand in hand across the lobby, trailing hat and sarong and gown, kissing again in the privacy of the lift and then once again in the corridor leading to their rooms. As the door to Riva's room clicked shut behind them, they stood in the small passageway and Aman carefully peeled off her damp swimwear before taking off his own. Then he led her to the bed, laying her down on the sheets as gently as though she were a baby. She reached up for him and she felt his hard length against the soft skin of her stomach as he lay on top of her. They made love passionately at first, making up for the last few days that they had wasted so thoughtlessly, and then more unhurriedly, with gentleness and slow mutual enjoyment.

Later, Riva lay back, lacing her fingers in and out of

Aman's hair as his head lay pillowed on her breast. 'Much more expert than you were at eighteen, Mr Khan,' she whispered.

He shifted his head to look up at her and give her the sweetest smile. 'You still hold that fumbling teenage experience against me, don't you?' he said. Then, moving his head onto the pillows next to hers, Aman added, 'It wasn't *too* bad for a first timer, though, was it?'

Riva shook her head and leant over to kiss his forehead. 'Except, before I could teach you any real tricks, you ran off back to India,' she accused.

'Broken-hearted and crying, mind you!' he reminded her.

'I don't for a moment believe you,' she laughed.

At this, Aman sat up, the expression on his face more serious. 'You didn't then and you probably still don't, Riva. You never once realised how badly I'd fallen for you back in college. And it's true what they say about the first cut being the deepest.'

Riva was silent for a few minutes. 'Are you really telling me that you never forgot me all these years? Seriously?' she asked incredulously.

'Absolutely seriously,' Aman replied with seeming sincerity.

'Was there never anyone else? And what about Salma?'

Aman fell back on his pillow at the sound of his wife's name. 'Of course there were others . . . I was only a normal hot-blooded guy. And I was in film school after all, everyone was sleeping with everyone else! And, yes, I did think I could love Salma when I married her, I really did. But . . .'

'But?' Riva asked gently after a long pause.

Aman reached out and dragged Riva back into his arms.

He spoke with his mouth muffled by her hair, his voice husky. 'But love never came, Riva. Don't ask me why. And whenever I made love to anyone, even Salma, they weren't anyone, Riva. They were you. I mean it. It was a kind of madness, I think.'

Riva lay still for a few seconds, trying to assess Aman's sincerity, before she put her arms around him again. She ran her fingers lightly over the muscles on his back before holding him close, hearing the sound of his heart emerge from somewhere deep inside his chest. After another few moments, Aman asked carefully, 'And you, Riva? Did you ever think of me?'

Riva wanted to be as honest with Aman as he was trying to be with her. 'I hardly needed reminding, Aman!' she replied. 'A movie of yours every couple of months – it was like watching you grow up and become a man from behind a glass door.'

'And you never once thought of opening that glass door?'

'How could I have, Aman? When uni finished, I did the expected thing and married Ben and then, soon after, I heard you were married too. What had happened between us was brief and magical, but over. I did watch every single film of yours, though, oh, and inveigle my way into events to watch you on stage when I found you were in London!'

'Did you?' Aman looked surprised.

'I was in the BAFTA audience when you were on stage there last winter . . .'

'You know, I wondered if I'd spotted you there! But, the thing is, whenever I travelled to London, I appeared to be seeing you everywhere – glimpsing you on pavements through my car window, or in the windows of cafés and restaurants as I was driven around.'

Riva sighed. 'If only I'd known, Aman . . .'

'Known what? That I'd have whisked you off in a jiffy, given the slightest chance? What would you have done?'

'I'm not sure,' Riva replied wistfully. 'But perhaps we could have saved ourselves some heartache.'

'We still can – future heartache, that is. Yours and mine, mainly!'

Riva laughed and then, picking up her wristwatch from the bedside table, said, 'I'll tell you what will be the most terrible heartache – if we miss Brad Pitt on the red carpet in an hour's time!'

Aman groaned. 'Please, please, let's not go! He's a nice guy but I promise you I'm much nicer. Let's just stay here. Please, Riva!'

But Riva was already halfway out of bed. 'Aman Khan, that's mean! You have a lifetime of red-carpet shindigs ahead of you but I don't know when I'll next get the chance. And I've brought a special DKNY outfit for this too!'

'Wear that to the closing ceremony,' Aman suggested hopefully.

'I have another gown for that. Dior, no less! Look, I *have* to wear everything I've brought, given the hole it's blown in my bank account!'

'I'll buy you all the Diors and DKs you want. And take you to all the red-carpet events you want too. Our time here is so limited, Riva . . . please let's just stay here, and make love, and order something from room service and go to sleep in each other's arms and wake up in the morning and start all over again!'

Riva felt terribly tempted by the thought. Aman was such a gorgeous man and his continuing adoration of her was like a soothing balm after the treatment she'd recently faced from Ben. But – perhaps it was the thought of her husband – suddenly Riva felt clear-headed and very guilty.

'I think we should go, Aman,' she said quietly. Aman must have noticed the serious look on her face for he stopped arguing and got out of bed.

Wrapping a towel around his waist, he said, 'Actually, I nearly forgot I have a press conference to attend too with the Indian media. I'll come pick you up after that for the premiere.' He looked down at his towel-clad frame. Do you think I can sneak down the corridor like this back to my room?' he asked. 'What a bore to have to wear all my clothes just to go there, have a shower and get changed.' Before Riva could reply, however, he had opened the door and, after a quick look up and down the corridor, he disappeared, holding his clothes in one hand.

Riva showered briskly, feeling a strange mix of both bliss and despair grow somewhere deep inside her. Conscious that she was indulging in exactly the same behaviour that had so enraged her in Kaaya recently, Riva could barely look at herself in the mirror as she towelled her hair dry. While getting ready, she told herself that Kaaya's infidelity was less forgivable because she had a husband who was kind and good to her, unlike Ben, who in recent days had been nothing but surly; uncommunicative and selfish. Besides, given the angry way in which he had last hung up on her, she probably had no marriage to go back to! But, as Riva saw Ben's face in her mind's eye, she found herself feeling less and less convinced by this thought.

Chapter Thirty-One

Ben laid two plates on the wooden kitchen table and took out a chunk of bread from the breadbin as his father came in, holding a casserole between oven mitts. They sat down and Ben waited while his father ladled a portion of stew onto both plates. They ate in silence at first and then talked about some of the goings-on in the village, mostly the latest events in the ongoing saga of Denby's school politics where Ben's father was a part-time counsellor. But, when they were clearing away, Doug Owen opened up the subject that Ben had known would not stay neglected for long. While scooping the leftover stew into an old glass dish, his father spoke in his customary gentle but direct manner.

'Is all well between you and Riva, son?'

Standing at the sink, Ben stiffened slightly. It was not that he did not care for his father's curiosity; they had always been unusually close for father and son. It was more a case of not being mentally prepared for what he knew would be the most tragic event of his life; worse even than his mother's death when he was a child (after all, he had still had a loving father) and far worse than losing his job at the bank (there was enough saved up from previous bonuses to last him a long time yet). No, losing Riva would be a lot worse than all that, quite simply because she was the only girl Ben had ever loved. He owed his father an honest reply.

Removing the dripping casserole dish from the soapy water, Ben said, 'No, things aren't great, to be honest. I knew you'd guess before long.'

'Well, it hardly requires the finest intuition. I haven't heard you talk once to her since you came.'

'She's in Cannes and probably quite busy, you have to admit.'

'Pah!' his father snorted. 'I may live in a village but even we've heard of global roaming mobile phones up here. What's wrong, son?'

Ben stopped to swallow hard before replying. The last thing he wanted was to start blubbing before his old dad, like a child. 'I'm not sure how it started, Dad,' he said finally, his voice trembling precariously. 'We were fine until about six months ago.'

'I know. You two were here at Christmas, remember?' Mr Owen said. 'And Riva looked her usual serene self then. Despite her father's death just months before that, come to think of it.'

'Yes, I remember Riva was really pleased to be getting away from her mum for a bit then. Sweet as Mrs Walia is, she has rather reverted to second childhood since Mr Walia passed away.'

'The strain must fall on young Riva's shoulders, then. Her sister – the glamorous one – she's not really one for nurse-maid duties, is she? Remind me of her name again . . .'

'Kaaya,' Ben replied. 'No, Kaaya's certainly not one for caring duties. Murder on the expensively manicured hands, you see,' he said sarcastically. He filled a glass of water before continuing. 'You're right, the strain has certainly fallen on Riva. But Riva sometimes has this way of practically pushing people away when she's stressed. I guess it's something to do with being efficient and in charge. She doesn't realise how alienating that kind of behaviour can be. But, to be fair, I don't think that's the reason for the current state of our relationship at all . . .'

'What is it then? Not your being made redundant, is it?'

Ben stopped to consider this possibility, but had to admit that Riva had never once complained about his wanting to be a writer rather than a banker. 'No, I don't think it's that, Dad. She's been quite a brick about the loss of my job. And, with my previous bonuses and her own earnings from the books, money has never been short.'

'Ah, but it does throw you together rather a lot, doesn't it?'

'We've never had a problem with that!' Ben protested. 'I mean, we were always inseparable, even back in our university days.'

'Time can make things look different; the mere act of growing up and developing individual interests and all that, you know. Not that I ever had much practice but I've always thought that the best marriages are those where couples give each other a bit of space. Not *too* much, mind! If you think of it like a garden, it's when there's just enough room for breezes to blow between the plants that you get the healthiest foliage.'

'Ever the poet, Dad,' Ben tried to joke.

'Ah well, Riva *has* credited me with the title for her next book, remember? "Slow Sunsets" – that's an Owen original. From here.' Mr Owen tapped the side of his forehead. 'When is the new book out, by the way?'

'Next month. The publishers are sending Riva for a book tour around Europe in June because she's being translated all over the place. She'll be back from Cannes barely a week before she'll be off again.' Ben tried to rein in his resentment but his father must have detected it in his tone.

'Don't hold her back, son,' Ben heard his old dad say gently, almost speaking to himself. 'Sometimes things are made worse by fighting them and you simply have to let go. That's how I coped with your mother's passing.' Mr Owen paused a few moments before gathering himself and speaking again. 'From what I've seen, you and Riva have a strong enough bond – if you stay steady, and give her the space to unfurl her wings, I'm sure as anything it'll be only a matter of time before she comes flying back to you.'

'You think?' Ben asked hopefully.

'Yes, I certainly do, son. Riva loves you too much. And she's one of the most decent girls I know. I can't see her upping and leaving with nary a word.' Ben was silent for a long time and so Mr Owen spoke up again. 'You certainly don't want to lose her, do you?'

Ben replied finally. 'Losing Riva would be pretty damned devastating, Dad. For both you and for me, eh? What say you I get myself packed and think about going home tomorrow?'

'Tomorrow? Good grief, that soon! It wasn't anything I said, was it?' his father asked in a voice of mock concern, but Ben saw that his eyes were twinkling.

Ben left his father pottering in the kitchen to go upstairs and begin his packing. Walking through the living room, he passed under the picture of his mother who was smiling her saintly smile as usual. This time Ben stopped and looked more carefully at the photograph, trying to imagine what it must have been like for his father to have loved this beautiful woman and then so tragically lost her. And through no fault of his own.

It was a stark reminder to Ben of how important it was to fight to save what he had with Riva. He ran up the stairs, hoping it was not too late to make amends.

Chapter Thirty-Two

Riva disconnected the hotel phone and held it against her chest for a few seconds, feeling her rapidly beating heart thump against it. Then she placed the handset back on its cradle with a slightly trembling hand. She was so excited, she felt almost giddy. Luckily she had been sitting down during her conversation with Walter Zuckerman or she would surely have keeled right over! It was incredible to think that as respected a director as Zuckerman would be interested in optioning film rights to her first book! He said he had been given a copy by Aman Khan at the Directors' Convention and had sat up every night since then reading it in his hotel room.

'Your book will make a stunning film, in my opinion', were his exact words and, 'When authors like you write so visually, you make my job as a film maker very easy indeed.'

Riva squeezed her eyes shut, trying to recall all the other fantastic things he had said about her book and its characters, feeling a happy glow radiate from deep within. It was Aman she should be most grateful to. It was typically kind and generous of him to have passed her book on to Zuckerman without even telling her he was going to do so. From what Zuckerman had said, Aman must have given it on the first or second day of the festival.

Riva looked at her watch, impatient at the idea of having to wait another hour before she could call Aman and thank him, but he would now be in his press conference. Riva flopped back on the bed, trying to quell her excitement. She had not felt so energised or exhilarated since her Orange win. That had been a mere two years ago but it felt like so much longer, given all the negative things that had happened between her and Ben since then . . .

The thought of Ben cast a sudden shadow over Riva's joy. She sat up and dangled her legs over the side of the bed, looking at the Mediterranean sparkling outside her window and remembering how genuinely overjoyed Ben was about her winning such a prestigious literary prize as the Orange. She still carried the image of him standing and applauding her from their table at the Royal Festival Hall, tears shining in his eyes. But all that had happened since then had changed their lives irrevocably – the loss of Ben's job, the failure of his writing career . . . Not that any of these things mattered a whit to Riva, but who would have imagined how much they would change Ben?

Riva lay down again, curling herself up as she felt a sudden chill. On the one hand, Aman's presence seemed to be transforming the very fabric of her life – joys she had thought long vanished were blooming gloriously in her mind again, like desert flowers. How easy it had been to forget she was married to someone else. As Riva's heart shrank inside her chest in fear and shame, she felt tears emerge hot and fast, rolling down her face and onto the pillow. Clutching her knees with her hands, she rocked herself, begging for forgiveness. What sort of fate was leading her to stand at the same crossroads she had faced as an eighteen-year-old? Then her choice had been between a boy from exotic, far-off India who represented things she had spent all her life yearning for, and an English boy who came from her world and made her feel safe. Neither of those boys was anything like the men they had become now. But the choice before her today wasn't that different. Aman brought the fantastic possibility of a glorious escape from the dull grind that her life had become, while Ben stood for Riva's more practical side, where she played important roles of wife, daughter, sister, friend. With Aman, Riva could revel in herself and discover all the potential life had always held. Whereas with Ben there was now the saddest sense that all the excitement in life had come to an end. Perhaps marriage was like a fixed deposit in which there was only so much joy and happiness to be had. It felt to Riva as though her account was already badly overdrawn.

Later that night, Aman stepped onto the red carpet and waved to the crowds, reminding himself not to either squint or frown at the flashing cameras. He turned to see Riva walking up behind him, wearing a cream silk gown slit all the way up one leg to her thigh. Despite the occasional flash of her left leg as she took her customary long graceful strides, she looked beautiful and dignified.

This time there was none of the high jinks Aman had so uninhibitedly performed with Riva at the opening gala. Perhaps it was because they had made love earlier in the evening but, suddenly, Aman felt shyer than he usually did before the cameras.

He turned to Riva and spoke in a low voice. 'Are you okay?' She smiled and nodded. 'Need my arm to keep from tripping over?' She smiled again and this time shook her head. Feeling a bit more mischievous now, he asked a question his old kindergarten teacher – a stern elderly Anglo-Indian – had often asked her group of five-year-olds: 'Cat got your tongue?' This time, Riva burst out laughing and the cameras flashed, catching what would no doubt look like a very intimate moment if it were ever published.

Riva finally spoke as they walked up the stairs to relative privacy. 'Among those camera flashes are at least a hundred pictures of you and me. Don't think they'll compromise us in any way, do you?'

'Don't care,' Aman replied, smiling, but Riva looked worried.

'You have more of a reputation to protect than me, Aman. Do be careful.'

'Absolutely no point trying to be careful, Riva. There are thousands of photographs of me with all sorts of women, taken at parties and premieres and shoots. These pictures of us will merely join that big album up in the sky, or wherever it is that all unused pictures go.' Aman looked at Riva's disbelieving face and added, '*Really*. Quit worrying. Anyway, as I said before, you're just as well known as me so don't worry on my behalf alone.'

'Ah, but my readers won't stop reading my books whatever I do. But a film star – especially in India – is another matter altogether; you know you're expected to maintain a spotless moral record if you want to keep your following.'

They had now reached the party venue inside the Lumière, a hall glittering with people wearing the most beautiful frocks and jewels. Waiters were weaving through the crowds carrying trays of Cristal and delicate *hors d'oeuvres*, each of which looked like a beautifully crafted miniature sculpture. Aman took Riva's elbow and steered her right through the crowds, grabbing a couple of flutes of bubbly along the way.

They stopped behind a couple engaged in conversation with a small group of people. Aman tapped the man on his shoulder, enjoying the look on Riva's face as he said, 'Brad, my man. I'd like you to meet a very dear friend. This is Riva Walia. She's a world-famous author, also on the jury this year. And, believe it or not, an old classmate of mine.'

After a few minutes of polite conversation, Aman moved Riva on and they walked away, Riva leaning her head briefly on Aman's arm.

'I feel quite faint,' she joked.

'I'm still Number One, though. Much handsomer than Brad Pitt, right?' Despite the jokey query, Aman looked at Riva with some uncertainty.

She screwed up her face as though having to think really hard before saying, 'Hmmm . . . okay, yeah, Number One and a Half, I guess . . .'

'*Half!*'

'You have to admit, Aman, Brad Pitt is . . . Brad Pitt!'

'I dunno,' Aman shook his head ruefully. 'What does that man have that I don't, huh?'

They circulated some more, stopping to chat with fellow novelists and Bollywood actors. Riva, concerned, spoke to Aman. 'Aman, you have to decide if it's all right for us to be seen so much in each other's company. There seem to be a lot more people from Mumbai over here than I'd have thought . . .'

'Ah, don't worry,' Aman tried to reassure Riva again, although he too knew there would be hell to pay from Salma if word did get back to her about his mysterious attractive female companion. More worryingly, he suddenly thought of his parents and his fans. Riva was right. An extramarital affair was not something Bollywood was ever too forgiving of. Bigamous marriages were another thing but it was one of those unwritten rules: in Bollywood, infidelity was never, ever flaunted.

Nevertheless, it was beyond Aman to even consider letting go of the precious girl he had lost when he had been too young to know better. For all these years, Riva had held the kind of special place in Aman's heart that he had hardly been able to explain to himself, possibly – he was willing to admit – because he had not found love with the woman he had married. And, now that Riva was here by some kind of miracle, Aman was not going to allow some distant fears to allow her to slip away again. He could not, in fact, wait for the party to be over so that he could return to his room with Riva. And it was only then, lying with Riva in his arms and listening to the swell of the sea blow in through the wide-open windows, that Aman knew he would feel he was finally at one with the world.

Chapter Thirty-Three

Riva sat on the edge of her hotel bed, holding her return ticket to Heathrow in one hand. The ticket that would tomorrow return Riva to her mundane old life that now, curiously, felt like a lost world. She thought of the often dull hours that had to be spent staring a laptop screen as she clicked away on the keyboard, of the growing silences between her and Ben. She thought of her mother's anxieties and ailments and the recent row with Kaaya. Then Riva tried measuring all that up against the last two luminous days with Aman, wondering why she was even the tiniest bit surprised at how wretched the comparison made her feel.

Today was her last full day in Cannes. Important not just for being her last day with Aman for the foreseeable future, but also for being the day of the jury's final deliberations before the awards would be announced. The jury members had all been asked to be ready by nine o'clock to be taken to the Château de la Napoule on the outskirts of Cannes. The debates would take place under strict security, with a brief break for lunch with the Mayor of Cannes, after which the final decisions would be made by secret ballot.

Riva had woken later than planned, exhausted and

hung over from the splendid bash of the previous night at the Hotel du Cap. Riva had never seen so many stars and big names jostle together under one roof but she had uncomplainingly allowed Aman to drag her away before the night had got too late. Even she had had no appetite by that stage for more star-gazing and so had willingly returned to the privacy of Aman's room, both of them filled with the desperation of parting lovers who knew that time was rapidly running out for them.

Riva had returned to her room in the morning to get ready but she had done so with none of the *joie de vivre* of the past two days, feeling instead as though her heart had turned to lead. Going silently through the motions of showering and dressing in her smart Chanel suit, she was painfully aware that her spell in the sun was nearly at an end. Listlessly brushing her hair, she felt as though she could see the storm clouds gathering on her horizon, pushing her away from Aman, tossing them both back to the lives they had before they had so miraculously met again.

A knock on her door brought her back to the present. It was Aman, standing in the corridor, also looking as though he were carrying the weight of the world on his shoulders.

'Ready?' he asked quietly. Riva nodded and turned around to collect her purse and laptop case. Emerging from her room a few seconds later, she found that Aman had already called for the lift and they travelled down-stairs together in silence. A flag-bearing car was waiting for them, its driver wearing a uniform complete with a peaked cap. They got into the back seat and Riva slipped her hand into Aman's, hoping it would not be visible from the driver's seat.

The Château was five miles west of Cannes and, as they drove down the sweeping Croisette, Riva looked out at the now deserted Cinéma de la Plage where, every night, fans of classic films had gathered to watch old favourites play out on the huge outdoor screen. Festival workers were clearing the beach of debris, readying the place for what would probably be the final screening tonight. Out in the distance, she could see a clutch of opulent yachts, bobbing and glittering like jewels on a bed of blue velvet.

'That one there is the Raheja yacht,' Aman said, pointing to a particularly large and sleek specimen called *Mastaani*. 'Apparently the whole Indian party leaves today for the Grand Prix at Monaco.'

'All right for some,' Riva said, throwing her eyes upwards.

'I wish I'd taken you on board the night of their party. You'd have enjoyed observing the excesses. They'd even flown shish kebabs in from London to serve with Scotch . . .'

'Which night was it?'

'The second day we were here. I went with Ritesh Shah only to avoid you, at that stage assuming you were happily married and sitting by your phone waiting for Ben to call! What a waste of a week that we could have spent together.'

Riva noticed the bitterness in Aman's voice and squeezed his hand. 'I did spend the first night hoping Ben would call, I must admit, Aman,' she confessed.

'Does that mean you would not have come to me that day on the beach if he *had* called?' Aman's voice was quiet but Riva knew it was a significant question.

She was silent, trying to consider her reply. Perhaps because she was taking too long to come up with something, Aman spoke again, his voice now sharper than before. 'Tell me, Riva. Am I just a stopgap while Ben sorts himself out and you go back to him, huh?'

Riva slipped her hand out of Aman's, unable to deal with his anger piling up on top of her own pain and guilt. After a pause, she said, 'I don't know, Aman. I just don't know what I want . . . or even what to think any more . . .'

'Well, you have to come up with something. We don't have that much time left, you know.' Riva heard the desperation in Aman's voice and closed her eyes.

She opened them a few seconds later to find that Aman was now looking out at the passing flat French countryside, his lips pursed and his expression inscrutable.

Riva spoke up finally, keeping her voice gentle. 'Aman, my darling. If I could freeze-frame my life in any one chosen moment, it would be this. It would be here and now, with you by my side. These past few days have been nothing less than a dream . . .'

Aman turned to her and took her hands in his again. 'Then come with me. Leave England. Leave Ben. Please.'

Riva looked at Aman, her expression anguished. 'You say it so easily,' she said. 'Where would we go, Aman? Mumbai? Where your wife and parents are? And the baby you adore? And what would your millions of fans say if you fetched up with me in tow?' Aman was silent and so Riva continued, still speaking softly. 'And what about me, my darling? My life is in England, Aman. My work, my mother . . . I couldn't possibly abandon all that to run away with you. Even if I left Ben.'

That silenced Aman and, as the tall castle walls of the Château de la Napoule rose before them, they knew their conversation had come to an end.

* * *

The rest of the day was sheer torture for Aman. It was unbearable to be within touching distance of Riva and yet be surrounded by other people all the time. The nine jurors had all been closeted together in a massive vaulted dining room and the discussions held around a large mahogany table. As befitted Aman's mood, an air of seriousness and secrecy pervaded the day's proceedings.

Riva and he had spent all morning with the other jurors, discussing the various films they had seen and the six categories they had to award prizes in. Aman was unsurprised by how incisive Riva's remarks were, even though film was not her chosen medium. She was a true intellectual but never dismissive of anyone else's opinion, he noticed. How lightly she wore her talents. He restricted his own remarks to areas he was familiar with from his own profession: acting, directing and cinematography.

At one stage the discussions became so involved that Aman needed to let himself out for a breather. Standing on one of the castle's many terraces overlooking the sea, he tried once again to absorb Riva's bleak words in the car about the future of their relationship. Or lack of. She was right, there was little hope for them – unless they set about building a life together with no regard for all the people who would be affected by their decision. But that kind of selfishness would not come easily to either of them. On the other hand, the thought of returning to the loveless marriage he shared with Salma was a sorrowful thought to Aman. If he did so, it would be mostly for Ashfaq . . . but such a decision could well be the beginning of emotional death for him. He smiled wryly to himself, realising how dramatic such a sentiment would sound if he said it out loud. But it was something Aman felt truly fearful of now that he had met Riva and seen what real love could be like.

He heard the sound of footsteps behind him and felt a gentle hand on his shoulder. Even without turning, he knew it was Riva. He heard her voice, soft and troubled. 'Aman, my love. Are you all right?'

Aman turned to her. Her eyes, large and dark in her face, looked unhappy too. He took a deep breath and replied sadly, 'Of course I'm not all right, Riva. How can you expect me to be? It's our last day together, for God's sake, after having found you again after so long.'

She dropped his hand and stood next to him, her hands gripping the stone balustrade as she looked out with him at the blue stretch of water lying calmly before them. After a pause, she said tentatively, 'I have a book tour coming up in the summer. Would you be able to come to Europe? I may have worked something out by then . . .'

Hope sprang alive in Aman's chest once again. He looked at Riva but saw only a deeply troubled expression. He knew this was harder on her because, unlike his feelings for Salma, she still had a semblance of love for Ben in her heart. Aman was no fool. He had lost out to Ben once before and knew that it was because Ben had essentially much more in common with Riva than he did. They came from the same place and spoke the same language; they read the same sort of books and enjoyed the same kind of pursuits. If Aman had lost out to all that once, it would be the easiest thing in the world to fail once again. Piecing together some of the things Riva had said, Aman gathered that her relationship with Ben had only recently hit a rocky patch. Aman was wise enough to know that all long-term relationships went through bad phases, most of them coming through eventually at the other end. He had even seen his normally devoted parents go through patches where they had seemed perilously close to walking out on each other. But here was Riva offering him a half-chance that she might leave Ben for him. How could he possibly not jump at it with both hands?

'I have a shooting schedule lined up for Europe too,' he said eagerly. 'June and July. Do you have your tour itinerary yet?'

Riva shook her head. 'It should be waiting for me when I get back. Do you know where you will be shooting?'

'Paris in June. And then four days in Venice, with Rohit Mirchandani's company. He's planning to shoot the Serenissima, which is a Grand Prix speedboat race on the canals. And use CGI to pretend I'm taking part in it.'

Riva finally smiled. 'Aman Bond?'

'Something like that,' Aman said with a rueful grin. 'Or James Khan, maybe.'

'And after Venice?'

'In July I'm in Tuscany . . . apparently the Leaning Tower has never made it onto a Bollywood film. But Salma has not been to Tuscany yet and she has said she wants to go too. I thought it would be good to spend time with Ashfaq . . .'

Riva nodded. He knew she had heard the helplessness in his voice when she replied, 'I understand, Aman. I'd also considered asking Ben if he would like to accompany me on the book tour. Just to cheer him up, you know, and have him feel less alienated by my work.' She sighed before continuing. 'I never got the chance to ask him in the end, because he was behaving so stupidly. But now . . . how different things look now . . .'

Before Aman could respond, a waiter arrived on the terrace with the message that their presence was required by the jury who were waiting to continue the discussions. Riva looked at Aman, who shrugged.

'Better go back indoors before we're dragged in,' he said, although he felt unenthusiastic at the prospect of pondering anything but his own dilemmas.

By evening, the decisions had been made and it was time for the jury to return to their hotels and get ready for the closing ceremony. After a quick rehearsal of the events that would later take place at the Palais de Festivals, the cars were summoned and Aman and Riva took theirs back to the Carlton. They sat side by side on the back seat, each of them silently mulling over the love they shared and how terribly it conflicted with their responsibilities back home. The fairy tale of Cannes was drawing to an inexorable close without – it would seem – the customary happy ending that all fairy tales and love stories ought to have.

Chapter Thirty-Four

Riva woke the following morning, feeling Aman's breath blow gently over the top of her head. Carefully, so as not to wake him, she eased herself out of bed and made her way to the toilet. Standing at the mirror, she looked at her naked form, still feeling the kisses Aman had rained on her face and neck and breasts. He had made love to her last night with even more passion than their first evening together in Cannes and, when she later held him in her arms, she had felt him weep. Whether out of sorrow or rage, Riva could not tell, but she made no mention of this, thinking it kinder to pretend she had not noticed.

When she returned to the bedroom, she found Aman awake, half-sitting up against the pillows, his hair tousled and eyes still filled with sleep, looking at her with an expression she could not read.

'Hello, love,' Riva said softly, climbing back into bed. He held the duvet up for her to slip in next to him and then wrapped his arms around her body, holding her so close she felt short of breath.

They had kept the French windows open all night and, as they lay entwined in silence, Riva could hear the sound of the sea wafting in. She wondered if that sound was one that would from now on always remind her of these halcyon days in France. That, and the musky smell of Aman's favourite Roger & Gallet cologne. She knew so many little details about him now: that his favourite after-shave was Gaultier, that he only ever ordered underwear from a Swiss company called Zimmerli, that his shoes were made by a bespoke shoemaker near Baker Street in London . . . such intimate minutiae, usually collected over years of living with someone, had now become hers to possess and own.

Riva closed her eyes, trying again to work out the nature of her feelings for the man whose mind and person she had grown so familiar with in such a short space of time. How easily she had given herself up to him. Why had she hardly questioned it and what did she really feel for Aman, Riva wondered, searching for some way to define the tumult she felt in her heart. Without a doubt, she knew that she could not bear the thought of never seeing him again. How unfeasible to even consider boarding her flight later this morning without some promise of a future meeting. It had become clear too, even if she had never admitted it to herself before, that a part of him had stayed with her since her youth. Now, after Cannes, she had so much more to hold close to her chest. She wanted to shut it away from everyone else, making it her most precious possession, a resource against all the sadness that might come. What did one call all that: was it love?

Feeling Aman kiss the top of her head, Riva looked up at him. She looked directly into his sleepy brown eyes and said softly, 'I love you, Aman. I haven't said it before but I do, you know. And I need you to know that, before we take our separate flights this morning.'

A tear emerged in Aman's eyes and started to slide down the side of his face. 'What will happen to us, Riva?' he asked. 'Please don't tell me it's over . . . not when we've only just started . . . there is so much more to come . . .'

Riva kissed his tears, tasting the salt in her mouth as she replied, 'I don't know yet, Aman, if you want me to be honest.' After a pause, she asked, 'Could it be enough for us to know we love each other? Can that sustain us as we fly into far-off worlds?' Aman was already shaking his head as she carried on speaking, 'I'm not saying it will work, Aman. But let's try it for now. Please. I see it as a moral choice for us. What is that happiness worth which comes at the expense of so much else?'

'How can you put everyone else before yourself? And me?' Aman asked in a choked voice.

'Oh, Aman, I know we've all grown accustomed to going out there and taking with both hands all the things that we want. It's seen as laudable to do that now, isn't it? But that old-fashioned thing – what shall I call it – decency? – that's not dead yet, is it?'

'But we've already crossed that line, don't you see, Riva?' Aman said, his voice rising.

'In the eyes of most people, yes, but we know what's compelled us,' Riva pleaded. 'It's what comes after this that I know we'll never forgive ourselves for. However happy we may think we can be . . .'

Riva felt Aman release her from his grip. He flopped back on the pillows with a loud groan. 'Go with your heart, Riva, for once, not your bloody head!' He threw his forearm over his eyes, as though unable to bear his frustration with her. But, after a few minutes, Aman shifted his arm to turn on his side and place his palms on either side of Riva's face. He looked directly at her. 'I love you,' he said more quietly. 'The life I've had without you so far hasn't been worth much. Yes, yes, I know, despite my successful career, which I'm not ungrateful for.' Riva reached out her arm to touch his face but he sat up now as he continued speaking. 'I'm willing, Riva, to take all the consequences of getting together with you. And there will be many consequences, for you and for me. I don't doubt that. Just tell me when you're ready and I'll come for you.'

With this he got out of bed and Riva silently watched him pulling on the clothes he had discarded by her bed last night. Then, without another word, he walked out of her room and Riva heard the door click shut.

Chapter Thirty-Five

Kaaya pulled her car into Heathrow's Terminal 1 and found a slot without much trouble. Walking into the arrivals area, Kaaya glanced at her watch. She was a lot earlier than required, determined not to miss her sister's flight from Nice and have her go straight to the taxi rank. Ben, typically, had not answered his phone when Kaaya had called to ask if he was planning to collect Riva and so she had finally sent him a text to say that she would do it.

After buying herself a skinny latte, Kaaya parked herself on a chair outside Costa Coffee from where she could get a clear view of all passengers arriving at Terminal 1. She had not stopped for breakfast in her haste to leave the house this morning and now took a welcome sip of the scalding hot coffee, thinking about the past ten days without Riva in London. Her sister's silence after their confrontation had been sheer torture and the possibility of a permanent rift with her had, in these past few days, grown into a thought far more unbearable than Kaaya had ever imagined it could be. Even Ma had not heard much from Riva after she had left for Cannes, beyond one hasty phone call, which also seemed ominous to Kaaya. Nothing but the most serious of problems would prevent Riva from calling their mother, surely.

For her part, Kaaya had faithfully kept the promise she had made to Riva on the day of her departure, resisting all of Joe's frantic efforts to revive their affair. And finally, after three days of stonewalling him, the calls and texts had finally stopped. Oddly, Kaaya had not missed Joe as much as she thought she might, the business of not having to sneak around Rohan suddenly becoming a huge relief. It was a terrifying thought, but Kaaya had even wondered if perhaps she had grown too old to enjoy the frisson of secret affairs any more.

Having finished her coffee, Kaaya squashed the paper cup and threw it into a nearby bin. What was really important now was to let Riva know that the affair with Joe was well and truly over. From what Joe had said, Susan did not seem to have guessed anything at all and so it was obvious that Riva had not told her about it before leaving for Cannes. In Kaaya's opinion, it would be best for Susan to remain unaware of what had happened but, if an apology was what Riva wanted, then Kaaya would be willing. She got up from her table and wandered out of the café, pondering why family relationships had suddenly grown so important to her. Kaaya stopped at the railings near the arrivals gate and concluded that her father's death probably had much to do with it. It stood to reason that an already tiny family unit of four was terribly depleted by the loss of one person. She could not let that shrink any more.

A bunch of arriving passengers was coming through the doors, wheeling trolleys and suitcases, and Kaaya scanned them for her sister. The electronic board showed that the flight from Nice had landed forty minutes ago, so Riva should be coming out around now. The first gaggle of passengers passed by and in another few minutes Kaaya spotted her sister, wearing jeans and a blue cotton shirt. She raised her hand to catch her attention. Even from a distance, she could see that Riva was startled to see her there. She looked drawn and despondent, Kaaya thought, even worse than when she had left. Kaaya wondered if, over the ten days that she had been away, Riva had allowed her anger over the affair with Joe to crystallise into sorrow. That, from Kaaya's experience, would be far more diffi-cult to deal with than a good old-fashioned shouting match. But, as Riva neared, Kaaya saw the shadow of a smile on her sister's face and, when Riva reached out for a hug, Kaaya felt her heart lighten at the indication that she had been forgiven.

'Hey, sis, it's good to see you,' Kaaya said, putting her arms around Riva and squeezing her tightly.

When they drew apart, Riva said, 'I wasn't expecting anyone and was about to make for the taxi rank.'

'That's why I was standing right here, so I could catch you before you did exactly that. I sent Ben a message to say I would pick you up, of course, to be sure we didn't both end up coming.'

Riva nodded. 'Have you seen him while I've been away?' she asked, pushing her trolley as she walked by Kaaya's side.

'Ben? We spoke a couple of times. Rohan managed rather miraculously to get through to him while he was at his dad's in Denby. Network coverage is zero out there, as you know, so they only spoke briefly but Ben called us again last night.'

'And Ma?'

'She's okay. As well as can be expected, I guess. The usual ups and downs. I saw her yesterday and I think she's hoping to see you later today.'

'I'll go across to her once I've unpacked a bit and had a shower.'

'So, was it good? Cannes?'

Riva nodded.

'You look exhausted,' Kaaya observed. 'Was the partying manic?'

'There sure was a lot of that,' Riva replied.

'Can't wait to hear all about it. Especially any stories you have about Aman Khan.'

Busy as she was helping Riva lift her suitcase into the boot, Kaaya did not notice the passing look of anguish on Riva's face at the mention of Aman's name. Once they were both settled in the front seats, Kaaya knew it was time to address the huge unspoken issue still lurking between them. She stuck the key in the ignition, took a deep breath and turned to her sister.

'Riva, I need to get this out of the way before anything else. We may be chalk and cheese but at least we've always been upfront with each other.' Riva nodded, her face solemn, and so Kaaya ploughed on, her voice wobbling with emotion. 'Riva, I'm so, so sorry for what happened with Joe. Don't ask me for explanations because I honestly don't have any. It . . . sounds crazy, I know, but it just kinda came to pass. Really. It wasn't planned or malicious or anything like that. I have nothing at all against Susan, you know that. It was just something stupid that *happened* and, now that I think about it, it was so meaningless and thoughtless and unkind and I'm so *so* sorry I did it. But what I really need you to know now is that it's over, Riva. Well and truly over. I haven't seen Joe since you left for France and he's stopped calling me too. It's over, so please, please forgive me . . .'

Kaaya's voice, cracking with emotion, trailed off. She

searched her sister's face but Riva was looking down at her feet, as though unable to make eye contact, and Kaaya wondered if that was a sign that her sister had still not forgiven her. It was possible that Riva would never entirely trust her again.

'You believe me, don't you, Riva?' Kaaya spoke again, her voice now wobbling as she broke down in tears. 'I promise you, it's the truth. And I can't bear you being angry with me any more . . . having lost Papa, I couldn't stand it if I were to lose your love too . . . won't you forgive me . . . please . . .'

Suddenly Riva reached out and clutched Kaaya's hand that was resting on the gear stick. She picked it up and, as she had sometimes done when they were small children, Riva held her sister's hand to her cheek and then kissed it. To her astonishment, Kaaya found that Riva was weeping copious tears too. It must mean she had been forgiven! Kaaya wanted to laugh and cry in sheer relief. For a few minutes, both sisters sat in the front seat of the Lotus, weeping and sharing tissues from a box on the dashboard, feeling closer than they had done in a long, long time.

Chapter Thirty-Six

Ben stood waiting in the living room, his nerves stretched taut with anxiety. He knew from the BA website that Riva's flight had landed two hours ago. She should be coming in at any moment now.

Ben surveyed the lounge, which – after three hours' effort – was spick and span, the piles of newspapers and magazines that had cluttered it for days now sitting in the recycler, a huge vase of pink Asiatic lilies, Riva's favourite, looking luxuriant on the mantelpiece. Someone had once told them that the word 'lily' meant 'forever in love' in Cantonese and Riva had taken to buying huge quantities of the flowers for all their anniversaries and birthdays.

Ben was glad he had remembered this while shopping at Waitrose yesterday. He had later even got down to his least favourite household chore: clearing the garden of the profusion of weeds that had taken over parts of it, catching an unusually warm May morning to rake all the winter leaves to one side and give the old wrought-iron tables and chairs a fresh lick of white paint. His plan – seeing that it looked set to be another fine day – was to serve dinner on the patio outside: prawns and pasta with a rocket and avocado salad. They would eat in the light of the two outsized tapers he had bought on his drive home from Denby.

He owed Riva an apology. Ben had known that, even before his father had gently guided him in that direction and sent him home. Driving back into London, Ben had recognised that he had allowed his own frustrations to grow into jealousy, not just of Riva's writing career, but the life she was developing quite independently of him. And how stupid to imagine that she would run away with Aman Khan merely because he had seen them on TV together! Even if Riva did have a flirtation with Aman, Ben knew he had virtually propelled her away from him with his recent shoddy behaviour, and at a time when she was probably still mourning her father. His bad moods these past few months must have been hell for Riva to live with and Ben cast about, still desperately thinking of ways in which he could make up for it. He was suddenly keenly aware of how close he had come to destroying one of the best things he had, which was, without a doubt, his life with Riva.

He looked out the window as he heard Kaaya's Lotus pull up outside the house. Both sisters emerged from the car but, once Kaaya had helped to get the suitcase out, she hugged Riva before getting back into the car and driving off. Ben was grateful for Kaaya's discretion, although her quick departure was more likely designed to avoid him. They had spoken tentatively a few times but had not seen each other since that row they'd had on the telephone before he had left for Denby and the memory of it now made Ben cringe. He owed apologies to a few people: Kaaya, his mother-in-law but, most of all, Riva . . .

Ben opened the front door and walked down the drive to help Riva with her suitcase.

'Hello, love, welcome home,' he said softly, reaching out to kiss her. He could not help noticing that she gave him a guarded look as they drew apart. She stepped back, allowing him to take the suitcase off her. 'Do you want it here or in the bedroom?' he asked.

'Er . . . if it's not too heavy, upstairs would be good, thanks,' she replied. 'It's mostly clothes.'

Riva did not follow him up the stairs but went into the kitchen. She was filling up the kettle when he returned to the ground floor.

'Do you want a cuppa?' she asked, taking the box of teabags out of the cupboard.

'Yes, please. Have you had breakfast?' he enquired. Riva shook her head. 'Do you want me to make you some toast? Or a cheese sandwich perhaps . . . there's some ham as well?'

After a moment's hesitation, she replied. 'Toast would be nice, thanks.'

Ben pulled the loaf out of the breadbin, acutely aware of the awkwardness that was cloaking their stilted conversation. He ought to be asking her about her time in Cannes, make it known that he was not feeling resentful any more. Of course, Riva would not have forgotten his conduct on the eve of her departure but Ben could not tell if she was still smarting from it. Perhaps her discomfiture was due to their lack of communication while she had been away. Or she may merely have grown wary of his changing moods these past few months, being constantly half in expectation of another swing this way or that. Ben cursed himself for forgetting how much he stood to lose by such behaviour. After sticking two slices of bread in the toaster, Ben turned around and, leaning on the kitchen counter, said, 'I have an apology to make, Riv.'

'Whatever for?' she asked, looking at the hissing kettle, rather than his face.

'Well, for the way I've been generally these past few months. I know I've been like a bear with a sore head much of the time. And it hasn't been fair on you, I know. It's hardly your fault things haven't been working out for me!'

Riva said nothing as the kitchen filled with the din of the kettle whistling. It clicked itself off abruptly and, as silence returned, she took a pair of mugs out of the cupboard. 'You don't have to apologise to me,' she said quietly.

'Of course I do. You've borne the brunt of it. And without complaint. I'm so sorry too that I didn't call you again while you were in France,' Ben said.

'Well, I didn't call either after that first night . . .' she replied, stirring the tea, her voice hesitant.

'I wasn't sure if you'd tried or not. I was at Denby and the coverage is bloody awful there, as you know.'

'I thought you might have gone up there. How's Dad?'

'Oh, his usual chipper self. He sends his love. Very keen to read your new book. Although I have to warn you, he's openly laying claim to the title. You may have an intellectual copyright case on your hands if you don't acknowledge him handsomely!'

Riva smiled briefly as she handed Ben his tea. A few drops of the beverage slopped over the edge as he briefly caught her wrist, startling her.

'I'm glad you're back, Riv,' he said, leaning over and dropping a kiss on her temple. 'No more moods, I promise,' he added, drawing away but keeping his eyes on her face to read her expression, desperate to see a hint of forgiveness.

Riva was silent, however, looking blankly at the tea stain

that had formed on the side of the mug Ben was holding in his other hand. The sound of the toast popping up made them both jump slightly, releasing the tension. Ben freed Riva's hand and turned to get the butter dish out of the fridge. Somehow he felt as though she had not forgiven him after all.

Riva turned to pick up her mug, feeling wretched beyond words. First Kaaya, then Ben. Everyone was apologising to *her* while she . . . Riva wasn't sure what she felt about herself right now. All she really wanted to do at this moment was to chuck her undrunk tea into the sink, run upstairs wailing at the top of her voice, crawl into bed and lie curled up under the duvet so that the world would simply pass her by.

But now she had to talk to Ben, accept his apologies and pretend (oh God, the terrible, terrible deceit) that Aman had never happened. It was *she* who should be going around apologising to everyone: Ben, for her shameless adultery; Kaaya, for rushing to judge her before going off and doing worse; her mother, for forgetting all the principles she had brought her up with; and Aman himself for leading him on to expect they could have a future together . . .

Riva's thoughts about Aman on the flight back to London had been so confused, she had even found herself wishing at one point that she would get home to find that Ben had indeed left her. That would at least half solve her dilemma – it was so much easier to be the victim and not the offender!

'Butter?' Ben asked as he transferred the hot toast onto a plate and popped in two more slices. Riva nodded gratefully, realising that she hadn't eaten anything since a few nibbles at the grand closing night party.

'There are a few messages for you on the answer phone,' Ben said. 'I've left them as they are so you can listen to them yourself.' He passed her the plate of buttered toast and she took it into the hallway to listen to her messages.

She jabbed on the red button and heard Gideon's nasal voice drift into the room.

'Oh hello, darling. I know you're still in Cannes. Just a heads-up when you get back that Fifth House is planning a little bash for you at La Portes des Indes to kick off your book tour. A few journos and literary editors from the broadsheets. They're looking at Friday the 12th. And your flight to Paris will be on the Sunday following. Paris, Barcelona, Lisbon, Amsterdam, Frankfurt, Rome. In that order, I think. More when you're back, darling. Super. Cheerio!'

The next message was from Selina, Riva's editor at Fifth House, stating more or less the same thing and saying that her tickets were going to be biked over in the week. The following few messages were all from friends: Chris, inviting them to Neil's 40th birthday party at a pub in Stroud, Steve, asking if she knew a good decorator and Vicki, who had managed to wangle tickets to the Madonna concert at the O2 through her event management company. There were no messages for Ben, unless he had already scrubbed them out.

'They're mostly about the forthcoming tour,' Riva said through a mouthful of toast as she wandered back into the kitchen.

'I know, I heard them. Quite soon, isn't it? You'll have barely got your feet under the table and you'll be off again,' Ben said.

'Never mind that feet-under-the-table is the only position Selina's ever happy to see me in!' Riva said with a wry laugh. Then, after a minuscule pause, she asked Ben,

'Did you want to come?' She realised how abrupt the invitation must sound. Besides, she had already half promised to meet Aman while on tour! Was she going mad, behaving like some sort of split personality?

Ben looked surprised and chewed on his toast for a few seconds before saying, 'For the book hoopla? Not for all of it, surely? From what you've told me of book tours, they're pretty exhausting affairs. Best treat it like a business trip, I think, Riva, or you'll just do yourself in. But, perhaps I can join you towards the end – whichever your last destination is – and then we can take off into the Alps for a bit of skiing or something. Would you like that? You'll need a break by then, I reckon.'

Riva thought about the prospect of a holiday with Ben; she had always adored travelling with him as he was great company – funny and energetic, dragging her away from her books and laptop into having all kinds of fun, and excellent with the pre-holiday research and organisation. They hadn't been away together for a while and Riva thought of how, normally, she would have jumped at the offer. But, of course, that was before Cannes and before Aman. And her suggestion that *they* meet in Europe during her book tour . . . dear God, what a total mess!

'You need to call your mum too,' Ben reminded. 'She phoned a couple of times yesterday, worrying about you. Seemed convinced you wouldn't be eating properly, even though I did try telling her that you'd be supping on the finest French dishes every night!'

Riva tried to cover her embarrassment by joking. 'It's rich for Ma to be worrying about *my* diet! Perhaps I'll go across and see her this afternoon. Do you want to come?'

'Sure,' Ben said. 'Seeing Dad was a stark reminder of how the old folks are all getting on a bit.'

'Why? He's okay, isn't he?' Riva asked, concerned.

'I guess. Just becoming a tad absent-minded, I noticed. There wasn't a drop of milk in the fridge when I got to Denby, for instance. And I found a bag of carrots all sprouting and soggy at the bottom of his veg tray. That's not like him at all, as you know.'

'Maybe we should bring him down here for a break. He may enjoy being fed and fattened up for a change,' Riva said.

'Not that London's his favourite place. But he'll definitely want to be here for your book launch,' Ben replied. 'He's already booked our guest room for that!'

Riva returned to the hall to call her mother and tell her they were coming.

'Hello, *beti*!' her mother's voice said, sounding a great deal more cheerful than she had before Riva's departure. 'Back safe and sound, thank God! Ben told me you were arriving in the morning but he did not say what time. When are you coming here? Have lunch with me. I have made *saag-aloo* and *moong dal*. Your favourites.' She said all this in one breath and Riva couldn't help smiling.

'Sounds lovely, Ma,' she replied. 'Only you could have known how much I'd missed *moong dal* in France! We'll arrive by one. Just need to unpack a bit.'

'Ben is also coming for lunch?' Ma asked, sounding pleased as punch.

Sticking her head into the kitchen a few minutes later, Riva said, 'I've said we'll have a spot of lunch with her, Ben. Hope that's okay? Sounds like she's been up since crack of dawn, cooking all your favourite stuff and mine!'

Ben, washing up at the sink, turned and nodded. 'She did say something about making *gulab jamun*s to welcome you home when she called yesterday. I'm not complaining!'

'Oh no, that must mean she's eaten at least six already; those things are sugar sponges and she loves them! Shall we leave in an hour? I'll go do a spot of unpacking and grab a shower.'

Riva went upstairs to the bedroom, noting how tidy everything was. Ben had obviously made a huge home-coming effort for her, and she suddenly felt touched to the point of tears. Without needing to be told, he had even lifted her suitcase onto the bed so that she wouldn't have to do it. Riva clicked open the latches and lifted the plastic lid. Her silver lamé cocktail dress, worn to the Palais des Festivals party on her last night in Cannes, lay right on top. She picked it up and held it to her face. Surely traces of Aman's cologne would still be lingering on it. She inhaled deeply, knowing that even the tiniest whiff of musk would bring back his presence and the last night they had spent together. But there was nothing at all and, for one strange moment, Riva felt as if Cannes and Aman had been no more than a dream.

Chapter Thirty-Seven

Aman's phone lay beside him on the leather car seat. It had been ringing incessantly since he'd landed in Bombay an hour ago: calls from producers, directors and financiers, all of whom Pillai had kept at bay during his visit to Cannes. Aman knew he ought to be grateful for the constant demands on his time; it was what every aspiring actor in this ambitious, thrusting city dreamt of and so few got. But, stupidly, irrationally, there was only one person he really wanted to hear from – Riva – and she had not called yet.

Aman had thought of her endlessly on the flight back from Nice, reliving every conversation, every moment of their time together in Cannes. Three hours into his own flight, Riva would have reached London. He worried about the state she was in and how she would cope. Without a doubt, the aftermath of what had happened in Cannes would be more difficult for her to deal with than for him. Riva was a principled person and – despite the occasional prodding – she had not once succumbed to criticising Ben in his presence. Aman calculated that Riva and Ben had been together for over fifteen years now. That must count for a lot. It wasn't at all like his loveless marriage to Salma. Besides, Riva had always been the loyal sort from what he could tell.

Nevertheless, the tenderness and passion Riva had shown him in Cannes had not been make-believe; she was incapable of such pretence. Why, she had even, on that last morning together, told him that she loved him. She would never lie about something like that. Surely there was some chance that the love Riva had for him would, somewhere along the way, outgrow the feelings she still carried for Ben? Aman was willing to wait for that; without that shred of hope, the future would have felt bleak indeed.

The car pulled into the drive of his Juhu home and Aman turned his phone on to silent mode, slipping it into his shirt pocket as Fareed held the door open for him. Aman sprinted up the wide marble stairs, nearly bumping into Hameeda at the front door who was dusting its intricately carved surface with a small feather-duster. Aman was always faintly uneasy in Hameeda's presence – in his more suspicious moments he saw her as Salma's chief mole, something like the spies that kings and queens of yore employed to keep them aware of all intrigues in their kitchens and courts. Aman asked her in Hindi where Salma was.

Hameeda's reply was brief. 'Pali Hill,' she said, her words barely discernible through a mouthful of freshly inserted *paan* leaf.

Aman sighed. He had no objection to Salma being at her parents' house but it meant that he would most likely get a summons to go there later at night. 'And Ashfaq?' he enquired.

'Pali Hill,' Hameeda said again, in a tone of extreme forbearance, making Aman want to throttle her.

He ought to be grateful to have the house to himself, Aman thought as he walked upstairs. No one around to distract him when he wanted a bit of peace and quiet to mull over the events of the past week. But he felt oddly sad and angry to find that only the servants were around to welcome him home. After all, he had texted Salma from Nice airport with the details of his flight. Aman had never expected his wife to be a doormat but it was curious that, as his star status grew, Salma's behaviour had become more deliberately dismissive of him. Perhaps she worried that fussing around him would make him self-important. Or was it plain stupid of him to look for excuses to explain Salma's selfishness?

Aman felt a sudden quiver of anticipation go through him as he felt his phone buzz with a text. Nearly tripping on the last step, he whipped his mobile out. But when he clicked it open, he found just an automated message from India-Tel offering him ringtones from his own film songs. He jabbed the delete button furiously and went into his bedroom. Fareed would bring his suitcases upstairs and someone would unpack them at some point. He wondered at the likelihood of their finding some incriminating evidence among his things, an item of Riva's clothing, perhaps – after all, they had virtually lived in each other's rooms in their last two days at the Carlton. If Salma suspected him of cheating, there would surely be hell to pay. But there was a part of Aman that was past caring. What was the worst that could happen, he asked as he threw himself down on the bed. Salma leaving for her parents' house? Well, she was there all the time anyway! He barely got to see his son even under normal circum-stances. Watching the vents of the air-conditioning system move gently up and down, Aman considered how Salma would surely use Ashfaq to punish him if he left her. But he could always line up a team of Bombay's best lawyers to prevent that . . .

Sitting up, he took a few deep breaths to calm himself. Then he picked up his mobile phone again and scrolled to its picture gallery. Riva had allowed him to keep just one photograph of her and he looked at it now. She was on the promenade at Cannes and had taken off her shades at his request. Smiling over her shoulder at him, he could see her long black hair whipping in the morning breeze as she looked into the camera from under her lashes. It was a lovely shot, full of sunshine and movement, and, the longer Aman stared at it, the more it seemed to come to life. It was almost as if the Riva looking at him so intently would suddenly break into a laugh or speak to him if he stared for long enough. But she didn't, of course, and the stubbornly unmoving stillness of that image made him want to hurl his phone across the room. After a few minutes' hesitation, Aman started to punch a message on its keypad.

Riva felt her phone make a buzzing motion against her thigh. She and Ben were still seated at her mother's dining table, though lunch had long segued into tea. Ma was offering them the leftover *gulab jamun*s to take home and Ben – taking Riva's signal that the sweets were better kept in their fridge than her mum's – said he would look for a box to transport them in. Riva pulled her phone out of her pocket to check her message, her heart stopping when she saw an Indian number. She hastily shoved it back into her pocket again. It could only be Aman, she thought, a sudden wave of panic washing all over her. Her legs went weak under her as she carried the sticky pudding bowls into the kitchen.

'Use one of those *dabbas*, Ben,' Ma was saying, pointing to a stack of Tupperware containers.

'I was thinking of using an ice-cream box, or something that you're discarding anyway,' Ben replied, rooting around among the shelves in the pantry.

Riva decided that both would be too busy to notice her sudden absence. 'Back in two ticks,' she said before going swiftly upstairs to her mother's bathroom. She slid the bolt carefully shut and clicked open the message on her phone. It was, as she had guessed, from Aman.

I miss you, Riva. Plz let me know u r thinking of me. I hv 2 c u again soon. Can I come to London?

Riva sat down on the toilet seat and held the phone to the side of her hot face as she covered her eyes. Tears pushed at the inside of her lids but she kept them tightly shut and swallowed the sadness back as hard as she could, feeling sick. While she had spent her time on the flight hoping Ben would have left her, she had spent the rest of the day hoping Aman would have forgotten her by the time he had returned to his life in Mumbai. What was wrong with her? She had never behaved like such a teenager in her life. Not even when she had been a teenager!

Riva started to compose a reply, her fingers trembling on the keypad. *Aman, pls don't do this. It's tearing me apart. I will tell you my Europe plans when I know. I promise.* She hit the send button and imagined her desperate message flying across the miles to Mumbai. It must be quite late in India by now . . . half past nine . . . what was Aman doing texting her when he should be with his wife and child? She reread her sent message, trying to see how Aman would receive it. Was it too reproachful? Would it offer him hope she was not in a position to give? On the other hand, perhaps it mattered not a whit because Aman had already made up his mind to come . . .

Riva, who worked with words and sentences, knew the

power they could carry, but here, in this sorry little exchange of text messages, they felt like the most ineffective little things. She read her words once again, trying to commit them to memory. Then she deleted both Aman's and her own messages and pulled the flush before leaving the bathroom.

Downstairs, her mother was still buzzing around Ben, helping him pack food and *rotis* into a variety of ice-cream cartons and plastic containers.

'Goodness, that'll last us three days at least!' Riva said, returning to the chaos of the kitchen. But her mother barely noticed her. Ben's presence in her house had made Ma unusually gleeful tonight and getting him to carry away half the contents of her fridge was making her half-hysterical with happiness.

Riva felt another text message buzz silently on her phone. It was probably Aman again but she could not possibly duck into the bathroom once more without having Ma worry she had upset her stomach. Ben was nearly ready to leave anyway, now fetching their jackets and fishing out the car keys from his pocket.

They drove the three miles home, listening to Radio 4 on the way. Riva's mind was behaving like a darting swallow; all she could think, as her husband drove her home, was that the phone in the pocket of her jeans contained the direction her future could take.

Back at their house in Kingston, Riva and Ben set about putting away all the food they had brought from her mother's into the fridge, then Ben turned on the MP3 player in the lounge and the sound of jazz music filled the house. It was an unusually warm night for May and Ben suggested that Riva choose a bottle of wine to take out into the garden. She selected a Syrah from the rack and Ben opened it while she fetched a pair of goblets from the glass cupboard. They carried their glasses out and settled on the wrought-iron garden furniture they had impulsively bought together on a trip one summer to the Cotswolds. Birds were coming in to roost on the laburnum that stood at the bottom of their garden and, as the evening slowly drew in, Riva wondered how any power on earth – even the phone in her pocket – could possibly ruin this peaceful picture.

Chapter Thirty-Eight

Susan dialled Riva's number, hoping she wasn't intruding on anything private. Susan had been meaning to call her friend earlier in the day but Joe had managed to get tickets to the theatre and they had only just emerged onto the South Bank. A pleasant breeze was blowing across the Thames as they walked back to where they had parked their car. Susan released her hand from Joe's as the ringing stopped and Riva's voice floated into her ear.

'Oh hello, Riva, it's not too late to speak, is it?' she said, placing her other hand around her ear to block out the sound of the pavement revellers gathered outside one of the restaurants.

'Sooz, darling! No, not late at all. So lovely to hear from you!' came Riva's cheerful reply.

'Not cutting in on anything, am I?' Susan asked.

'Not at all. Ben and I are out in the garden, drinking wine and nibbling at some rather nice Manchego cheese . . . care to join us?'

'Ooo, jammy. But we wouldn't dream of it, not on your first night back!'

'You can be gooseberry any time, you know that,' Riva laughed. 'Where are you, anyway?'

'Somewhere near Waterloo Bridge. South Bank

315

Centre. But never mind that,' Susan said impatiently, 'how *was* it?'

'How was what?'

'Cannes, you goose! What else? *Nothing* more moment-ous has happened to any of us in years!'

'Oh, it was good. I'll tell you all about it when we meet,' Riva said rather vaguely.

'Of course you'll tell us all about it! Goodness, sounds like I'm gonna have to sit you down and worm it all out of you. I want every single detail about everyone you met and what they wore and what you said and ate and did,' Susan said. There was a pause before she asked, 'Did you meet Aman?'

'Course I did,' Riva said briefly.

'And?'

'And what?'

'Oh, for God's sake, Riva, did he remember you? What's he like now? You *know*! Cripes, you're not going all discreet and secretive on us when it comes to your VIP friends, are you?'

Riva laughed again in response. 'Let's meet up one of these days, Sooz. It's too late now and I'm knackered and festivalled-out now.'

'Say when,' Susan demanded.

'Er . . . next weekend?' Riva asked.

'Not waiting till then, sunshine – you'll have forgotten half of it by then. I can meet you midweek, one day after school, if you like?'

'Okay, I'll give you a call,' Riva said, laughing at Susan's persistence.

After they had hung up, Susan dropped her phone into her jacket pocket and slipped her hand back into Joe's. She leant her head on his arm as they strolled up the stairs leading to Waterloo Bridge. In the distance, the lights of Hungerford footbridge were reflecting and shimmering in the river below, looking like hundreds of fallen stars. On Susan's left was tourist London – the giant Ferris wheel of the London Eye and the glowing friendly face of Big Ben that always reminded her of nursery rhymes. To her right, lay the businessman's city with its vaulting skyscrapers and glittering lights overlooked by the serene moonlit presence of St Paul's. Everything looked peaceful and orderly, as it was meant to be. With her hand safely tucked into her husband's, and the knowledge that her best friend was sitting happily in her garden with her own husband, Susan felt as if the world had finally righted itself again. For a while everything had teetered and seemed ready to collapse but perhaps they had all just been through an unfortunate patch. Now, crossing her fingers inside her jacket pocket as Joe unlocked the car, Susan looked fervently at St Paul's cathedral – tonight seemed as good a time as any to ask God to desist from wandering off again.

Back in the garden at Kingston, the night was getting cold, a light dew starting to settle on the grass under their chairs. Ben had brought a couple of Riva's shawls out when the second bottle of wine had been opened and they were both wrapped up from head to toe. Riva was sitting curled up on her chair, her feet stretched out and tucked under Ben's thighs.

'Don't you want to turn in?' Ben asked, feeling Riva's toes with his hand. 'Your feet are frozen.'

'My feet are always frozen,' she responded. 'It's heavenly out, isn't it? How many such nights can one hope to get in a year?'

Ben looked up at the inky sky dotted with stars. 'Too right. This week could be both the start and the end of the summer. Remember what a washout last year was?'

'I don't think we sat out here once.'

'Still, time for beddy-byes, I think,' Ben said, getting up and arranging the debris from their snacking into a neat pile. 'I'm surprised you're not more tired than you seem, Riv, given you were on a flight this morning.'

She stretched her arms above her head. 'Something to do with being home, I guess. I feel quite agog!'

'C'mon, upsy-daisy,' Ben said, standing behind Riva and slipping his hands under her armpits to haul her up. She finally put her feet into her clogs and stood up, tottering slightly.

'Didn't realise how strong that Syrah was,' she said, clutching her head.

'Are you all right?' Ben asked, concerned.

Riva nodded but he saw that she was picking her way carefully indoors, stepping over the doorstep quite deliberately before going in.

'Never mind me,' Ben laughed. 'I'll just clear away after you and wash up and bring you hot chocolate and a hot-water bottle. Anything else before milady turns in?'

But there was no response from inside the house and Ben guessed that Riva had gone upstairs. Whistling under his breath, he picked up the bowls and glasses and took them into the kitchen, leaving the washing up for the morning. All he wanted to do right now was to follow Riva upstairs, get into bed and make passionate love to her. It had been too long and Ben had thought many times about this moment for the past couple of days.

The stairwell lights were all on and so Ben clicked them

off one by one on his way upstairs to their room. He smiled wryly as he looked across at the bed. All that was visible under the duvet was the top of Riva's head, but the soft gentle breathing told him that she was fast asleep.

Chapter Thirty-Nine

Riva blinked at the bright sunshine as she woke, imagining for one moment that she was back in her room at the Carlton – before she saw the framed caricature of her and Ben on the opposite wall. The artiste had hammed up her over-wide smile as well as Ben's toothy grin to make them look like the cheesiest, happiest couple in the world. It was this that had amused them enough to get the picture framed a couple of weeks later in an exaggerated shiny red fibreglass surround. Deliberately placed so that it was the first thing they saw as they woke up every morning, today the two smiling faces made Riva want to turn her face into her pillow and have a good sob.

She wondered where Ben was as she tentatively raised herself on her elbows and looked around their bedroom. There was no sign of him – only a vase of lilies on her chest of drawers and her suitcase from Cannes, now stashed more neatly against a wall, still waiting to be unpacked. On her bedside table was a mug of coffee, long grown cold, and next to it was a note. *Gone for a run. Didn't have the heart to wake you from your slumber. Will bring fresh croissants from Luigi's on way back so DON'T eat! x B*

Riva flung her head back on the pillows and felt a

moment's relief at knowing she was alone in the house. She pulled out her phone from the depths of her bedside table – even in her half-drunken state last night, she had remembered to store it carefully out of Ben's sight before getting into bed, leaving it in silent mode. Riva checked the phone and found no new text messages, but the one Aman had sent last night was still there. So much for being hyper-careful; a message like this would be incriminating at a glance, even to a stranger. *Can't w8 till w meet in Eur. Coming to Lnd next week. Staying Claridges. Will call.*

Riva lay back on her pillows, thinking again about what she had done and the juggernaut of events that had been set uncontrollably in motion. Was it unfair to blame her adultery on Ben's behaviour before she went to Cannes? It would certainly be the easier way to deal with it, but Riva knew how perilously close she would have been to embarking on the affair anyway, even if she had been happy with Ben. Aman was such a handsome man and Riva could not very well pretend she had not remained terribly nostalgic about their teenage love for all these years. And Aman had shown he was still kind and sweet and funny and – incredibly – still madly in love with her. What superhuman self-control would have been needed to turn all that away? And, if Riva had turned him down for the second time, would she not live to regret it every single day that followed?

Riva heard the bang of the front door as Ben returned from his run, and hastily deleted Aman's text message before getting out of bed to go to the bathroom. While she was brushing her teeth at the basin, Ben came upstairs, his T-shirt dripping with sweat, approaching her with arms open wide, pretending to want a hug. Riva played her part, squealing and ducking away, her mouth full of toothpaste.

Ben said dolefully as he started to strip off his clothes and got into the shower, 'What is it with twenty-first-century women that a man can't embrace his own wife, huh?'

Riva went downstairs, tying her hair into a loose knot on the nape of her neck. A bag of bakery-fresh croissants was sitting on the kitchen table. She arranged them on a baking sheet and turned on the oven while she made a fresh pot of coffee. After she had poured the boiling water from kettle into cafetiere, Ben came in and this time she did not object when she felt his arms wind around her. Droplets of water were still shining on his arms and chest as he turned her around to kiss her. Riva could taste toothpaste in his mouth. He was all minty and soapy and wholesome. This was the man Riva had loved from what now felt like Year Dot. From a time of innocence, when life ahead seemed filled with uncomplicated pleasures and the only thing of importance was that they should be together.

Riva felt near grief as Ben slipped off her nightshirt and kissed her neck and shoulders and whispered that he wanted her back in bed so they could make love.

'It's been too long, Riv,' Ben muttered into her hair sprung free from its knot. 'I'm so sorry to have been such a wanker these past few months.'

'You're not . . . don't be . . .' she whispered, trying to make herself less guilty by postponing the inevitable. 'The croissants will burn . . . the coffee's getting bitter . . .'

But Ben clicked the oven off behind Riva and led her by the hand into the lounge where they made love among the cushions on the carpet.

Two hours later, Susan saw Riva's name flash up on her phone and quickly left the staff room so as not to disturb the other teachers.

'Heyyy,' Susan said, stopping when she heard the sniffle. 'Riva?'

'Sooz . . .' Riva's voice emerged, distraught and tearful. 'I've gotta talk to you . . .'

'Riva, what's up?' Susan asked. Hearing only a few sniffles in response, she asked suspiciously, 'It's not Ben being a bastard again, is it?'

'God, no, it's not Ben. I can't blame him this time, Sooz. Oh God, what have I done?'

'What *have* you done, sweetie?' Susan asked, starting to feel panicky at how bleak Riva sounded.

'I can't talk about it now . . . can we meet, please?' Riva asked.

'Sure, honey. Just say when.'

'Now? I mean, after school, of course . . .'

Susan glanced at her watch. 'Yes, of course. Can you come here? The usual place – Casa Madeira? Four-ish.'

'Okay, ta. See you then,' Riva said, still sounding desolate as she hung up.

At the end of the school day, Susan piled her papers together and put them away on her desk Then she walked towards the school gates, telling the school porter that she would be back later to collect her car. She walked down the leafy road in the direction of the Madeira on the high street. There were cafés nearer the school but these were frequented by its students and teachers and Susan preferred the privacy of the Madeira. She suddenly remembered that tearful meeting with Riva when she had told her about Joe's suspected affair. That was well and truly over now, Susan knew that for sure – and it wasn't just her heart telling her, but her head too. Joe was thankfully back to being his old self, kindly and absent-minded, leaving his silly old phone lying around in the most un-expected places. Susan thought about the rational advice Riva had given her at the time. It had seemed so unlike the kind of thing Riva would come up with – to refrain from accosting a partner who was quite likely to be cheating! But Susan now knew that, when such a deep love as hers and Joe's was at stake, a little leeway was not a sign of weakness but of humanity and affection.

Susan quickened her footsteps when she saw Riva's car parked down a side street near the Madeira. She was early. What on earth had transpired to cause this sudden SOS from Riva, Susan wondered – when they had spoken on Sunday, Riva had not sounded in any tearing hurry to meet. Something had obviously happened since then. Riva clearly stated it wasn't anything Ben had done. And Riva was far, far too sensible herself to do something stupid.

Susan hurried into the café and looked around to see Riva sitting at a table right at the back. She looked terrible, her face all blotchy, her hair uncombed and pulled roughly back into a ponytail.

'Oh, heavens, what is it, darling?' Susan asked as Riva took one look at her and started to weep. She clutched her friend when she neared, sank her face into her shoulder and sobbed her heart out for a few minutes. Alarmed, Susan held her tightly. Looking around, she saw that the woman who ran the café was wearing her usual resigned look as she carried two cups of coffee in their direction.

Riva finally released her grip and Susan sat down before her, still holding her hands.

'What is it, Riva, tell me!' she queried, trying to keep her voice calm despite feeling frantic. But Riva wept and hiccuped some more before finally calming herself enough to sip at her coffee. Then, taking a deep breath, she said, her voice wobbling, 'Sooz, you'll never forgive me for this . . .'

'Don't talk like an eejit, Riva,' Susan said, panic rising within her again. 'I'll forgive you anything, you know that.'

'Not this,' Riva said with certainty, wiping her nose with the paper serviette that had come with the coffee.

Susan gave her a few seconds before asking again, 'Please, what is it, Riva?'

'It's . . . I've . . .' Riva stopped and then started again, her voice small. 'It's . . .' Finally, she blurted, 'It's Aman.'

'Aman? What about Aman?' Susan was still completely baffled.

Riva was silent for a couple of seconds before she whispered, 'Aman and I . . .' She trailed off again, a fresh tear starting to slide down her face.

'Aman and you . . .' Susan echoed dully as the import of what Riva was trying to say slowly started to dawn on her. She stared at Riva in disbelief, feeling her insides churn. Of course, the pair of them had joked about Aman often enough and Susan had openly confessed to envying the affair Riva had had with Aman back at uni, especially since she herself had 'zero flings to her credit', as she often put it. But what Riva was saying to her now was not the same thing. Riva was now married, and so was Aman. What Riva was talking about was what Joe had done, it was what – less than three months ago – Riva and she had agreed was the most terrible thing to put a partner through. Was Riva really confessing to adultery? An affair with Aman was so thoughtless, so *meaningless*, when measured against the years and years that Ben and Riva had been together!

For Susan, who had just about come to terms with the idea of her husband's possible infidelity, it was just too much to bear that Riva, her best friend whom she admired so enormously, should go and do the same awful thing. She got up from her chair so abruptly it banged hard into the table behind. Overcome by waves of nausea, she ran outside for some fresh air.

Chapter Forty

Aman looked out of his cab at London's wet streets. It was bizarre to be travelling by himself in an ordinary black cab, rather than in his customary cavalcade of limousines. But Aman had not informed any of his staff of this particular trip; the last thing he wanted was to be ferried around with a whole posse of supporters. Aman recognised the pillared front of Selfridges as the cab turned off Oxford Street and headed for Claridge's. He had only a small overnighter with him as he had asked for his clothes to be sent straight up to Paris along with the film crew who would be travelling there at the start of the week. Wangling this one day in London had been easier than he imagined. He had told Ritesh Shah that he had personal business to attend to and anyone who tried contacting him on his mobile would not know that he was in London, rather than Paris.

Aman had already sent Riva a text, telling her that he had arrived at Heathrow, but she hadn't replied yet. He paid the cab driver and walked into the Mayfair hotel that he had carefully chosen and booked on the internet. Aman had not had to make his own bookings for tickets and rooms ever since he had become successful and he had been pleased that he'd eventually managed to make all the necessary arrangements without any help. He usually stayed at the Mandarin Oriental whenever he was in London but too many people knew him there. Aman hoped it was safe to assume that no one would recognise him here at Claridge's. He looked briefly around the lobby as he was checked into the Brook Penthouse. No one was looking at him and the receptionist, though polite to a fault, seemed disinterested in all but the check-in details. Aman knew that he was often mistaken for a rich sheikh whenever he was among people who did not recognise him – and rich sheikhs were probably a dime a dozen in places like this.

Turning down the services of a bellboy, Aman wheeled his overnighter into the lift and then into his room. He closed the door, wondering if he ought to text Riva again or call her. And then his phone rang. His heart thudded as he saw her number flashing up on his screen.

'Riva?' he asked urgently as he answered the call.

'Hello, Aman,' she said softly and Aman sat down on the edge of the bed, deeply relieved to finally hear her voice. He had kept his word and they had not spoken once since their last morning in Cannes. There had only been those couple of texts but his resolve had held out a mere week before he had set about planning this trip, knowing by then that he could not bear the thought of waiting until Riva's book tour the following month.

'Riva, where are you?' Aman asked, hearing what sounded like a thousand people milling about in the background.

'Selfridges,' Riva replied, 'round the corner from you.'

'Come here, for God's sake. What are you doing there?' he asked, both amused and exasperated.

'I got on the tube when your message came and didn't want to come to the hotel.'

'Well, I'm here now, so you can safely come.'

'No, that's what I meant . . . I didn't want to come to the hotel,' Riva repeated in a small voice.

'Why not? I'm here now, my darling . . .'

'You don't understand, Aman . . .' Riva said tearfully before trailing off.

Aman stood up, beginning to understand what Riva was saying. 'Riva, please,' he said, 'I've got to see you, talk to you . . . please come to me.'

She paused for a minute before speaking, 'I know it sounds silly after all that happened in Cannes but . . . I can't, Aman . . . it feels wrong . . .'

'Well, I can't very well come to bloody Selfridges, can I?' Aman exploded. There was a strange pulsing sound in his ears. Then he calmed himself, closing his eyes; there was nothing to be gained by frightening her off. 'Riva, listen,' he said more calmly. 'I need to talk to you. Please come to Claridge's. It's quite safe here and no one will recognise us. I'm in the Brook Suite on the top floor. I'll see you in ten minutes, yes? I'm waiting for you . . .' Then he hung up before she argued any more. Riva would come, he was sure of that.

Nevertheless, Aman paced around restlessly in the suite, walking from one window to the next, stopping every so often to look out in frustration at the bright blue English sky. He felt trapped, like a caged animal. Opening a door that led to a terrace, Aman stepped out into the sunshine and looked down at Mayfair's crowded streets, not feeling very much better for it. While all of life unfolded colour-fully and gloriously on those streets below, here he was trapped in this penthouse suite, unable even to go to the woman he loved. What he would have done to be another faceless, anonymous man in the crowd, able to take his girl for a coffee and a wander down Oxford Street. And people were envious of film stars!

A knock on the door had Aman bolting back into the room. He ran through the living room and hurriedly opened the heavy wooden door. It was Riva. To his utter and complete relief, there she was, wearing jeans and a fitted black T-shirt, a woebegone expression on her face. Aman opened his arms and she walked into them, starting to weep.

'Shh . . . shh,' Aman said softly, rocking Riva in his arms and breathing in the leafy smell of her shampoo as he sank his face into her hair. After her sobs had quietened slightly, Aman kicked the door shut behind her and led her into the living room. 'Do you want something to drink?' he asked, gently propelling her by her shoulders onto the sofa.

'A glass of water please,' she said.

Aman fetched a bottle from the minibar and placed two glasses on the table before them as he sat down next to Riva. He filled one and gave it to her before pouring another out for himself. Watching her drink all of it in one long swallow, Aman observed how tired she looked. In Cannes, she had virtually glowed with vitality but, here, she looked listless, with shadows under her eyes that indicated she had not been sleeping well. He hoped that Ben wasn't treating her badly. On the other hand, if Ben *was* treating her badly, perhaps she would be more easily persuaded to leave him . . . Aman thought it best not to voice such thoughts aloud, silently pouring out another glass for her and waiting for her to gather herself together. Riva did not drink the second glass, however, leaving it on the table while she wound her arms around her chest in a miserable huddle.

'Riva, what's wrong?' Aman asked gently. 'You look terrible.'

There was a shadow of a smile at that as she looked at him and replied, 'I thought you were practiced at making a girl feel like a million dollars.'

Aman took Riva's hand and kissed it before playing gently with her fingers.

'Are things okay with Ben?' Aman asked, feeling strangely fearful about what she would say in reply.

'Never better,' she responded, but Aman noticed that her words were accompanied by a humourless laugh.

'You're joking, right?' he asked hopefully.

But Riva shook her head and looked directly at him. 'No, Aman, that wasn't sarcastic or ironically stated at all, I'm afraid. Ben really has transformed himself while I've been with you in Cannes.' She took a deep breath. 'He'd gone to stay with his father and did a bit of thinking there. He's been just lovely ever since I got back . . . and it's tearing me to shreds. As though . . . as though I've been robbed of all the rationale I had to be with you. If Ben's good to me then my being with you suddenly becomes so selfish . . . so low . . . you know?' She looked up at him, tearful and pleading.

Aman silently absorbed this information but, after a few seconds, he asked, 'How do you know it will last? This good behaviour from Ben may just be temporary, to keep hanging onto you. How do you know he won't soon revert to his old ways again?'

Riva shook her head. 'I don't get the impression it's a passing thing, Aman. You see, he's back to being his old self now. What I had from him in the run-up to Cannes was the aberration . . . maybe it was *because* of Cannes, who knows . . .'

'So that means you're back to being in love with him,' Aman said abruptly, his voice bitter. Riva shot him a look and Aman knew how piteous he must have sounded. Nevertheless, he looked stubbornly back at Riva, willing her to change her mind and revert to the way they were in Cannes – so much in love that the consequences did not matter. But Riva held his gaze for a few moments before dropping her eyes and extricating her hands gently out of his grip.

'It's not like that at all and you know it, Aman.'

Her gesture and the flatness of her tone infuriated Aman.

'What is it like then, Riva?' he snapped. 'Enlighten me. You're the clever one who knows everything, aren't you? Just like before. I'm the stupid boy from India while you . . . you and your Ben are so sure of yourselves!'

'I think I should go, Aman,' Riva said softly, picking up her bag and getting up from the sofa. 'I've said what I had to.'

Aman knew he had to think of something, anything to stop Riva walking out of the door. He had not come all the way to London, taking so many risks, just to have her walk out on him. Besides, he was Aman Khan. Nobody walked out on him any more. He knew his thoughts were incredibly arrogant but he couldn't stop himself now. 'Well, you've said what you had to say to *me* all right, Riva. But what about Ben? Have you told him what you have to say to him?'

Riva looked confused. 'What do you mean?'

Aman was now almost shouting. 'Have you told your husband about us, Riva? Isn't that something you should do? You, who claims to be so *decent.*'

Riva stopped and stared down at Aman, her dark eyes suddenly inscrutable.

'No, I haven't, Aman. But perhaps you plan to do it for me,' she replied in an even voice.

Aman leant back on the sofa, crossing his arms over his chest as he felt them trembling slightly. 'Shall I? Shall I tell him?' he challenged. 'I have your home number too, don't forget,' he added.

Riva stood a few feet away from him, looking very pale and vulnerable next to a flamboyant arrangement of vivid yellow roses. After a long silence, she spoke.

'I can't stop you from doing whatever you want, Aman. Do what you think is best.' Her voice was cold but Aman could detect the fear in it.

Now he could not prevent the angry words that came pouring out of him, unbidden and unplanned, as if he had to lash out at Riva because of the pain she was causing him. He took a deep breath.

'Because if Ben does find out about us, Riva, he *will* leave you,' Aman said, his voice sounding loud and harsh even to his own ears. 'You know he will. And *then* you'll come to me. Won't you? Asking to be taken back. But what if by then it's too late for us, huh? What if by then I don't love you any more . . . because you only seem to want me when it's convenient for you . . .'

But this time Riva did not reply, not even waiting for Aman to finish his sentence before turning to flee the hotel suite without another word.

Riva tumbled out of Claridge's into the sunshine and pelted down Brook Street without pausing to see where she was going. Nearly getting mown down by a street-cleaning council vehicle on New Bond Street, Riva continued to run until she reached Hanover Square. There she finally stopped and flung herself down on a park

335

bench, heaving for breath. Bending over, Riva held her head between her hands and waited for the nausea to pass.

Thoughts returned gradually as her breathing steadied again. She deserved all this censure, Riva thought tearfully: yesterday Susan, today Aman. Riva felt sure she would slowly lose everyone and everything. And she deserved it too. Aman was right, Ben would certainly leave her if he knew what she had done in Cannes. He wasn't like Susan, able to take a magnanimous view of a partner's infidelity because of all that had gone before. Ben expected total and complete dedication from a relationship. Why, even her writing career seemed to sometimes represent a threat to him and he had barely been able to ask a few questions about Cannes before closing the subject!

Riva looked around the square, teeming with jolly tourists and shoppers, feeling like the only person in London whom life was buffeting about so inconsiderately. She was still reeling from Aman's sudden turn. It had shocked her to see him swing from tender to spiteful in a matter of seconds. Had he really meant his threat to call Ben? Or was it merely his anguish making him sound so bitter? Surely he would do nothing to deliberately hurt her . . . but Riva could not be too sure. At this moment she was not sure of anything. Everything felt tenuous and temporary, treacherous even.

Riva reached for her handbag lying below the bench to search for a tissue and jumped as her phone started to ring. She wondered frantically if she should answer it if it was Aman. But it wasn't him at all . . .

'Gideon,' she said as she clicked the green button.

'Darling, marvellous news, I have your tickets!' her agent said in a bright voice.

'Oh, I thought Selina said she was biking them over to me?'

'Did she? Inept editors – *gaah!*' Gideon said, using one of his standard catch phrases. 'Well, the itinerary and tickets are here now. What do you want me to do? I can have them couriered . . .'

'Okay,' Riva said before she had a sudden thought. Anything was better than going home and facing Ben – who, dear God, may be having a revelatory conversation with Aman at this very moment! 'Oh, actually, Gideon . . . are you in for a bit? Or will someone be there in the office in the next hour or so? I could collect the tickets. I'm not far, as it happens, near Oxford Street at the moment . . .'

'Sure, darling, come right over. And have a swift half with us down at the Nellie Dean on this lovely sunny afternoon. It's just Penny and me today. We could do with a spot of amusing and authorly diversion.'

'Oh, I can do diversion with no trouble, but I can't promise to be amusing,' Riva said, mustering up a laugh.

'Darling, you are not just amusing but downright hilarious. Come right down!' Gideon ordered.

'Okay, I'll see you in about ten minutes.' Riva gathered up her bag and made her way out of the square, feeling slightly better. At least she still had a writing career and an agent who liked her, even if her love life was in a total shambles.

Gideon's office was a minuscule space in the heart of Covent Garden, crammed with books and manuscripts. The main room – once an Elizabethan printing press – hung precariously over a pub, its ancient bow window sticking right out into the street. Riva climbed up the single flight of stairs, hoping the redness of her nose from that small weeping fit in Aman's room would have subsided

337

by now. She received a gratifyingly raucous greeting from her literary agent and his assistant. Everyone at Gideon's agency adored her for having brought them their first literary gong with her Orange win two years ago and it always uplifted her tremendously to be in this ancient book-lined space that had launched her literary career.

'Look who's here, it's our star writer!' Penny said in her usual effervescent manner, kissing her warmly on both cheeks, while Gideon nipped out from behind his desk to give her a hug.

'Ahh, love and appreciation, bring it on,' Riva said, hugging both Penny and Gideon before sinking into a sofa.

'Why do you say that, aren't they looking after you at Fifth House?' Gideon demanded, putting on his angry ferret expression that reputedly regularly sent publishers running for cover.

'Well, Fifth House wouldn't shower you with these if they didn't adore you,' Penny said, waving a large manila envelope in the air.

'Ah, lovely, my tickets!' Riva said, trying to look enthused. She took the envelope from Penny and slid the sheets of paper out: a set of e-tickets and a detailed itinerary.

Penny peered over her shoulder, reading. 'Paris, Barcelona, Amsterdam, Frankfurt, Rome, Venice . . . looks like they've dropped Lisbon. Any idea why, Gid?'

'Hmm, must be an oversight. I'm sure Gradiva wanted you to visit. I'll get onto it. But they've added Venice, I notice.'

Penny squealed with excitement. 'That's an unusual venue for a book talk, how very thrilling! Have you ever been, Riva?'

Riva nodded, trying unsuccessfully to absorb some of

Penny's enthusiasm. 'I've been backpacking to Venice once, in my gap year, but yonks ago obviously. Is it an unusual place for book events?'

'Well, the British Council were looking for a young author to include in the Biennale and I jumped at the chance. Don't worry, darling, you won't have to do anything at all,' Gideon said breezily. 'Just turn up looking pretty and watch those Italian men elbow each other out of the way to get to you. Can't think of an easier way to sell books.'

Riva laughed good-naturedly and looked again at the tickets, growing sober as she remembered Aman telling her about his own plans to shoot in Venice in the summer. She could not remember exactly when he said he would be there but it was something to do with a speedboat chase on the Grand Canal. While Penny and Gideon chattered on over her head, Riva sat on the sofa feeling faint. How strange a thing fate was, insistently sending her path ricocheting into Aman's. Perhaps this was her punishment for having played so carelessly with both Aman's and Ben's lives.

Chapter Forty-One

Susan put her book down, unable to pretend any more that she was concentrating. Rachmaninoff's Second Piano Concerto was swelling through the speakers and, as she looked around the cosy, lamplit living room of her Wimbledon home, Susan knew she ought to feel grateful for the perfect picture it made. Joe was sitting in a pool of light in his favourite armchair, reading *Private Eye* and chuckling occasionally while the dishwasher whirred gently in the kitchen. She and Joe had eaten their usual weekday dinner at the kitchen table, talking about their respective working days while both their phones had sat side by side on the kitchen counter, as though proudly making known that there were no secrets in this household any more.

But Susan knew it took little for the pain and her sense of betrayal to return. Every so often something would happen to remind her of it, such as Riva's revelation at the café that day. Susan had always prided herself on being nonjudgemental about most things, but she was still trying to process the shocking information of Riva's affair with Aman. She had tried to understand her reaction, rationalising that Riva had never been as conservative in her views about marriage as she herself was; not to mention that Susan knew better than anyone else that Ben had been a complete bastard to Riva recently, resenting her hard-earned and truly deserved success. So, given all that, should she feel so livid at finding out that Riva had had a fling with Aman in Cannes? For surely that's all it was – an impetuous and meaningless fling. Should she, as Riva's best friend and the person she had turned to in her desperation, have tried to understand and help, rather than rush to judge?

Susan looked at Joe as she heard him sniggering again at his magazine. Normally she would be asking him to tell her what the joke was. But tonight she looked at him sitting comfortably in his chair, having eaten a lovely dinner cooked by her, and felt a sudden inexplicable surge of anger towards him. The strength of it startled Susan at first, for her overwhelming feeling these past few days had been one of relief at seeing Joe coming out of whatever madness had recently possessed him. Susan had even convinced herself at one point that Joe's affair was *her* fault – after all, it was she who had put off having children so far in the interests of her career. Perhaps if Joe had been a father by now, as he had always wanted, it would have prevented him from straying into some other woman's arms . . .

Susan picked up her book again and frowned at it, struggling to concentrate. It was stupid and delusional to let Joe off the hook for what was essentially plain bad behaviour. How naïve she had been to assume forgiveness would come merely because she still loved her husband. And, stupidly, she had gunned for Riva because she was an easier target than Joe. Susan pressed her fingers against her temples, now deeply ashamed that she had let her best friend bear the brunt of her angst. After all, it was Riva who had helped her deal with her own recent marital problems, and this despite being put through the wringer herself by Ben. It was Susan's support and counsel Riva needed at a time like this, not her censure.

She got up to go in search of her phone. Joe looked up. 'Where are you going?' he asked.

'Just getting my phone,' she replied.

'Why? Who're you calling this time of night?'

'Hmm . . . no one particularly,' Susan replied vaguely, picking up her phone from the counter in the kitchen. She opened the door to the back garden as she needed privacy to speak to Riva, and apologise to her. Susan smiled, feeling a little evil as she thought about the fact that Joe would be puzzling over whom she was speaking to in the garden, in the dead of the night. She almost never played the mysterious-woman-with-secrets-of-her-own card with Joe. But, tonight, still feeling mildly resentful as she was, Susan thought it would do no harm to keep *him* guessing for a while. Why, she still did not even know who the woman on the phone was that night at the River Café, and now probably never would. It was one of those secrets that someone had once said all marriages were littered with, even the seemingly happy ones . . .

Susan saw Joe's frame appear at the kitchen window and make a questioning gesture. She turned her back firmly on him as she walked to the bottom of the garden, phone to her ear. When Riva answered, Susan could hear a doubtful tone in her voice; the poor girl was probably imagining she was still angry and calling to berate her some more.

'Riva, darling,' Susan said softly. 'I'm so, so sorry about the other day at the café. I should have called earlier. But

343

you know I'm here for you, as I've always been, don't you? Can you talk now? I want to help . . .'

Indoors, Joe turned away from the window, puzzled and a little anxious. Although he had told Kaaya before their break-up that Susan had never suspected a thing about their affair, deep down he knew that was not true. Susan had almost certainly guessed he was up to something, although she had probably never realised the identity of the person he was having the affair with. It was plain that Susan had been far too decent to confront him on the basis of a mere suspicion. That was typical of her. And her love for him had obviously, eventually, overridden everything else . . .

Now, turning to look again at the figure of his wife standing in the back garden as she talked into her phone, Joe felt another familiar wave of shame and revulsion at his actions. Beautiful, beautiful Kaaya had been irresistible and few men would have remained impervious to her charms. But Joe knew he had had it in him to resist, and that was surely what he should have done. Even when he had briefly considered himself truly in love with Kaaya . . .

Joe sighed deeply and returned to his armchair in the living room. He had huge amends to make and would make them as tenderly and sincerely as he could. But, even if Susan forgave him, Joe couldn't help wondering if he would ever be able to forget the utter vileness of what he had done.

Across in central London, Kaaya sipped on her wine as the waiter served the desserts. Her colleagues – some of whom, in her opinion, would do well to never touch another dessert in their lives – had decided to order one between two and she watched now with wry amusement as they set about, reaching across each other with their spoons to scoop into goblets of passionfruit tiramisu and something chocolatey that Kaaya would have sworn had enough calories to sustain a human being for one full calendar month.

Indrani, sitting next to her, offered her a spare spoon. 'Ohhh, try this, Kaaya, it's just heavenly. I tell you, the puds in Yauatcha are to die for. Better almost than the mains . . .'

But Kaaya shook her head. 'I was born without a sweet tooth, luckily,' she said, tossing her glossy hair.

'Okay, at least have some of this raspberry sorbet then,' Indrani insisted. 'It's more tart than sweet and there's zero fat content. But, God, this chocolate mousse is just fabulous, I tell you. It's got some flavour that really uplifts the bitterness of the chocolate . . . what is it . . . oh, lime flower it says here on the menu . . .'

Kaaya's attention lapsed as Indrani wittered on. Food was not her favourite subject at the best of times and she found it both curious and a bit pathetic when people — especially porkers like Indrani — expounded on the subject at such length.

Indrani turned to her again a few minutes later, talking through a mouthful of chocolate. 'Hey, I meant to say, Kaaya, that Bollywood director Ritesh Shah came in again today. He wanted to discuss a few plans for the Aman Khan film before firming up the deal with us. You'd gone to the Paramount offices so I put him onto Arabella.'

Kaaya felt peeved. 'Arabella didn't mention it. She wouldn't have a clue about Bollywood. I'd better go speak to her right away. If she isn't too pissed, that is.'

'No, no, don't worry. She knows the account's yours if

it comes to us. It was just a holding thing,' Indrani paci-
fied.

Kaaya considered getting up to make her way across to
the other end of the table where she could see Arabella
digging deep into a bowl of tiramisu. But there was probably little point trying to discuss business with an old soak
like Arabella; she spoke absolutely no sense once she'd
downed half a bottle of wine.

Her attention turned back to Indrani who was still
chirping on between great mouthfuls of pudding.

'Apparently the gossip magazines are full of it . . .' she
was saying '. . . no one's ever been able to get anything on
Aman Khan before, you see. I mean, it's a well known fact
that his marriage to Salma Khan has been on the rocks
for years. But there's never been a whiff of scandal about
him. I mean, the man's reputation has been so clean, some
papers in India once tried suggesting he might even be
gay. Which is a joke. I mean, look at the man! Not a gay
bone in his body. So obviously there's bound to be much
excitement now if he is having an affair. What a lucky
woman, eh?'

'Aman Khan's having an affair?' Kaaya asked.

Indrani nodded. 'Apparently he was all over her at the
Cannes Festival. Some woman who was also a jury
member. They haven't named her yet but *Cineblitz* column
said they were inseparable there, hand in hand on the
beach and canoodling everywhere. It'll be major news in
Bollywood if it's true. But you never know with these
gossip columnists. Actually, it might even be some kind
of publicity ploy to get people talking before his next film.
We should know about that kind of thing, huh? And
they're a rule unto themselves, these film *wallahs*, oper-
ating like loose cannons and pulling off their own PR

stunts. Be fun if you do get the Aman Khan account actually, especially while all of this is going on.'

But Kaaya wasn't listening to Indrani any more. Her head was reeling. It was Riva. Suddenly, she knew it was Riva who was having the affair with Aman Khan. Perhaps it was some sixth sense but – in the same way that Riva had guessed so easily at Kaaya and Joe's affair – Kaaya now knew without a doubt that the mysterious woman spotted canoodling with Aman Khan in Cannes was her sister. It would also explain why Riva had done such a quick volte-face over her affair with Joe; why there had been no anger at all since she arrived back in London. Riva's tears in the car when Kaaya picked her up from Cannes had been not tears of forgiveness, but of guilt!

Chapter Forty-Two

Aman looked down over Paris from his aircraft window. The Eiffel Tower was catching the afternoon sun, gleaming and looking exactly like the small brass ornament his mother had on her mantelpiece back at home, a souvenir from a European holiday he had insisted they take when he was home one summer from film school. Aman remembered booking his parents' trip with a tour operator who specialised in taking large Indian groups around Europe and smiled as he recalled his father's delight at finding himself served with Indian food every night.

Not that he blamed them, Aman thought as his plane now banked over Paris. He too missed his *daal-chawal* on the longer film shoots and had been relieved to find that both directors he would be working with on this trip had organised to have Indian chefs cooking for the crew on the sets. As far as Aman was concerned, he had done all the required sampling of French cuisine on his very first shoot in Paris, and it had left him unimpressed.

The aircraft seemed to be taking forever to land and was now lazily circling the city once more. Aman wondered if it was a deliberate ploy on the part of the Air France pilot to show off his country's beautiful capital on this sunny day, or perhaps the man was just enjoying his own ride through summer skies. Looking down at the city, Aman could spot many famous landmarks – the Sacré Coeur gleaming white over there on the left and the golden Seine winding through squares of grey and green. It was strange that Aman had only ever visited Paris with film crews. Although Salma had once planned to accompany him, that trip had fallen through because she had been pregnant with Ashfaq. She had subsequently visited Paris with her parents and, from what Aman had been able to tell, had spent all her time visiting *haute-couture* boutiques, racking up a hefty bill at the Chanel store on the Rue Cambon.

Paris, city for lovers, Aman thought wryly, leaning his head back on his seat. For the umpteenth time since the previous afternoon, he remembered Riva, feeling sorrow and remorse twist his heart once more. No more than five minutes after she had left his hotel room at Claridge's, Aman had bitterly regretted his outburst. Wondering what had possessed him to be so nasty to Riva, he had tried chasing after her but there was no sign of her at all on the streets outside. He had ventured as far as Selfridges, hoping she might have gone there to recover, rather than straight home, but she had been nowhere among the thronging shoppers either. Amazingly, he had wandered unrecognised among the shoppers at Selfridges and tried to take his mind off Riva by looking at the clothes and shoes. When that failed to work, he tried dialling her number twice, but there had been no reply.

Then, when he returned to the street, wondering where to go next, Aman saw another woman look enquiringly at him. By habit, he quickened his steps, even though he thought it unlikely that a white Englishwoman would know Bollywood films well enough to recognise him. But she followed him at a safe distance, finally catching up with him at a traffic light. She had tapped him on the arm and said, 'I think I know you.'

'Ma'am, you must have mistaken me for someone else,' Aman replied politely, starting to cross the road. But by now the woman had a firm grip on his arm as she insisted, 'I know! You're the man on the telly, ain't ya? That feller in *EastEnders*!'

Aman had beaten a hasty retreat back to his hotel after that. It was the sort of story that would have amused Riva no end and Aman wanted to rail at the thought that he could not tell her about it; to see her throw her head back and laugh. It was perhaps just as well that he did not know Riva's address because Aman knew that it would have taken all his self-control to keep from turning up outside her house. Not that he wanted to harm her. Despite what he had said about Ben, Aman truly had no wish to destroy Riva's life. If Riva did come to him, he wanted it to be with love, and because she had willingly put aside everything else to be with him.

The aircraft was finally landing at Charles de Gaulle airport, its tyres screeching on the tarmac before they gradually slowed and started to taxi towards the terminal. Aman disembarked along with the other first-class passengers and followed the group into the terminal. Ritesh Shah had promised that his luggage would be awaiting him at the Four Seasons and Aman looked around for his driver. Spotting his name on a placard, Aman walked towards it and within minutes was in a limousine headed into the city.

Evening was falling when Aman arrived at the hotel affectionately called 'Le Cinq' by Parisians. It was not his first time here, so he was familiar with the huge flower arrangements and opulent wall paintings that were the hotel's features, barely noticing them this evening as he checked in and was shown up to his room. Ritesh Shah would be along later that night and Aman left a message to say that he would be in the health club.

After a brisk half hour workout, Aman sank into the whirlpool, feeling some of his tension and fatigue gradually diminish. Then, showered and changed into a fresh set of clothes, Aman walked around the hotel, investigating the elegant courtyard restaurant and the bar before deciding to have his sundowner served to him on one of the terraces overlooking the Eiffel Tower. He was shown to a small table covered in snowy white linen that bore a huge bowl of red roses. Ahead of him, Paris's famous tower rose into the night sky, lit with a thousand lights and looking as though it were encrusted with a profusion of diamonds. It was a beautiful balmy night and Aman could not have asked to be anywhere more lovely. He took in his stunning surroundings and then looked into his ruby-coloured Virgin Mary, thinking of the number of people who would envy him his good fortune. But only Aman knew of the gaping hole in his heart that was intent on sucking away his happiness. It would be easy to blame Riva for it but somehow he baulked at this. Perhaps it was because he still loved her too much and he cursed himself for doing so.

Chapter Forty-Three

After a sleepless night, Kaaya waited till nine before calling the office. It was Indrani who answered the phone and Kaaya could not help marvelling at how effervescent the woman sounded, despite the vast quantities of food and wine that she had put away at Yauatcha the previous night.

'Oh, Indrani, I feel just terrible,' Kaaya said, trying to croak convincingly.

'Oh dear, what's wrong?'

'I don't know. Must be something I ate. It's my tummy. I've been up and down all night.'

'But you hardly ate anything!' Indrani responded unhelpfully.

'I had at least four of those scallops. Sometimes seafood does that to me. But, anyway, I can't come in. I'll be useless in the office, feeling the way I do.'

'Okay, sweetie, don't you worry. You stay home and take a rest. I'll field your calls today and keep an eye on your emails too, if you like.'

'Oh, Indrani, you're such a doll. A giant box of Krispy Kremes for you when I come in. Tomorrow, hopefully. I'm sure it'll pass by this evening, whatever it is.'

'You can't be too careful if it's food poisoning. Take a

rest, honey, don't worry about a thing here. And let me know if I can do anything else.'

Kaaya hung up with only the faintest flutter of guilt before getting out of bed and walking into the shower. Rohan was in Japan again on business and Kaaya had been proud that she had not felt even a passing temptation to call Joe in the four days she had been alone. The affair was well and truly over and, as Susan and Joe were not people she saw on a regular basis, Kaaya knew it was only a matter of time before the awkwardness and embarrassment would fade away too. Luckily no damage had been done to either her own marriage or to Joe's.

Brushing her teeth, Kaaya knew she had Riva to thank for getting her to see sense . . . She stopped brushing for a minute to gaze unseeingly at her reflection. So now what was she to do with her knowledge of Riva's affair with Aman Khan? She could taunt her with it, of course, seeing how crummy Riva had made her feel when she had been found out for the same misdemeanour . . .

An hour later, Kaaya pulled up outside Riva's house. Ben's car was not in the drive but, from her earlier phone call, she knew Riva was in. Riva had been clearly puzzled at why she was taking a sickie to come and see her but Kaaya had not wanted to talk about it on the phone.

Riva opened the door, clad in a navy tracksuit, her hair tied tightly back from a make-up-free face. She looked pale, as though she hadn't been sleeping properly. In this state, Riva certainly did not look the most likely candidate for an affair with a glamorous film star, Kaaya couldn't help thinking as she was let in.

'In time for brekker,' Riva said. 'I've just finished my yoga. Not that you'll have anything but a few pumpkin seeds for breakfast, of course . . .'

'Not true. I had a pot of yoghurt before leaving home actually. I keep thinking I should restart yoga at some point,' Kaaya said, following her sister into the kitchen. 'But I've probably forgotten everything we learnt back at the Ashtanga Centre.'

'I'll give you a refresher, if you like. It's easy once you're back in the swing of things. And you have a body like rubber anyway, far more supple than mine,' Riva said, turning on the kettle. She turned to face Kaaya for the first time. 'What's up, sis? Is all well?' she asked in her usual direct manner.

Kaaya took a deep breath. 'Riva, I know about you and Aman,' she said, quietly.

The expression on Riva's face as she stared back at her sister turned from one of anxiety to panic and then guilt. After a few minutes of silence, broken only by the rising hiss of the kettle, she whispered, 'How do you know?'

'Never mind that for now,' Kaaya replied. 'Just tell me – is it true?'

Riva looked down at her bare feet and nodded. Kaaya saw that tears were rolling down her cheeks to fall onto the limestone floor.

'Oh, Riva,' she said, reaching out and gathering her sister into her arms.

Behind them, the kettle clicked itself off but neither woman moved. Kaaya, feeling Riva's body shake as she broke down in anguished tears, had a sudden flash of their father watching them from somewhere far off, shocked and saddened by what both his beloved daughters had done. That thought was enough to make Kaaya start to weep too but, after a few minutes, she disengaged herself and asked gently, 'Would you like some coffee, sis?'

Riva nodded, wiping her eyes with the back of her hand

before reaching out for the kitchen roll. She handed a sheet to Kaaya and wiped her own face while Kaaya made the coffee. They took their mugs into the living room and sat at either end of the sofa, their legs stretched towards each other. Riva pulled a woollen throw from the back of the sofa and covered their feet with it as she used to do when they were children.

Kaaya opened the conversation again as Riva sipped silently on her coffee. 'I'm not going to ask what possessed you to embark on an affair, Riv, because I think I know there's sometimes no answer to that sort of question.' She stopped with a wry laugh before continuing, 'But I think it's a fair question to ask what you might do next?'

Riva was silent for a few seconds before replying quietly, 'Nothing, Kaaya. It happened while we were there. It was more magical than I'd ever imagined such things could be. And I was completely swept off my feet. But it's over now.'

'Are you sure of that? And is that what you want? For it to be over?'

Riva nodded again. 'Yes. There is no other way.'

'Do you love him? Aman, I mean,' Kaaya asked.

'Of course, in a manner of speaking,' Riva replied sadly. 'Or I wouldn't have done what I did. In that respect, I guess you and I differ, Kaaya. I couldn't have slept with someone I didn't love.'

'Then why do you want to finish it?' Kaaya asked, choosing to ignore Riva's assumption that she had not had any feelings for Joe.

Riva considered her reply. 'Because I think I love Ben more than I love Aman. And I owe him more . . .'

'Despite his shitty behaviour recently?'

'Yes – I married him for better or for worse, Kaaya. If

356

we all upped and left the minute we hit turbulent patches, there'd be no marriages left in the world.'

'Bloody hell, you sound so conservative and so *Indian*! That's the kind of thing Papa would've said,' Kaaya laughed.

'Well, he'd have left Ma many times over if he'd chosen to walk out every time she behaved like a child. And where would that have left us, huh?'

'Papa was simply the most decent man in the world, Riva. They don't make them like that any more.'

'Decent . . . strange you should use that word,' Riva said. 'I used it to Aman too, to explain why I needed to come back to Ben. But I'm not sure he understood . . .'

'Was Aman cut up then?'

Riva nodded. 'He seemed to believe, more than I did, that our relationship had some kind of future. But then he's desperately unhappy with his wife so I guess that's where that hope came from. His marriage sounds nothing like what I have with Ben.'

'And Ben hasn't guessed?'

'Don't think so. Or, if he has, he's decided to overlook it. He seems to have undergone a bit of a transformation himself in the ten days I was away in Cannes.'

'I did wonder – he was unusually pleasant when we spoke just before you returned from Cannes.'

'Well, he'd gone up to see his dad in Denby when I was away and I think they must have talked things over. His dad's always had a calming influence on him.'

'Glad to hear it, Riva. Ben was really snarly when I called him soon after you'd gone. I mean, we've had our moments but I'd never heard him as agitated as that. Quite startled me, I can tell you.'

'My being in Cannes must've had something to do with

it,' said Riva meditatively. 'His mood just seemed to get darker and darker as my departure loomed.'

'How will he deal with your forthcoming book tour, then?'

'Oh, he seems far more relaxed about that. I guess he sees it as much more a part of my life as an author and we're planning to end it with a holiday together somewhere too. Besides, there'll be no Aman Khan on my book tour for him to worry about!'

'Oh, was that why Ben had his knickers in such a twist about you going to Cannes?'

'Without a doubt. He must have hated the idea that Aman and I were going to be together in Cannes. You see – I've never told you this – but, before Ben, Aman and I went out together for a bit in our first year at uni. Ben knew that, of course.'

'*What?* You and Aman *Khan?*' Kaaya's screech was loud enough to make Riva smile through her sniffles.

She nodded. 'I know . . . seems bizarre now that Aman's so famous, doesn't it? But if he hadn't been a film star, it would have been the most normal thing in the world: a short affair in college before the real thing came along . . .'

'Was that all it was then; an exploratory fling?'

Riva looked pensively into her mug, trying to be truthful. 'Well, you know me, Kaaya, I don't do things by halves, do I? I did love Aman deeply back then – well, as much as eighteen-year-olds are capable of loving – but I couldn't help wondering all along if it was just his foreignness that had attracted me. His Indianness, you know. I was also very confused by that Indianness, though. It was all the things I wanted to be but knew I never could. Anyway, in the midst of that teenage angsting and mulling, Ben just kept persisting. And suddenly one day, he seemed – especially by comparison to Aman – so uncomplicated and familiar and *safe*, so, in the end, I merely plumped for him. I don't suppose too much thought went into it but we were all so young then . . .'

Kaaya laughed ruefully. 'Women, we're all the same! Total suckers for feeling safe. Even if I had fallen for Joe, I too would probably have stayed within the safety of my life with Rohan.'

'It's over with Joe, then?'

'Yes, sis. Well and truly over,' Kaaya said. After a few seconds, she turned the question back to her sister. 'I take it it's the same between you and Aman?'

Riva took a split second before nodding. 'Yes, it's over,' she said softly. But Kaaya thought she could detect just the tiniest trace of regret in her sister's voice.

Chapter Forty-Four

The first leg of Riva's book tour was on board the Eurostar. She hastily kissed Ben goodbye as she jumped out of their car at the traffic lights on Euston Road. Trundling her wheeled suitcase through the gleaming new terminal at St Pancras, Riva bought herself a coffee before surveying the electronic board for details of her train to Paris. There it was: the 11.32 that would get her into the Gare du Nord at 14.47.

She walked to the platform, the excitement finally growing in her. Riva had spent the past couple of weeks feeling more miserable than she had in a long time; almost on a par, she realised with some astonishment, with the way she had felt after her father had died. But, when the first day or two had passed, and Aman had not made good his threat of calling Ben, Riva started to breathe easily again: not merely because she did not want a showdown with Ben but also because it meant that Aman had forgiven her. She had seen two missed calls from him after she had left Gideon's office that day and, a day later, Aman had sent a text message apologising for his outburst and asking her to call him whenever she was able to. Perhaps that was what she had needed to start recovering again, even though there were still moments when she remembered their stolen moments in Cannes with sudden tears overwhelming her. As the days had progressed, however, Susan had made up with her and Kaaya too had been so comforting during their heart-to-heart. And so Riva had slowly returned to her usual self, even getting on with preparing the spiel she would use during her book tour and peppering it with humorous anecdotes about the business of writing. She had, however, not returned Aman's calls for fear it would give him renewed hope that they could be together.

Now, on board a train speeding towards the English Channel, Riva couldn't help wondering how Aman was getting on with his film shoot in Europe, and where he was. He had said he would be in Paris sometime in June but she had no idea where or when. She herself was only in the city for two days, staying at a small hotel on the Left Bank and signing books alongside Françoise, her French translator, at the WH Smith on Rue de Rivoli. The chances of her bumping into Aman were remote indeed – Paris was hardly a village and, given the totally separate worlds they occupied, they may as well have been on different continents. Nevertheless it still felt weirdly serendipitous to Riva that both she and Aman would be wandering the same city in a few hours. She tried to quell the sudden frisson that overcame her at that thought.

She looked out at the Kent countryside, blurred green and gold by the speed at which they were travelling, and told herself again to stop thinking of Aman and to stop being so fanciful. There could have been any number of occasions on which she and Aman had been in the same town, perhaps just streets apart, even seconds apart from meeting each other. Such things must happen all the time – when lives crisscrossed and intercut and, at other times, narrowly missed doing so, all of it without any of the participants even knowing.

'Ships that cross in the night,' Riva muttered to herself, returning to the book she was struggling to read.

In the heart of Paris, Aman's phone started to ring. He could see Salma's name flashing and clicked the mouthpiece open. The reception was scratchy, perhaps because he was slap-bang in the middle of the Palais du Louvre courtyard, surrounded by tall buildings.

'Wait a minute. I can't hear you, Salma, say that again,' Aman said, walking away from the steel and glass pyramid to see if that would reduce the interference.

'I have to know when to book our tickets for Pisa,' he finally heard her say.

'Pisa?'

'That's where we have to come. For Tuscany. You've forgotten!'

'No, I haven't forgotten. But have you checked if Pisa is the best airport? Not Florence?'

'Of course I checked, what do you think? From here to Paris and then connect to Pisa. Shahsahib will have to send a car there. We will need at least two large cars.'

'Okay, yes, I'll ask him.'

'But *when* should I book tickets for, Aman!'

'Hang on, Shahsahib may be around here somewhere. I can ask right away.' Aman thought he heard Salma sigh loudly. But there was no sign of Ritesh Shah in the vicinity so Aman returned to the phone. 'No, sorry, he's not here.'

'Ooffo, can't you just decide?'

'No, I can't just *decide*, Salma. It does depend on the shoot, you know.'

'Of course, you can decide, Aman, you're the star!'

'Look, I'll find out the schedules as soon as I can,' Aman replied, sounding more brusque than he intended. 'And don't forget I'm committed to Rohit Mirchandani for the Venice shoot too. That will only be a short one, though, maybe four days.'

'So you'll just keep us hanging till then?'

Aman tried to mask his irritation. 'No, I don't intend keeping you or anyone else hanging, Salma. I just need to be sure that I complete the job I'm committed to before taking a holiday.' Salma was silent and Aman tried to sound more placatory when he said, 'I'm looking forward to seeing Ashfaq and you, Salma. It's been really lonely, these ten days in Paris . . .' But, from the ongoing silence, Aman realised that Salma had either hung up or been cut off.

Aman returned to the set, feeling even more dejected than before. The scene he had been preparing for was a rather over-the-top action shot in which a stuntman, pretending to be him, would scale the glass pyramid while the villain and his gang infiltrated the Grand Gallery below in order to steal the *Mona Lisa*. Preparations were still ongoing and so Aman took a chair to wait for them to be finished, looking at the considerable number of bemused tourists who had gathered to watch the shoot. It was quite amazing that Ritesh Shah had managed to acquire special permission to film at the Louvre. Aman spotted the rotund director approaching him with a suit-wearing Frenchman in tow, and wondered whom he was schmoozing now. Shah was almost breathless with excitement as he made elaborate introduction.

'Aman-ji, this is Mr Philippe Leconte, a very senior official from the French Ministry of Culture. Mr Leconte, please let me introduce you to our industry's biggest and brightest star – the world-famous Mr Aman Khan! You know he has just come from being a jury member at the Cannes Film Festival. He is soon going to be a big name in Hollywood also, you take it from me, sir.'

Faintly embarrassed, Aman tried to wave Ritesh Shah's hyperbole away by shaking hands and exchanging pleasantries with the Frenchman, remembering also to thank him for granting permission to film in this beautiful setting.

'Aman-*ji*, I am taking Mr Leconte to L'Arpège for lunch. Please do us the courtesy of joining us,' Ritesh Shah said.

Aman declined politely, knowing it would be a very long, liquid lunch. 'Very kind of you, Shahsahib,' he replied, 'but I think I will carry on with the shoot. The scene is already delayed, you see.'

Ritesh Shah did not hide his relief. 'Quite right, quite right, Aman-*ji*,' he said before turning to his guest. 'See, this is why actors like Mr Aman Khan become great stars, Mr Leconte. What a director gets from someone like Mr Khan is total dedication. Total dedication.'

Shaking his head from side to side to emphasise his appreciation, Ritesh Shah patted Aman's arm gratefully before turning to leave, but he stopped when he saw that Aman had a question for the Frenchman.

'Er, sorry, Mr Leconte, before you go,' Aman said, 'I wonder whether you can help me with something.' He hesitated, hoping it wasn't a stupid question, and then took the plunge. 'Mr Shah said you were from the Ministry of Culture. So . . . is it possible that you may have some information about book events taking place in the city these days? You know, book talks . . . or signings . . . anything to which British authors have been invited?'

His query elicited an understandably puzzled look from

Ritesh Shah who had, quite accurately, not seen Aman as an avid reader of books. The Frenchman's reply, in accented but otherwise perfect English, was predictably disappointing.

'I am so sorry, Mr Khan, but books are not the responsibility of my department at all. There is the Direction du Livre et de la Lecture who oversee such things. I am certain someone will be able to help you in that department so, if there is any specific information you are seeking, I can try to get it for you later today?'

But Aman shook his head. Riva's was probably a privately organised book tour anyway and, apart from combing every book store in town, Aman could not think of any way to find her – if she was in the city at all. Even if she was still angry with him, he owed her an apology for the way he had shouted at her in his room at Claridge's.

The walk from the Metro station at Rue du Bac was short and Riva soon found the Hotel De L'Academie, a grand name for a small *pension* with the tiniest reception area she had ever seen. After checking into a very girlie room, crowded with intricately carved furniture and pink flowered valances, Riva freshened up before escaping back onto the street. The street was typically Parisian: pharmacies and cafés and a very fancy chocolate shop all sitting cheek-by-jowl. Clutching the map that had been provided by the pretty girl at reception, Riva walked in the direction of the river, going through the lively Latin Quarter as she aimed for Ile de la Cité. She wanted to view the Notre Dame before evenfall as she had only managed to see it in the dark on her last visit to Paris. Catching her first view of the cathedral today as she turned a corner, Riva thought it looked a lot less atmospheric, lit by the evening sun and heaving with tourists and worshippers streaming out of the main doors on the western side. Riva walked around the side and stood looking up at the carved apse and the stone gargoyles, caught in midair as they leapt off the side of the building. Gothic architecture was a strange, ugly thing but very stirring for a writer's imagination, Riva thought, envisioning what would happen if the gargoyles did all suddenly come to life and fly around the streets of Paris. She contemplated going in to explore the cathedral's interior but decided instead to locate the bookshop on Rue de Rivoli where she was due to be at ten o'clock in the morning. In Riva's view, it was so much better to be well prepared for all eventualities, rather than rushing in somewhere all breathless and flustered. She thought of her sister who was the polar opposite. Kaaya certainly seemed to manage her life very well minus the cautionary dry runs, not only always being late for appointments, but even making rather a stylish art of it!

Riva walked on, smiling as she remembering how wonderful Kaaya had been to her these past few days, calling regularly to check on how she was coping in the aftermath of Cannes. Never for one moment had she judged her, even though Riva recalled with embarrassment the haste with which she had censured Kaaya over the affair with Joe. Of course, that was partially due to her loyalty to Susan, but she now realised that she should have tried to see things from Kaaya's point of view too.

Riva sighed in relief at how that situation had resolved itself. She and Ben had recently dined at Joe and Susan's and it had seemed as though the pair had never been happier. Susan had even whispered to her as they washed up that Joe and she were now trying for a baby. Riva, who knew she would take to her grave the knowledge that

Kaaya had been Joe's lover, was astonished to think that infidelity could actually cause a marriage to be energised in such a manner. It certainly didn't seem to be having that effect on her for she merely felt sick at heart whenever she remembered Aman.

Riva turned her map upside down and cricked her head in an awkward position as she tried to get an idea of the direction in which to walk. She remembered Ben's crabbiness at her complete lack of navigational skills as they had got more and more lost on the narrow back streets of Paris on their last trip to the city. But the memory of it now made Riva grin. Dear old Ben had, over the years, learned to cope with her failings too. Perhaps that was what happened in comfy old relationships, couples compensating for each other's flaws and learning to slot into mutual inadequacies rather than railing against them.

'But where the hell am I to go now,' Riva muttered to herself as she looked around and saw a sign for Jardin des Tuileries. Gideon had told her that the WHSmith was close to the Jardin end of Rue de Rivoli and, thanks to that being represented by an unmissably large green rectangle on the map, Riva felt marginally more confident about the direction to take. Rue de Rivoli turned out to be a much longer road than anticipated and Riva started to flag after fifteen minutes of trudging up it. She also needed a loo and so, on spotting a Quiksilver shop, she ducked into it. Remembering that Ben's favourite old wallet had started to fray, Riva decided she would purchase him a new one before asking for the toilet. She rehearsed the phrase in her head – *Où sont les toilettes?* – feeling pleased that she still remembered her GCSE French. She had got some practice while in Cannes and it had impressed Aman no end. Riva examined a few wallets, thinking of how easily Aman still slipped into her thoughts. Where was he and was he all right, she wondered. Seeing that he had not made any attempt to contact her recently, she could only conclude that he too had decided to move on with his own life. She ought to be happy with that thought . . .

Ten minutes later, her gift for Ben purchased, Riva was back on the busy shop-lined Rue de Rivoli with its endless procession of cars. She started to walk again, hoping she was still travelling towards the Jardin rather than away from it. No doubt a road sign or Metro stop would soon offer a clue. To her left, she spotted signs for the Musée du Louvre and was briefly tempted to take a detour and look at Pei's glass pyramid. From this distance, she could see large crowds gathered around it and guessed that some outdoor performance was probably going on. Riva looked at her watch. It was already well past six and she was not sure what time W H Smith was likely to close. It was important to meet someone who would know what was expected of her at the book reading – that would be better than wandering off and delaying herself further. For now it was best not to allow Paris's many attractions to distract her. Riva turned away from the sign for the Louvre and carried on walking up the Rue de Rivoli in search of what she was really meant to be looking for.

Chapter Forty-Five

After returning his credit card to his wallet, Ben threw it down on the table in a flourish that indicated his pleasure at having finally completed the booking. Passo dello Stelvio sounded terrific. Ben had spent the past two hours researching the best deals for summer skiing in the Dolomites and had eventually found a charming ski chalet in what was described on Wikipedia as 'the highest mountain pass in the Eastern Alps'. Both he and Riva were reasonably confident skiers and Ben hoped they would be able to try the more advanced piste at the top of the pass.

He checked the time on the corner of his computer screen where, at the start of Riva's trip, he had saved Central European Time on the world clock. By now, she would be back in her hotel room as her meeting with the German Book Office was to have been no longer than an hour. He called her mobile, keen to tell her about the holiday.

'Hi, Ben,' she said through a crystal-clear line.

'Hi, sweets, are you able to speak?'

'Yeah, I'm in a cab at the moment, headed back to the hotel.'

'Is it good? Frankfurt, I mean.'

'A bit bland, to be honest. None of the charm of Paris

and not half as bookish as I'd expected for some reason. But I was taken to the venue where the book fair is held every year and that was fantastic, I have to say. So huge it's like a strange nether world populated only by readers! Must be quite amazing when the fair's on. Is all well there?'

'Very well. I played squash today with Rohan at his club and even your sister dropped by for a drink. And I called your mum an hour ago – she's fine. Just worrying about you as usual. *But*, I have news . . .'

'Oh?'

'The skiing holiday's been booked!'

'Oh goody! Where are we going?'

'The Italian Dolomites. You have to travel quite far up to get the summer snow so it's three thousand metres high. It looks fabulous, Riv. If you have wi-fi in your hotel room, look up Passo dello Stelvio.'

'Goodness, three thousand metres, that'll be something,' Riva exclaimed. 'How do we get there?'

'It's a four-hour drive from Milan. So, when you're finished with Venice, you should bring yourself to Milan and I'll meet you there. At the airport, if we can coordinate our flights.'

'Must we drive up the Dolomites? I mean, those high mountain roads sound a bit daunting . . .' Riva said apprehensively.

Ben laughed. 'Believe me, I hadn't exactly forgotten that I'm not married to an ace navigator, so I looked up the alternative. Which is a two- or three-hour train journey to Tirano from where we'll have to take a bus to Bormio. From there you get a cable car to get to the lodge. So it's either that or a car, you decide.'

'Oh dear, a car does sound a better bet, doesn't it? I just

have this horrible image in my head of us wandering around the Dolomites, lost forever.'

'Don't you worry, sunshine. I'll print off detailed directions from Google Maps.' Ben stopped, hearing Riva sigh. 'Okay, and investigate the possibility of hiring a taxi. As a special treat for you, my sweet!'

'Oh, that does sound much better,' Riva said with audible relief, making Ben laugh again. He could hear sounds of traffic in the background as she said, 'Oh, I'm at the hotel now, Ben darling. I'd better hang up so I can pay.'

'Okay, sweetie. I just wanted to tell you about the holiday. Speak to you later tonight . . .'

Ben rung off, feeling pleased with himself. This was the tonic he and Riva had needed for a long time. He had spent far too long moping about his job situation, and his nonexistent writing career. Ben was determined now to return their marriage to the blissful state it was once in. Having nearly lost Riva, he vowed to never allow that to happen again.

Chapter Forty-Six

Riva arrived at Marco Polo airport at noon. Seven cities in ten days had left her feeling drained and exhausted but she felt no more confident about finding her way around now than she had at the start. She was to present herself at the Ca'Foscari University's Department of Foreign Languages and Literature, which (she looked at her notebook again) was located on the Grand Canal between the Rialto and San Marco. The names were all quite familiar to Riva from her previous two trips to Venice but getting lost in Europe was by now *de rigueur*.

Rolling her suitcase along on its wheels, Riva followed signs for the shuttle bus, thinking of how much time she had spent in the past ten days losing her way only to be bailed out by kindly passers by. Apart from that, the tour had gone off without a hitch, decent-sized crowds turning up at all her readings.

When a bright blue Venezia shuttle arrived, Riva loaded her suitcase on board and took a seat. The guidebook had said that the ride into the Piazzale Roma was no more than twenty minutes but the challenge of getting to the university awaited, so she sat back, deciding not to think of that right now. Riva took out her mobile phone to call her mother but the line was busy. She slipped the instrument back into its case. Ma was probably talking to either Kaaya or Ben, the pair of them apparently taking efficient charge of their mother's affairs in Riva's absence. It suddenly occurred to Riva that she had stopped worrying about her mother on a daily basis. Why, Ma herself seemed altogether more cheery these days, taking particular joy in finding out that Riva and Ben were soon going off on a holiday together. The impending anniversary of Papa's death was bound to cause renewed pain but something told Riva that they had all turned a corner in some important way.

From the bus window, Riva now watched as they approached the busy hub of Piazzala Roma and the red-tiled rooftops of Venice came into view. In the distance, she could see the towering russet Campanile and, near it, the Gothic dome of Santa Maria della Salute. After hopping off the bus, Riva surveyed the scene, trying unsuccessfully to get her bearings. From the route Riva had marked out for herself on board the flight from Rome, she could see she needed to find a bridge called Ponte Tres Ponti before tackling the rest of the labyrinth.

'One pont at a time, Riva Walia,' she said nervously to herself before looking around for a likely saviour. At least the name of the pont was easy to pronounce. She spotted a ponytailed man who was leaning on a scooter, apparently in no hurry to get anywhere.

'*Ah scusi, Ponte Tres Ponti, per favore?*' she asked, tapping her map. The man's eyes flicked appreciatively over Riva's khakhi shorts and white T-shirt as he left his scooter to wander across. Using the excuse of having to share her map, he stood so close to Riva she could smell his body odour. She contemplated stepping back but, reluctant both to appear rude and to hand over the Venice guide that was now firmly in the man's grip, Riva stood her ground, continuing to cling to one corner of her map.

'Ponte Tres Ponti? *Nessuno problema, l'aiutero*,' the man said, showing more interest in Riva's legs than the map.

'Er . . . *scusi, no Italiano. Parli inglese?*'

'*Ah lei e inglese? Molto bella*.' Now he was looking not at her shorts-clad legs but her T-shirted bust instead.

'*Si, si*,' Riva replied weakly. Clearly, the conversation was not headed in the direction she needed it to go and so she snatched her map from between the man's fingers and started backing away. '*Scusi, grazie, ciao*,' she said, smiling apologetically.

'*Non c'e problema*,' the man replied, shrugging as he turned away. Greatly relieved, Riva hurried away, roughly dragging her suitcase over the cobblestones.

She spotted a small humpbacked bridge ahead of her. 'Who would've thought – Ponte Tres Ponti!' Riva said, reading the sign and delighted at having found her first target with no help at all from the locals.

It was only half an hour later, still wandering and by now completely lost in Venice's maze of high-walled streets, that Riva started to panic. Finally, two hours and five long conversations later, Riva found herself rather miraculously standing before a large sign that read Università Ca'Foscari Venezia. She wanted to weep. But she dragged herself up the stairs, lugging a suitcase after her that now felt like a ton. A young woman wearing a worried expression was waiting for her in the reception.

'Oh, Ms Walia? I am Claudia Ercolani from the Faculty of Foreign Languages and Literature,' the woman said, approaching her, and Riva had to control her urge to fling herself bodily into the woman's arms to express her over-whelming relief.

'I am so, so sorry I'm late,' Riva said.

'Did you get lost?'

Riva nodded. 'I really should have paid someone a few euros to guide me here. Stupidly, I tried using a map and I'm afraid I'm very, very stupid with maps,' she said apologetically.

'Oh, don't worry, everyone who comes to Venice gets lost,' Claudia replied pleasantly. 'But, good, you are here now. So I will take you to your room, yes?'

Riva nodded. 'I'd be so grateful, Ms Ercolani,' she said, following the woman back out into the sunshine.

'Oh, Claudia, please.'

'In which case you must call me Riva.'

Claudia looked at Riva with a smile. 'You look very young,' she said accusingly. 'I was expecting someone much older. And not so pretty!' Riva laughed as Claudia continued. 'The students will love you,' Claudia promised. 'So nice to have a woman for a change, and one so young and lovely. And they've all read your last book.'

'Oh, you do flatter me,' Riva said, adding modestly, 'I promise I won't look so young when I change out of these shorts into formal wear! At what time is the event tomorrow?'

'We start in the morning with a lecture by the French poet, Yves Bonnafoy, and then, at midday, we will have your lecture. Ah, here we are now . . . this is one of the old *palazzos* used by the university to house visiting academics . . .' Claudia stopped outside a wrought-iron gate and fished out a large iron key to unlock it. Riva followed her into a small walled courtyard covered in tiny pink rambling roses. A few green-painted doors surrounded the quadrangle and Claudia was now unlocking one that led into a tiny studio apartment with a low-beamed ceiling. Everything was white, from the painted walls to the wooden bed, desk and dresser, except for a bunch of mauve peonies stuck in a small glass vase atop the dresser.

'Oh, so pretty,' Riva exclaimed, 'it's like a doll's house!'

Claudia laughed. 'Well, shall I leave you to freshen up? There's a bathroom through there and this set of keys is for you. Would you like me to come and get you on my way to the lecture in the morning?'

'Oh, yes please,' Riva replied. 'Is this evening free then? I wasn't sure if I'd be needed for anything . . .'

'The evening is yours to use as you would like. You probably want to explore the charms of Venice?' Claudia smiled. 'Have you been to Venice before?'

'Twice actually. And I absolutely loved it both times. But there's always new things to discover in a place as lovely as this. So no fear, I will find plenty to amuse myself.'

'Well, if you've seen all the famous sights, I would recommend the Musica a Palazzo at Fondamento Barbarigo – the theme is love duets from the famous nineteenth-century operas. You know, exploring the many kinds of love: the passionate love of *Tosca*, the fatherly love of Giorgio from *La Traviata*, jealous love from *La Bohème* . . . Just wonderful if you are a music lover.'

'Or even just a lover!' Riva responded lightly. 'I'm no opera buff but I'm familiar enough with the more well-known pieces. Musica a Palazzo at Barbarigo, you said? I must write that down . . .'

As Riva delved into her purse for her notepad and pen, Claudia added, 'Oh, and I mustn't forget – I was saving it up to tell you because I know you write about India – but there is also a big Indian film shoot going on at the Grand Canal these days. Today may be their last day in fact. They have been practicising some fight scenes on boats near the Santa Maria della Salute and it has been of much interest to the local people. We are not used to Indian cinema over here, you see, but it looks like much fun – and totally free, no queueing for tickets!'

With that, and a cheery *ciao*, Claudia was gone. Riva stood in the middle of her small, white room, hearing the deep, deep hush of Venice blanketing her. No traffic sounds, no car horns, no rumbling trains; the stillness of Venice had always been the most evocative thing about the place. But the silence was now ringing strangely in her head as Riva sat down on her bed, feeling suddenly weak at the knees. It was over a month ago that she had run out of Aman's room at Claridge's. She had heard no more from him after the two missed calls and the text he had sent on the day after their row. But Riva had thought about Aman so often, it was as though he was still nearby. Perhaps her thoughts had insisted on returning to him because she knew he too was in Europe somewhere. Or would their time together in Cannes haunt her forever more, just as their short spell together in uni had? Her two chances with Aman, both thrown to the winds. Surely her feelings would slowly die away if she could only leave them well alone? What a crazy idea it had been in the first place to imagine they could snatch so greedily at a love that had never been intended for them. Claudia Ercolani had talked about many different sorts of love but adultery – so wrong, so forbidden – wasn't it wrong to even think of it as *love*?

Riva got up and wandered out into the sun-filled courtyard, trying to warm her suddenly cold bones. She turned her face up to the sky, closing her eyes and willing the warmth to permeate her skin. Of course, love came in all sorts of forms, not always convenient and prettily packaged up. And perhaps that was why, even though Riva knew all about right and wrong, she was having such difficulty letting the thought of Aman slip away . . .

The Grand Canal was liquid gold as the sun sank behind the Rialto Bridge. Behind Aman, the grey dome of the Santa Maria basilica was catching the last rays before it too would lapse into the shadows of the night. From having spent the last three days at this location, Aman knew that evenings drew in slowly here, gold gradually giving way to grey as the mists rolled in from the sea. Rohit Mirchandani had already got all the evening shots he needed and the crew was now awaiting the final wrap. Even the local crowds and tourists had drifted away by now, having satisfied their curiosity about Bollywood in these past few days. The gruelling month-long schedule was finally coming to an end. Tomorrow Aman would travel to a remote medieval village called San Gimignano for a two-day shoot that would be followed by a well-deserved break. He felt satisfied at having spent the past month working as hard as he possibly could and was now looking forward to spending precious time with Ashfaq, who was already ensconced with Salma and their entourage in a villa near San Gimignano. Salma had, fortunately, expressed her satisfaction with the converted farmhouse Ritesh Shah had found for them, apparently set amid miles of vineyards and olive groves and quite beautifully appointed. Aman imagined going for long walks in the Tuscan countryside carrying his son on his shoulders. Ever since Ashfaq had started to talk, using one or two words to form small sentences, his company was growing ever more varied and interesting. Aman reminded himself of how lucky he was to have a healthy and lively child like Ashfaq and resolved again to try getting on better with Salma, if for nothing else than his son's sake. There was no other choice. Aman had done a lot of thinking since that last meeting with Riva in Claridge's and had come to the conclusion that it had been truly foolhardy to imagine – even during that glorious spell in Cannes – that he and Riva could ever have had a future together. There was too much to lose. For her, it would be the loss of her family and friends and perhaps her own self-respect. For him, his son, his career, the adulation of his fans . . . It had been a close shave when one of the gossip magazines had reported a sighting of him with a woman on a Cannes beach. But no one else seemed to pick up the story and the news was soon buried.

Aman got up from his chair and stretched himself. 'Rohit, *yaar*, just stretching my legs a bit. Not going far,' he called out to the young director who was a good friend of his. Rohit, busy examining the shots of the day in his viewfinder, gave him a thumbs up and Aman strolled slowly around the mammoth basilica, now shut and barred for the night. He turned a corner, intending to walk up to the road that overlooked the wide blue gulf. And that was when he saw her in the half-shadows, leaning on a mossy half-wall and facing him, her back to the luminous sea. For one split second, Aman wondered if it was merely some kind of fevered vision, but – as he neared – he saw, without a doubt, that it really was Riva. Riva, looking oddly like a lost little girl, wearing shorts and sandals, looking at him from across the road as if she had never gone away.

'Riva?' he called softly, still half-fearful that she would turn and run, or melt into the gathering shadows.

Riva stayed where she was, however, and Aman walked

closer, coming to a halt inches away from her. She was near enough to touch, to reach out and kiss, but Aman kept his hands by his side, feeling weakened by his overwhelming relief at merely seeing her again. The look on Riva's face told him that she was not angry with him any more. She was not smiling but her expression was gentle and, when he stood before her, she reached up a hand and touched his cheek. He cupped her hand with his before pulling it towards his lips to drop a kiss on her palm. His gaze stayed on her face and he saw her eyes start to well up. One large tear escaped and coursed slowly down her face.

'Don't cry,' he whispered, using his thumb to wipe it away as it made its way past her nose. But another tear had now started to roll down the other side of her face.

'I'm so sorry, Aman,' she whispered.

'Don't be sorry, Riva, you haven't done anything wrong to me.'

'Maybe I shouldn't have led you on . . . made you hope?'

Aman was silent for a minute, thinking of many things he wanted to say but, more than anything else, he wanted Riva to stop crying. He smiled and took on a jokey tone, 'Yeah, that was pretty heartless, actually; seducing me like that, when all I wanted was to watch some decent films at Cannes.' Aman was only trying to make Riva laugh but she was crying in earnest now. 'You really should stop crying, you know,' he said, glancing over his shoulder, 'or some muscular Italian man will come along and beat me up for making a pretty girl cry.'

'I'm not pretty at all when I cry,' Riva said, fishing a tissue out of the pocket of her shorts to wipe her nose.

Aman held her face between both hands and examined it as though he were a plastic surgeon. 'Hmm, it's pretty enough. But your pink nose – that's a bit scary.'

Riva finally managed a half-hearted laugh. She wiped her eyes and nose and then said in a sad voice, 'Oh Aman. What'll it be like watching your movies and feeling you in the room and not being able to touch you or talk to you . . .'

'Don't watch my movies. They're all crap anyway,' he responded. Aman got another shadow of a smile for that. Then Riva showed a flash of her old spirit by saying, 'Okay, I won't watch your films if you promise to never read my books.'

'No problem,' Aman responded cheerily. 'Your books are too clever for the likes of me anyway.' Still trying to lighten things, he added, 'Which is why I think you did the best thing by marrying Ben, and not me. At least he can read your books.'

At that Riva started to cry again and so Aman carried on speaking swiftly. 'Listen, Riva, this might sound like *filmi* shit but I really want you to be where you're happy. I mean that. Just – if Ben ever misbehaves – give me a call and I'll come with a gang of Bollywood *goondas* to beat him up and whisk you away. On a white horse. With an A.R. Rehman score playing in the background and lots of backing dancers. Just like in *Slumdog*.'

Riva smiled through her tears but, refusing to give up, asked, 'What about you, Aman. Will you be okay?'

'Ah, I'll manage,' he replied. 'At least I'll no longer be wondering what happened to that angry Union leader who looked so damn cute in a red miniskirt at university and who briefly gave me her heart. I shall also thank God every day for having given us Cannes. At least now I can die in peace knowing that you and I would have driven each other crazy if we had got married. You a mad Brit writer and me a mad Bollywood actor. Different worlds, different journeys . . . but I'm glad we met, Riva. First time and second time. And I guess, wherever I go in the world, there'll be a part of me hoping we'll meet again. In fact, I'll never be able to turn a corner without wondering if maybe you'll be standing on the other side, leaning like this on a wall, waiting for me . . .'

Riva stopped Aman's ramblings by wrapping her arms around his waist, putting her ear against his chest as though listening for his heartbeat through her sniffles. He felt the length of her body lie against his and held her shoulders. But he refrained from putting his arms around her too tightly for fear that it would be hard to let go. After a while, she finally released him, looking up at his face one last time before slipping her arms away and turning to leave. Aman did not move while Riva walked away from him and out of his life, as she had done before, at a time when they were too young to know any better. He continued to stand where he was while the white of her T-shirt melded slowly into the night.

Epilogue

He picked up the magazine as her name caught his eye. It was unsual for her to get a mention in a film rag. But it was unmistakable, her name, right here on the contents page: 'Riva Walia's latest novel picked up by Dreamworks,' it said. 'See page 36.'

Aman riffled swiftly through the magazine, searching, and there Riva suddenly was, looking out at him. It must have been an old picture the magazine had kept on file somewhere. She looked younger than when he had last seen her in Venice, three years ago. Her hair was shorter, her face filled out a little more. But her smile was the same; a big sunshiny one that still had the power to make his heart skip a beat. He ran his eye over the small news piece that accompanied the photograph: film rights optioned by Spielberg to award-winning novelist Riva Walia's latest novel, Past Love. Spielberg was quoted describing it as 'an old-fashioned love story' and a 'Brief Encounter for our times'. He had gone on to describe it as a story that crossed cultures and continents, an unfulfilled love affair that provided a new twist on the theme of infidelity . . .

Aman looked at that word – infidelity – a big word for what had happened between him and Riva. A cruel word, in fact, for what had merely seemed the most decent thing to do.

In Conversation with Jaishree Misra

1. If you were stranded on a desert island, which book would you take with you?
Something fat and deliciously detailed and long-running, with that essential goose-bumpy quality to remind me that I still had feelings. Probably a big, sweeping historical romance like 'Gone With the Wind' or 'The Thornbirds'.

2. Where does your inspiration come from?
Oh, from all over the place. Stories abound in the most surprising corners of life. I've found them in chance encounters, casual chats, overheard conversations on a bus . . . sometimes even the sight of a passing stranger looking sad can set off a whole saga in my head.

3. Have you always wanted to become a writer?
As far back as I can remember, yes. I was good at it too, always getting top marks in English and essay writing, to the detriment of all other subjects at school. My first published piece was a short story in the magazine section of an Indian newspaper when I was thirteen. My father was so overjoyed to see my name in print, he forgot to ask when I'd managed to research a soppy love story.

4. What's the strangest job you've ever had?

Without a doubt, my most recent one at the British Board of Film Classification. Friends never got over the fact (or their envy) that I was actually paid to watch films before they got to see them in the cinema.

5. When you're not writing, what are your favourite things to do?

I love travelling, experiencing new things, sampling different foods and meeting people. I could kid everyone that I was researching new novels by doing so but, really, novels are the last thing I'm thinking of sometimes when I'm out there enjoying myself.

6. What is a typical working day like for you? Have you ever had writer's block? If so, how did you cope with it?

Usually a typical working day only allows for writing in the crevices of time that may or may not emerge in between a bread 'n' butter job, running a house, engaging with hubby, daughter, friends, family etc. But I must be thinking about my book and characters all the while because, sometimes, my eyes will snap open at the crack of dawn and I will find that I have a whole chapter ready at the back of my head, waiting to be spilled out. Writer's block would be too much of a luxury when writing time is so short.

7. Do you have any secret ambitions?

To be a screenwriter as clever and witty as Nora Ephron and have Hollywood come panting after me.

8. What can't you live without?

Books. Despite having managed many years without it, the internet. If I'm allowed to mention human beings, my husband, daughter, family and friends. Oh, and chocolate.

9. When you were a child, what did you want to be when you grew up?

Briefly, an air-hostess (because I liked to travel), a night-club crooner (because I craved the limelight), a model (because I wanted the glamour), a psychologist (because I thought it would be fun to walk around inside people's heads), a journalist (because I wanted to write). I never became any of those but, oddly enough, I manage to meet all those requirements by being a novelist.

10. Which five people, living or dead, would you invite to a dinner party?

Archbishop Desmond Tutu, Joan Rivers, Alan Bennett, Victoria Wood and the Bollywood actor, Shah Rukh Khan (not because he's dishy but because he's witty, I promise). You can imagine how much we'd laugh and, somehow, I can imagine all of them being easily persuaded to join in with some post-prandial Bollywood bopping too. What a party that would be!

What's next?

Tell us the name of an author you love

> Jaishree Misra   **Go** ▶

and we'll find your next great book.

book army

www.bookarmy.com